THE LONG FIRM

THE LONG FIRM

Jake Arnott

F

First published in Great Britain by Hodder and Stoughton

Copyright © 1999 by Jake Arnott

Published in the United States by

Soho Press, Inc.
853 Broadway
New York, N.Y. 10003

Library of Congress Cataloging-in-Publication Data

Arnott, Jake.
The long firm / Jake Arnott.
p.   cm.
ISBN 1-56947-169-X (alk. paper)
I. Title.
PR6051.R6235L66   1999
823'.914—dc21   99-26932
                                                        CIP

10 9 8 7 6 5 4 3 2 1

What's a jemmy compared with a share certificate?
What's breaking into a bank compared with founding one?
Bertolt Brecht, *The Threepenny Opera*

1

The White-Hot Poker

'You know the song, don't you? "There's *no* business like *show* business".' Harry gets the Ethel Merman intonation just right as he heats up a poker in the gas burner.

'"Like no business."'

Turning the iron slowly, sheathing it in blue flame.

'You know?'

I nod with enough emphasis to cause the chair I'm tied to to edge a little across the room. This only brings me closer to Harry. The gas roars softly. Blue flame looking cold. Poker looking hot. Glowing now, already brighter than the fire that feeds it. Getting red hot, white hot.

'Well what if there *was* a business like show business. *Like* show business. You know?'

Nod nod edge edge.

'There is, Terry. There is.'

I can feel the heat of it on my cheek now as he points it at my face. I feel sick.

'You know what it is, don't you?' Harry asks in a hoarse whisper. 'It's what I do.'

'Harry,' I croak.

'Shh,' he insists. 'You'll have a chance to talk. Don't worry. You'll want to tell me the whole story. But first the show. I'm going to show you something.'

My brain is throbbing with terror. I've got to think. Work out how all of this happened. Put it all together and find a way out. Think.

Remember.

*   *   *

3

Johnny Remember Me.

The Casbah Lounge. Pine panelling, tattily upholstered benches around the walls, a fish tank embedded in the central partition. Sipping bitter black espresso. Boys sitting or standing around in groups clattering transparent glass cups and saucers. Looking. Checking out who was in the place. Checking out who other people in their group were checking out. And checking out who was being checked. Dull eyes twitching, slightly glassy from speed and coffee and cigarettes.

'Johnny Remember Me' wailing mournfully from the jukebox. Last year's hit still haunting. Strange girl's voice calling out of the echo-chamber wilderness.

My first year in London. I had to start somewhere. A crummy bedsit in Westbourne Grove. Working as a messenger in an advertising firm. I'd escaped suburbia, that was the main thing. I found places that I could go. A handful of theatrical pubs and seedy coffee bars. The Casbah Lounge was one of them.

A group of Earl's Court queens there with cheap polari sophistication. Vada this, vada that. Casual bitchiness judging anybody's fleeting object of affection.

Then he came in. Thick set in a dark suit and tightly knotted tie. Looking out of place amidst all the loud clothes the young homos were sporting. Standing out sombre and heavy among the bright shirts and hipster slacks from Vince or Lord John. He looked around the coffee bar, negotiating all the signals, all the brief flashes of eye contact with a weary frown as if his imposing presence was a burden. He looked clumsy and awkward, intimidated for all his toughness. All the looks, the staring. In places he was more used to, spielers, drinking clubs, heavy boozers like the Blind Beggar or the Grave Maurice that level of eyeballing would have seemed an affront, a prelude to combat. Here, he had to get used to the fierce looks and learn a new way of staring. He had to come off guard in order to make contact.

He had dark, oil-slicked hair, a battered face that made him look older than he was. An extra tuft of hair joined his eyebrows so they furrowed in a single line. You couldn't say he was pretty. Handsome, in a brutal sort of a way. Impressive. Something about him I found rather attractive. Something dangerous. The style he had in the way he held himself, holding himself up against any embarrassment. The way he looked. Like he meant it. It inspired some arch glances amongst the queens. *Get her*, someone murmured.

As I looked over he caught my stare. His face tightened and drew back a touch. I smiled and his frown narrowed for a second then opened up. A lopsided grin brought out the crease of a scar in his right cheek, then thinned out to a sad smile as he continued to scan the room.

His gaze moved into a more professional line of vision and a flurry of communication flashed from one face to another. *Trade*, another voice muttered coldly. *Johnny Remember Me*, howled the jukebox. Someone coughed significantly and went over. As I watched the casual intensity of the negotiations the man seemed to look over at me. I turned away thinking not so much that it was rude to stare but that it was bad for business. I didn't want to interfere. So I looked at the fishtank. Huge carp mouthed silently. A stream of silvery bubbles trailed to the surface.

Someone nudged me. The queen had returned, a faint smile on his lips. He nodded petulantly at me

'He wants *you* dear.'

The poker throbs with heat and light. Harry blows on it and a few tiny sparks fly off and quickly die in the cold air of the lock-up. He plunges it back into the brazier.

'You stupid fucker,' he says. 'Thought you could have me over, didn't you?'

I start to say something. Harry slaps me hard across the face.

'Shh,' he hisses at me again. 'I know, I know, you want to explain it all. But I ain't interested in some story you'll come up with. I want the truth. The whole truth. And by the time I've finished with you by Christ I'll get it.'

Harry comes up close to me. My head is twisted to one side from the slap, one cheek still sore from the blow. He grabs my jaw and forces me to look directly into his stare.

'You've been a naughty boy, Terry,' he whispers into my face. 'We need to teach you a lesson.'

Breaking a person's will, that's what it was all about. He'd explained it to me once. Harry didn't like to do business with anybody that he couldn't tie to a chair. He liked to break people. Sometimes it was a warning, sometimes punishment. Always to make one thing very clear. That he was the guvnor. That's what all the violence was for. That was the point of it. That was the one gruesome detail that was missed out in the trial. All the press reports, the TORTURE GANG BOSS headlines. All the lurid stories to tease the punters. The beatings, the pliers, the black box for giving electric shocks. They all missed the point. He liked to break people.

'But how can you tell?' I'd asked him back then. 'Don't people just fake it?'

And Harry had laughed. A little spasm of knowledge.

'Oh, you can tell,' he had assured me softly. 'They become like children. Crying and that. Calling for their mummies.'

The Casbah Lounge. That's where it all began. I walked across the floor, nodded at the man and we went out together into the night air. He had a big black Daimler parked outside. A driver awaiting instructions. He held the door open for me. I felt flash. And completely reckless.

I'd never done it for money before, never even thought about renting it. I was a nice boy from the suburbs, passed the eleven plus and everything. But I'd always been drawn to trouble. Ended up getting expelled from Technical High School. I left home, left a semi-detached life for the longed-for city. I craved some sort of excitement. I think carrying around the secret that I was a homo had something to do with it as well. That part of me didn't really exist until I moved down to London.

We got into the back of the motor together. The man nodded to his driver. As we pulled away I felt a sudden surge of trepidation in my stomach but I tried to ignore it.

'Harry,' he whispered as introduction, taking my hand in his.

'Terry,' I responded.

'Hello, Terry,' he breathed huskily, stroking my leg.

I remember us pulling up somewhere off Sloane Square. Harry had an expensive flat in Chelsea. He poured us both a large brandy and showed me his photograph collection. Harry with Johnnie Ray, with Ruby Ryder, Tom Driberg MP, Sonny Liston. Pictures of him looking stern faced next to film stars, singers, boxers, the great and the good.

Then we had sex. He fucked me up against a full-length mirror. My breath misted the glass but I could make out his reflected face clenched in need as he came into me. Afterwards we had a smoke and he spoke softly. His voice lost some of its gruffness and took on a high-pitched almost child-like tone.

'You're a nice-looking kid,' he whispered.

'Thanks.'

'I ain't very pretty am I?'

He touched his battered face sadly.

'Oh, I don't know,' I replied, not quite knowing what to say.

He drew a finger across his brow.

'And me eyebrows join. I look like a bloody werewolf. You know what my Aunt May told me? What it means if your eyebrows join?'

I shrugged.

'It means you're born to hang.'

The next morning he saw me off, casually handing me a five-pound note. He said he'd like to see me again. He was a businessman, he claimed, and a club owner. He invited me to a party at his club, The Stardust in Soho.

'What do you think I'm going to do with this?' Harry asks, waving the poker in front of me. 'Eh?'

I squirm about a bit against the ropes that tie me. Tony

Stavrakakis stands behind me. It was him that had secured me to the chair. The big Greek rests a heavy hand on my shoulder to stop me from moving about too much and to concentrate on what was going on. Harry fiddles with the brazier thing. I don't want to think about it. I don't want to think at all. I want to break down and blubber uncontrollably. To give in and give up the truth that Harry would insist upon. I want to break. But Harry's right. You can't fake a thing like that.

'Show business is in my blood, Terry. Did I ever tell you about my grandad? Billy Sheen. The Canning Town Cannonball they called him. Champion bare-knuckle fighter he was. But he wasn't just a fighter, he was a showman as well. Had a strong singing voice and did a strongman act in the music halls. He could leap out of a barrel, break a stack of house bricks with his bare hands. But you know what the climax of his act was? Licking a white hot poker. Yeah, that's right. Has to be white-hot mind. Just red hot and it'd shrivel your tongue off and no mistake. He learnt it off this big black fellah doing it before a crowd on Mile End Waste. And he taught it me.'

Harry laughs and moves the poker in the flame again.

'You watch this carefully now,' he insists

He brings the metal to the tip of the flame, its hottest point. At the same time he moves his lips and tongue, making spit in his mouth.

'Have to make sure your gob's good and wet too. Hard to do if you're scared. Nothing like fear to make your mouth dry. Nah, you have to make sure your mouth's good and wet and the poker's white hot. Then you can't go wrong.'

He chews and sucks, moving his tongue to the front of his mouth as he watches the poker glow. Tiny bubbles of sputum dribble at the corner of his mouth and his tongue darts out to draw them back in again.

'You watch carefully now.'

The Stardust. Harry was out front, flanked by two huge doormen, greeting people. He grabbed my hand with both of his. Gave me a wink as I passed through into the club.

'Glad you could come, Terry. Get yourself a drink, I'll see you later.'

The Stardust. Not exactly my scene. Mostly an older crowd, overdressed and out of style. Heinz and The Wild Boys were performing that night. I went to the bar and ordered a rum and Coke. A modernist kid to the left of me in a two-piece tonic mohair. Three-buttoned single-breasted jacket, narrow lapels, flap pockets, from Harry Fenton's no doubt. He wore his hair *en brosse*, in a french crew. He nodded at me. I felt shabby standing next to him. I want some of that, I thought to myself. Something more than that.

Bleached-blond Heinz was dragging his backing band through a medley of Eddie Cochran songs.

'Pretty, ain't he?' said the mod kid.

'Yeah,' I shrugged. 'I guess.'

'Shame about the voice. Still, Joe Meek's so in love with him he's convinced he's going to be big.'

He nodded at a tall quiffed man sitting at the main table watching the performance intensely. Joe Meek, record producer, famous for his ice-rink-in-space electric organ sound. He'd had a big hit with 'Telstar' by The Tornadoes.

'Joe should stick to instrumentals,' muttered the modernist as the blond singer crooned 'C'mon Everybody' slightly off key. 'So should Heinz for that matter.'

Harry had come into the club with his entourage. He beckoned me over with a jerk of his head.

'Come over and join us,' he said and led me to a large table.

The party was an assortment of celebrities. Along with Joe Meek there was a boxer or two, someone from television and Ruby Ryder the film actress. Equally famous and with their own brand of glamour were the people pointed out with names like Alibi Albert and Jack the Hat. 'Faces', Harry referred to them as. And as it turned out that was what Harry was. A face. *Mad* Harry, I was slightly disconcerted to learn, was his also known as. Every so often a flashbulb would go whoosh and the main group would go into a fixed expression for a second. Showbiz eyes and teeth. Underworld jaws and suits.

I was introduced to Joe Meek. Being the official young person present, he was keen for my opinion on Heinz. I hesitated.

'Love the peroxide riah,' I declared with genuine conviction.

'It's great ain't it?' Joe had a high-pitched west country accent. 'Got the idea from *Village of the Damned*. You know, those spooky kids from outer space.'

He was as tall and thick set as Harry but his movements had a kind of jerky thinness to them. He had big farmboy hands that fluttered at you. I didn't have the heart to tell him that I didn't think Heinz was going to work. The dyed hair, the shiny jacket with silver piping. Wonderfully camp. Woefully out of date. Something new was happening. The Beat Boom, people were calling it. Rock and Roll, well, that was for the die-hard leather crowd and Heinz certainly didn't impress them. Apparently in Birmingham a gang of rockers had chucked tins of beans at him. Rhythm and Blues, that was what everyone was talking about. Something new was happening but Heinz definitely wasn't it.

Heinz finished to polite applause. He came over to the table grinning awkwardly. Joe fussed around him for a while and then chatted, wide-eyed manic, to Harry. Pupils like sharpened pencil leads. Pilled on amphetamine, no doubt about it. Blocked, we called it. They talked business. Management. Heinz sat between them and they furtively eyed him like confection as they talked. Harry was drawn to Tin Pan Alley, a way of breaking into legitimate show business. Maybe thinking of becoming the next Larry Parnes or Brian Epstein. And why not? He was a homosexual Jewish wide boy just like them. But maybe a bit too wide. Not quite smooth enough. Harry would never look right in a camel-hair coat somehow. He was too much of a performer to be a successful impresario. You could never see him in the background. Too conspicuous, too much of an act himself. In fact all the faces seemed to have more confident a turn than any of the showbiz lot. The gangsters were the real stars at The Stardust.

I got drunk. I wasn't used to boozing. I staggered into the gents, splashed some cold water in my face and dried it on the towel machine. Jack the Hat was handing over a huge bag of pills to the modernist child.

'Fancy a doob, mate?' he called over to me.

I rejoined the party with a purple heart melting on my tongue. Around the table stories were being offered up. Showbiz secrets and behind the scenes gossip swapped for tales of fixed fights and doped dogs. Frauds and rackets and heavier jobs were alluded to as all the tricks of the trade seemed open for discussion. Like conjurers taking apart an illusion confident that their public was elsewhere. The audience, the punters. The mugs.

One of the villain's women got up and gave us a song to much encouragement. She had a clear sad voice. You could see that she had been pretty once but now looked a bit washed out. As she sang 'Cry Me A River' without accompaniment I wondered what kind of a life it would be being the woman of one of these hard-faced men.

When she'd finished there was applause and banging on the tables. Everyone was far gone by now. Music started up and Jack the Hat got up and danced on the table. I could hear Joe Meek next to me bawling about the record industry in the mod kid's ear over the noise.

'They're trying to steal my sound! The rotten pigs! I'm still the bloody guvnor!'

Jack the Hat was starting to strip off and two of the boxers tried to gently coax him down off the table. Harry came up and put his arm around me.

'Enjoying yourself?'

I nodded. Actually I was. It wasn't a trendy scene but there was something altogether furtive and exciting about The Stardust. It reminded of that bit in Pinocchio where all the bad boys bunk off school and go to Playland where they don't have to do any work and can just fuck about all day. As a child I'd always longed for that sort of cheap utopia. When the funfair came to our local common every year, I'd be drawn to the cheap thrills of the waltzer and the dodgems. I spent as much time simply gazing at the gypsy lads as they casually hopped amidst the spinning machinery, collecting fares. Showing off. Danger and glamour. Greased-back pompadours and muscled arms marked with tattoos and stained with engine oil. I'd always fancied the rough boys who ran the fairground rides. The Stardust scene seemed a version of the playland I'd dreamt of as a child and I wanted to be a part of it. I'd conveniently forgotten that, in the story, all the lazy boys are turned into donkeys in the end. I should have been warned.

Anyway, the speed had sobered me up. Given me confidence. When the party was over and people began to stagger out of the club, Harry asked me to go back with him and I said yes.

At the door a bloke in a heavy overcoat came across and muttered something in Harry's ear. They whispered gruffly to each other in the doorway.

'All right, I'll deal with it. Terry,' Harry said, turning to me, 'Jimmy will drive you to my flat. Wait there for me. I won't be long.'

He nodded to a sandy-haired man who was waiting outside. I recognised him as Harry's driver from the night we met at The Casbah. Harry said a few words to him, turned and winked at me and then went off into the night.

From the back of the Daimler I saw Jimmy's eyes slotted in the rear-view mirror.

'All right son?' he asked with a little nod of the head.

There was a weary edge to his voice.

'Yeah,' I replied. 'I guess.'

Jimmy unlocked the door of the flat and held the door open for me. He wrinkled his nose in an obliging sneer.

'Make yourself at home,' he said. 'Harry might be a while.'

Then he was gone and I was alone in Harry's flat.

I poured myself a large brandy and looked through Harry's record collection. Judy Garland, Dorothy Squires, some opera and Winston Churchill's Wartime Speeches. On the coffee table was *A History of Western Philosophy* by Bertrand Russell and a well-thumbed edition of *Physique Pictorial*. I collapsed into the leather-buttoned chesterfield and flicked through the magazine. The speed had begun to wear off and I started to feel drowsy from the brandy. A second glass sorted me out and I fell into a light sleep on the sofa.

I woke up with a start to find Harry standing over me still in his overcoat. He prodded me gently with his foot.

'All right?' he whispered.

He had a slightly crazed look about him. His face twitched with the strange distracted playfulness that a cat displays when it's just killed a mouse.

'Where have you been?' I asked rubbing my face awake.

'Shh,' Harry ordered with a finger in front of his mouth. 'Never you mind.'

I sat up and he grinned at me.

'Come on,' he said softly, taking my arm and leading me into the bedroom.

When I next woke up it was eleven o'clock.

'Shit,' I said sitting up in the bed.

'What's the matter?' asked Harry blearily.

'I'm late for work.'

'Fuck them.'

'I should phone in sick or something.'

'Nah. What you want to work for them for? Phone them up and tell them to stuff their job.'

I laughed.

'You could work for me,' Harry suggested.

'Oh yeah? Doing what?'

Harry grinned slyly.

'You could make yourself useful round here. Look after the place for me. Look after me a bit and all.'

Harry pulled me back under the covers and nestled up close to me.

'What do you say?' he asked, with a big sloppy grin.

'All right,' I said.

And that's how it happened. I chucked in my job. Harry looked after me. I became kept.

He bought me things. We went shopping for clothes. Harry disapproved of Carnaby Street. 'Too cheap, too lairy,' he insisted. Instead he took me to Blades in Dover Street. There Rupert Lycett Green combined bespoke tailoring with the latest tight silhouette style and colourful cloth. He paid for me to have a couple of suits made up there. And a Pierre Cardin off the peg from Dougie Millings in Great Pulteney Street.

Harry's taste was more conservative. He had his suits made at Kilgour, French & Stanbury in Savile Row. Charcoal-grey wool or dark-blue chalkstripe. But I persuaded him to go for a two piece. Waistcoats were out and the watch chain he sometimes wore looked far too old fashioned. And we got the tailor to taper his cut a little so that he looked slightly taller and less thick set than he actually was.

We bought hand-made shirts from Jermyn Street. Turnbull & Asser, Harvie & Hudson. Ties from Mr Fish in Clifford Street.

I was spoiled rotten. I got to know about *haute couture*. And that wardrobe was an essential part of the way that Harry operated. Being so well dressed was the cutting edge of intimidation. A sort of decorative violence in itself.

And I got to meet the main faces on his firm. Jimmy Murphy, who had driven me to Harry's flat. Tony Stravrakakis who was generally known as Tony the Greek or Bubble, and Jock McCluskey, a huge Glaswegian. Also Manny Gould, Manny the Money, a little bloke with round glasses who dealt with accounts such as they were. There were many other minor faces he could call upon to go in plenty handed when needed. But generally Harry liked to keep things small and tight. The fewer people he had to trust or pay off the better.

Harry's queerness seemed to be something that the firm accepted. Not that they had much choice. He'd often berate them with his opinion that hanging around with women made you soft. My status was less secure. But, of course, I was a threat to nobody. At that time

I simply belonged to Harry as far as they were concerned. I suppose, for the most part, they treated me as they treated the many women who were connected to members of the firm. I got the impression that Jimmy Murphy didn't exactly approve of me, though. Nothing was said directly just the occasional glance or comment.

Anyway I was on the firm in a more or less unofficial capacity. Sometimes called upon to deliver messages and packages or to find out information. Other times when Harry was calling on someone I'd go in ahead to let them know that he was on his way. Smooth the way as it were. Harry disliked awkwardness or anything 'unnecessary'. Like a true gentleman he was never rude or brutal by mistake. I knew that Harry had other boys who did similar things and more but I had to live with that.

I even had my own little racket for a while. Joe Meek was paying Harry to help get his singles into the charts. It was simple enough. There were about sixty or so chart-return listed shops in London whose sales the Hit Parade was based on. You could buy a hundred copies to get it into the charts, buy a few more the following week to push it up a bit more, then get on to the deejays to say it's in the charts and give them a backhander so they'd give it airplay. I was put on to the job, being the firm's official young person. The only problem was some shops, if you bought, say, ten, they wouldn't mark it down because it looked like an obvious fix. It was then that I'd persuade them what was good for business. I'd learnt how to put on the casually threatening manner from Harry though I often took Big Jock McCluskey with me for good measure. Also, every other record company was up to the same thing so we'd try and target other record fixers, muscle in on them, even get them to buy Joe's records instead of the ones they were supposed to be fixing. It was a minor league racket, for sure, but I have to say I got a real kick out of throwing my own weight about for once. I could see the attraction in leaning on people, the aura of power that it gave you. It was a thrill, something almost sexual about it. Once, I vada this kid in a listening booth as I'm walking out of a record store on Shaftesbury Avenue. He's gaping at me through the glass and it's obvious he thinks that I'm a bit tasty like. So I give him a wink and wait for him outside the shop. I act all tough and he loves it. We end up back at his flat in Bloomsbury. It was the first time I'd had sex with someone my own age in weeks.

I'd take all the records back to Joe's recording studio on the Holloway Road and he'd hand over a wad of cash. I'd get a percentage and the rest would go to Harry. Sometimes I'd take a load of pills round as well. Amphetamines. Joe was mad for them.

But my main job was to be with Harry. For sex and for companionship. Harry liked to go out to smart restaurants, to the racetrack, to the opera even. There were so many flash places that I went with him where we were treated with almost grovelling respect. So many people who hid their fear by looking pleased to see him.

Then there were nights at his club, parties at his flat where boys were served like canapes to his queer friends in high places. More often than not descending into a clumsy orgy. Harry would never get involved himself. He enjoyed the organising side of it. Manipulating things.

There was an attractiveness that went with the fierceness. He drew people to him. He had a sort of threatening charisma that made you want to be close to him, an aura that you could feel safe within. A bit like those fish that swim right up close to sharks, you felt protected being in his slipstream. I remember him saying that, in a fight, the best first move is always to go in close rather than back away. If you give space to your opponent, he'll have room to take a proper swing at you. 'Always be near to them but make sure they're far away from you.' It was advice that I took to heart.

There were things that I kept from him. I kept the bedsit in Westbourne Grove without telling him. If the worst comes to the worst, I thought, at least he doesn't know where I live. And, of course, our backgrounds were very different. He used to joke that I'd 'been to clever school'. I'd left all my safe suburban upbringing behind me. I didn't really keep in touch with my parents, for obvious reasons. But this baffled Harry.

'Your poor old mum,' he'd berate me. 'I bet she worries about you.'

I remember once him taking me to a Boys' Club in the East End that he patronised. It was for a boxing tournament that he had donated the trophy for. He was sort of a guest of honour. I tried not to wince as I watched wiry adolescents with huge upholstered fists clumsily batter away at each other.

Harry chuckled darkly when he noticed my unease.

'Bet you never been in a real fight, have you Terry?' he goaded.

And he was right. I was soft. A hundred playground humiliations played back in my mind. *Sissy. Poof.*

After the final bout Harry went back to congratulate the scrawny little lad who had won.

'Well done, Tommy,' he said, ruffling the blond curls of the young fighter.

Tommy blinked, still half dazed from combat and slightly shy of Harry's obvious affection. His grey-blue eyes looked far older than my own. I felt awkward standing in this makeshift dressing room that stank of youthful sweat and stale liniment. Something I couldn't ever really understand or be part of.

But I loved the image of it all. Harry's masculinity. Being fancied by such a tough and dangerous man. The danger of it. It seemed so real compared to my privet-hedged experience of life. There was something sexy about it. Though the sex itself was really quite gentle. I know in some of the trial reports they made him out to be some sort of sadist but I don't think he was really into that. That was just business.

But then there was the waiting. I never really knew what he was up to. A lot of his work was done at night. I was expected to be there for him at all hours at his flat. Sometimes he'd never turn up. He'd be away somewhere or simply staying over at his mother's house in Hoxton. There would be no explanations. I was expected to understand this part of Harry's life and yet be completely ignorant of it at the same time.

One night he and Jimmy Murphy came to the flat at four in the morning covered in blood. They looked wild eyed

'What the fuck's happened?' I cried.

'Nothing,' replied Harry. 'Nothing's happened. Help us get out of our clothes.'

'What?'

'You heard me. Undress us. We mustn't touch anything in the flat.'

I reached out a hand to unbutton Harry's jacket and touched a clot of blood and tissue. I recoiled.

'What have you done Harry?' I gasped.

Harry lost his patience and slapped both sides of his hand against both sides of my face. I fell onto the hallway floor. I touched my cheek and a smear of blood came away on my fingertips. Somebody else's blood.

'Do what you're told and don't ask any stupid questions,' Harry ordered softly.

I looked up at Harry glowering down at me and Jimmy Murphy with a faint smirk on his lips.

'Look at that.'

Harry pointed with the toecap of his boot. At first I thought that he was going to kick me and I started to curl up. Then I saw where he was pointing with his foot. There was a mark on the hallway floor where I'd put my hand out as I'd fallen and smeared the blood and stuff from Harry's coat onto the polished tiles.

'Look,' he said. 'Fucking forensic all over the floor. Get up,' Harry ordered. 'Go and get a bowl of water and clean this mess up.'

I picked myself up off the floor. This was the first time Harry had laid a finger on me. And he'd done it without losing his temper, that's what was really chilling about it. How calm he could be with violence. Up until then I hadn't really thought about the real nastiness of what Harry did. The ugliness behind all of his charm. What lurked behind the scene in all of his rackets. I kept my head down and sloped off to the kitchen.

'And put some Savlon in it,' Harry called after me. 'I don't want fucking germs all over the flat.'

'Watch.'

Harry stands with his legs slightly apart. One foot slightly in front of the other. Back foot slightly turned out. His weight is on his back foot, his centre of gravity lowered as if squaring up to something. Like a boxer. Or a showman.

He heats up the poker once more then brings it out of the brazier in an arc. Displaying it. Bringing it slowly down in front of his face like a fire-eater or sword swallower.

His eyes are wide and bright. Tiny images of the glowing metal burn in each one. His tongue, wide and drooling, unfurls to his chin. He looks demonic.

He holds this mask of expression as he brings the poker up close. His face reddened with heat and concentration. Cords of sinew stand out in his neck. Veins bulging out on his forehead. Then he licks it. Drawing it down slowly and tossing back his head. There's a short sizzle. Like a drop of water in hot fat. *Shh.* A nimbus of saliva vapour disperses above his head as a drop of sweat goes cold on my neck.

Tony Stavrakakis gives a slow heavy laugh of appreciation, slapping me absently on the shoulder. Harry breaks his showman poise and sighs.

'See? Nothing to it.'

He puts the poker back into the flame and wipes his mouth with the back of a hand.

'Right then,' he says, looking over at me with a grin. 'Now it's your turn.'

Then came Harry's black moods. His evil brooding moods. It was Jimmy who warned me the first time. He knew the signs. The signs that Harry was 'going into one' as the firm phrased it. A slow but sure descent into half madness. The Mad Harry nickname didn't simply refer to his gameness, his readiness to have a go whatever the odds, although it was a convenient reputation for obtaining money by extortion. There was more to it than that. Turns out Harry was certified insane in a prison hospital psychiatric wing when he was doing time in the fifties. Diagnosed manic depressive. The manic side could often be expressed in violence and action. Sometimes he'd flare up and throw stuff about the flat. Sometimes he'd lash out at me. But I think he found ways of channelling that side of his nature. Putting the frighteners on people and that. It was what he was good at.

But the depressive side hit him really badly. He would sit brooding, filled with all kinds of horrors. Morbid thoughts. He would listen to his opera records. His eyes wet and bulging as divas shrieked their arias of distress. Then he'd get out his LP of Churchill's wartime speeches and play them over and over. He seemed soothed by the gloomy voice offering nothing but blood, toil, tears and sweat.

The anti-depressants helped. But they also made him drowsy and a bit puffy about the eyes and face which of course he hated. And he had this Harley Street shrink that he saw. Thing was, Harry was paranoid that anyone outside the firm might find out about his mental illness. A sign of weakness to his enemies, I suppose, but also he did have a terror that he might get committed and locked up in a mental home. So no one was to know. He couldn't go to this doctor's place in case anybody saw him and the doctor couldn't come around to the flat for the same reason. So the doctor was picked up in the Daimler and Jimmy Murphy drove around the West End as Harry and this shrink had a consultation in the back of the limo.

The paranoia got more and more intense. Harry was liable to lash out at anyone or anything. As word got around the firm that the boss had 'gone into one' they generally stayed away. It was left to Manny the Money to bring over the takings of all the various businesses and rackets in a huge suitcase. They went through it together, arranging different piles of money all over the bed. Once I saw Harry grab the little man by the throat, convinced that some of his money was missing.

'Where is it, you little fucker?' Harry hissed as he asphyxiated Manny.

Somehow Manny managed a shake of the head and his habitual shrug. When Harry finally released him he merely straightened his tie, pushed his glasses back onto the bridge of his nose and began counting out the takings again. He knew that the best way to respond to Harry's outbursts was to not respond at all. Just wait for it to come to an end. And indeed this was the best way to deal with him. Just to wait for him to calm down and hope that you lived that long.

I was the closest person to him during this time. Long brooding silences would be punctuated by his morbid reflections. Doping himself with brandy and handfuls of anti-depressants he'd talk of violence, boastful confessions of how he'd hurt people. Awful stories. It was then that he'd told me that he liked to control people by breaking them physically and mentally. It made me sick to the stomach to hear him talk like that. When I complained that he gloated over causing pain he took a knife and drew it slowly and deliberately across the back of his hand. He cut himself quite deeply and I had to get a crooked doctor that the firm used to come over and sew up the wound.

Once he held a loaded revolver to my head.

'When I go, you're coming too,' he said softly as he cocked the hammer.

I closed my eyes and counted in my head, trying not to move at all until I felt air on the spot made by the pressure of the barrel. I opened my eyes. Harry had wandered off into the bathroom. I traced around the little circular dent in my temple.

And yet, despite all the delirium, this was the time that I really got to know Harry. He was vulnerable, not a big tough guy any more. For once his guard came down and a frightened little child peeped out at me. He was ill and needed looking after. I'd never felt that kind of responsibility to another human being before. And no matter how difficult it was I couldn't help feeling emotionally protective towards him. It was a practical sort of affection. I cared for him because, quite literally. I cared for him. I didn't really have a choice about it and so sensitive feelings that hadn't really occurred in our relationship before just sort of happened. He needed to be held, to be reassured. A soothing voice to calm him. There. There. There.

And then, quite suddenly, he came out of it. He started doing exercise to get rid of the fat he'd put on during his illness. We went down to The Stardust for the first time in weeks. The firm started having proper meetings again and Harry got involved in all his big plans once more. He was back to his old self and he treated me. He brought me clothes and took me out. It was as if to compensate for how he'd been in the last few weeks though the period of depression was never mentioned directly. He talked of getting away for a while. Of going on holiday to Greece or Morocco. Everything seemed happy once again. But I found it hard to adjust to his recovery. His illness had seemed more real than anything else. I resented the cheeriness that people greeted him with, as if nothing had happened. And, I suppose, I started to resent Harry too.

One day a smartly dressed woman came to the flat. She was a shoplifter, a 'hoister' as Harry would put it. Harry didn't usually fence but this woman stole to order. She specialised in thieving *haute couture* from the fashion houses of Knightbridge and Bond Street. She had Harry's mother's measurements so she could lift whole outfits for him to spoil his dear old mum with. It was worth all the effort, not just for the money Harry paid but also for the protection he could offer should she ever need it.

'Ooh!' Harry cooed as this hoister woman held up a silk blouse by Tricosa. 'That's lovely!'

I suppressed a giggle. Harry could be quite camp at times but it was best not to draw his attention to it unless you were sure that he was in a good mood. As it happened he was. The woman had brought over a whole bundle of stuff and Harry thought that now was as good a time as any to go and visit Mother. He handed me the clothes and the keys of his brand-new Jaguar Mark II and I went out and put them carefully on the back seat as he paid the woman off. When I came back up to the flat Harry was getting ready to go. He called me into the bathroom.

'Why don't you come with me?' he said, looking at me through the mirror.

I shrugged. It wasn't something he'd ever suggested before. And I suppose it was then that I got to thinking, not without a certain amount of dread, that Harry was beginning to see me as a permanent fixture. Part of his life that he could take home to Mum.

We drove out east. Past the Angel and up the City Road to Shoreditch and Hoxton. Harry nodded moodily at the familiar scenery and pointed out a weed-covered bombsite. There was a council sign posted on it: Temporary Open Space.

'That's where our house was. Where I was born.'

He sighed.

'Bombed to fuck.'

Mrs Starks was an immaculately dressed wiry little woman. She was taking tea with Harry's Aunt May in the front room of her terraced house when we arrived. She made a fuss over Harry as soon as we were in the door. He got out all of the hoister's ill-gotten wares and there was a shrill fuss made over the clothes as they were laid out on the sofa not least by Harry himself.

'He spoils me, he does, May,' said Harry's mother.

'He's a naughty boy,' replied Aunt May coming over and stroking his forehead. 'Born to hang, that's what he is.'

'Hello dear,' his mother said to me warmly as we were introduced.

I wondered what she knew.

'I'll put the kettle on, make a fresh pot,' I suggested wanting to appear useful.

'What a nice boy,' I heard her comment as I went into the kitchen with the tea things.

While I was in the kitchen a middle-aged man shuffled in.

'*He's* here then,' he muttered.

He was swarthy looking with greying curly hair. He wore a collarless shirt with braces. A copy of *The Morning Star* was under one arm.

'I'm the old man,' he announced. 'Don't suppose he's mentioned me.'

And it was true, Harry had never talked of his father. He'd often spoken of his mother without any paternal reference. I'd somehow assumed that he was dead or permanently absent.

'There's some biscuits by the breadbin,' came Harry's voice from the doorway. 'Hello Dad,' he added flatly, noticing his father.

'Son.'

They nodded at each other cautiously.

'How's business?' inquired Starks the elder.

'Oh,' Harry shrugged. 'You know.'

'Yeah, I know,' he turned to me and shrugged. 'Still, it's a shame my only son turned out a gonnif.'

'I make a good living. You and Mum see enough of it.'

Harry's father grunted and turned his head to me again.

'He was a bright kid. Could have got an education, done something with his life.'

'Well maybe if you had been around a bit things might have been different. You were on the run half the time.'

'Yeah, but that was on principle. The Party was against the war so I had to avoid the call up.'

'The Party was against the war up until 1941. We didn't see you till VJ Day.'

'I was a pacifist. I wasn't going to fight in no capitalist war.'

'Yeah, but you ran a capitalist spieler, didn't you?'

'I suppose you blame me for your criminal tendencies.'

'No Dad. Fact is we all learned to run rackets in the war. The black market, everyone was in on it, one way or another.'

Now Harry turned to me.

'I was the youngest spiv on Shoreditch High Street,' he said proudly, then turned back to his father. 'Just lay off with all that principled pony.'

'Yeah, well, you can come back here with all your bourgeois trappings, just don't forget where you're from.'

'Well, Dad,' replied Harry, wearily, 'I don't suppose you'll ever let me. Now come in through and have a nice cup of tea and we can pretend at being happy families for a while, eh?'

'Mum liked you,' said Harry as we drove back west.

The words chilled me. There was a cold feeling right down in my guts. I realised then that I had to get out, that I would have to leave him. I'd never really thought about how long me and Harry would last but I certainly didn't fancy myself as part of the family. Perhaps I was scared of the prospect of going through his madness again.

But fear prevented me from coming up with any properly thought-out way of leaving. It would have been stupid to confront him. I didn't rate my chances in a showdown with Harry. So I resorted to guerrilla tactics. I could niggle him, wind him up, it wasn't difficult. I somehow figured that if I got up his nose enough he would tire of me altogether.

I would undermine him. Harry hadn't managed to lose all the weight he'd put on during his depression. All the booze and lack of exercise had taken its toll. And the anti-depressants. As he sighed at himself in the mirror I would hold back from reassuring him that he didn't look so bad.

I started to affect an indifference to the sex that we had together. I got into the habit of sneaking out into the bathroom and wanking off before spending the night with him just to make sure that my boredom seemed genuine. Then I'd deliberately go through the motions in a way that reduced it to just a functional level. Robbed of any illusions it became an empty pleasure for Harry. And I knew that that was not what he wanted. Nobody does, let's face it.

And I stopped keeping the flat in the kind of order that Harry insisted upon. He hated mess and so I just let the housework go until it became too much for him.

'Look at this fucking place!' he finally exploded at me. 'It's a fucking dump!'

I let him stomp about the flat a bit, picking up clothes and papers that had been strewn about the drawing room.

'Well?' he demanded.

'Well what?' I replied a bit cockily.

'Well, are you going to tidy this pit up?'

I shrugged and let out a long sigh and started to collect up some of the debris in a listless way. And he snapped. He came over and clouted me across the ear and I went down on the carpet.

'Behave yourself!' he bellowed.

I acted all hurt, which wasn't difficult with a thick ear.

'You can't treat me like this,' I sobbed. 'I'm not your bloody slave.'

I looked up at him from the floor as he seethed above me. I had to be careful. I wanted to goad him enough into saying something reckless but not so much so he'd kick the shit out of me.

'It's not fair, Harry,' I whined at him.

He stared down his nose at me, nostrils wide with anger like a double-barrel shotgun.

'Well if you don't like it, you can piss off,' he declared and with that I got up off the floor and walked to the door.

'Terry!' he called after me. 'Come back here!'

But I was gone. I didn't look back once. That was it, I thought, finish.

So I went back to the bedsit in Westbourne Grove. I'd never officially given it up nor told Harry where it was. He'd never asked. To be honest I didn't expect that I'd be able to get back into it. I hadn't paid rent in nearly three months and my landlord wasn't known for his leniency. Tenants in arrears were likely enough to be called upon by his heavies and a couple of alsatians for good measure. I was surprised to find that my key still fitted the lock and my possessions, meagre as they were, hadn't been tampered with. Two dingy, damp rooms in a run-down Victorian terrace. Its squalor reminded me of the luxury I had briefly been familiar with. I put a shilling in the meter and tried to make myself at home. The unaired rooms smelt of cat's piss and sour milk but it was my own place, at least for the time being, and Harry didn't know where I lived. Or so I thought.

I'd scarcely taken anything with me when I'd walked out of Harry's. Just the clothes I was wearing, a Rolex watch he'd bought me and a bit of spending money that I had in my wallet. And I had no work to go to. Thoughts of the leisurely life that I'd almost got used to hung around in my head, mocking me. I'd have to get some kind of dreary job again. I'd go back to being the sort of person that villains would ridicule whilst they preyed upon them. A mug.

And I couldn't understand why the landlord hadn't sent anyone around about the rent. Stories I'd heard from other tenants about his rent collectors were far from reassuring. He wasn't likely to have merely forgotten one of his godforsaken slum dwellers. He was the type that got rich from counting every penny. Waiting around to be knocked about and thrown out in the street started to drive me crazy. I figured that I had nothing to lose by meeting my fate head on.

I pawned the watch Harry had given me and sold my Dansette gramophone player to a junk shop on Golborne Road. A few weeks' rent and some bluffing might hold some sway. I'd learnt from Harry that a direct approach with as much front as possible could often get results.

The estate agent's office was in Shepherd's Bush. The clerk on the lettings desk ran his finger down a ledger and frowned up at me.

'There's no rent owing on that address,' he informed me.

'What do you mean?'

He smiled coldly at me.

'You have an arrangement with Mr Rachman.'

This threw me. I'd been all geared up to plead my case. Sudden relief, then sudden uneasiness. I got flustered.

'What do you mean, *arrangement*?' I demanded.

The clerk turned the ledger around so that I could read along the row that he had his finger on. There was my name, the address, and RENT FREE written in red ink across the payment columns.

Just then Rachman himself came out of his office in the back. One of his heavies loomed behind him. Rachman was short, fat and bald. He looked over at the desk sourly.

'Is there a problem here?' he hissed in a thick Polish accent.

The clerk pointed at the ledger and Rachman walked up and leaned over. The heavy stayed where he was but stared at me morosely.

'Hm,' mused the Pole looking to where the clerk's grubby finger now smudged the page. 'No problem at all.'

Rachman smiled at me with dead eyes.

'You see, many of my properties I let without financial remuneration. To my friends, you understand. And friends of friends. Mr Starks has proved to be a very useful friend to have. Don't you agree? You will give him my best regards when you see him next, won't you?'

I grinned and nodded at Rachman and got out of the estate agents as soon as possible. It was midday. I went into the first pub I came across and tried to drink away some of the fear and paranoia. Had I been followed? Had he known for some time about the bedsit? Whatever. I'd underestimated the scope of Harry's power and the booze didn't calm me down any. They closed for the afternoon and I staggered back to Westbourne Grove. To where he knew I was.

Two days later, sure enough, a knock came on the door. It was Jimmy Murphy. He cocked his head towards the street.

'Come on,' he said. 'He's in the motor.'

I got into the back of the Daimler. Harry scarcely acknowledged me and didn't start to talk until we'd been moving along for a while.

'You shouldn't have walked out like that,' he said softly. 'It was out of order.'

'I'm sorry.'

Harry shrugged.

'Well maybe I was a bit out of order myself,' he said.

We looked at each other properly. Harry gave a sad little smile and cupped my cheek with an open palm.

'So are you going to come back and behave yourself?'

'I don't think that would be a good idea Harry.'

His hand dropped from my face and he sighed. He sat back and let his head rest against the leather of the seat, his face turned from mine, gazing out of the window.

'I'm sorry Harry.'

He shrugged against the upholstery.

'Yeah, well, that's the way it goes I suppose.'

He turned to give me a little sneer.

'You're nothing special,' he hissed.

He leant forward and told Jimmy to drive back to my place. We sat in silence as we went around a block. Then, when we were back on Westbourne Grove, he spoke again.

'So, what, you working?'

'No.'

Harry nodded thoughtfully.

'You want a job?' he asked.

'What kind of job?'

'One of my businesses. Needs an assistant manager. You've been to clever school, should be able to handle that. What do you say?'

'What kind of business?'

'Electrical goods. Wholesale, retail.' Harry sniffed. 'Legitimate.'

Dominion Electrical Goods occupied a warehouse on Commercial Road. I had to get the tube right across the city. Westbourne Park to Whitechapel on the Metropolitan Line. Manny the Money met me there and showed me around the office. Mr Pinker, the manager of Dominion Electrical, wasn't in.

'He's off sick,' little Manny muttered.

Manny went through my duties. It was simple. Signing delivery notes and filing invoices. Manny would come in from time to time to keep the books up to date but all the records needed to be kept in their proper box files. Now Manny wasn't involved in Dominion in an official capacity. Turned out none of the firm was. This he made clear and that Jimmy Murphy would come in every so often to keep an eye on things.

Mr Pinker wasn't in the next day. Or the day after that. It was just me and a couple of labourers who genially sat around playing cards until a lorry arrived and there were fridges to shift. There wasn't much for me to do. It struck me that this was the sort of job

I might have ended up doing if I'd stayed on at school. Except that, with Harry involved, there was bound to be some sort of angle.

Jimmy came around and we had a cup of tea in the office. He brought out a hip flask and gave us both a shot.

'Everything all right?' he asked.

I nodded.

'No visits or phone calls?'

I shook my head.

'Right,' he said, getting up and draining his laced tea. 'Keep up the good work. I'll see you.'

And he left.

With time on my hands I started to think about what was really going on. I tried to work out what the angle was. Every aspect of a legitimate business seemed in order. We weren't doing much trade, that was for sure, but there's no law against that. I'd thought at first that the warehouse must be fencing for lorry hijacks. I'd heard gossip amongst the firm in the past of how they dealt in gear knocked off that way. The jump up, they called it. But deliveries at Dominion were nothing of the sort. All the paperwork seemed in order, invoices properly made out and everything. The only thing I could think of was that this was a legitimate business funded by dodgy money. That would make sense after all.

Harry came in with Jimmy at the end of the week. He looked around. He seemed happy enough with how things were going. He asked me how I was getting on.

'Fine,' I replied. 'We haven't done much trade, though.'

'Yeah,' said Harry vaguely. 'We'll have to do something about that. In the meantime keep it all kosher. Know what I mean? Anything else?' he asked as he made for the door.

'Just one thing,' I said. 'This Mr Pinker. He hasn't been in at all.'

Harry grinned and looked over at Jimmy.

'Well,' he said. 'If you do see him, let us know.'

And both him and Jimmy Murphy laughed.

That little shared joke got me thinking. Mr Pinker was the set up. The joke was on him. I guessed that he was some straight businessman that they were taking for a ride. That he was the mug. But that didn't stop me, in the last couple of hours of Friday afternoon, from searching the office for more clues before I locked up for the weekend.

There didn't seem to be anything of interest though. Minutes of an annual general meeting revealed that Sir Paul Chambers DSO was on the board as a non-executive director. A meticulous treasurer's report obviously compiled by the diligent Manny Gould. Everything looked in order. Then, when I'd just about given up I found an envelope at the back of the bottom drawer of the filing cabinet. Central Registry of Births, Deaths and Marriages was stamped on it. I took it out and laid it on the desk. I fished inside and pulled out a long form. It was a birth certificate. James Nathaniel Pinker was written in the column headed Name, if any. Under when and where born was scrawled: Eleventh March 1929, 304 Fore St., Edmonton. It made no sense, except to confirm that my as yet invisible boss actually existed. I slipped my hand under the flap of the envelope again and came out with a similar form. Except that this was a death certificate. It too bore the name James Nathaniel Pinker. He'd died of meningitis on the Ninth of June 1929. All his paperwork was in order. Delivery note and final demand. The manager of Dominion Electrical Goods had only lived for three months.

I put the birth and death certificates back in the envelope, shoved it into the filing cabinet, locked up the warehouse and went back to Westbourne Grove. I spent the weekend getting drunk and trying not to think about Mr Pinker or Dominion Electrical Goods. I was getting a good wage, I had a rent-free flat, I knew that even thinking about what was really going on would only get me into trouble. So I tried to block it all out with booze. Two bottles of gin but I was still haunted by my boss the dead baby.

The next week reminders of unpaid invoices started to pile up. We continued to get deliveries. There was hardly space left in the warehouse to put all the stuff. Harry came in on the Wednesday.

'Seen Jimmy?' he demanded tersely as he strode into the office.

I shook my head.

'Right,' he went on, beckoning me out of the office. 'I need to do a bit of shopping.'

He wandered about the crowded showroom. He pointed out a couple of fridges, a cooker and three television sets.

'I'll take all of them,' he said, peeling some notes of a wad.

'You're going to pay for them?' I asked.

'Course I'm going to pay for them,' he frowned at me. 'And I want a proper receipt and all.'

I got the labourers to load up the stuff in the van. Harry gave the driver a list of addresses. He tapped one of the TVs and nodded at me.

'Put this one in the back of the Daimler.'

I lugged it out to where the motor was parked. Tony Stavrakakis was leaning against it having a smoke. He helped me heave it into the boot. Harry came out and opened the back door of the limo. He looked over at me.

'Come on,' he said.

I got in the back beside him and Tony the Greek pulled away. There's something soothing in the smooth motion of a limousine at cruising speed, something comforting about being driven around in a big powerful car. Harry always seemed most at ease in the back of a motor. It was an intimate space for him. He'd used it as a consulting room and no doubt a confessional as well. It was the place we'd first met and where we'd finally split up. I suddenly thought of all those times in between when we'd be all dressed up and chauffeured off somewhere flash.

Harry gave me a sideways look and patted me absently on the leg.

'All right?' he asked.

There were so many questions that I wanted to ask Harry but just then I didn't want to say anything awkward. I didn't want to spoil the moment. There were some things that I really missed about being with Harry. So I just smiled.

'All right,' I replied.

Our destination was Willow Nook Old People's Home in Stepney. Harry went in and spoke with the matron then we carried the telly in through to the lounge. A few wrinkled inmates gaped at us with yellowed eyes. Perched on high-backed chairs that lined the room they looked like lizards sunning themselves.

'Look at all these coffin dodgers,' Harry muttered under his breath as we put the television in place.

A podgy, red-faced man came into the room and went around leaning over and smiling at the inmates.

'Look at that silly cunt,' Harry muttered again. 'Shaking hands with all these half-croaked fuckers.'

'Who's he?' I asked.

'Benny White. Local councillor. Second-rate politician, thinks he's fucking important. Still, he has his uses.'

'Harold!' the councillor declaimed across the room. 'What a fine gesture. Local business putting something back into the community.'

Harry shrugged as Benny White rubbed his podgy hands together. A reporter and a photographer arrived ushered in by the matron. The councillor drew himself up in front of the gathering and gave a little speech.

'Isn't this lovely,' he began. 'Look at this, ladies and gentlemen, a magnificent new television set!'

There was a muted response. A bit of orchestrated groaning from the senile assembly. Harry beamed beside the TV set. The reporter who had been scribbling away in shorthand came over.

'All right Joe?' asked Harry. 'Got all you need?'

'Yeah, sure,' he replied. 'Just the photo.'

'Course. Let's get this over with. Benny!' he called over.

The councillor came over and a few pictures were taken of them shaking hands over the television with the matron and one of the better-looking inmates in the foreground.

Driving back, Harry asked me how the business was going.

'Everything's fine,' I lied.

Harry nodded thoughtfully.

'There are a few things I'd like to know about, though,' I ventured, thinking about my dead baby boss.

Harry touched my arm in a placating fashion.

'Of course Terry,' he assured me. 'We'll talk,' he promised. 'In the meantime, as I've said, keep everything kosher.'

They dropped me back off at the warehouse.

'And when you see Jimmy,' Harry said in parting, 'tell him I want to see him.'

I read the story in next day's *East London Advertiser*. A HELPING HAND was the headline with a photo of Harry, the TV set and the councillor. *Benjamin White, councillor for Stepney East, launched his 'Old Folk's Appeal' today and one of the first to make a donation with a gleaming new television set was local businessman – Harold Starks . . .*

'All right Terry?'

It was Jimmy Murphy. I held up the paper for him to look at and he nearly pissed himself laughing.

'Charity,' he said scathingly. 'Yeah, Harry's big on that. Good for public relations, he says.'

'He's looking for you, Jimmy,' I informed him.

'Yeah, yeah,' he replied as he sat down on my desk.

'So,' he announced, pulling out a hip flask from his jacket pocket. 'How's it going?'

'Well,' I replied and pointed to the pile of invoices on my desk. 'There's all these unpaid bills, what am I supposed to do about them?'

Jimmy took a slug from his flask and sighed.

'Don't worry about them,' he said and passed me the curved metal bottle. I took a swig myself.

'So what am I supposed to do? Pay them?'

'Mr Pinker will sort them out when he gets back.'

'Mr Pinker?'

'Yeah.'

'When he gets back?'

'Yeah,' Jimmy took back the flask. 'What's the matter?'

'Jimmy, I know about Mr Pinker.'

'What you mean?'

'I know he's dead.'

Jimmy laughed lightly at me.

'Oh yeah,' he said casually. 'That.'

There was a pause in which we both looked around the office.

'Jimmy,' I said. 'What the fuck is going on?'

'Don't you know?'

'No, of course I don't know.'

'You mean you haven't been told?'

'Haven't been told what?'

'What a long firm is.'

'What?' I implored.

'A long firm,' replied Jimmy, screwing the cap back down on his hip flask. He got up off the desk and made for the door.

'Don't worry,' he said as he walked out. 'You'll find out soon enough.'

Harry holds the poker up in front of me.

'You've seen how it's done. Now you can have a go.'

I start to hyperventilate. As I shunt about in the chair its rubber feet squeal against the concrete floor.

'Hold him down, Bubble,' Harry whispers to Tony Stavrakakis and the big Greek puts both of his heavy hands on my shoulders.

'The thing is, Terry,' Harry goes on, 'it's a question of trust. You've got to trust me now so that we can do this right. And if you can trust me enough to do that, well, maybe I can trust you and all. It's all a bit medieval, I suppose. Trial by Ordeal. You know, the punishment itself sorts out whether you're guilty or not. If it goes wrong, well that's proof of a sort. It would be a shame, but then, if you do lose your tongue—'

He smiles over at the big Greek.

'Well, you won't be able to grass, will you?'

*   *   *

The warehouse was becoming ridiculously crowded. There was scarcely any showroom space any more and walking through the building was like going through a maze the walls of which were cardboard boxes stacked high and filled with all kinds of electrical goods. One of these walls had nearly collapsed and I was helping the labourers to make it safe when Harry arrived team handed. Most of the firm was with him, Manny, Jimmy and Tony Stavrakakis. They looked around and muttered to each other a bit.

'We're having a board meeting,' Harry announced. 'We'll be in the office.'

'You want me to come up?'

'Nah. Carry on with what you're doing. We won't be long.'

We restacked the boxes and I realised that with all the shifting around I'd lost track of a lot of the stock. I'd left the clipboard with the stock list on it in the office so I went upstairs to fetch it. I was about to rap on the frosted glass door when I realised that I could hear the firm talking. I carefully pressed my ear against the door jam and listened.

'. . . so we're all ready then?' It was Harry's voice. 'We hit the floor next Wednesday.'

'And the kid?' came Tony's Cypriot accent. 'He doesn't know nothing?'

'That's right,' Harry replied. 'And let's keep it that way. Don't want him worrying his pretty little head this stage in the game.'

'What if he has to take the fall?' asked Manny. 'He won't be any trouble to us, will he?'

I could barely hear Harry's deep chuckle.

'Nah,' he said. 'And we can make sure of that when the time comes. At the moment him knowing nothing is our best cover. So, let's get going.'

I heard them all getting up to come out of the office so I tiptoed down the stairs as quickly and silently as possible.

'Right,' said Harry coming up to me. 'We're having a closing-down sale. Next Wednesday.'

He grinned at me.

'Everything must go.'

Jimmy had the clipboard I had gone to fetch in his hand. He nodded at Harry.

'Right,' Harry continued. 'We'll be off now. Jimmy's staying behind to do a stock check with you. Why don't you come for a drink tonight?' he asked, all full of affable charm. 'At the club.'

Jimmy and me spent the afternoon going around the warehouse and ticking off stock. When we had finished on the fridges he glanced sideways at me.

'So,' he said. 'You worked it out yet?'

'What?'

'What the scam is.'

I shrugged.

'Are you going to tell me?' I asked.

Jimmy smiled and took the hip flask from out of his jacket pocket. He unscrewed the metal bottle and took a shot. He gave a sharp sigh and smiled again.

'Well that depends son,' he said. 'That depends. You see I'd be doing you a favour, see? I'd expect a favour in return. Know what I mean?'

'I'm not sure.'

I felt myself being drawn into a dangerous game. I was already out of my depth but my curiosity was getting the better of me.

'What do you mean, a favour?'

Jimmy handed me the flask and I took a swig. The whisky burned the back of my throat and I coughed. Jimmy tapped the clipboard.

'What I mean is, we could be a bit clever with these figures. It could be worth our while.'

'Well, I don't know.'

'Look, do you want to know what a long firm is or not?'

I hardly dared to say anything but my head nodded automatically. Jimmy took back the flask and screwed back the top on.

'Right,' said Jimmy, giving me a satisfied glare. 'You owe me. Right?'

The scotch glowed in my empty sinking stomach. Jimmy started to explain it all.

'A long firm's a good racket. Simple, see? All it needs is a bit of capital and a legitimate front. You found out about Pinker, didn't you?'

'Yeah.'

'Well he's dead but his birth certificate is still valid. You see, they keep records of births and deaths in different files. That's the beauty of it. So if you get hold of a birth certificate of someone who died when they were a kid, no one's going to know from it that they're really dead. There, you've got yourself a front man. You can get all the essential documents you need from a birth certificate. Driving licence, passport, bank account. With a bank account set up you can open a business account. Register a firm at Companies House. Bribe a few influential faces on to the board as non-executive directors. Rent a warehouse, get some tasty-looking stationery printed with all your friends in high places prominent on the letter heading. Deposit some cash into your business account, move it about a bit so it looks like you're trading. And you are, at first. Buy in a load of gear wholesale, pay on the dot for the first delivery then work up a bit of credit. Delay payment on all the stuff that comes in after that until you've got a warehouse full. Then, bosh, hit the floor.'

'Hit the floor?'

'Grand slam. Everything must go. Cut rate, strictly for cash. Sell the whole lot off in a single day. Make a withdrawal from the business account the same day and then disappear. The whole operation's been fronted by someone who died years ago so you can't be traced. You can make ten grand, twenty grand, who knows?'

'Right,' I said, trying to take it all in.

'Thing is Terry, nobody knows for sure how much the scam will bring. Everything moves so quickly when you hit the floor. You're selling in quantity and for cash so there's bound to be some leeway.

Harry isn't going to be anywhere near the warehouse on the big day. He can't afford to be associated with this set up.'

'Wait a minute.'

'I know what you're thinking. But it's not like we'd be having him over in any big way. He won't know, for fucksakes. A couple of grand. Three or four maybe.'

'I don't know.'

'Listen, you reckon everything's going to be all right if you just keep your head down. You're scared of what Harry might do if he found out. Right? Well, yeah, you've got good reason to be. But what do you think you're doing here in the first place?'

'What do you mean?'

'I mean, you walk out on Harry Starks, next thing you know he gives you a cushy little job like this. That was quite a liberty, you know, walking out like that. He was choked.'

It was embarrassing hearing this from Jimmy and I think he knew it. I couldn't look at him.

'Right choked he was,' he went on. 'You think he'd just let it pass? You think he'd just forget about it and give his old boyfriend a job just for old times' sake? Hasn't it ever occurred to you that you've been set up?'

'What?'

'Whose signatures are they on all those invoices and delivery notes? If this little racket is ever investigated, who's the one person they can finger for it? You, that's who. You're the mug here, Terry, and no mistake.'

'Harry wouldn't.'

'Harry wouldn't what? Let you take the fall? Do me a favour. And what are you going to do about it? You ain't going to grass him up, are you? He'll make sure of that. He always does. It's what he's good at. And you aren't going to grass me up to him neither. So it's up to you son. I'm taking a piece of this scam and if you're in, you can have your fair whack.'

'And if I'm not?'

'Then you keep fucking quiet about it.'

39

Jimmy brought his face up close to mine and hissed halitosis and whisky fumes at me.

'Otherwise I'll fucking do you, nancy boy!'

It seemed such a long time since I'd been to The Stardust that I was surprised that the doorman recognised me. He nodded me through with an expectant grin. As I went downstairs into the nightclub I felt none of the charm that I'd once associated with the place. It was just a tacky dive. I guess I'd grown old in the past few weeks.

I got myself a drink and looked out across the room. I clocked a few faces I vaguely remembered. Harry was at his usual table, holding court. He casually waved over at me. I drained my gin and tonic, straightened my tie and wandered across.

'Terry,' Harry announced amiably, indicating a chair opposite him. 'Have a seat.'

There was a young man sitting next to him. He wore an expensive mohair suit and his blond hair was cut in a short college-boy style. Harry's new boy, I assumed. My replacement. The new boy looked at me shiftily, trying to affect some sort of professional sneer. I gave him a fierce stare and he looked away. He was pretty enough, I thought, and convincing in his role of Harry's kept boy. He looked to be doing a better job of it than I ever managed. He had a cheap haughtiness, an eagerness to be spoiled that I'm sure Harry fell for.

'So, how's it all going?' Harry asked.

I glanced across the table. The new boy was looking disdainfully bored. I kind of hoped Harry would give him some spending money and send him away but maybe he was part of the night's proceedings. A gesture to show me what had been between us was all passed. It certainly reminded me of how expendable I was. It was then that I resolved not to tell Harry anything. Maybe I felt some spite at him for casually showing off his new boyfriend as he was setting me up to take the fall for the long firm. But mostly I figured that, if Harry knew that I knew, things would be a lot more dangerous for me. It would mean telling him of how I'd snooped around behind his back. I decided that I'd go along with Jimmy's plan. I deserved to get something out of all this, after all, given the risk I was taking. So I resolved to play dumb. Looking over at the new boy, I realised that that was another thing he was better at than me. I shrugged.

'It's all going fine, Harry,' I lied.

'So we're all ready for the big day?'

I nodded.

'Right. Well, as you know, I won't be there on the day. I'll be otherwise engaged. Remember, I'm not officially connected with Dominion Electrical Goods. I'm like a silent partner. Silent,' he repeated, putting a finger to his lips. 'You understand?'

'Sure.'

'Right, well Jimmy will be there but Manny will be coming around later to pick up the takings. Jimmy's going to be organising security, can't be too careful with all those takings. But it's Manny that looks after the money. You clear about that?'

'Yeah.'

'Good. Don't worry, it'll all go fine. I'll explain it all later. You'll get a bonus and everything. OK?'

'Yeah.'

'Good. You're a good kid.'

Harry leant over the table to give me a friendly pat on my cheek. I involuntarily flinched away from his heavy hand. The new boy watched and sniggered. Harry frowned.

'Relax,' he said. 'Have another drink.'

I had plenty.

I spent the next few days getting the warehouse ready for the big sale. There were huge gaps in the stock check that me and Jimmy Murphy had done. I tried to cover them up amongst all the paperwork in the office hoping desperately that I could maintain my assumed ignorance of everything.

The last thing to do was to put up signs on the outside of the building. CLOSING DOWN SALE. LAST FEW DAYS. EVERYTHING MUST GO. I tacked them up on the shopfront with a sense of doom. They reminded me of those signs you see religious nutcases carrying about. You know, THE END IS NIGH, stuff like that.

The big day. I was as nervous as fuck. Jimmy arrived with a couple of heavies I'd never seen before. Freelancers. Harry wanted to keep any connection between him and the long firm to a minimum. But we needed some sort of muscle, just in case. The amount of money expected to change hands that day would be tempting for any outside team to heavy into. Jimmy gave me a wink, implicating me. I sighed heavily.

'Don't worry, son,' he assured me. 'It'll soon be over.'

And things did move fast that day. After weeks of doing very little trade we were suddenly very busy. It wasn't called a long firm for nothing. This sort of fraud required a lot of patience. A long wait and then a quick killing.

They came from all over town, our customers. Word must have gone out: a gravy train on Commercial Road. And it was well worth their while. They were getting goods at criminally low prices, it was like legalised fencing. And everyone got a receipt so no one could be accused of receiving stolen goods. Even though they were. Everything went dirt cheap but then we were getting a hundred per cent profit on everything we sold. Harry had a very pure sense of business.

They came in vans, lorries, high-sided pantechnicons. Even a flat-bed truck that we loaded up and tied down with a tarpaulin over it. And everyone got their receipt. As I signed them I was reminded that each one was evidence against me. That I had been set up by Harry. And so I could feel justified in being part of Jimmy's scam. He would nod over at me at particular parts of the stock that we sold that he hadn't included in the stock check and I would destroy our copies of the receipts for that sale.

I can scarcely remember any really clear details of the day we hit the floor. Everything happened so quickly, what with all the activity, but I think the time passed swiftly also because I dreaded the end of it.

When we were cleaned out I took all of the money into the office. I paid off the labourers, gave them a bonus that Harry had suggested. They went off happy, no doubt to the nearest pub. I envied them as I set to work sorting out piles of cash on the office floor. I'd never handled so much money in my life before or since. The smell of all those fingered notes was vaguely disgusting. Jimmy peeled off some notes for his freelance heavies and they were gone too. Just me and him. We put the money we planned to take for ourselves to one side and counted it up. It was nearly three thousand pounds. Jimmy scooped it up and shoved it into a holdall. He took out his hip flask, had a slug himself and then passed it to me.

'We'll divvy up that later,' he said as I took a swig myself.

Manny arrived with a battered old suitcase, no doubt to carry the takings in to Harry. We counted through the takings together as Jimmy watched by the door. Manny was very systematic. He went through the original delivery notes to check all the stock that had been sold. He was completely in his element as we sorted through the piles of money. He seemed instinctively able to keep different columns of figures in his head as the day's takings were calculated. I noticed a frown growing on that little round head of his as he realised that some of the cash was missing. He was implacable, starting the count from the very beginning again as he noticed some of those columns in his mind just didn't add up. His formidable little head started to shake from side to side as deep down, on an almost unconscious level, it realised that something was wrong.

'Is this *all* the money?' he demanded, sniffing at the piles of notes on the floor.

'Yes, of course,' I replied, trying not to shake with the real fear that I felt.

'Then we must count it all again,' he insisted and got back down on his hands and knees.

I looked over at Jimmy who was feigning nonchalance. He shrugged back at me. Manny looked up, perhaps sensing something. His little eyes pierced through me. He stood up.

'Look,' he said. 'Maybe there's been some mistake. Something you've forgotten.'

He shrugged amicably.

'It's not too late,' he said reassuringly. 'Things move fast. Money gets lost in all the fast dealing of it. Just hand it over and there'll be no more said.'

Manny was moving towards me with a soothing smile on his round little face. I backed away and as I did so saw Jimmy come up behind him. I tried to say something but my mouth was dry. It was like pantomime. *Behind you.* I saw Jimmy take a cosh from out of his jacket pocket.

'Don't worry,' said Manny. 'We can work this all out.'

I stuttered something unintelligible and then Jimmy whacked Manny with his cosh, putting that troubled little mind to rest.

It was like slow motion. Manny's eyes rolled white in their sockets. He shrugged fatalistically then fell to the floor scattering piles of notes around the office.

Jimmy slapped the shot-filled leather cosh in the palm of his hand and looked down at Manny.

'Fuck,' he said thoughtfully. 'Fuck, fuck, fuck.'

I was down on my knees checking on Manny and trying to extricate the notes trapped under his heavy little frame. I was worried that Jimmy might have killed him but the little man seemed indestructible. Semi-consciously gurgling something that sounded like Yiddish. Jimmy moved swiftly then, gathering up the money on the floor and stuffing it into his holdall.

'What are you doing?' I demanded.

'Change of plan,' he announced. 'We're going to take the lot. Do a runner.'

I looked up at him and frowned.

'What?'

'We've got no choice now. We can take the fucking lot and go.'

'Go where?'

'I don't know. Over the water. Belfast. Dublin. There's enough here to get us sorted.'

He caught my stare.

'So, are you in?'

He looked down at me fiercely.

My hesitation was answer enough.

'Well, you ain't going to stop me are you?'

He'd finished collecting all the money. His cosh hanging out of his trouser pocket. He took it out.

'Turn around,' he said.

'Jimmy, no,' I replied but he poked me in the face with it so that I turned away and tensed up.

'You'll thank me for this,' he said and whacked me on the side of the head.

The blow caught my temple and I went down, blacking out as I hit the floor. I woke up grabbing hold of a five-pound note that Jimmy had missed underneath the desk. I was only out for a couple of minutes. I heard the warehouse door slam downstairs as Jimmy made his getaway.

'Fuck,' I groaned and closed my eyes again, my head throbbing with pain and trying to think what to do.

There wasn't much that I could do. I knew that I would have to face Harry about all this. I got up and felt the bruise on the side of my head. Jimmy was right of course, giving me a whack was doing me a favour in a way but I knew that it wouldn't be nearly enough. I tried to think of what to say without giving too much away of my own guilt. It seemed pretty hopeless. Manny was still prone on the floor. He had got a much worse whack than I had. Jimmy had really taken a proper swing at him. So I sat him up against the desk and phoned Harry.

Harry answered and demanded to speak to Manny. I had to tell him that Manny was unable to come to the phone. There was a pause, then Harry said that he was coming over. His voice was cold and matter of fact. I was scared shitless.

He arrived with Tony Stavrakakis. He didn't even look at me at first but went over to Manny and tried to talk to him. Manny was still slumped down against the desk, muttering incoherently. Harry crouched down and slapped the round head a while until he realised it was a waste of time.

'Jimmy,' he finally said, looking up at me.

'He's gone,' I replied, rubbing my face, trying to make as much as I could of my own wound.

'And the money?' he demanded.

'Gone,' I said, mournfully.

Harry stretched his legs and stood upright. He nodded thoughtfully and looked over at Tony the Greek. He sighed and shook his head. He tutted, tongue against teeth. As if ticking off all of the bad things that had happened. All of the bad points. Tick, tick, tick.

'Well, Terry,' he said calmly, his voice soft as if to indicate disappointment rather than anger. 'We need to have a little chat. Don't we?'

Harry made some phone calls as I sat with my elbow on the desk cradling my dazed head. The doctor that the firm used came over to check on Manny. And Jock McCluskey arrived with a minor face I didn't know the name of. He briefed them to go after Jimmy. They were both armed.

'Right,' said Harry as the doctor led a semi-conscious Manny out of the office. 'Let's get out of here.'

He cocked his head at me sharply.

'You're coming with us.'

I was made to get into the boot of the Daimler. By the time we arrived at our destination I was sick with fear and petrol fumes. It was a lock-up garage beneath the arch of a railway bridge. Harry unlocked a padlock and we went inside.

A light was flicked on. The bare bulb revealed an almost empty room. There was a table to one side with some bottles and old chip wrappers scattered on it. A brazier with a gas canister stood by the arched end wall. In the middle of the cavernous space was a wooden chair. It looked lonely, sat there all on its own. A few lengths of rope lay curled around its legs.

'Take a seat,' Harry insisted.

As I sat down he went over to the table and picked up a bottle of Johnny Walker.

'Fancy a drink?' he offered and I nodded.

He poured the scotch into a chipped mug and passed it to me. It was about half full. I drank it down in two or maybe three quick gulps. Harry then took the mug off me and nodded at Tony. The Greek started to tie me to the chair.

'Right. Let's get started.' Harry bared his teeth at me in a grin. 'Showtime.'

'So, now it's your turn, Terry,' Harry says, heating up the poker again. 'Trust me.'

He smiles at me playfully as if the whole thing is a childish dare.

'Now, we want to get this right, don't we? Don't want to burn your tongue off. You're going to need that later to tell us the whole story. Open wide. Give him a hand, Bubble.'

Tony pulls me head back by its hair. My jaw hangs open. Harry holds the poker over the flame until it's white hot. Then he advances, pointing it at me.

Panic. A spasm of breathing. I'm panting like a dog. Can't speak.

Please, Harry. Don't Harry.

'Come on. Stick your tongue out.'

I do as he says. My mouth feels so dry. He holds the poker in front of my nose. Heat and light press against my face. Harry gently draws it down. It slides against my tongue with a rasping hiss. A whisper of steam stings my eyes. I feel only the pressure of the luminous metal. No heat. But I'm sure that it's searing into me, burning my tongue from out of my head. I black out for a second.

I come to suddenly. A numb, gaping mouth heaving out heavy sobs. My tongue is still there. I lick at my lips to make sure. Swooning with relief I feel a lovely warm feeling in my cock. I realise that I'm pissing myself. Through the tears, I see Harry nodding at me. There's piss running down my legs.

'There, there,' he says, patting me on the shoulder. 'That's it. It's all over now.'

I continue crying as Harry walks over and tosses the poker back into the brazier and turns off the gas. Then comes back over to me. Tony's let go of my hair and Harry strokes it back into place using his splayed fingers as a comb.

'It's all right,' he says, softly. 'You can tell us all about it.'

And I do. I tell him everything. I try to tell him everything at once but he gets me to start at the beginning, occasionally stopping me and asking questions. And it all comes out. All of it. The whole truth.

Tony unties me and Harry pours me another drink. This time the scotch burns against my swollen tongue. I cough most of it out down my front.

'I'll tell you what happens now,' Harry says, reading my mind. 'You can go now. We're quits. You don't talk to anybody about anything. You've had a taste of what will happen if you do.'

And that was it. I never saw Harry again, though years later, what with the trial and that, he became quite famous, or rather, infamous. As I left he peeled off a few notes at me. About fifty quid. As if to remind me that I owed him. I got a taxi back home. Next day I got a rash of tiny white blisters all over my tongue. Made it difficult for me to talk. Not that I had any inclination to.

2

Dissolution Honours

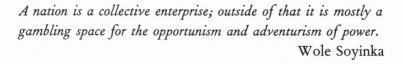

A nation is a collective enterprise; outside of that it is mostly a gambling space for the opportunism and adventurism of power.
Wole Soyinka

1964

Monday, 2 November

To the House of Lords for Ceremonial Introduction. Black Rod leads the way, his ebony shaft of office surmounted by a golden lion rampant. The Garter King of Arms carries the patent conferring my imminent status of Lord Thursby of Hartwell-juxta-Mare. Flanked by two peers I approach the Woolsack.

Always had a craving for preposterous ritual & you don't get much better than this. Teddy Thursby taking his seat in the Upper House. Joining the lords temporal, the lords spiritual. I'm wearing all the gear of course. Ermine, knee britches, silver buckled shoes, silk stockings. Try to move with processional rhythm. The slow gentle dignified sway. But it's hard not to swagger a bit.

Ceremonial introduction is so solemn & ridiculous. Useless, stupid, bloody beautiful ritual. So calm and soothing. I love it. Maybe it's the High Church upbringing. But then I always played that up a bit. Went through a big Anglo-Catholic phase at Oxford. Dead give-away, I suppose. Still, it always pays to send out the right signals, the right codes. That way you can make your intentions known whilst still remaining discreet. And that's what I've always been. Discreet.

Present the patent & the writ of summons to the Lord Chancellor. Sign the Test Roll, take the Oath, kiss the book. The strange purity of detail. Each tentative, futile gesture an escape from the everyday.

Feel like a new boy again. Like my first day in Parliament back in 1924 when I took my seat in the Commons. There had been ceremonial introduction then as well. No dressing up though. I remember other rituals equally important if slightly less formal. Chips Channon showing me round the Members' lavatories. 'The most important rooms,' he had announced with mock solemnity, vainly trying to affect a sparkle in those deadly dull eyes of his.

That was forty years ago. I've had some success, I suppose. Never lived up to my potential though. Early days held such promise. That stupid scandal back in the thirties. Failing to declare a business interest. Misleading the House. Had to resign from Cabinet & I never got a government post again. Became the flamboyant backbencher instead. Glad to be out of it now, to tell the truth. All those years of service & all I've got to show for it is a measly life peerage. Kicked upstairs. Some wag said that it was entirely appropriate, given my reputation, that I should be given a peerage in Sir Alec's Dissolution Honours List. Oh well, I'm a fucking Lord now. I can lord it about a bit.

Met Tom Driberg in the Lobby afterwards. He congratulated me. Genuine warmth there, I'm sure of it. Always felt a sort of cross-bench camaraderie with old Tom. Pure disinterested brotherly, or rather sisterly, affection. Nothing physical you understand. Shared interests. He's High Church too, of course. And we both have a taste for a bit of rough. He always wants to go down, mind you, being a socialist. I suppose he sees fellatio as an expression of democracy. He once confided his conviction that ingesting young & vigorous semen counters the effects of ageing. He was quite serious about it. I replied that it was probably the closest he'd ever get to transubstantiation. I'm not averse to it myself but I usually like to maintain a proper posture when mingling with the masses, rubbing my honourable member up against the constituency. Mutual masturbation, I think, is the tedious technical term. I hate these modern definitions. Makes everything sound coldly medical rather than deliciously sinful. There's an ancient word that far better describes my pleasure. *Slicklegging*.

Of course I've always been more discreet, which isn't saying much when it comes to Driberg. Don't know how he's managed to get away with it all these years. I've always been very careful, furtive perhaps, but then that's in the very essence of pleasure in slicklegging. I've always acted with caution. Never caught wet handed as it were.

'How are you celebrating?' Tom asked.

I shrugged. I hadn't gave it much thought. All that ceremony seemed enough. Frankly, I'm a bit too broke at the moment to throw a proper party. A few drinks in White's later on perhaps. Tom suddenly looked at me conspiratorially.

'Well, you must come to a party tomorrow night, Teddy,' he insisted. 'I think you'll find it interesting.'

He writes down an address & presses it into my hand with an implicative smile.

'Be there around ten,' he said.

I went back to Eaton Square & picked up my mail. A few telegrams of congratulation. One from the constituency association. Won't have to deal with that dreary lot any more. Two ominous-looking letters. One from Ruth, one from the National Provincial Bank.

Sir,

Can I remind you that the borrowing on your account is creeping ever upwards and that the overdraft is now about £1,000 higher than a year ago.

I feel sure that you are as concerned as I am about this. It is not merely a question of credit squeeze or of the absence of security – this borrowing is costing you something in the region of £150 per annum in interest. Is it not possible to re-budget and reverse the trend? Otherwise, without some assurance of an improvement in this situation I would feel compelled to seek the advice and guidance of my head office.

Yours faithfully,

George Budgen

Manager.

Teddy,

I really have had enough of you avoiding facing up to our situation. I'd much rather talk to you directly but I doubt if we'd be able to manage that with any civility so I am forced to write.

I am sorry that our marriage has turned out so very badly. I feel that I have played my part well enough but I am constantly undermined by your behaviour and your extraordinary mode of life.

It has always been me that has had to make compromises in order to maintain your precious veneer of respectability but I no longer feel that I can go on in this way.

A final break between us would probably be for the best but I realise what effect a separation would have on you professionally and socially, so I will agree to continue with the charade under certain conditions.

As soon as you are in a position to do so, I would like the sum of £250 paid into my account at Chase National Bank on a Banker's Order each month. I want a separate provision made for me financially. I'm sick of having to deal with your increasingly irate creditors and of never being sure whether the cheques I write will be honoured or not.

For my part, I will be with you occasionally at Hartwell Lodge, say, the first Sunday of each month so that we can go to church together. Also I agree to go with you to such functions in London and elsewhere that will serve to keep up the facade of happily married life in our new roles of Lord and Lady Thursby.

For the rest of the time we can be free of each other. You can be free to carry on with your selfish and dissolute lifestyle and I can be free of any useless expectations of your duty as a husband.

Ruth.

Well, with all the pomp & circumstance over it's back to ghastly fucking reality, I suppose. I suddenly felt completely deflated. Pour myself a large gin & start to make dreary calculations. Incoming: no MP's salary, odd bits of journalism beginning to dry up (no one interested now I'm no longer the flamboyant backbencher), expenses for attendance in the Lords (but the less time spent at that Darby & Joan club the better), BBC work poorly paid & notoriously slow in actually coughing up. Outgoing: my 'selfish and dissolute lifestyle', as Ruth calls it. Could make some economies there I suppose though I'm loath to do so. And that bitch wants £250 a month! Just where she thinks I'll find that kind of money is beyond me. Ungrateful cow. I never asked anything of her. Though, on reflection, that could be seen as the root of our problems. Repairs on Hartwell Lodge. Dry rot, wood beetle, estimated costs £2,000. Get up and pour myself another gin.

Depressing that I should have to be thinking of how I can balance the books on the very day of my glorious investiture. Maybe I could write a book. Get an advance on the royalties and pay off a few debts. What about, though? Still too young to be writing my memoirs even though I am almost as old as the century. The obvious thing, of course would be to sell the house. Hartwell Lodge. The baronial seat of the first (& last, let's face it) Lord Thursby. No, it would never do. Besides, I love it too much even though its Tudor foundations are falling to bits.

Get rotten *fou* brooding over such matters. And so to bed. Gin melancholia well & truly set in.

Jake Arnott

Johnson in the White House with a landslide. Yanks obviously had no stomach for this Goldwater creature & I can't say I blame them.

Evening & I'm off to this 'party' Tom D. mentioned yesterday. Find the slip of paper he handed me with that salacious grin of his in my pocket. A Chelsea address & a name. Harry Starks. The name means nothing. Sounds Jewish. Still, Tom's contacts always hold some strange promise.

Arrive about ten thirty. Shown into a large, rather over-furnished drawing room by a blond-haired young man. Some sort of a houseboy maybe. A hideous stone fireplace had been constructed around the chimney breast & a bar, complete with optics, had been built into a connecting wall but apart from that there hadn't been too much vandalism. There were a few quite agreeable pieces of furniture that one would guess had been here when the present occupier had moved in but, my goodness, the place was stuffed with all manner of junk. Boxing & horse-racing memorabilia, African & Oriental kitsch, trashy porcelain figurines & lots of gilt-framed photographs. Each one showed a heavy-set man with slicked-back hair caught in stillness with any number of what one would call, I guess, 'showbusiness personalities'. Next to each professional smile, the man, whom I guessed must be our host, held an equally professional stare. Defiant & direct yet shyly cautious, as if superstitious of the camera & somewhat wary of being identified. A lonely expression amidst the cheap & flashy glamour, looking out from the glossy surface as if in search for something more.

The blond boy brought me a gin & tonic & I looked around the room. Quite a crowd. A close-knit group of men with battered faces who looked like retired boxers or doormen. A few flashy-looking types, someone I'm sure I recognise from the television, more sombre men mingling with them, & lots of young men. Boys. I caught sight of a clerical collar. I saw our host talking with Tom Driberg. An imposingly powerful-looking man. His Savile Row suit gave him an air of savage nobility. It was a dark-blue chalk stripe just like my own.

Tom caught my eye & beckoned me over.

'Harry,' he said, 'let me introduce you to Lord Thursby.'

His joined-up eyebrows raised as one. I could see he was impressed. Probably took me for full-blooded aristocracy instead of just a kicked-upstairs life peer. There's a strange sort of bond between the lower-class tearaway & the upper-class bounder. A shared hatred of the middle classes I suppose. He shoved out his hand, adorned with chunky rings & a big gold wristwatch.

'I'm honoured, your lordship.'

I grinned. It was the first time I was referred to by my title since the ceremony.

'Call me Teddy,' I insisted & took his strong grip.

'Harry,' he grinned back & I just knew we'd get along.

'Harry does a lot of charity work in the East End,' said Tom.

'Really?'

Harry shrugged.

'Boys' clubs, that sort of thing,' he explained.

His own sort of *noblesse oblige*, I suppose, with its optional *droit de seigneur* one imagines.

Two of the boys were setting up a film projector & a screen at one end of the room. One of the pugilists had assumed the role of major domo, arranging the seating, giving orders to the other boys & glancing over to Harry, who appeared to be directing everything from afar whilst still engaged in conversation with me.

'Come on Teddy,' he said with a wink, gently taking my arm & leading me to a seat. 'The entertainment's about to begin.'

The party slowly got seated as the room was darkened. The film was a series of vignettes. Short scenes of innocent depravity. An old-fashioned, almost prelapsarian quality about them. More like drawing-room farce than any of this modern art-house pornography. There was as much emphasis on costume as on nudity in their erotic content. Dressing up was as important as undressing. Master & footman were depicted amidst the golden age of Edwardian romanticism complete with chaise longue & french windows. Sailors on shore leave wrestled with each other in playful brutality. Even a scene with leather boys, despite its bondage & mild sadism, had a naive quality to it, a child-like *nostalgie de la boue*.

Gasps of delight & muttered comments of approval from the room as the film proceeded but also other sounds that indicated that what was on screen was merely dumbshow for the main drama of the evening. There was already some groping in the darkness. The celluloid clattered to an abrupt end leaving a bright white square on the screen. Two of the boys started undressing each other. The beam of the projector caught their tight little bodies in a harsh chiaroscuro. Wanton flesh outlined with charcoal-thick shadow. One boy knelt to take the other's cock in his mouth.

Harry distributed the boys among his guests as largesse. They went into service or were themselves served. One of the businessmen was on his knees in front of the broken-nosed major domo. Some of the party were content in their role of audience. Touching themselves as they looked on. They also serve, those who watch & wait.

A young lad was propelled towards me by our host & we found a quiet corner in one of the bedrooms. He leant back against the wall with a lazily arrogant look on his tough little face as we indulged in a little slicklegging. I grabbed at his crotch & kneaded it through the cloth.

'Get your cock out,' I ordered softly as I undid my own fly.

I spat on the palm of my hand & rubbed our cocks together vigorously, coaxing some languid groans from the hoarse-voiced youngster.

'You naughty boy,' I muttered harshly as I brought the two of us off. 'You naughty, naughty boy.'

I gave a strangled cry of delight & relief as my mind darkened

& sperm spilled out through my hand onto the front of my trousers. The youth gave an indolent sort of grunt then was off, no doubt to continue in his duties. I pulled out the handkerchief from my top pocket & wiped myself off. Felt a sense of calm & no little exhaustion from my exertions. Takes it out of you at my age. From every part of the flat could be heard the strange sounds of sexual indulgence. I felt drained & in need of refreshment. A gin & tonic would do the trick, I thought. Wandered out through the gloom of the bedroom. Nearly tripped over Tom Driberg, honourable member for Barking, on his knees, energetically sucking away.

Wednesday, 11 November

I got a call from Harry in the week suggesting that we meet for a drink. So I invited him to White's. I knew he'd be impressed, not just because it was London's oldest & most prestigious club. It retains a touch of aristocratic raffishness that has all but vanished from the rest of clubland, a quality that I instinctively knew Harry would be drawn to. Just as I was drawn to his own kind of style. Such a change from the dreary businessmen, the constituency-party Tories I've been used to dealing with. Boring me to death in the Hartwell Conservative Club. I suspected even then that Mr Starks wasn't exactly, shall we say, kosher despite his Yiddish name. He was dangerous, but that was part of his charm.

I saw him catching his own reflection in the huge mirror on the stairway as I showed him around. Seeing himself framed by its baroque elegance he permitted a wistful smile to play across his lips. We walked through the collonaded entrance into the games room. Harry walked over to the billiard table. He seemed drawn to it, reassured by its familiarity.

'White's is one of the few clubs in London with a billiard table,' I explained.

He looked absorbed as he gently fingered the green baize.

'I used to have a billiard hall,' he declared. 'Well, I was part owner. The bloke who ran it offered me a partnership. He was having a spot of bother.'

Harry grinned over at me.

'Fancy a game, Harry?' I asked.

'No thanks, Teddy,' he replied, slapping the side of the table. 'Solid enough things, billiard tables. Still, so easy for the felt to get ripped.'

Harry caught my eye with a blank stare. A well-practised look. One that can intimidate & yet draw one in at the same time.

'Let's have a drink,' I suggested breezily & we walked through together. Harry leant back in his leather armchair, taking a sip of brandy & soda, casually surveying the fixtures & fittings.

'Nice place,' he commented. 'Wouldn't mind joining myself.'

I smiled, hoping that he was joking. The club has a two-year waiting list & Harry's background wouldn't exactly support an application. I had a vague horror of him making White's some sort of offer. Then he frowned with the thick line where his eyebrows joined. He took another gulp of brandy & sighed sharply.

'So, Teddy,' he said.

I could tell he enjoyed the familiarity just as he savoured the formality. The combination was irresistible.

'I was wondering if we could talk business.'

'Business?' I countered with a casual cautiousness.

'Yes, business. I have a proposition. I wonder if you'd be interested in becoming involved with a new company I'm starting up. As a director.'

'Well, I'm a bit tied up at the moment, Harry. Otherwise.'

'Oh, I don't mean that you'd be involved in an executive position, Teddy. I wouldn't expect you to take part in the day-to-day running of it. Just, you know . . .'

He shrugged.

'The occasional board meeting?' I suggested helpfully. 'Turn up to the annual general meeting. That sort of thing?'

'Yes,' he replied with a smile. 'That sort of thing.'

Friday, 13 November

To Bristol to record *Any Questions?* With me on the panel – Dingle Foot, Tony Crosland & Violet Bonham-Carter. Excellent dinner before the programme.

One of the questions was 'What do you think will be the effects of a more permissive society?' I replied that the twenties had been a bit of a wild party but we'd got away with it then because we didn't ask anybody's permission. Much laughter and applause.

Tuesday, 17 November

Have officially been made a director of Empire Refrigeration Ltd. Appointment confirmed with a cheque for £2,000 brought around to my flat in person by one of Harry's boys. And it wasn't only the money that was delivered by hand.

So, I'm out of a hole financially, for the time being at least. I can keep the bank & Ruth off my back for a while. Things are looking up. Harry's desire for legitimacy definitely has its possibilities for me. The name Lord Thursby is bound to look good on his letter headings. His strong-arm stuff can get him respect but friends like me can get him respectability.

Saturday, 21 November

By way of reciprocation, Harry takes me to his club. 'It ain't exactly White's, Teddy,' he explained. The Stardust is located at the unfashionable end of Soho, south of Shaftesbury Avenue, virtually in Chinatown. A nice enough place, I suppose, if a little on the kitsch side. Still, if its decor lacked the bohemian charm of some other Soho haunts, this was more than made up for by the real danger of some of its clients. A photographer was on hand, of course, to record my visit. And so I finally enter Harry's gallery of 'personalities', grinning with bow-tied & puffy-faced affability next to a stern Harry & a coloured boxer.

Jake Arnott

Monday, 23 November
Today I joined the board of Victory Electrical Goods. Took rather a shine to the young man that Harry sent around. His name is Craig. Good-looking in a rough sort of way that I find irresistible. Trouble written all over him of course but something shy & vulnerable about him as well. A nervous sensitivity. After some very satisfactory slicklegging we have a little chat. Turns out he's got nowhere permanent to stay. Suggested that he could stay with me. I would pay him to keep the place tidy, do the odd job here & there. He seemed taken with the idea but said that he'd have to check with Harry first.

Friday, 27 November
To Hackney Dog Track with Harry. Rather jolly. Must confess that I enjoy slumming it just as much as Mr Starks relishes a taste for high society. Exciting to be amongst hard men & tough little boys.

Harry suggested that he start paying me a monthly fee. 'As a business consultant', he explained. Occasionally I'd be asked favours. An introduction or merely my presence at a meeting or a business lunch. I agreed. He also gave the OK for Craig to move in.

A lucky night. I came away with £30 winnings.

Monday, 30 November
The Albany Trust are lobbying me for my support in advocating homosexual law reform. Said that I agreed with them in principle but I have to be careful in involving myself in anything that might cause people to draw any unfortunate conclusions.

Repairs have started on Hartwell Lodge.

Thursday, 3 December
Craig has moved in. Meagre possessions, poor boy. Just two battered suitcases in the spare room. Embarrassing moment when, seeing

him looking with interest at my bookshelf, I started to talk about various volumes & he meekly confessed his illiteracy. Promised to help him to learn to read. He appears as interested in matters of taste & breeding. He is always trying to glean bits of knowledge of etiquette or culture. Has a particular curiosity in the curios and *objets d'art* in the flat & seems to have a passing knowledge of antiques.

Monday, 7 December
Lunch with Harry at the Lords. He loves all the pomp & circumstance of the place, of course. Harry's charm is that there is absolutely nothing bourgeois about him. Instead he exudes a rough feudal charm. He refers to his neighbourhood, indeed his whole milieu, as his 'manor'. I wonder if he had played at being a pirate lord as he scrambled about the bombsites of his childhood just as I had done in the more salubrious landscape of my own youth.

He is fascinated by the world of privilege. A patriotic desire to be part of a really big racket, I suppose. He wants a piece of the action. He actually asked my advice on how one got on to an honours list. 'I wouldn't want a peerage,' he confided to me. 'A knighthood would suit me.' I think its martial aspect appeals to him, the notion of nobility of arms. He has a great admiration for upper-class men of action like Lawrence of Arabia or Gordon of Khartoum. Empire heroes and explorers he no doubt read of in picture books. And in his own way he sought to emulate them, to find some respectable and gentlemanly way to demand money with menaces. Some way of jumping the counter of middle classness straight into aristocracy.

Wednesday, 9 December
Managed to have a civilised telephone conversation with Ruth. She is very content with the new arrangements by which she will be financially provided for. So she should be.

The repairs to Hartwell are now in full swing. 'The place is like a building site, Teddy,' she said, which conjured up delicious images of sweating workmen for me. We have decided not to have Christmas at Hartwell Lodge due to the state of the place. She is going to friends and so I will be able to spend the time with Craig. We agreed that I will come down for a weekend some time in the new year once all the repair work has been completed. I have also resolved (to myself) to get her out of the way some time later, so I can host a 'party' there.

Saturday, 12 December
Took Craig to see Olivier's *Othello* at the Old Vic. Larry a frightful old ham affecting some ludicrous West Indian accent. Craig enjoyed himself. Thought L.O. very talented. 'He could be in the Black and White Minstrels,' he said.

Tuesday, 15 December
Dinner at Quaglino's with Harry. First really serious chat about business. Present arrangements are fine but there are opportunities to expand. To be honest I'm worried about the precarious nature of Harry's entrepreneurial activities. I dread being embroiled in some sort of ghastly scandal. Harry wants legitimacy & the way to this is in doing business on a grand scale. And so we can both benefit from this approach.

We went through the facts together. Harry's various business concerns have accumulated capital which has been constantly moved around in order to avoid the attentions of the Inland Revenue & other interested parties. Now is a time for expansion, I argued. A big project to invest in. Preferably overseas.

Harry was enthusiastic at the notion of founding a business empire. The adventure of it appeals to him. Some way of making a mark on the world. He has an atavistic sense of economics. Dull commerce bores him. He has a desire to conquer, to carve something out for himself.

'Maybe I could get a Queen's Award for Industry, Teddy,' he commented drily.

Saturday, 19 December

Worried about Craig. He went out the night before last and I saw nothing of him until he rolled back into the flat late tonight filthily drunk. We had a row. He has been, of late, lazy & derelict in his duties. When I diplomatically pointed some of this out he became obstreperous. 'I'm not your bloody servant, you know,' he snarled at me with a beery breath then slunk off to bed.

I can understand that the inequality of our respective status can make him insecure & even bitter towards me. But I did so much hope that we could get on without class resentment rearing its ugly head.

Monday, 21 December

The Commons tonight voted overwhelmingly (355 to 170) to abolish the death penalty for murder. Given the size of the majority it does not look like the Lords will try to frustrate this decision. This is the last important business of Parliament this year.

Friday, 25 December

Christmas. Craig went over to Bethnal Green to see his mother during the day & then back here for the evening. We had a pleasant evening together. Talked about ways that we could get on better. Craig was very sweet, apologising for his bad behaviour etc.

1965

Friday, 8 January

To the Colony Casino Club in Berkeley Square with Harry. One of the many new casinos that have opened up since the new gaming laws. Lots of overdressed Americans in the place. Apparently the film actor George Raft was present but I'm not sure who he is anyway. Harry introduced me to a charming New Yorker called Dino Cellini. 'It's an honour to meet ya, Lord Thoisby,' he said in that cartoon Brooklyn drawl. All wonderfully Runyonesque. He & Harry then went off in a huddle but not before H. had handed me a big stack of chips to play with.

Haven't played roulette since Monte Carlo in the twenties. It all took me back rather. I'd gambled recklessly back then. A young man's vice. Squandering one's inheritance to order to fuel one's own ambitions. *Faîtes vos jeux*. Had a winning streak then lost it all by the end of the evening.

Friday, 15 January

A sort of eager solemnity in the Smoking Room. News is that Winston is v. ill. A stroke or something. Still, the old bugger made 90 only last month.

Saturday, 16 January

Craig has gone & done his disappearing act once more. Left the flat in an utter mess. And we had planned to spend time together this weekend. Really it is too much. Felt quite depressed. Had enough of waiting around so I went out to the Colony Casino again. Found out that by using Harry's name I can have an account with them. Lost about £500. Felt cathartic though, somehow.

Sunday, 17 January

Still no sign of C. so I cleaned up the flat myself. Found a holdall of silverware under his bed in the spare room. His interest in antiques obviously more professional than I'd imagined. Worst fears realised. I've a thief living under my roof.

Tuesday, 19 January

Craig rolled in late, drunk. Confronted him about the silverware. He got very indignant & finally quite tearful, saying that he'd had a rotten life, never had a chance, etc. I ended up comforting him, but saying that he really must start to behave.

Thursday, 21 January

Awful day. The police turned up at the flat. That is to say a thuggish little man with beady eyes calling himself Detective Sergeant Mooney. Wanted to interview Craig but Craig wasn't in. So instead he started to ask me all sorts of impertinent questions about our 'domestic arrangements' etc, making all sorts of ghastly insinuations. When I asked him if he knew who I was he just nodded with a nasty smile & replied, 'Oh yes, I know all about you.' The upshot is, of course, that the grubby little policeman wants money. £200 pounds! Laughed in my face when I suggested payment by cheque. I'll have to see Harry. Haven't got that sort of cash to hand at the moment. Also, things as they are with Craig cannot go on. He'll have to go.

Friday, 22 January

Went to see Harry at his Mayfair flat. Told him about yesterday's unpleasantness. He seems to know this Mooney fellow. 'He's known for the fit up,' H. commented. 'Don't worry, I'll straighten things with him.' Felt relieved & thankful but when I said, 'Thanks, Harry, I owe you for this,' Harry gave me a rather fearsome grin and said v. softly, 'I know, Teddy, I know.'

Sunday, 24 January

Had it out with Craig. Asked him to leave. Terrible scenes, him shouting and becoming abusive. Then he went all quiet & just started packing. Left very quickly, muttering 'You'll regret this' on his way out. Queen Anne carriage clock & some silver candlesticks seem to have left with him. *C'est la guerre.*

Felt v. depressed. Nursed a bottle of gin & listened to home service. News came on that Winston has finally croaked. Strange morose feelings about it. Not grief for him so much as a sort of mourning for my own failed career. I was one of the few people that stood by him in the wilderness years & yet when that undeclared assets business came about he froze me out. Can't blame him for that, I suppose but I always felt a slight sense of betrayal.

Couldn't stand moping about any more. Brooding about the past. Went out to the Colony to play the tables for a bit. Always gets me out of myself. Of course, by the time I got to the casino I was absolutely rotten *fou.* Have to watch this. Can't even remember how much I lost.

Saturday, 30 January

Winston's big send off. Full State junket at St Paul's. Wanted to avoid the whole thing to be honest but Harry insisted that I go around to his for drinks. Turns out he was holding some sort of wake for the old bugger. Harry's a big Churchill fan, of course. Got all of his LPs. I became the guest of honour, having known him personally. Was able to regale the assembled group of villains & 'personalities' with some anecdotes. Told of how, when W. was holding forth at the Oxford Union back in the twenties, F.E. Smith had heckled him, hissing, 'Shut up, Winston. It's not as if you've a *pretty* voice.' Harry was in a more reverent mood, though. Proposed a toast. 'To the last great Empire man,' he announced. 'We shall not see his like again.' All of the East End lot quite dewy eyed. One thing the Socialists will never fathom. The deep loyalism of the genuine working classes.

Saturday, 6 February

Repairs completed on Hartwell Lodge so I travelled down to Hartwell-juxta-Mare by train. Good to get out of London for a couple of days. The Lodge is back to its former glory, I'm glad to say. How I've missed it! It's such a strange hybrid of architecture. A Tudor end that had been built in the 16th century & a Georgian half added about 200 years later. Wonderfully secluded with a belvedere on top that gives a simply marvellous view of the coast. I wish that I could have it for myself.

Ruth & I dined agreeably enough. She still retains a sharp sense of humour, tinged though it is with bitterness. But as the day wore on to gloomy darkness things began to get awkward. We both had a lot to drink & it released the venom. I've never approved of women getting drunk. Especially Ruth. It makes her all the more ugly.

'You've never cared about me, Teddy,' she slurred at me. 'It gets so fucking lonely out here.'

'Then why don't you divorce me?' I countered.

'That's what you want, isn't it? Well I'm not going to give you the pleasure.'

'You mean that you stay married to me just to spite me?'

'Is that what it does, Teddy? Spite you? Our little arrangements, all I've put up with. Oh, no, you won't get rid of me so easily. I'm Lady fucking Thursby now.'

'Then you should start behaving like her.'

'Don't you start lecturing me about behaviour. I know what you've been up to.'

'Now Ruth, don't be tiresome.'

'I've heard all about you and your *friends*.'

She used the word as if it were a curse.

'I've heard,' she went on, 'that you're in with some sort of thug. Been seen at the dog track together, importuning young men.'

'That's a damned lie!' I protested loudly.

She let out a hideous, eldritch shriek of laughter at this.

'Oh, Teddy,' she continued, hatefully. 'You're such a fucking joke. You and your precious discretion. You think anyone's taken in by your ridiculous façade? Everyone knows you for what you are.'

I said that I'd had quite enough of this & got up to leave the room.

'I didn't marry a man,' she called out after me. 'I married a boy. I wonder if you'll ever grow up before you die?'

Sunday, 7 February

To St Matthew's at Hartwell-juxta-Mare for Mass. Ruth & I play at being Lord & Lady Thursby for the benefit of the parish. All teeth & smiles. Try to ease myself into the tranquil gloom of the village church. The solemn, calming ritual. Harbouring murderous thoughts towards my wife hardly puts me in a state of grace though. Go through the motions. Have a chat with the vicar afterwards, shake hands with a few dimly recognised parishioners.

Catch the afternoon train back to London. Nagging fears of gossip. I dread any kind of scandal.

Friday, 12 February

Went to Leicester Square Odeon for a charity showing of *Lawrence of Arabia* that Harry had organised. His favourite film, apparently. At drinks in the interval Harry all misty eyed & sombre. Some wag, a famous comedian or pop star or something, one of Harry's 'personalities' had secreted sand into his shoe from a fire bucket & proceeded to pour it out theatrically at the bar. 'Bleeding sand gets everywhere!' he declared in a loud South London twang to much laughter. But Harry was not amused. For once he was entirely unimpressed by all the showbiz types crowding out the bar & foyer. He turned his back on the frivolity & muttered darkly to me, 'Lawrence was a real man. He faced adversity with real bottle. And he was bent, like me.'

Harry feels an obvious attraction to the television-age celebrity that he often surrounds himself with but is really drawn to a deeper sense of fame.

Within him dwell dreams of high renown & adventure. We spoke of Arab culture & Harry talked about N. Africa. He had been in Tangiers in the fifties when he'd worked for Billy Hill, the king of the racecourse gangs.

Monday, 15 February

Lords debate on overseas aid. Afterwards talked to Lord Chilvers about Africa. Tony Chilvers is a newly ennobled captain of industry with plenty of ideas. We talked about the situation in Rhodesia. Both agreed that if Smith strikes out on his own the Tory party could be split in its response. Then he went on to the newly independent black states. 'The thing is Teddy,' he told me, 'we want to make sure that they don't turn commie. All of their nationalist intellectuals tend to look to the Soviet Union as an example of development and industrialisation.' He went on to talk about theories of growth, 'conditions for economic take-off' etc. I was a bit lost but then he started to tell me about the opportunities for investment. Especially in Nigeria, apparently. Huge country, rich in resources wanting to modernise. He knows of many schemes that promise generous dividends.

I suddenly thought of Harry & his considerable ill-gotten capital. Such a venture would surely appeal to his strange imperial vision. It seemed ideal. The new government in Nigeria is, by all accounts, unstable & already rife with corruption. I said that I'd be interested in such an enterprise & knew of potential investors. Tony Chilvers promised to introduce me to a prospect.

Wednesday, 17 February

Miserable grey day. Sunk into gloom. Coming down with the 'flu I fear. Feel old and lonely. I miss Craig for all his faults. News on the wireless – Gambian independence. Africa again. Coincidence or a sign that this investment idea is meant to be.

Jake Arnott

Thursday, 18 February
Stayed in bed all day, feeling ghastly. Plenty of medicinal scotch. Horrible feeling of being alone with one's illness. Who will look after me when I am old & infirm?

Saturday, 20 February
Feeling much better. Went for a bit of a stroll amongst the drizzle. Spoke to Tony Chilvers on the telephone. Arranged a meeting with some Nigerian fellow. Colony Casino in the evening. Won £1,200!

Sunday, 21 February
Phoned Harry to mention African idea. Seemed v. keen. Also mentioned recent illness & H. said, 'If I'd have known I'd have sent one of the boys around to nurse you better.' 'Well, now you come to mention it,' I joked, 'I haven't made a full recovery.' 'Right then,' he said & put the phone down. At around six, a blond-haired youth appeared! Gave him a drink & we quickly got on with the slicklegging. Very brusque and methodical but felt that was all for the best. Didn't want to feel in any way engaged emotionally, what with all the awful consequences that stemmed from my attachment with C. Went to bed feeling wonderfully sated.

Tuesday, 23 February
Invited over to Tony Chilvers's huge modernist mansion in Kingston-upon-Thames to meet this African chap. Expected a much older man. John Ogungbe looked like he was still in his twenties. Short & lithe in a tightly cut fashionable suit with an open-necked silk shirt. He wore dinky little slip-on crocodile-skin loafers. His hair was cut short to his scalp which, with his well-defined bone structure, prominent mouth & flat nose, accentuated his skull. As if the skin had been stretched tightly over his face with some economy. He is very striking.

We shook hands & his thick lips peeled to reveal an impressive set of teeth. But as he gave me this flashing white smile I noticed that his eyes remained impassive, cautious. They were yellowish & slightly bloodshot.

John has come from Nigeria to London to study engineering. Since qualifying he has divided his time between here & there & has been involved in various building schemes. He is determined, he tells me in great earnest, to use his education to improve the lot of his own people. We talked of development & I tried to make all the right noises.

His current project is to build a township near Enugu in southern Nigeria. The plan is to construct 3,000 houses & a shopping precinct. He has secured government approval but lacks enough investment to get started. He wasn't disappointed when I told him that I don't have that sort of capital at my disposal. He said that he thinks that my title & status will be of use in attracting support for the scheme. And that I might be able to help him find potential investors in London.

Tony gave us lunch. John Ogungbe asked us what we thought about Ian Smith and the Rhodesia situation. We were both v. diplomatic & rather skirted around the issue. Tony changed the subject & bewailed the fate of business under a Labour administration. Apparently Wilson is planning to introduce a Corporation Tax in the budget. Gave serious warnings to J. Ogungbe against Nigeria embracing socialism. Also invited me to join a special group looking at party policy on overseas aid that the Advisory Committee on Policy has set up. I accepted.

Wednesday, 24 February
Went to see Harry at his flat. Explained to him what had been discussed yesterday. Suggested that he meet with John Ogungbe & he agreed. I thought of arranging some sort of civilised luncheon at White's or somewhere but Harry had his own ideas.

'Why don't you invite him to my club?' he proposed.

'The Stardust?'

'Yeah, why not? He can be guest of honour.'

'Are you sure that's a good idea, Harry?'

I was determined that we should make a good impression. I dread any vulgar behaviour from Harry. Of course, I couldn't say this to him. He could get so touchy.

'What's the matter with my club?' he retorted indignantly.

'Nothing Harry. It's just that . . .' I sighed. 'We need to be on our best behaviour.'

Harry laughed heartily at this.

'Don't you worry, your lordship,' he said. 'I'll behave myself.'

Thursday, 25 February

1922 Committee have approved new system for choosing the next leader – a vote by MPs. Sir Alec is bravely hanging on but only a matter of time before he will have to announce resignation.

Saturday, 27 February

At The Stardust Club with John Ogungbe as guest of honour, Harry fussing about as host, trying maybe a little too hard to make our guest feel welcome. But he managed to invite a few of his business friends who he thought might be interested in investing some money into the scheme. Of course there were the inevitable photographs.

Mr Starks & Mr Ogungbe eye each other up a little suspiciously at first. I could tell that Harry found John attractive, not just as a business proposition. When I first introduced them he slyly winked at me as if in complicity. There was something over-friendly in Harry's manner that worried me. Not sure about Harry's feelings about race. I knew that he was touchy about his own Jewishness but I didn't quite know whether he himself harboured prejudice in other areas. He seemed completely unabashed about talking about colour though. He quickly turned the conversation to boxing. I suspect that this is the one area where Harry has contact with blacks. He reeled off a list of coloured pugilists as if John might know them personally, readily conceding their superiority. 'White boys just ain't hungry enough any more,' he lamented. I wasn't sure if this concession covered for an overall feeling of superiority that he might have. I feared that he might say something uncircumspect.

John Ogungbe appeared to enjoy himself. He laughed loudly at all of Harry's jokes and oft times gave that glazed-eyed grin I'd first noticed on meeting him. Harry was very taken with him.

'What a find, Teddy,' he confided to me. 'He's the son of a chief, you know.'

We all got very drunk. Harry's strategy was to entertain lavishly, if a little crudely. Not being sure of Ogungbe's proclivities, Harry had made sure that there were some pretty boys on hand as well as a few available tarts. When John showed an interest in one of the women Harry made sure that the lucky girl went home with him.

Sunday, 28 February

Dreadful hangover. Felt sullied & spiritually dissipated. Went to Evensong at All Saints in Margaret St. It's Quinquagesima. The service had a marvellously calming effect upon me. Felt grateful to have a moment of peace for one to pray quietly to one's Redeemer. 'Bow, stubborn knees, & heart with strings of steel, be soft as sinews of the new-born babe. All may be well.'

Monday, 1 March

Ogungbe appeared at my flat in Eaton Square quite out of the blue.

'Harry was quite taken with your scheme,' I told him. 'And with you, if you don't mind me saying.'

Ogungbe grunted & nodded. Much more sullen now.

'He tells me you're the son of a chief.'

Ogungbe laughed sharply.

'My father worked on the railways. I gave him that chief story because I knew it would impress him. I also told him that I had six wives but he didn't seem so interested in that.'

I couldn't help laughing myself.

'He's something of a tribal chief himself, isn't he?' he suggested mischievously.

'What do you mean?'

'Come on. I'm not stupid. You think I haven't worked out where he gets all his money? And that whore the other night. She told me plenty.'

'I hope that this doesn't put you off doing business with him.'

Ogungbe laughed again.

'Don't worry. I know all about the British sense of fair play. You think we Africans are innocent natives? We know how things operate. We've had it done to us for long enough. We've learnt from it.'

I'm less enamoured by this new Ogungbe that was sitting opposite me in my drawing room. I'm not sure of what the proposed business deal would entail & what would be its consequences but I didn't like the thought of him having the upper hand. Despite this I arranged for a proper meeting to go through the scheme.

Friday, 5 March

Meeting at Ogungbe's offices in Euston. A large table laid out with architects' plans & engineering drawings. He even had a little model of the scheme. He went through the whole thing in detail.

Harry sat with Emmanuel Gould, who takes care of his finances. Little Manny sat quietly, intently blinking through his round spectacles as Ogungbe laid out all the plans in front of us. Harry, by contrast, was agitated and enthusiastic. Pointing at things & eagerly asking questions.

The conversation moved on to money & then Manny took an active part. The initial investment was to be £25,000 & then further payments as construction was undertaken. In the long run, a profit of over £200,000 could be realised from the project. Manny stroked his chin & looked cautiously over at Harry who nodded almost absently. A company would be set up to oversee the investment. I had my doubts about the whole thing but then it wasn't my money. I just hoped that my name on the letter heading of this new firm would bring me a handsome commission.

Then everyone stood up & shook hands. Harry hovered over the model of the township and rubbed his hands together.

'What's it going to be called?' he asked.

'That's yet to be decided,' replied Ogungbe.

'Tell you what,' Harry went on, gazing down at the tiny blocks of flats. 'We could call it "Starksville".'

Ogungbe gave Harry his impassive grin. As he looked over at me his yellowy eyes glared.

Monday, 8 March
West African Developments came into being today with me nominally on the board. Drinks around at Harry's to celebrate. After initial euphoria H. looked a bit grim faced. 'I'm putting a lot into this, Teddy,' he said. 'I'm going to have to call in a few favours.'

Thursday, 11 March
Terrible news. Harry has been arrested. One of his boys came around to tell me the news. Apparently he has been charged with 'making an unwarranted demand with menaces'. Horrible sinking feeling. This could ruin me. Need to make sure that I can distance myself from any unpleasantness.

Friday, 12 March
Visit from Manny Gould. The latest is that Harry has been refused bail and is on remand in Brixton prison. Manny made all sorts of reassuring noises about it being a 'very flimsy case'. I'm not so sure. Told Manny that my reputation wouldn't allow me to be caught up in all this & the little Yid just shrugged and said, 'Well, if Mr Starks goes down, so might you, your lordship. And we want to avoid that now, don't we?' He insisted that I made sure that the Nigerian project went ahead as planned. 'Business as usual,' he said. 'That's the order of the day.'

Saturday, 13 March
Very depressed about how things have turned out. Oh, why have I allowed myself get caught up in all this? Feeling strangely reckless. Went to the Colony Casino & played the tables as if tempting the fates. Bumped into one of Harry's cohorts. Seemed casual about the

whole business. 'I wouldn't worry,' he said with an affable grin. 'People can be got at.'

Monday, 15 March

Went to see J. Ogungbe at his Euston office. He was very perturbed about the Harry situation. I reassured him that West African Developments would be able to fulfil their commitment to the project. 'That's good, Teddy,' he said. 'We have an agreement, after all, and if it were to fall through I would hold you personally responsible.' He's off to Nigeria this week to oversee the start of construction on the scheme.

Thursday, 18 March

Harry's application for bail to a judge in chambers turned down.

Friday, 26 March

Bad week for the Tories. Liberals win Roxburgh, Selkirk & Peebles by-election. If we can't win seats in the Borders where can we win them? Knives out for Sir Alec. *Daily Telegraph* running a front-page story suggesting there could be a leadership contest before Easter. With Sir Alec goes the last of the old school, I fear. *Après?* – the inevitable rise of the grammar school boys.

Wednesday, 31 March

Judge Griffith-Jones at the Old Bailey turned down another application for bail. They were going to take it to the Lord Chief Justice, apparently.

Friday, 2 April

Manny came around to see me to persuade me to support Harry's application in the Lords. I am extremely reluctant to do this but once again oblique references to my being implicated etc. M. suggested that I should table a question along the lines of asserting the rights of an individual in being held in custody for such a long period without trial. Eventually agreed to do what I could. Didn't really have any choice. Feel quite sick about the whole business.

Wednesday, 7 April

House of Lords. A bit unsteady on my feet as I asked the question. Had a few drinks beforehand. Dutch courage. My question v. badly received. Challenged as to whether I held any kind of brief for Mr Starks. Denied this vigorously, saying that I have always fought for the right of any person not to be held without trial. Catcalls. Viscount Milburn declaring that 'such a question has no place in being asked here'. Felt thoroughly humiliated by the whole thing, though managed to maintain a posture of righteous indignation throughout. Application denied in any case. Trial date has been set for April 15.

Thursday, 8 April

To Little Venice for lunch at Diana Cooper's. She was as charming as ever but confessed that she felt awfully depressed at getting old. 'I feel posthumous, Teddy,' she confided to me. Made me conscious of my own decline, too. All the other guests were of a younger generation. Some television presenter & new friends that D. had made in the neighbourhood. We talked of Duff and reminisced about Philip Sassoon's weekend parties at Trent Park in the '30s. Like a dream of another world.

Thursday, 15 April

Good news as to opening day of Harry's trial at Old Bailey. Key prosecution witnesses failed to turn up. Judge ordered adjournment.

Friday, 16 April

Prosecution case against Harry has completely fallen apart. Judge threw the case out of court. *Evening Standard* reported Harry's comment leaving the Old Bailey: 'It's a case of police harassment, pure and simple.'

Big celebration at The Stardust in the evening. Lots of now familiar faces. And 'personalities'. Film actress Ruby Ryder & radio comedian Gerald Wilman. Wilman very camp. Told a funny story about a repentant homo actor being caught *in flagrante delicto* with a hotel bellboy. 'I'll turn over a new leaf,' the queer thespian declared. 'Just once I've got to the bottom of this page.' Also noticed Detective Sergeant Mooney amongst the gathering greedily quaffing the champagne. Harry very grateful about my support. 'You've been very staunch, Teddy. I appreciate that.' Showed his gratitude in the form of a new boy for me to take home. Feel tremendous relief (in more ways than one!).

Friday, 16 April
Good Friday. Away for a weekend at Hartwell Lodge. Went to St Matthew's at Hartwell-juxta-Mare for the Mass of the Pre-Sanctified. Gave thanks for how things have turned out this week.

Saturday, 17 April
Fine spring day. Went for a walk with Ruth along the coastal path. Wild flowers in bloom everywhere. Sea air marvellous. Good to be out of London for a spell. Good to be away from all this business with Harry. It really has been too much. Must try to maintain a safe distance from his intrigues in the future.

Monday, 19 April
Board meeting of West African Developments. Harry had initial report on the progress of the township project from Ogungbe. It all sounded a bit vague to be honest. Harry seemed pleased enough though. Passed around some photos of workmen digging out the foundations & grinning for the camera with relish. Grandiose illusions – they were carving out the footings of his new empire. Mentioned the matter of my commission. Harry said that this would be paid once the scheme had started to realise some return on investment. Not what I had in mind.

Tuesday, 20 April

Craig turned up on my doorstep late last night. It had been raining & he was all wet & dishevelled in a rumpled and dirty suit with the collar turned up. He looked terrible. 'I was just passing,' he muttered & managed a mirthless smile. Should have told him to get lost, really. But he looked desperate & I feared some sort of scene in the street. So I invited him in & he stood in front of the fire in the drawing room as I poured him a brandy. He shivered & mumbled something about 'needing to get back on his feet'. Let him stay over in the spare bedroom. When he left this next morning I slipped him a five-pound note.

Saturday, 24 April

V. warm day. Went for a stroll. Saw a pretty youth on the King's Road with long hair, frilly shirt & bell-bottomed trousers. Reminded of Oxford days & the dandy style we wore in those days. Oxford bags – trousers flared out to 28 inches in bright hues. Quite as outrageous as any of this 'swinging' style. Young people always think that they've found something new. Had wistful thoughts of when one was young & fashionable & desired. Now I'm just a flabby-faced old buffer in a bow tie. Playing the Lord.

Wednesday, 28 April

Craig turned up again, looking a good deal smarter. Said he wanted to borrow some money. I gave him twenty quid and told him not to worry about paying it back. I can hardly convince myself that this is the end of it though.

Wednesday, 5 May

In the Lords for a debate on the Finance Bill. Saw Tom Driberg in the Smoking Room later, eager for gossip & making none too oblique references to Mr H. Starks. I chided him that gossip should, by its nature, be confined to talking about others, not oneself. When parting he suddenly became serious. 'Be careful, Teddy,' he said. Sudden paranoia. Driberg urging caution is not a good sign.

Tuesday, 10 May

Craig at my flat again. No good deed ever goes unpunished. Talked of some 'business' plan of his. Some fairy story about setting up a car-hire firm. What he wants is someone to invest in it.

'Maybe you'd like to put some money into it,' he suggested.

'I'd like to help,' I tried to assure him. 'But, you see, all my money's tied up at the moment, I'm afraid.'

'Well, maybe you could get one of your friends interested.'

'Craig, please.'

'Look, Teddy. The thing is I need some cash. Someone I know, a journalist, he says he could pay me quite a lot of money. A human-interest story, he calls it. Says I'd make a very good subject. Plenty of colour, if you know what I mean. Well, I told him, I'm not going to rat on my friends, am I? I wouldn't do a thing like that, would I Teddy? Not unless I was really desperate.'

'How much do you want?'

'Five hundred pounds.'

'And that would be the end of it?'

'Yeah.'

'Look, I'll need some time to get the money.'

'Of course, Teddy. There's no hurry. I'll give you till the end of the week.'

Wednesday, 11 May

Went to see Harry about the Craig business. I didn't know what else to do. He was in an ugly mood. Worried about the Nigeria project. He'd heard nothing for weeks & is seething with suspicions of treachery. He's not the most well tempered of men, I must say. And there are rumours of psychopathic tendencies.

I finally got around to mention C.'s blackmail & I really wish I hadn't. Harry went into barely controlled rage.

'I thought I told that little slag to lay off,' he spat out, pacing about his flat. 'Well he's asking for it now.'

I tried to placate him.

'Maybe just a warning,' I suggested.

'He's had his fucking warning. You leave this to me. You won't have to worry about that little fucker.'

Then he returned to his brooding & I made my excuses & crept out.

Friday, 14 May

Went to White's. Saw Evelyn Waugh there, looking grim in a loud dogcheck suit. I asked how he was. 'Toothless and melancholic,' was his reply. He had all his teeth removed apparently & dentures have proved v. unsatisfactory. 'These false snappers ruin my appetite for solid food,' he said, looking like he was compensating with liquid intake. He appeared utterly desperate. 'I'm a wreck, Teddy,' he told me. 'I hardly sleep though I'm full of dope. I get up late, try to read my letters, have some gin, try to read the paper, have some more gin. Then it's lunch time.' He gave a ghastly smile, his mouth an empty rictus. Eyes cold, unblinking, vigilant.

Came home with an overwhelming sense of decay. My generation is dying out. All the Bright Young People of the twenties have become old and hideous. In my own decline I'm left with an abiding sense of failure – a wasted political career, a rotten marriage, constant worries about money, scandal, blackmail. I've utterly failed to resist temptation, I've given in to beastly lusts. The flesh is weak & going flabby. I feel resigned to the slow surcease of life, clinging on to some hope of redemption yet wallowing in a descent into final decadence. This is my fate & I must bear it with all the courage I can muster. Mine are dissolution honours, after all.

Monday, 17 May

Meeting of the group Tony Chilvers is chairing on party policy on overseas aid. Bit of a talking shop really, full of dreary types going on about 'modernising the party'. There's all manner of small groups meeting about new policy. Any recommendations go to Shadow Cabinet via the Advisory Committee on Policy. The chairman of the ACP is Ted Heath – obviously building a power base for the inevitable leadership contest.

Jake Arnott

Spoke to Tony after and he asked how the Nigeria project was going. I said something vague about problems in communication. I really have no idea what's happening.

Friday, 21 May
Constant jabber about the direction of the party. Lots of talk about the need for new policies & 'modernisation'. An obsession with becoming 'classless' which merely means middle class. Classless in the v. worst sense. Indistinct. One particularly gruesome comment: 'We must become the party of the consumer' – which brings to mind bodily function rather than any real political vision. The Blasted Heath, needless to say, is behind most of this 'reform'. Manoeuvres, more like. Reggie Maudling will run against him for the old school, I hazard. A scholarship boy, but at least with some ballast.

Wednesday, 26 May
Harry invited me over. There was boxing on the television broadcast from America & Harry was having a little party. When I arrived I recognised some of the people from the first of Harry's 'parties' that I had attended & there were quite a number of young pugilists. From a Boys' Club boxing team, apparently. Lots of masculine & youthful energy as we crowded around the screen. Harry v. partisan for one of the fighters, Sonny Liston, an acquaintance, he proudly announced, passing around a photograph of them together at The Stardust Club. I rather favoured his opponent, Cassius Clay, a good-looking fellow Harry dismissed as a 'mouthy coon'. Anyway, the whole thing was over in the first round! Clay floored Liston in about two minutes, standing over him arrogantly, refusing to retire to a neutral corner & delaying the count. The room filled with catcalls of disappointment & indignant comments. Discussion followed as to whether the fight was fixed. Then we all had more drinks.

The brevity of the evening's entertainment after all the antici-pation charged the atmosphere. Harry was animated. He has a tremendous manic energy & charisma. A noble savage demeanour that is such a palliative to the dull mediocrity that seems to be taking over everywhere. Something atavistic about him. He confirms ones worst fears but in a way this is somehow reassuring.

We all started to get drunk & the horseplay began. Starting with demonstrations of boxing moves & combinations, some light sparring between the younger boys, moving on to more erotic play. I had thought of asking Harry about the Nigeria business but I know he's worried about it & I didn't want to spoil his mood. Instead H. brought up a subject that I'd much rather forget. Craig. He became part of the banter.

'Had an accident, didn't he?' Harry asked in mock innocence. 'What was it Frank, fell down the stairs or something.'

'Something like that,' replied one of the older men laconically.

'Or slipped on the soap,' Harry went on. 'Was that it?'

'Yeah, could be.'

'Slipped on the soap and fell down the stairs.'

Laughter. I suddenly felt sick. Somebody was plying me with brandy & I didn't refuse. Harry came up to me & whispered in menacing mockery.

'See? I can get things sorted for you.'

Then the business started in earnest. Older men pawing at the youths. Harry kissing greedily at a boy with bright red hair. I had no stomach for it. I felt horribly drunk. Completely *fou*.

I got up & staggered towards the door. Harry noticed & pushed the redhead in my direction.

'Go on,' he ordered. 'See to his lordship. He'll only want wanking off.'

Before I knew it the boy was guiding me into one of the bedrooms & was starting to roughly knead at the crotch of my trousers.

'Whatsmatter?' His voice high pitched. 'Can't get it up?'

Harry had followed us in.

'He can't get it up,' the youth observed, shrilly.

I swayed in the spinning room.

'Get him on the bed,' Harry ordered tersely.

They both heaved my flaccid body onto the awful softness of the mattress.

'Get his clothes off,' Harry hissed sharply.

I felt a tugging at my vestments. My shoes thudded onto the floor. I lay helplessly inebriated. More muttered orders at the doorway. Suddenly the darkened room was filled with light. My eyes smarted. The red-haired boy pulled off my remaining clothes then stripped himself & got into bed with me. There seemed to be many people in the room now. Low cackles of laughter & underbreath comments. Whispered directions from Harry. The naked youth stuck his cock rudely in my mouth to the sound of soft clicks & ratchets. Someone was taking photographs.

Thursday, 27 May

Woke up late in the afternoon in my own bed with no idea how I got there. Strange feeling of lethargy throughout my body & thick drowsiness in my head. Was I drugged last night? Awful recollections of shame, humiliation & most of all fear. Quite glad to be in a state of sedation.

Monday, 31 May

Detective Sergeant Mooney turned up at my flat again. Something deeply unsettling about this man. All of the physical threat of H. Starks but none of the charm. His beady little eyes were always darting about, taking everything in. I asked him what his business was.

'I was hoping that we might co-operate, sir.'

'Yes, yes,' I replied impatiently. 'How much do you want?'

'Oh, it's not money I'm after, your lordship,' he retorted, as if affronted.

Then he got to the point. Influence. That's what he was after, & offering a 'reciprocal arrangement' as he called it. I asked him to explain.

'Well, if I start by the way I could bring my influence to bear in a way that could be of benefit to you. Now, there's a whiff of scandal in the air regarding connections that you have with some, shall we say, rather colourful characters. There's still a great deal of sensitivity about any kind of intrigue involving sexual immorality. Remember all that Profumo business. In no time you've got the gutter press stirring things up. Nobody wants that. I've got a pal in the Criminal Intelligence Branch. There's an increasing concern about organised crime. Apparently, they've been asked to investigate an alleged connection between a peer of the realm and a well-known figure in the criminal underworld. Racy stuff, wouldn't you say? If the tabloids ever got hold of it.'

I groaned audibly. Mooney's little eyes gleamed.

'But if I was to use my influence . . . convince my friend at C11 that it's all nonsense and hearsay. As I've said, no one wants a scandal like this. It only makes the general public lose faith with the establishment. Gangsters are always trying to cultivate friends in high places. They think that it gives them an air of respectability. I could suggest that you're merely a dupe in all this. Persuade them to drop the inquiry. And in return, you could use your influence for me in a certain matter.'

'And what would that be?'

'Well, I'm in a spot of bother myself. Years of keeping London's streets safe to walk along and I'm being accused of impropriety. That's the thanks I get. Left-wing trouble makers taking advantage of the British system of justice and sense of fair play.'

'What's happened?'

'I arrested some demonstrators who were making a nuisance of themselves outside an embassy. Now they say I planted evidence on them and tried to force them to make untrue statements. Turns out one of them belongs to some sort of civil liberties group. A diabolical liberties group, more like. Making accusations. The British Police Force is the envy of the world. Any other system would have them rounded up and shot.'

'So what do you want me to do?'

'Well, they're demanding a police inquiry. If you could use your influence.'

'I'm afraid that I don't actually have very much influence on the affairs of state.'

'Well, every little helps. But I was thinking that maybe you could have a word with your friends in the press. An article about trouble makers trying to blacken the name of authority, that sort of thing. Everyone knows that these people are always just stirring up trouble. Something that might put me in a favourable light and counter some of these scurrilous accusations. I've brought some of my press clippings. They might be useful.'

He handed me a sheaf of grubby newsprint.

'Well, I'll see what I can do.'

He finished his drink and got up to leave. We shook hands. Mooney's palm was cold and clammy.

'I suggest,' he added as I showed him out, 'that you don't mention our little arrangement to Mr Starks. He might take advantage of the situation.'

Thursday, 3 June

Lunch with the editor of *The News of the World*, obvious choice for what Mooney wants & I've done some articles for them in the past. I fed him the story. A plot by subversives to discredit the forces of law & order. One of Mooney's cuttings mentioned personal courage in breaking the Ricardo Pedrini racket in 1962. We talked the story into shape – a dedicated & courageous fight against crime & vice in Soho, extolling an impeccable service record & hinting that sometimes unconventional methods bear fruit. British police the best in the world etc., trouble makers just want to undermine authority. He agreed to run it & quite out of the blue asked if I was interested in doing a weekly column. Bluff stuff. Old values in a modern world, that sort of thing. Said that I was definitely interested.

Saturday, 5 June

Have agreed to do column for N.O.T.W. Not exactly intellectually challenging but it means a weekly income & opportunities to get other bits of journalism. Feel that this is really what I should be concentrating on. A chance to air forthright views with a detachment gained from being out of the rat race of politics. And regular money might help to keep me out of trouble.

Suggestions for name of column – *Points of Order* (a bit dull), & *Entitled Opinions* (which I hate – a cheap joke against the peerage).

Monday, 7 June

Board meeting of West African Developments. Latest progress report from Ogungbe extremely vague – no sense of when actual construction is to commence. Harry manically optimistic about it all, though. The whole project seemed to represent something v. important to him & so he refused to accept any possibility of failure. Ambition. It's dreams we believe in, after all. Much talk of drastic measures to be taken unless there was more clarity about the scheme. 'We'll fucking sort it out,' he said, his usual business acumen hopelessly inapplicable in these circumstances. V. glad not to have any of my own money invested in this.

Sunday, 13 June

First column published – *Being Reasonable*. Bringing a bit of respectability to what is, I have to say, a very trashy rag. Elsewhere in the paper news that some pop group have been all given MBEs in the Queen's Birthday Hons. Just shows how dreadful things have become.

Monday, 14 June

Called to an emergency meeting at Harry's flat. All his cohorts there. H. seemed to be delegating all sorts of tasks & activities to his gang. V. animated again, apparently in a good mood but difficult to tell. His temperament is so unpredictable.

'Right then,' he said, slapping his hands together. 'That ought to keep you lot occupied. Make sure that you behave yourselves. Don't get involved in anything unnecessary. All right?'

Grunts & nods all round.

'Right then, Teddy,' he said, looking over at me for the first time. 'It's all sorted.'

This unknown certainty made me feel uneasy.

'Er, what's all sorted, Harry?'

'I've decided what to do about this African business.'

'Really? Well that's good.'

'Yes it is, Teddy, it is. We're going to go there. Sort it all out.'

'Ah,' I said. 'So when are you going?'

'We, Teddy. I said "we". Me and you.'

'Well, thank you for the offer but . . .'

'You don't want to come?'

'Well, much as I'd like to accompany you, I've er, other commitments. You know, business in the House, a column to write, that sort of thing.'

Harry smiled & shrugged. I forced a grin back.

'Suit yourself then. But since I'm sorting my affairs out you might want to look at this.'

He nodded to Manny who shuffled through his papers, fished out a handful of markers & passed them over to me. I stared at them blankly.

'Gambling debts,' Harry went on. 'From the casino you've been frequenting. I sanctioned your account, I own an interest in the place after all, but since I'll be away I'll no longer be able to act as guarantor. I'll have to hand them back and let the parties concerned deal with them themselves. They are, of course, debts of honour, and as such have no real legal binding. So I guess the people concerned will have to find their own ways of securing payment. Some of them are quite imaginative, I believe. And if that doesn't persuade you . . .'

He held out his hand to Manny again. The little Jew handed him a pile of glossy photographs. He waved them at me, shaking his head & tutting loudly.

'Naughty Teddy,' he taunted.

He held one up to my face. I flinched and looked away but not before I'd caught an awful glimpse of myself naked on the bed in a grotesque posture of supplication.

'Harry, please,' I begged.

'No. You listen. And listen good. This African business was your idea. Remember? I've poured a lot of gelt into this scam and I want to know what the fuck is going on.'

'But what can I do?'

'You can be with me. I don't know what these jungle bunnies are up to but I guess having a peer of the realm along for the ride might help putting them in their place.'

'When are you planning to go?' I asked wearily.

'In a couple of days. Manny's sorting out tickets. Hope your passport's up to date.'

I flapped the scraps of paper in my sweaty hands impotently.

'I don't really have any choice about this, do I?'

'No Teddy,' he replied brusquely. 'You don't.'

Friday, 18 June

Lagos

BOAC flight to Kano, in northern Nigeria, then connecting flight to Lagos. V. travel sick. Awful heat & closeness. Ogungbe met us at the airport. Took us for drinks at the Lagos Polo Club. The best club in town, he assured us. Faded colonial atmosphere which Harry loved but made me feel uncomfortable. Pre-Independence, Ogungbe explained, its membership had been, of course, mostly white but now its exclusivity was based on rank & means. Nigerian military and police officers, white civil servants & members of the diplomatic corps & businessmen of every colour and nationality. The ideal place to make business connections.

H. wandered out of the bar to watch a chukka of polo & Ogungbe took me to one side.

'Your friend is worried about the project,' he said softly.

'He is rather.'

'Try to reassure him. These things take time. There is a lot of, shall we say, bureaucracy.'

'You mean people to pay off?'

'The notion of a free economy in this new country of ours is an illusion. Officials on every level want their share.'

'So, how far has construction of the scheme developed?'

Ogungbe shrugged.

'Well there have been some delays. We've had to wait for the end of the rainy season to start work proper. And I've had to secure import licences for the building materials.'

'More "bureaucracy", is it?' I said scathingly. 'I suppose every petty official's got his hand out for the backsheesh.'

Ogungbe's yellowy eyes flared at me in indignation.

'Don't presume to lecture me, Teddy. Your people have taken plenty. And years of colonial rule have left us with no political or institutional framework to regulate growth. People who have struggled all their lives to earn a few pounds now find millions passing through their hands. What do you expect?'

I coughed.

'I'm sorry. It's just that this whole project, well, we want it to go smoothly, don't we?'

'Of course. You must try to reassure your friend Harry. It's very important that his investment in the scheme continues. Otherwise we could all lose out.'

'I'll do my best,' I replied.

Suddenly I felt hot & sweaty. Wandered out of the club room onto the veranda to get some air. Galloping hooves of polo ponies thundered across the field beyond.

Saturday, 19 June

Enugu

Morning flight from Lagos in a light aircraft. The plane bounced up & down in the air above the jungle canopy. Felt quite sick by the end of the journey. An official reception to greet us at Enugu as we dizzily staggered out onto the runway. A motorcade drove us through the town to the President Hotel where we were staying.

There, the regional minister, Dr Chukwurah, gave a welcoming speech & there was a party. All the local dignitaries lined up to greet us. One man, enthusiastically shaking our hands, said: 'Welcome Lord Thursby, welcome Lord Starks. It is a great honour.'

Harry laughed.

'It's just Mr Starks,' he explained.

'You're not Lord?' the man asked, unable to hide his disappointment.

'Well.' Harry smiled mischievously. 'I'm something like that. You can call me Harry.'

The man smiled & shook his hand again.

Dr Chukwurah announced that we would visit the project on the outskirts of Enugu the next day.

'But while you are in the city is there anywhere you would like to visit?'

Harry thought for a moment.

'Yeah,' he said. 'There is one place I wouldn't mind having a look at.'

'And what would that be?'

'The jail. I wouldn't mind having a look around your jail.'

Dr Chukwurah frowned.

'Really, Mr Starks?'

'Well,' Harry went on, 'I've a keen interest in criminology, see? One of my hobbies if you like. It certainly would be interesting to compare prison conditions here to those of back home.'

'Very well,' said Dr Chukwurah & motioned over to the Chief of Police.

'Harry, really,' I muttered chidingly under my breath.

He grinned back at me.

'You want to come too, Teddy?'

I certainly didn't. I need to take a rest. Exhausted from all this travelling. And this appalling heat.

'Suit yourself,' he replied & went over to where the police officers present were organising themselves into a guard of honour.

When he had gone, Chukwurah came over to me.

'Lord Thursby.'

'Call me Teddy, please.'

'Very well, Lord Teddy. I thought we might have a quiet word.'

He led me into an empty room away from the reception area.

'Lord Teddy, my government and particularly the government of this region are very keen to encourage investment from overseas in development.'

'Well, that's good.'

'Yes it is. But it is important to make sure that any expansion or economic growth is controlled and regulated for the benefit of the people. We don't want people coming over here trying to make, what the Americans would call, a quick buck.'

'Of course not.'

'Of course not, yes. What we want is long-term commitment otherwise such schemes are not viable. As a politician, I'm sure you understand.'

'I think so.'

'Ogungbe is a very ambitious young man. He has, as we say here, got a big eye. As such he is not to be trusted fully. And your friend Mr Starks with his keen interest in criminology . . .'

'I assure you Harry's intentions are entirely honourable.'

'I hope so. For both your sakes. I wouldn't want you to get out of your depth. You're a long way from home out here. Might I ask how much you have personally invested in this scheme?'

'Well, I've not exactly put any money into it myself. I'm more of a consultant to the whole enterprise.'

'A consultant? Yes. That's good. Well I hope you can maintain a certain objectivity in that role. If things don't turn out the way they seem. Now, let's rejoin the party, shall we?'

I agreed. I needed a drink. Jet lag & poor air conditioning made me light headed & a little nauseous. The booze didn't help but I needed something to stop my head from spinning. The party began to wind down. I made my excuses & went to my hotel room to lie down. I took off all my clothes & lay down in bed under a single sheet. Felt hot & sticky. The air around me was heavy with a humid dread. I got up, wetted a face flannel & rested it on my eyes. Slept fitfully, my mind crowded with half dreams. Confused thoughts made lucid with anxiety.

After a few hours there was a tapping on my door.

'Come,' I droned into the darkness.

It was Harry. He stood over the bed.

'Teddy?' he whispered.

'Yes?' I groaned, taking the flannel away from my eyes, blinking at the light.

'What a fucking hell hole,' he announced.

'What?'

'The prison. Makes the Moor look like Butlin's. I pity the poor bastards banged up in there.'

I groaned again & rolled over. Harry patted me on the shoulder.

'That's right Teddy, you get some sleep. Need to get up tomorrow to go and look at our investment. See how the natives are getting on with building Starksville.'

Sunday, 20 June

Next morning we rode in a motorcade to the outskirts of Enugu & the development. Dr Chukwurah made another speech & then motioned to me and Harry with expectation.

'Go on, Teddy,' Harry urged me. 'You're good at this sort of thing.'

I can't really remember my address. It all came out on cue. All the *thank yous, great honours, wonderful opportunities for a young country in the modern world* & all that crap. When you've been at this game as long as I have you don't even have to think. Which is just as well as my mind was racing with uneasy imaginings. The heat constantly getting to me. Head throbbing. Brain fever.

We stood before a large billboard announcing the development. There wasn't much behind it. A huge clearing had been hacked into the jungle. A few earth movers & dumper trucks were parked here & there. The foundations had been dug & various plots marked out with pegs & string. Ogungbe led us around the site with a copy of the plans in his hands. In a determined way he pointed out each section of the scheme as if conjuring an image of it before us. I looked down into the earthworks thinking of archaeology rather than construction. As if history had already left this pitiful site behind & moved on somewhere else. The earth a very red clay. Monsoon water in the trenches, its rustiness made me think of corrosion.

'Of course we haven't been able to start work properly because of the rainy season,' Ogungbe explained.

Harry frowned & nodded. Unconvinced.

'Yeah.' he said. 'But that's over now, isn't it?'

'Yes, just over.'

'So why haven't we started?'

'We're waiting for the cement.'

'Cement?' asked Harry, incredulously.

'Yes,' replied Ogungbe with a placatory grin. 'There's been a hold up. I'm going over to Lagos today to sort it out.'

We continued our tour. Harry sidled up to me.

'Cement,' he muttered disdainfully.

I shrugged, not knowing quite what to say.

'I don't like the look of this. Cement? What can be the problem with that. I know all about cement, Teddy.'

Monday, 21 June

Drove out into the bush to visit a tribal village. Treated to a display of ceremonial dancing. Strange ritual processions in huge raffia masks. Harry was quite absorbed by it. Plentiful supplies of palm wine that dulled my headache somewhat.

After the performance Harry was all smiles, mingling with the natives & showing off a few boxing tricks to the young men of the village. Seemed quite at home. Natives seemed drawn to his charisma. Surrounded by smiling piccaninnies. Looking like Kurtz.

Later, he was more stern and subdued.

'Where's Ogungbe?' he asked.

'He's already gone back,' I replied. 'He's flying back to Lagos tonight.'

'I've got a bad feeling about all of this,' he said. 'I think we should pull out.'

'Let's sort this out when we get back home,' I suggest.

'I think we've been had over, Teddy,' he said with a soft fierceness. 'And I don't like that. I don't like that one bit.'

The motorcade took us back to the President Hotel in Enugu. We were due to fly back to Lagos in the morning & get a connecting flight back home. Drinks in the hotel bar. Harry became involved in deep conversation with the Chief of Police. Dr Chukwurah took the opportunity to speak to me directly.

'I hope that your visit has been a success Lord Thursby.'

'Yes,' I reply cautiously. 'I think so.'

'And, no doubt, you'll be anxious to get back home.'

I nodded. You can say that again.

'And your friend Mr Starks. I hope he is satisfied with the way things are going.'

'Well . . .' I shrugged.

'If there are any discrepancies between your investment and the actual progress of this project I'm sure you realise that this is best dealt with by the proper authorities. I, for one, am keeping a close eye on Ogungbe so you mustn't worry on that account.'

'Quite.'

'But your friend Mr Starks. He strikes me as an impetuous sort of a fellow. It wouldn't be a good idea for him to involve himself in the internal affairs of this country.'

'Most certainly not.'

'I hope you can convince him of that. Well,' he said, raising his glass. 'Here's to a safe passage home. And if you do happen to find yourself caught up in any, shall we say, difficulty . . .'

He handed me a slip of paper surreptitiously.

'You can get in touch with me on this number. You might find it hard to get through. The telephone system here is a little primitive. But if you do find yourself in any trouble I advise you to persist.'

Tuesday, 22 June
Lagos
Flew back to the capital in the morning. Again tossed around in a light aircraft & I was sick this time. Too much palm wine & too little sleep. A constant state of anxiety. But some sort of relief as with my head between my knees, vomiting, I thought: at least we are going home.

Landed at the city airport & I found out that Harry had booked us into the Excelsior Hotel by Lagos Harbour. There were some delays in the connecting flight, he explained. We took a taxi & booked in. I went straight to my room & to bed. The air conditioning here was much better than in Enugu. I fell into a deep and thankfully dreamless sleep.

Wednesday, 23 June
Packed and ready to go but no sign of Harry. Not in his room. Boy at reception said that he'd gone out early this morning. I went back to my room & waited. What the hell is going on?

Thursday, 24 June
Still no sign of Harry this morning. Anxious thoughts only relieved by bouts of impatience & boredom. Started drinking after lunch. Tried not to think about what might have happened. Sweaty hand nervously fingering the slip of paper with a telephone number on it. Decided to give it a bit more time. Went to my room and had a nap.

Woken about six by Harry.

'Where the hell have you been?' I demanded. 'I've been out of my mind with worry.'

'Just needed to find out a few things,' he replied casually.

I got dressed.

'When's our flight? I want to go home.'

Harry gave me a rather disturbing little grin.

'We ain't going home, Teddy,' he said. 'Not just yet.'

'What? Harry, this is intolerable.'

'We've got some unfinished business to attend to.'

'You might have. I've had enough.'

I picked up my suitcase.

'I'm going to the airport.'

Harry blocked my path.

'I'd advise against that, Teddy.'

'Get out of my way!' I seethe and tried to push past him. Harry wrenched the case from my hand & threw it onto the bed. Then he grabbed me.

'Get your hands off me you bloody hooligan!' I shouted in his face.

With an open palm he slapped my face. His nostrils flared a little but otherwise his expression was calm & measured. Cold. He threw me onto the bed and I crumpled into a ball, knocking my head against my suitcase. The bedsprings creaked a little. I was helpless. Like a child. Suddenly overcome with memories of prep school cruelty. The ghastly humiliations when one is small & utterly powerless. Being beaten. Wanting desperately to please the older boys. I started to sob.

'I want to go home,' I wailed.

Harry sat down on the edge of the bed & gently stroked the cheek he has struck.

'Shh,' he implored, softly, suddenly becoming an older boy even though he is half my age.

He waited for my sobbing to subside, patting my shoulder slowly. I felt sick to my stomach.

'Listen,' he whispered. 'We've been had over. Well and truly. But if these fuckers think they can get away with it, then they've got another think coming.'

'But what can we do? We're out of our depths here, Harry. Let's get home and try and sort things back there.'

'That'll be too late. We need to act now.'

'I really think we should walk away from this one, Harry. You know, put it down to experience.'

Harry's face suddenly darkened.

'You silly old queen. You think I can just walk away? Wipe my mouth and say, "Oh well, fifty grand down the drain"? What kind of a wanker do you take me for?'

He handed me a handkerchief & I wiped my face.

'So,' I ventured fearfully, 'what are you going to do?'

'Tomorrow,' he said, 'I've got something to show you.'

Friday, 25 June

Drove down to the docks. Harry in his element, looking along the waterfront & nodding as if in recognition. He had the driver stop by a quayside & he pointed out a group of cargo ships moored out in the bay.

'There's our cement, Teddy,' he announced

I frowned & squinted at the distant ships.

'So what's it doing out there? Shouldn't they come into port to be unloaded?'

Harry grinned.

'Yeah, well, that's what you'd think, isn't it?'

'I don't understand. What's going on?'

'You'll see,' he replied & gave the driver an address to take us to.

We pulled up in front of a line of ramshackle bars that were built haphazardly between two large warehouses.

'Come on Teddy. There's someone I want you to meet.'

We got out & walked over to one of the fearsome-looking drinking dens. *Highlife Bar*, was garishly daubed in red paint over the entrance. The place was full of white merchant seamen, drinking noisily in groups. A few black men stood at the bar talking intently, staring sidelong at us as we walked in. Some tartily dressed Nigerian girls at a table in the corner looking bored. Harry nodded at the barkeeper, who looked up & cocked his head at a room in the back whilst polishing glasses & lining them along the counter.

A beaded curtain clattered gently as we went through into a grubby little room with a dirt floor. A swarthy-looking man was seated at a table drinking beer. He stood up and greeted Harry.

The barkeeper came through with a bottle of cheap brandy & three glasses. He set them up on the table & Harry handed him a few notes. Harry poured us all drinks. He introduced us. His name is Rico.

'Salud,' he said, lifting his glass & draining it in one.

'Rico is the captain of one of the ships out there,' Harry explained. 'It didn't take me long to find our precious cement. And why it's still here and not in Enugu. Thanks to our friend here. Rico, why don't you tell Teddy what you told me?'

Rico nodded as Harry poured him another drink.

'Is simple.' Rico shrugged, taking a sip of brandy. 'We bring cement from Cadiz. This man he say bring it here to Lagos. He say bring but not unload. Stay in Lagos harbour for a month or so then take it back.'

'I don't understand,' I said.

'We make more money waiting in the harbour than we would by unloading. This man say there is problem with import licence. He probably sell licence to someone else. So is not possible to put into dock. Instead, we wait. Come ashore, have a few drinks, have fun with local putas. Then we go home.'

'I still don't understand. How can you make more money by not unloading the stuff?'

Rico laughed, showing a blackened front tooth.

'No comprende? Is old trick. Demurrage clause.'

'Demurrage clause?'

Rico explained it all in broken English. An agent for a company procures cement for a fixed price. The cement arrives at port but waits offshore & is never actually unloaded. The company issuing the purchase order is then liable for payment for all the time that the ships have been waiting to discharge their goods. This is the demurrage clause in the contract, a common procedure in shipping. If they wait long enough they end up getting more money than if they had actually delivered the stuff. Then they can sail off with the cement & sell it somewhere else. And the agent gets to keep the money from the original purchase order.

'You've got to admit, Teddy,' Harry commented, 'it's a brilliant racket.'

'Well yes,' I agreed. 'But in this case we're the ones that have been, how would you say? Had over.'

'Yeah. And we ain't the only ones. Are we Rico?'

Rico frowned.

'At first,' he said, 'I think, the longer we wait the more we get out of the deal. But then I hear nothing. My men are sick and tired of waiting around. They get drunk, get into trouble and I start to worry. I think maybe this agent man, he not honour his agreement.'

They started to talk more intently, their faces up close. I found myself being ignored. I took a sip of the brandy in front of me & winced. It was foul but I was glad to have something alcoholic to comfort myself with. Harry and Rico spoke softly, almost lovingly, of vengeance. This was what I'd feared most. I poured myself another glass of the vile spirit.

I looked towards Rico. Tattoos, scars, strong-looking oil-stained hands. He looked as capable of violence as I knew Harry to be. I couldn't quite follow what they were saying. Harry was giving brusque instructions quietly to Rico with a solemn grin on his face. Finally they leant back from each other & finished their drinks.

'Right,' said Harry as he got up from the table. 'Phone me at the hotel when you know. Come on, Teddy.'

We went back through the main part of the bar. An argument had started between a merchant seaman & one of the Nigerians. A glass was broken. We hurried out into the hot muggy night.

It was getting dark. On the waterfront we could see the lights of the cement ships out in the bay. Black water lapped against the sea wall. The sky was streaked with purple clouds. We stood in a pool of yellow light from a streetlamp on the quayside. Above us huge moths battered against its sickly glow. A whiff of sewage & gasoline hung in the humid air.

'You can always find what you want down at the docks,' said Harry.

'Harry ... What on earth is going on?'

'We're going to sort out our business problems, that's all.'

'Wouldn't it be better to inform the authorities?'

Harry laughed.

'You've got to be joking.'

'I could try pulling a few strings with the Consulate.'

'It's too late for that. Look Teddy. You've got to trust me. All right? Don't you worry, we'll sort this out. Then we can fuck off home.'

'I'm not sure.'

'We've got to stick together. We're on our own out here. Sorry I knocked you about.'

He patted the cheek he had slapped. I sighed.

'That's all right, Harry. You're forgiven.'

And it was true. I bore him no malice. I just felt a sickening fear & a desperate longing to go home. Harry smiled at me.

'Thanks Teddy.'

He pulled me to him & hugged me. As he slapped me on the back I felt something hard digging into my stomach.

'What's that?' I asked.

'What?'

Harry pulled away from me, frowning.

'That.'

I tapped gently at his stomach with dread. Harry grinned & opened his jacket to reveal the butt of a pistol lodged in the waistband of his trousers.

'I told you, you can always find what you want down at the docks. I found something else, too.'

I closed my eyes & shook my head.

'Oh, God,' I muttered to myself.

'Cheer up, Teddy. Come on. I've got something else to show you.'

He led me to another bar. It was full of uniformed sailors & young black boys. There seemed to be a few women as well but on closer inspection this proved not the case. On a small stage a drag act was miming to some torch song.

'Come on.' Harry cocked his head at me as I hesitated at the doorway. 'The fleet's in town. Let's enjoy ourselves.'

Harry seemed to be indulging his own recklessness to the limit. Like my own predilection to gambling, I suppose. *Faites vos jeux*. I didn't have much choice but to go along with it. For the time being, anyway.

Drank a good deal though I didn't really feel the effect. My mind was racing too fast. We chatted with the sailors. Harry animated, laughing & joking with them. Making all sorts of suggestions. He persuaded a couple of them to come back to our hotel with us for a nightcap. We found our driver & went back to the Excelsior.

We went to my room & Harry produced a bottle of brandy. We had a few drinks together then Harry paired off with one of the sailor boys, gently leading him out of the room & along the corridor. I heard them giggling softly, like children.

The remaining jack sat on the bed looking languidly up at me, a cigarette drooping out of the corner of his mouth. I must confess, of all the services, I've always rather had a thing for sailors. Guardsmen are always greedy, asking for more money & threatening to turn nasty. But there's an almost innocent generosity about sailors. Perhaps it's just that the short bursts of shore leave mean that they've got plenty of money & vigour & very little time to spend either. There's something wild & abandoned about them, maybe something about being away at sea for so long that frees them from dreary landlocked virtues. And the uniform. Especially the trousers. The way that they taper up from loose bell bottoms into the tight crotch with its exquisite buttoned fly flap. Undoing this quaint device, seemingly designed for the very purpose of slicklegging, produces such a frisson of pleasure in itself. I rubbed the boy off as he lay back on the bed and groaned listlessly. I couldn't get a hard on myself. I was still too anxious & the booze hadn't helped. So I just watched as he went into little spasms of delight from my ministrations.

Went into the bathroom & washed my hands. Splashed some cold water in my face & looked up into the mirror. Puffy features staring incredulously back at me. I dried them on the towel & went back into the bedroom. The sailor had rolled over on the bed & was already snoring in a deep slumber.

Sat on the edge of my bed for a long time, trying to think everything through. I could hear Harry and his boy in the next room. I fished out the piece of paper from my jacket pocket & picked up the telephone.

Saturday, 26 June

Woke up this morning & the sailor had gone. Dreadful hangover & the heat oppressive. Harry insisted that we wait so I had some tea & a copy of *The International Herald Tribune* brought to my room. Spent hours sitting on the bed sipping luke-warm tea & gazing at the paper. Not able to focus on anything for long. I was going out of my mind.

Finally Harry came into my room full of grim purpose.

'Right,' he ordered. 'It's the off. Let's get going.'

'Do I really have to come as well?'

'Of course. We've got to stick together.'

We went downstairs & Harry waved to our driver. Obviously being kept on a retainer. Harry had planned everything with his usual precision. But I don't think he noticed as we pulled away from the hotel that we were being followed.

We picked up Rico from a quayside then drove around the harbour crossing over to an island across a huge bridge.

'Where are we going?' I asked, nervously checking behind to see that we were still being tailed.

'We've found Ogungbe,' Harry replied.

'We make him give us our money,' Rico added darkly.

'Yeah,' Harry growled & stroked the gun in his waistband.

'Harry,' I croaked. 'I cannot abide violence. I'm just no good at that sort of thing.'

'Don't worry,' Harry said. 'We'll deal with that side of things.'

105

'But there's no need for me to come along. I'll only be a liability.'

'Oh no, Teddy. We need you. You see, me and Rico here, we'll do the hard stuff. We need you to do the soft stuff. Quiet persuasion combined with a lot of menace. Never fails.'

I was suddenly overcome with a surge of nausea. I wound down the window & puked onto the dusty tarmac. The driver sucked his teeth audibly. Harry patted me on the back.

'Yeah,' he said encouragingly. 'Better out than in.'

I turned my head to see that we were still being tailed by the car that followed us from the hotel. A hot wind flowed over the back of my head. I puked again. Only bile came up. I'd hardly eaten in the last twenty-four hours. My stomach groaned but I felt an odd sense of calm. Everything that was happening was now completely out of my control. All the danger that surrounded me was just some horrible gamble. Nothing was predictable. As I watched a line of nondescript office blocks file backwards in my field of vision I realised that this is how we travel. Looking backwards. Seeing what has just passed.

'Teddy,' Harry called to me. 'Are you all right?'

I slumped back into the car seat & wiped my mouth with a handkerchief.

'Yes. Just getting some air.'

We pulled up in front of a low-rise whitewashed concrete flatblock. Thought I recognised the design of the dwellings and wondered why. Then I realised that it was the same architecture on the plans for the residential part of the Enugu scheme.

Rico pointed out a flat.

'Are you sure that's the right number?' asked Harry.

Rico nodded. Harry leant forward & gave some instructions to the driver. Then he sat back in his seat & all was still for a while. Harry closed his eyes for a couple of seconds. His face became very calm, he breathed deeply a couple of times. Then his heavy lids slitted open. His jaw clenched and his mouth tightened. His face had become a mask.

'Let's go!' he hissed sharply.

All at once we moved quickly out of the motor car. Onto the street. We looked ridiculously conspicuous but Harry led us swiftly up to a doorway & banged heavily against it. Five seconds & then he banged again, harder. A few curious black faces gazed up from the street. Harry took a couple of steps backward & charged at the door, forcing it open with his shoulder. He rushed in & we followed. A half-dressed Ogungbe was trying to scramble out of a window at the back of the flat. Harry grabbed him & dragged him across the room.

'Not so fucking fast, Sambo!' he shouted.

He was using his fists on him now & kicking him into a ball of submission on the floor in front of us. Harry grabbed a chair and planted it in the middle of the room. He pulled out a few lengths of rope from his pockets & handed them to Rico.

'Tie him to the chair,' he ordered.

Rico pulled Ogungbe off the floor, seated him & proceeded to bind him in place. Harry rubbed at his skinned knuckles thoughtfully. He nodded at Rico who started to slap Ogungbe's face.

'Hijo de puta! You fuck me with your fucking demurrage clause!' he shouted.

Ogungbe's head twisted from side to side, trying vainly to avoid the blows. Rico stopped & looked towards Harry who nodded slowly. Ogungbe's screwed-up face loosened a little. Harry waited until he opened his eyes then he pulled out the gun, worked the action on it & then pointed it at the end of Ogungbe's nose. His yellowy eyes widened and went cross eyed towards the barrel.

'I say we kill this little bastard now,' he said coldly.

'No, please,' Ogungbe begged.

'Shut up!' he snapped.

He drew the pistol down Ogungbe's face. Forcing it against the lower lip he shoved it into his mouth. Ogungbe shut his eyes, his face trembling, sweat pouring down his brow. A muffled sound came from the back of his throat. Harry turned around & smiled at me. With his free hand he beckoned me over and nodded. *Your turn.*

I gently extricated the gun from Ogungbe's mouth & rubbed his bruised face.

'Now, now,' I said. 'There's no need for all this, is there?'

Ogungbe started breathing heavily.

'W-w-what do you want?'

Harry clouted him on the ear with the pistol. Ogungbe shrieked. He looked up at me plaintively.

'Make them stop,' he sobbed.

'Now, be reasonable John. They're very upset. And understandably so.'

Rico punched him in the stomach & he collapsed, groaning horribly, held up in the chair by his bonds. I somehow felt terribly calm amidst this violence. I had a part to play. I had to reason with him.

'Now John,' I continued softly. 'You owe these gentlemen money. It's only fair to expect that they want it back. Isn't it?'

Ogungbe's body started to shake. At first I thought that he was having some sort of a fit. He was panting like a dog. Then he lifted his head & we could see he was laughing.

'What's so fucking funny?' Harry demanded, moving towards him.

I held him back. I smiled at Ogungbe & cleared my throat.

'My friends here don't quite get the joke, Ogungbe. Maybe you'd like to explain it all.'

'Your friends thought that they could make plenty money out of stupid Africans. Think we're dumb natives. My country is a land of negative miracles. So rich in resources that are stolen from us and then sold back at a profit. We've learnt well from our colonial masters, our imperial gangsters.'

'Well, that's a fine speech, Ogungbe. But it doesn't really help. You see, we invested money in your scheme in good faith.'

'You wanted a quick profit from crooked money.'

Harry raised the gun again, pointing it at Ogungbe's temple.

'That's enough fannying around. Give us our cash back or I'll blow your fucking head off.'

Ogungbe flinched. I cleared my throat.

'I would suggest that you comply with my friend's demands,' I implored.

Suddenly there was the sound of people coming in through the broken front door. Everyone swung around. Three men in khaki fatigues rushed into the room with service revolvers drawn.

'Hold still, everybody!' the leading one shouted.

He waved his revolver at Harry.

'You! Drop your weapon!'

Harry let the pistol fall to the ground.

'Police?' he asked.

'Na so police. At all. We soza.'

Ogungbe laughed.

'Behold our country's glorious armed forces, gentlemen.'

The leader of the soldiers came forward and slapped Ogungbe hard.

'Shut up! You not get mouth. No more palaver from you. You think you clever. Go to England college. Learn big big grammar. Well, I go England college too. Sandhurst. Learn big big grammar too. Maintain military discipline at all times. Implement counter-insurgency tactics. And so on. We learn order. This country is a mess. Tiefman taking over everywhere. Chopping big big bribe from everyone. People like you. Soon soza take over. Restore order.'

'Thank you, lieutenant,' a voice came from out of the room.

Dr Chukwurah entered. He looked around the room, nodding.

'Well,' he said, smiling. 'Here we all are.'

He lit a cigarette & nodded over at me.

'Thank you for leading us to Ogungbe. I don't think we would have found him so quickly without you.'

Harry frowned at me.

'You?'

I shrugged back.

'So, we'll take over from here. You'll be escorted to the airport and put on the next flight home.'

'What about our fucking money?' Harry demanded.

109

Chukwurah took a sharp draw from his cigarette.

'You have caused quite enough trouble in our country already. And broken many of its laws. I'm sure that you've seen enough of our penal system not to want to hang around and face the consequences. All the assets of Ogungbe's little scheme will be confiscated by the proper authorities. Believe me, he's tried to embezzle as much from the government grant I secured for him.'

Chukwurah walked up to Ogungbe, flicking ash at him.

'You have a big eye, Ogungbe,' he said. 'And a long throat. But ambition and greed have got the better of you.'

He stubbed the cigarette out in Ogungbe's face. There was an awful scream. Chukwurah turned his head. He glared at us.

'Now, fuck off back to your own country,' he said.

Sunday, 27 June

Lagos Airport, 3 a.m. Long wait for the next flight home. Harry v. sullen. Dreams of his little empire, his place in the sun, all gone. Me v. relieved to be finally getting out of this god-forsaken place.

Yesterday, as we were being escorted back to our hotel to pick up our belongings, Rico was dropped off at the dockside. We looked out at the ships for the last time. Rico pointed out one that was listing badly in the water. He became agitated, cursing loudly in Spanish. They had been moored there for so long that moisture had got into the cement, solidifying it, adding more & more weight to the cargo. The ships were starting to sink.

3

Jack the Hat

Open the soap duckets. The chimney sweeps. Talk to the sword.
Shut up; you got a big mouth. Please help me up.
Henry . . . Max . . . come over. French-Canadian bean soup.
I want to pay, Larry. Let them leave me alone.

Dutch Schultz's last words

Soho Square. Park the cream and blue Mark II Zodiac and walk around to The Flamingo on Wardour Street. Mod club. Spade music blaring out below the pavement. R&B. Soul, they call it. Tip some hat brim at the doorman and slip him a note with a sly grin. In. Downstairs. Check the bag in the inside suit pocket. Pills. All kinds. Purple hearts, french blues, nigger minstrels, black bombers. Enough to keep all those mod boys and girls dancing all night to that spade music. Uppers, leapers, they call them. And sure enough there they all are leaping around on the dancefloor. Doing The Monkey or The Hitchhiker or whatever. But this mod thing is changing. Hair getting longer, clothes getting more lairy. Still a demand for the pills, though. That's the important thing. Keep some of the black bombers for myself. Keep me going. Keep me together.

New record starts. Needle scratch static. Engine noise. Rat-tat-tat gunfire. Car tyres squealing. Crash. A lairy spade voice mouths off. AL CAPONE'S GUNS DON'T ARGUE. Then this funny old beat starts jumping along with horns wailing over the top like sirens. All the mod boys and girls jerk about like spastic. Cagney moves. Shoulders shrugging, fingers pointing two-gun style. This ain't soul. This is something else. Funny rhythm, moving on an up beat like. The kids kind of stomp around to it. What the fuck is this? What have the spades gone and come up with now? No singing, just this Jamaican coon going *chicka, chicka, chicka.* And fannying on like he reckons he's a bit tasty. DON'T CALL ME SCARFACE. MY NAME IS CAPONE. C.A.P.O.N.E. CAPONE. Silly cunt. But it's catchy. *Chicka,*

chicka, chicka, chicka a boom a chicka. Picks up on that black bomber buzz I've got inside. I do a little waddle myself as I cross over to the bar. A bird on the dancefloor checks the hat and grins. I dance around her a bit and give her the old leer.

Get to the bar and order a bacardi and Coke. Lean back and take it all in, pushing the hat back from my brow. Slow number now and suddenly all the young things find a partner and sway about a bit, the blokes grabbing at these tarts' arses as they stagger about the floor. Slow, mournful church-organ chords as a spade sings when a man loves a woman, she can do no wrong. Now this is soul. It's like some sort of hymn except this blackie's talking about love and all the trouble it brings. And I kind of well up. As if I've got anything to feel sentimental about. Maybe it's guilt thinking about what a bastard I've been with birds. Madge. That horrible accident in the motor. Shudder and remind myself it *was* an accident. Christ's sake, Jack, pull it together. Maybe it's just the booze. And the black bombers.

'All right Jack?'

It's Beardsley come over and I give him the nod. He's wearing some crap light-blue seersucker. Cut far too tight on him. Kind of eye-tie look. He's still into the mod thing. If anything his hair's shorter than usual. I'm wearing my check serge number. I cut enough of a dash with this crowd, I reckon. Could teach them a thing about dancing too. I wander over to the gents for the drop and expect him to follow in a decent enough interval.

Run some cold water in the basin and take off the hat to splash some in my face. It's steaming hot in this dive or is it just me? Check the mirror. Count the wisps of hair on top. Bald. No two ways about it. Bald. Old Jack is bald as a coot. Fucking joke. All these kids growing their hair long just as I'm losing mine. Diabolical. Put the hat back on. Get the angle right. Become the Hat. Jack the Hat.

Beardsley's here by now and I pass over the bag of pills and he hands me a wad. Slip it in the suit without checking.

'Might be a while before I get more of these.'

Beardsley shrugs and downs a couple of blues himself. I make to leave.

'Jack.'

Beardsley whispers. Serious.

'What?'

'I want a shooter.'

I make a face. Wide boy mod acting tough.

'You don't want a shooter.'

'Get me a gun, Jack,' he insists, folding another wad into my top pocket. I shrug, give him a pat on the cheek and push the notes down since they don't match the tie.

'All right.'

I get out of there pushing my way past all the jigging kids giving a few Cagney shrugs for good measure. Go round to The Stardust. Mad Harry's club. More my scene really. Not many people about. A few second-rate faces. Matt Munro on the jukebox.

Someone gives me the nod. Gets me a drink. Respect. I like that. Some wankers think I've lost it. But I'm still there. Jack the Hat. I down another bomber with bacardi surreptitious like, and there's Harry.

Grins as he sees me. Scar crease criss-cross smile lines.

Chicka, chicka, chicka.

DON'T CALL ME SCAR FACE.

'Jack, you lairy bastard.'

'Who you calling lairy? You big poof.'

Harry laughs. *He* can take a joke. We go back. Dartmoor. Did time in the Moor together in the fifties. And in Exeter. Harry saw me deck that screw in the exercise yard. Knows I've got bottle.

'You want to watch that, Jack. People have been known to get topped for mouthing off like that.'

Cornell, he means. Common knowledge Fat Ron topped George Cornell. Went a bit moody over a snide remark.

RONNIE KRAY'S GUNS DON'T ARGUE. DON'T CALL ME FAT POOF.

'Fat Ron's got no sense of humour.'

Harry laughs.

'Well, he is a bit touchy. You want to watch yourself there.'

'The Twins don't scare me.'

Harry knows I'm off their firm for the time being. Glad to be out of it, to tell the truth. Don't fancy being one of their cronies on a twenty-five quid a week pension, doing their dirty work. Fuck that. I'm a freelancer. That's me.

'Just don't push your luck.'

Chicka, chicka, chicka.

'I ain't afraid of nobody.'

Reach into my suit pocket for a bomber, pull out a bit of lint.

'Sure, Jack. Fancy a drink?'

Harry's got some sort of a proposition, I can tell. We grab a table and I wait for the spiel.

'Still pushing pills?'

Shrug.

'It's a living.'

'Well I've got something lined up. Need a bit of muscle.'

Nod and grin. A job. I'm your man.

'What?'

'The Airport.'

'Heathrow?'

Harry gives this Jewboy shrug.

'Heathrow, Thiefrow, whatever. The Richardsons out of the picture. It's up for grabs.'

The South London mob used to run the Airport. Now they're all sent down after that stupid gunfight in Catford. Charlie and Eddie Richardson, Roy Hall, Tommy Clark and Frankie Fraser. Best of that firm all wiped up. Shame about Frankie. He was in the Moor and all. Chinned the governor for the kicking I got after the exercise-yard business. But Harry's right. They're out of the picture for now. Only one problem. The Other Two.

'The fucking Krays will want to move in.'

'Eventually. We could muscle in for a while though.'

Chicka, chicka, chicka. I give him a big lairy grin. Fuck the Twins.

'Look,' says Harry, reading my wicked mind. 'All I want to do is make a bit of easy gelt then fuck off out of it. I don't want to mess with the Twins if I can help it.'

'Those freaks don't bother me.'

'Jack, for fuck's sake, take it easy. Don't get involved in anything that's not necessary. All we got to do is put the frighteners on some bent car-park attendants and baggage handlers for a while, then we're away.'

Sounds reasonable. Harry's known for his powers of persuasion.

'I want some cash to put into legitimate business. The club could do with some capital and all.'

The Stardust is half empty. A band starts up. Some geezer crooning Burt Bacharach over chintzy electric organ. Easy listening. A few bacardis had taken the edge off the black bomber buzz so I can relax into it. No mad chicka, chicka, chicka beat in my head no more. Grab some nosh. Chicken in a basket. Harry's not happy.

'Look at this. This place is fucking dead.'

Shrug. Breadcrumb-coated skin caught in my teeth.

'I need to get some class acts on in here. Get the punters in.'

Suck grease off fingers.

'You could turn it into a strip club.'

Harry wrinkles his nose.

'That's the way Soho's going Harry. Either that or like a mod club or something. If you ask me, a strip club is where the money is. And porn. Real money to be made there.'

Harry looks pained.

'Jack, this is my club. I want it to be a place where I'd like to go. I want it to be a bit classy like.'

'Well, the punters want filth. Especially porn. Ship it in bulk from Scandinavia and sell it at a mad profit. Need to pay off the Dirty Squad of course.'

Harry's ignoring me so I drop it. No point saying wake up, this is fucking Soho we're on about. He's off on some showbusiness dream.

'I need to get some proper cabaret on here. Big-name draws.'

Nod. Yeah Harry, sure.

'I was thinking Dorothy Squires. She's got a residency up at The Tempo on Highbury Corner. You know it? Freddie Bird's club.'

Know it? I'm fucking barred from it. Got into a row. They were using Geordies as doormen. Fucking northerners coming down here doing what they please. I was pissed of course. And pilled.

'I was thinking of going over and checking her out tomorrow night. Fancy coming?'

'Yeah, sure,' I says.

No one bars Jack the Hat.

Few more drinks. The bacardi takes the edge off it all. The club closes. One or two faces left sitting around the table. Couple of tarts. Catch up on the chat. Tony the Greek's fucked off back to Finsbury Park. Bought a restaurant. Gone straight. Big Jock McCluskey's away on a two stretch. Receiving. Jimmy Murphy's disappeared. Common knowledge he had Harry over on a long firm. Diplomatic shrugs all round. Maybe he's propping up the brand-new Westway flyover. No body, no case, though. And nobody sure where the body is. Where the nobody is. Like Ginger Marks. Shot in Cheshire Street then bundled into a motor and spirited away. Only a few spots of blood, his glasses and a couple of cartridge cases left on the street. No body. Should have used a revolver, though. Automatics leave too much forensic.

Harry's making a fuss over some pretty blond boy. Mouthing off showbiz gossip. Friends in high places. Stroking his leg under the table. Feel randy myself. One of the tarts is still working so I leave with her.

Back at her seedy little flat. On with the gas fire. Thump. Give her a bit of a feel standing up as she takes off her clothes. Pushes me away and gets into bed. I get my clothes off and come around the other side. Fucking freezing.

'You going to wear that in bed?' Her screechy voice.

Still got the hat on. Take it off and spin it chairwards. Hits the floor. Bald head showing. Supposed to be a sign of virility. No such luck. All the pills and the booze. Can't get it up. Can't.

Suddenly feel awful. Need to hold on to her. Jaw all clenched. Sobbing gently. Face in her tits. There, there. Touches my neck. Been there before. Another useless punter. Poor Jack. There, there. No hair to stroke so she pats my bald head. No Jack the Lad tonight. No chicka boom a chicka. Can't get it up. Can't. Oh God. Hold on to this tart. Think of Madge. How I pushed her away. How I pushed her out of the car door.

Can't sleep. Tart rolls over and starts to snore. Long lonely night. Cold grey morning. Get up, get dressed. Check the hat in the mirror. Straighten tie. Top pocket wad. Thirty notes. Beardsley. What's that toe-rag want a gun for? Take out five and put them on the bedside table next to an old packet of Durex.

Get out and retrieve the motor. Drive around a bit. Buy a paper. Find a caff. Fry-up breakfast. Place full of workers stoking up for the daily grind. Splat ketchup over snotty egg. Then use sauce bottle to prop up *Daily Mirror*. Headline: CUT-UP BODY FOUND DUMPED IN 2 SUITCASES. *Yard men in hunt for boy's killer. The naked torso of a youth was found in a battered suitcase yesterday. Nearby was another suitcase, containing the limbs.* Eat as much as I can stomach. Speed comedown. Misery.

Drive home. Vodka mouthwash. Collapse into bed. Wake up and it's already starting to get dark again. Four o'clock. Feel like death. Take a couple of bombers and pick up a bit. Yeah. Have a bath. Shave. Watch a bit of telly. Find a half-clean shirt and give it an iron. No clean underwear so I put on a pair of swimming trunks instead. Dab the suit down a bit. Get ready. *Chicka, chicka, chicka.* Get suited and booted.

Phone Harry. Arrange to meet him in The Mildmay Tavern on Ball's Pond Road. Have a few before going on to The Tempo. Barred? What a joke. Ready to go. Down a couple more bombers just to be on the safe side.

Get to the pub about eight thirty. Harry's there. And Jimmy Briggs and Patsy Murphy. And one of the Lambrianou brothers. Tony.

'Tony's just got out of the boob,' Patsy says.

Been in Bristol Prison. Slip him a few notes. The done thing.
'Anything I can do for you?' I say.

Harry's keeping shtum about the Airport which is just as well because the Lambrianous are getting well in with the Twins. Word is they're being courted by the Other Two. I fanny on about helping Charlie Wilson escape from Winson Green.

Get to The Tempo mob-handed and a bit tanked up. Bother on the door. Some fucking Geordies in monkey suits don't want to let me in. Freddie comes out.

'Look,' he says all reasonable and shit. 'We don't want any trouble from Jack.'

Harry intervenes. One club owner to another like.

'It's all right, Freddie. He's with me. I'll look after him.'

Freddie lets me in grinning nervously. You know he's thinking about his fixtures and fittings. I put up with this shit and stroll in, unimpressed. Feel a bit wound up, to tell you the truth. Down a couple more bombers, chase them with a bacardi and Coke. That's better. Stay out of trouble, Jack. *Chicka, chicka, chicka.* Fuck them. The Tempo is all red walls and chairs sprayed gold. Trying to be classy, I suppose. All fur coat and no knickers if you ask me. At least the teenagers I push pills to know how to enjoy themselves. All this poncing about in dinner jackets. Don't impress me.

Me and Harry grab another drink and a table. Dorothy Squires has started her act. Short blond hair. Looks a bit washed out to tell the truth. Hoarse voice singing some sad song. She's past her best but she can still belt it out good and proper. Harry loves it. But then queers always seem to go for this sort of thing. Some washed-out old bint wailing on about what a mess they've got themselves into. Like old Judy Garland. Harry's a sucker for her and all.

Dorothy's taking swigs from a bottle between numbers. Pretending it's water, I suppose. It's obviously booze. Looks like she's had a few already. Harry looks a bit concerned. Unprofessional, he'd call it.

'She's pissed Jack,' he says a bit affronted.

'Maybe The Saint ain't giving it to her enough,' I reply.

You see Dot's married to Roger Moore who plays The Saint on the telly. Harry doesn't see the joke and goes to take a piss. Dorothy's beginning to slur her words. I feel the speed and the booze surge up inside me. Feel great. Poor old Dot looks fucked, and the crowd's getting a bit restless.

'Where's The Saint?' I shout.

Laughter. Then lots of shushing. Dorothy looks out blearily across the crowd, rotten drunk. *Chicka, chicka, chicka.* I can't stop myself.

'What's he like in bed then?' I shout over. 'The old Saint?'

Get a few laughs. A bit more shushing. Dorothy loses her rag.

'You mind your own business!' she yells, her voice thick with Welsh. 'He's a lot better'n you!'

Laughter. No more shushing. I'm part of the floorshow now.

'Come down here, darling!' I call back. 'We'll soon see!'

'I'll come down and have a fight with you!' she screams, her accent getting Welsher all the time.

More laughter. Everyone turns around to look at me. I stand up. The whole club does a bit of a spin around me. Faces everywhere. Looking at Jack. Jack the Hat.

'Come on then, darling!' I shout out.

I move forward. Knock over a chair and kick it out the way. A couple of doormen are coming over.

'All right, Geordie boy!' I call out to the biggest one. 'Me and Dorothy are just working on our double act.'

This thick northerner's grunting something in a stupid accent but no one can hear a thing because Dorothy's giving the whole place a mouthful.

'Fuck the lot of you!' she's screeching as she leaves the stage.

Game girl. I give her a clap and a cheer. The doormen are moving in but people are getting up and walking out. Lots of pushing and shoving. A ruck starts and the thick Geordie boys go off to deal with it. Booing and whistling from the back of the hall. Some prat of a compère in a crap shiny tuxedo announces the next act over

the row. An exotic dancer. I move towards the stage. The row's
been settled. The doormen are dragging someone out.

The dancer's music starts. Some mad Turkish racket. Drums
going like crazy. *Boom ba di boom ba di boom ba di boom.* And this
bird's on stage in a gold bikini shaking it all about. I'm jerking
about to this wog rhythm going *chick, chick, chick* on the offbeat
as I get nearer the front. Tits shaking along to the beat on stage.
Hypnotic.

'Yeaaah!' I call out, showing my appreciation. 'Get them off,
darling!'

The bird on stage ignores me. 'Sit down!' someone shouts and I
ignore them. Everything's coming up in a mad rush. *Boom ba di
boom ba di boom ba di boom. Chick, chick, chick, chick, chick.* I'm
climbing onto the stage. What the fuck am I doing? I'm climbing
on the fucking stage, that's what I'm fucking doing.

I'm moving about with her. Shaking it all about.

'Come on, darling,' I say to her.

'Fuck off!' she hisses back at me.

Charming.

Suddenly she stops shaking her tits about and walks off. Booing
and whistling from the audience. People shouting for me to get off.
Throwing things. A glass smashes on the stage. Look down at the
sea of faces. Cunts. I'm not scared of you. I'd fucking take the lot
of you on. The music's still going so I start dancing in front of all
these nasty cunts. Take off the jacket and duck an ashtray. Have
to do better than that. Loosen the tie, slip it off and whirl it about
my head like a stripper's feather boa. Throw it into the crowd and
start unbuttoning my shirt. I'll show this lot I've got bottle. I'll
show you.

Take off my jacket and shirt in one go and people stop chucking
things. Big cheer as I drop my trousers. I'm entertaining these
bastards. A lot of laughter when they see the swimming trunks.
Keep the hat on, of course, and dance about a bit to the music.

The Geordies are on stage with me now. One each side, moving
in. Take a swing at one of them and down he goes, crashing into

a table near the front of the stage. I turn and catch a punch from the other fucker on the side of my face. Stagger back. Manage to chin him with a hook as he comes forward. Follow with a cross and he's down too. Just about to kick the fucker when someone's got me from behind. Both my arms are pinned to my sides and I'm being dragged back.

'Jack! For fuck's sake!'

Harry.

He drags me backstage. Bundles me past the dressing rooms with his coat over my shoulders. The bird in the gold bikini is screeching filthy words at me. Dorothy's taking another swig from the bottle, tired, seen-it-all-before look on her face. Harry pushes me out through the stage door into the freezing night air.

'Come on you stupid cunt!' he says, holding on to my arm.

'Get your hands off me, you fucking poof!'

WHACK. Had that one coming, I guess. Get it right on the hooter and go down. I'm on my hands and knees in this filthy dog-piss back alley with Harry's steamy breath in front of me.

'Want me to leave you here?'

Wipe my nose with the back of my hand. Blood. It's fucking freezing out here and I'm bollock naked but for the overcoat and the swimming trunks. And the hat. Get up and brush myself down a bit. Straighten the trilby.

'I'm sorry, Harry.'

'Yeah, sure. Come on then.'

The stage door bangs open behind us. Shouting. Freddie Bird and the Geordies.

'You're fucking barred, Jack!'

He throws the rest of my clothes out after me. I gather them up.

'Don't fucking come back here!'

One of the Geordies mouths something unintelligible. And another voice, not northern, a London voice, not Freddie, don't know who it is, a whisper hisses in the piss-stained alley: 'You've got it coming to you, Jack the Hat.'

I snarl back.

'Leave it, Jack,' Harry whispers and off we go.

Harry's Jag is parked just around the corner so we go in that. I'm in no fit state to drive. I'll pick up the Zodiac tomorrow. We motor down Upper Street towards the Angel. Streetlights throbbing in my head. Feel like shit. Suddenly need to spew so I wind down the window and lean out. It all comes out. Try to aim at the gutter away from Harry's well-waxed paintwork.

The wind hits my face. Blow-drying the puke around my mouth. It hits me. I'm hanging out the window and it hits me. Madge. The moment I pushed her out of the car. Just gave her a shove. Didn't mean to push her out of the fucking motor. She was yacking on at me. Yacking on and on. Told her to shut up. To fuck off out of it if she felt like that. Gave her a push. I didn't know the door wasn't closed properly. I just meant to give her a shove. But I pushed her clean out of the car.

Remember the sound as she flew out and hit the tarmac. The wind rushing past. The thump of her body against the Great North Road. I didn't mean it. Honest. She's in the hospital. Broken spine. Going to be crippled. Worst thing is no one blames me. I know she won't grass. And nobody else will. No blame. An accident. Everyone agrees. Though everyone thinks I've done it deliberate. Little comments I hear behind my back. 'He chucked his last bird. Gave her the shove.' Big joke. Ha ha ha. No one says anything directly. No one blames me for it so I can never say that I didn't do it on purpose. Even though that's what they think, they never blame me for it. No one does. Except me.

I'm hanging out of Harry's motor. Streetlights screaming past my head. I think. Why not? Go on. Push yourself out. Get it over with, you useless slag. All the pills and the booze. Going bald, can't get it up any more. You're not a face, you're a fucking head case. Go on, get it over with. If you've got any bottle left at all, you'll do it.

I push the door handle down. The door swings open.

'What the fuck!' Harry shouts.

I'm holding on to the door for dear life. Can't let go. Haven't got the bottle. Car brakes screech and as it comes to a halt I get catapulted out backwards. Land on my arse in the gutter.

'What the fuck happened there?'

Harry's leaning through the passenger side to look down at me grabbing hold of the kerb.

'The door just opened, Harry.'

Harry shakes his head at me. Must look a state. Bloodied nose, dried puke round me chops, bruise swelling up where that Geordie thumped me, knuckles skinned where I decked them. There I am sitting on the kerb in swimming trunks and Harry's velvet-collared crombie. Fuck. The hat. Where's the fucking hat? I'm as bald as a cunt. Retrieve the trilby from the gutter, give it a bit of a brush and put it on.

'Come on, get in.'

Yellow streetlight blur. King's Cross. West End. Then Harry's flash Chelsea drum. Intercom buzzer then up in a poxy little lift, just a cage really. Door opened by blond boy Harry was feeling up in The Stardust the other night. Trevor. Harry's new houseboy? Looks at me a bit disgusted like. Get used to it, nancy boy.

Harry chucks me in the shower. Tosses me a poncey silk dressing gown. Trevor makes some coffee. Tie the robe and come through. Probably look a right woofter in this thing. Catch the mirror. Hammer horror. Bela Lugosi eyes, Uncle Fester hair.

Sit down on the sofa. Silk rides up on buttoned leather. Pull the gown down to cover my knees. Talk. Harry: What's it all about, Jack? Me: Madge. It all comes out. Spills out like puke. Tumbles out like Madge rolling out onto the Great North Road. And I really lose it. Boo hoo hoo. Blubbering away like a brat. Harry puts his hand on me shoulder.

'It's all right, Jack. Like you said, it was an accident.'

Sobbing nearly done. Sniffing up salt tears and tobacco phlegm.

'Come on,' he whispers, little pat on the arm. 'You can pull it together.'

Then Harry gives me this stare.

'We all done bad things, Jack,' he says coldly.

A chill shudder brings me out of it. Someone walking on my grave. *You've got it coming to you, Jack the Hat.* Harry's dead eyes. Nothing behind them. Look into them and think: he's topped people. He's seen it and it doesn't bother him. He can hurt without feeling. Use the fear without fearing it himself. He could kill you and the last thing you'd see is those dead eyes, staring at you, feeling nothing about it.

Then he snaps out of this look and grins.

I smile back. Harry's still got faith in me. And I need that faith. Someone who knows I've still got it. Somewhere.

'Sorry I called you a poof, Harry.'

Trevor looks over. Eyebrow arched. Harry laughs.

'Don't worry,' he says, shooting a grin at Trev. 'I ain't as touchy as Fat Ron. Now, get some kip. We got work tomorrow. You remember? The Airport.'

Wake up midday. Wash and shave in Harry's huge bathroom. Load of pills in the cabinet. Check a bottle. Stematol. Never heard of it. Wonder what Harry's on?

Trevor sorts me out a fry-up. He's sponged down the suit and given it a press. Harry's onto a good thing. Better than any bird. Borrow a shirt from Harry's triple-figure collection. Check myself out in the full-length mirror. Get the hat. A bit crumpled so I knock some shape into it. Harry comes in. He's wearing a sports jacket, open-necked shirt.

'You ready?' he asks.

I pull a bit of trilby brim down.

'Yeah.'

Harry in the mirror frowning.

'No one wears hats any more, Jack.'

'Well, that's because no one's got no style no more.'

And I ain't got no hair no more.

'You look like a fucking movie gangster.'

'Well.' Cagney shrug, catch my stupid grin in the mirror.

'Well, come on. We're only going for a shufti.'

Lift cage down to the entrance hall.

'Now look, Jack.' Harry's voice all soft and serious. 'You've got to cut down on the booze. And all those fucking pills.'

'I can handle them. I just got a bit lairy last night, that's all.'

Harry's not buying it.

'Oh, come on Jack.'

'Yeah. Well. What about you? What are all those things in your bathroom then?'

'What things?'

'You know, all them pills of yours.'

Harry's face suddenly goes fierce. Eyes narrow, nostrils widen.

'They're anti-depressants, Jack.'

Deep voice angry but not at me. Matter of fact.

'I need them.'

Harry's famous black moods and crazy outbursts. Not just called Mad Harry because of his reckless skill at violence. Winchester Jail crack-up in '59. Screws think he's working a cushy number to do his time in. Even his own mum thought he was playing up for a change of scene when she visits. Prison shrink tells it different. It's for real. Harry certified. Long Grove Mental Hospital, strait-jacket, the lot. Terror of madness and the authorities denying a definite release date. If you're a loony they can lock you up for good. He gets better and gets out but madness still haunts him.

Lift gate swishes open. Brass trellis shh like relief. Out into the street. Grey afternoon. We get into Harry's gleaming black Jag. Trevor's obviously waxed off the puke from last night. Tan leather upholstery. Lovely motor. Purrs into life.

Go west. Acton, Chiswick, get on to the Great West Road. A VC10 screams overhead, tail lights blinking through the gloom. Coming in to land.

'Thiefrow,' Harry announces as the Airport's control tower comes into sight.

And so it was. There were two main rackets. The car park, where the attendants were helping themselves to a considerable percentage of the takings. Given the amount of motors in and out of that place it was quite a wad. Then there were the crooked baggage handlers. Theft of valuables in transit. The best thing about this was that valuable items of cargo were specially tagged. For security reasons! Might as well slap on a label saying PLEASE STEAL ME. And who were the guardians of law and order amidst all the arrivals and departures? The British Airports Authority Police. Second-rate plod if ever there was. Might as well have had the Royal Botanical Constabulary at Kew Gardens minding it. Didn't even have to pay them off they were that stupid.

Now Harry wasn't planning to do any of the thieving himself. Oh no. He worked in what he would describe as a 'managerial capacity'. A thieves' ponce, more bluntly put. He would rob the robbers. Take his share of the rackets in return for protection and security. A certain amount of persuasion might be needed in negotiating this arrangement. The mugs hard at work nicking might not want to cough up at first. But this was where a villain like Harry came into his own. His well-known powers of persuasion could be brought to bear. Apply a bit of pressure. Be brutal if necessary. Scare the fuckers. Use the fear. And Harry had a real talent in putting the frighteners on. It was all 'psychological', he insisted. I don't know about that. It's diabolical, that's for sure. Harry definitely has a diabolical mind.

So we're wandering about the airport, having a general shufti, clocking faces, checking out how things run. We walk up to the big Departures and Arrivals board. Foreign names clattering into place like some mechanical card sharp shuffling a deck and dealing a hand. PARIS, MILAN, CAIRO. And Harry's looking up at it all wide eyed.

'Amazing, how it does that,' I say, trying to break him out the trance.

'Yeah,' he replies all vague like.

Then I realise it's all those far-off places that are mesmerising Harry. Like he's thinking of doing a bunk or something.

'Imagine,' he starts saying, 'you've made enough of a wad to just step on a plane and fuck off for ever. Disappear.'

I give him a shrug.

'I don't know. Don't know if I fancy that train-robber lifestyle. I'd miss getting a good cup of tea.'

Harry winces and heaves a big sigh.

'Oh, Jack,'

As we walk back to the car park Harry starts talking up our plan of action.

'We need to get another body. No one who's connected to any firm. No one who's being courted by any firm. Preferably no one that's known at all. Any ideas?'

'Well you know me, Harry. I'm a freelancer. But everyone knows me.'

'Yeah, but I don't want anyone to get to hear about what we're doing.'

I grin at him.

'Especially you-know-who.'

'Yeah, especially them.'

Fuck the Twins, I think, but I don't want to rile Harry.

'So,' he says. 'Give it some thought, eh?'

'Yeah, I'll give it some thought.'

We get in the motor and drive up to the kiosk. Harry winds the window down and, as a hand comes down to take the ticket, Harry very deliberately crumples it up and tosses it at the attendant.

'Tell Mr Charles we're going to pay him a visit,' he says, staring hard at this berk.

The berk looks worried. He knows.

'All right?' Harry sing-song with menacing grin.

Berk nodding furiously. Harry nods at the barrier.

'Now, put that fucking thing up,' he commands and we screech off.

Harry drives me up to Highbury Corner to pick up the Zodiac. Says to come around the club later if I fancy it. Walk past the puke and piss-stained back alley of The Tempo club. Half memories of last night's lairyness. Retrieve the motor and head east along the Ball's Pond Road. Another body, I think. Someone unconnected.

The Lambrianou brothers are being seriously courted by the Other Two. Who else? Get back home. My drum's a fucking filthy mess. Try and tidy up a bit but just end up throwing a few things into heaps. Need a bird to look after me. Someone like Madge. I can't stop myself fucking thinking about it. Take a slug of what's remained of the vodka bottle. Take a look at the *Evening News*.

SUITCASE MURDER: HOMOSEXUAL LINK. *Detectives investigating the body-in-the-suitcase murder now believe that there might have been a sexual motive behind the killing. The victim, who has been identified as 17-year-old Bernard Oliver from Muswell Hill, North London, was a prostitute who frequented various haunts in Soho used by known sexual offenders. Police are now following up leads in a thorough investigation that will turn a searchlight on the twilight world of homosexuals . . .*

Put the paper down. Think about something else. Someone who's not known. Suddenly think of Beardsley. Snotty-nosed, think-I'm-a-bit-tasty, get-me-a-shooter-Jack, Beardsley. Nah. Then I think, why not? He's a bit wet about the ears but he'd be a right little thug in his own way. Nothing special but he can handle himself. And he's not a known face except to all his mod mates. Bit of borstal form, no doubt. Could train him up. He could be my, like, apprentice.

Get something to eat. Fray Bentos meat pie, instant mash and tinned peas. Feel a bit sluggish after, so I take a few bombers. Think about it. Yeah. Beardsley, my little hooligan. Frightened of me though he tries hard not to let it show. Could be handy having someone else. My own little firm. Pace about. Bombers starting to work. Maybe he's down The Flamingo. Could go and suss him out. No time like the present

Get in the Zodiac and bomb down to Soho. Tip the doorman at The Flamingo a note and go in. Wailing guitar music and funny-coloured inkblot lighting projected on the walls. Clothes seem even more lairy, hair even longer. Bastards. Like they're taking the piss out of old Jack. No Beardsley. See a likely looking mod type with his hair all brushed down over his face, nehru suit and granny-framed sunglasses. No lapels to grab hold of on his paki jacket so I take hold of the front of the coat and pull him towards me.

'Where's Beardsley?'

'He don't come down here no more.'

'So where is he? La Discotheque?'

'Nah. He ain't into this scene no more. He'll be down the Ram Jam.'

'Where the fuck's that?'

'Brixton.'

I get an address and get back to the motor. South London. Never like going over the water. Injun country, the East London firm always call it. And Brixton? Well, that's fucking jungle land. Take a couple more bombers and head way down south.

The Ram Jam is in a crumbling dancehall on Coldharbour Lane. Spade doormen look me up and down as I go in. Give them my best Jack the Lad grin and hand over a ten-bob note. Inside and it's that mad chicka chicka chicka music echoing around the peeling decor. Full of black kids jerking around to that funny old beat. A few whiteys too but they're all gathered in one corner like. It ain't exactly racial harmony but there are one or two white girls showing out to the better looking coons on the dancefloor.

I make my way over to the white corner. A new song starts. *Changa changa changa* it goes and I sort of slope along to it. WALKING DOWN THE ROAD WITH A PISTOL AT YOUR WAIST, JOHNNY YOU'RE TOO BAD — WHOA OH. Catch sight of Beardsley in the thick of it, checking out the floor, swaying along to the beat. *Changa changa changa.* Beardsley catches sight of me. Surprised grin then a nod in my direction. ONE OF THESE DAYS YOU'RE GONNA HEAR THEIR VOICES CALL, WHERE YOU GONNA RUN TO? — WHOA OH.

'Doctor Livingstone, I presume?' I shout in his ear and he frowns, not hearing or not getting the joke or both.

'What you doing down here, Jack?'

'What you think? Missionary work? I came down to see you, you berk. We need to talk.'

Beardsley nods. He's booted but not suited. A pair of steel toe caps, tight jeans held up with braces, button-down shirt with no tie, crombie coat and on top of it all, would you believe, a fucking hat. A stingy-brim trilby, no less. *No one wears hats any more, Jack.* Well this fucker does. It's either the new height of fashion or else old Beardsley is taking a leaf out of Jack's book, stylewise. I nod towards the exit and he follows me out.

Out on the street, I look him up and down. He looks like a Jamaican pimp.

'So what's up?' I ask. 'You turning black or something?'

He grins and shakes his head.

'Nah. All that mod stuff, they're turning into hairy fairies. At least the spades have got style.'

'And what's this?'

I make a grab at his pork-pie hat. It's in my hand leaving him bareheaded. Bareheaded's the word, because there's his shaved bonce beneath. Boneheaded like old Jack.

'Are you taking the piss out me?'

Beardsley chuckles. Dedicated follower of fashion. Looking like a rude boy with his cropped hair and long coat. Wanting a gun to go in the waistband to complete the look. Question is: would he be any good for real?

'So,' I start.

'The shooter? You got me the shooter?'

'That depends. First you got to prove you could handle it. If you think you're tough enough, I've got a proposition for you.'

'What sort of proposition?'

'Need a little extra muscle on a job.'

Beardsley grins. Evil little youth.

'Thing is,' I go on, 'I don't know if you're hard enough, do I? This ain't just a bank holiday beach fight.'

He gives me his best sneer. Then this big black fellah comes over.

'What you want? Weed? Speed? Black hash?'

I try to wave him away. He sucks at his teeth.

'Wh'appen, man? You don't want buy nothing? Then move. This is *my* pitch.'

Then it comes to me. Beardsley can prove himself right now. I smile at the black geezer and step back. I shove Beardsley in front of me.

'See him off, son,' I say.

Beardsley stumbles a bit from the push then shapes up in front of this guy, hard eyes, the lot. I'm not sure that he'll be able to deal with this loud-mouth coon but it's worth a try. I can always step in if he bottles out.

They move around each other on the curb. Fierce eyeballing.

'Ras clat,' the black guy fannies.

But Beardsley's fast. Lively. He don't waste no words. A hand comes out of his overcoat pocket and lashes out. A Stanley knife comes from nowhere and slashes the black face with an upward backhand.

Nasty.

The black man's on his knees in the gutter clutching a bleeding cheek. Claret dripping all over the kerb. Beardsley follows through with his boots. Steel toe caps making contact with the bloke's rib cage. He's squealing away and the doormen of the Ram Jam hear the commotion and start to leg it over. I pull Beardsley back by his coat.

'That's enough, son,' I say. I've seen enough.

We make a dash for it, followed by a whole gang of spades. The Zodiac's parked on the corner of Electric Avenue and Atlantic Road. We jump in and tear away.

Drive back north. Over Albert Bridge. All lit up with fairy lights. Pretty. Nice to be back over the right side of the water. Out of Injun country. Up through Victoria, into the West End.

Get to The Stardust and we can't find Harry. He did say he'd be here. See Trevor sitting at a corner table. Waiting for H obviously. Get a couple of drinks and go over.

'Where's the guvnor?'

'He's upstairs in the office.'

'Right. I'll go up.'

Wink at Trev.

'You can keep each other amused,' I say, patting Beardsley on the back.

I go out to the foyer and start going up the steps. One of the doormen cocks a chin at me.

'All right?' he says, all cautious like.

'I'm going up to see Harry. He's expecting me.'

'Careful.'

His eyeballs roll upward.

'There's Old Bill up there.'

'Oh yeah?' I say, coming down a couple of steps to cock an ear. 'Anyone I know?'

'Mooney.'

That filth. Detective Inspector George Mooney. Remember him back in the fifties when he was just a Detective Constable in the Flying Squad. Liked to think he was tasty. Ex-Met light-heavyweight champion with a reputation for heavying into villains. Arresting officer for an armed blag I got pinched for. Tried to get me to name names. Do a trade. I told him to fuck off. Got a kicking in the cells and a three stretch for my trouble.

Then he made his name as a DS working out of West End Central. Number one fit-up merchant. Planting evidence and beating statements out of minor-league villains who haven't been keeping their payments up. Broke a Maltese racket back in 1962. Now he's OPS. Obscene Publications Squad. The Dirty Squad. Aptly named. Skimming off all the porn in Soho. Taking a percentage on all those smudges, yellow backs and rollers being touted down Old Compton Street. 'Licence fees' they called it.

Get to the landing and the office door is half open so I can hear the chat.

'So what's all this got to do with you, George? You're not Murder Squad.'

Harry.

'Yeah, but they reckon there's some sort of sexual angle. This lad, Oliver, he was a rent boy. So I've been seconded to their inquiries.'

'Your specialised knowledge?'

'Something like that.'

'So you're checking on all the homos?'

Mooney coughs. Embarrassed.

'Well, I can be very discreet in your case.'

'Don't bother. I ain't ashamed of nothing.'

'Yeah, well, they're checking on known homosexual offenders. And they asked me and the Dirty Squad to sniff around a few known haunts. Murder Squad are concentrating on a period of eleven days unaccounted for. Where and who this kid was with in that time.'

'So, what's this got to do with me?'

'Come on, Harry. Bernie Oliver was one of your boys. He's been known to attend some of your, er, parties.'

A pause. Harry coughs.

'So. I don't know nothing about what happened to him.'

'I don't care what you do or don't know. This is just a warning. Cover your tracks. You don't want to be implicated in any of this. It's bad for business. Speaking of which . . .'

'Yeah?'

'Well, I was wondering whether you'd be interested in expanding in the bookshop trade.'

'Depends on the competition. What about the Maltese?'

'Don't worry about them. They're still mostly running old-fashioned vice. You know, clip joints, prostitute flats. To be frank, I don't much like dealing with the spicks. The thing is, though, the porn racket's growing. But it's not organised. I'm having to deal with every Tom, Dick or Harry down Old Compton Street. It would be easier to have someone running the whole thing. Easier to regulate. To keep the lid on things.'

'And easier to collect off.'

'Yes. But you need to keep your nose clean. Cover your tracks on this Suitcase business. Make sure everyone connected to you keeps their head down. There's a big "searchlight on vice" operation going on to keep the papers happy. It'll soon blow over. Murder Squad aren't going to waste too much time on this one.'

'Unless they find the sick fucker what did it.'

Mooney coughs.

'Quite. So, think about it. Once this has all died down maybe we can do business.'

Sounds of Mooney getting up out of his chair. He comes out of the office. Nearly walks into me.

'Well, well,' he says, beady little eyes twitching at me. 'If it isn't Jack the Hat.'

I sort of grunt. Don't want to appear too rude. Not if Harry's planning to do business with him.

'Keeping out of trouble, Jack?'

'Yeah, yeah.' Give him a big cheesy grin. 'I'm a reformed character.'

Mooney laughs and shakes his head. Makes his way down the stairs. Cunt. I wander over and rap on the open door.

'Yeah?' Harry's voice weary.

I go in.

'Jack,' he sighs. 'You hear any of that?'

'Some of it, yeah. You thinking about moving into porn then?'

'Yeah. Maybe. I don't mean that. I mean this.'

He taps the *Evening News* lying on his desk. SUITCASE MURDER headline. I nod. Seen something about it myself somewhere.

'Yeah. I heard some of that.'

'Well keep it to yourself.'

Harry rubs at his face. Tired.

'Thing is, I did know the kid. Bernie. Poor little fucker. He was only seventeen, Jack.'

Only seventeen and cut up and turned into luggage. Sick. I frown. Think: Harry's not involved in all this, is he?

'So, Jack.' Harry stretches, yawns. 'What do you want?'

'It's what we want, Harry. And I got it.'

'Yeah, yeah, get to the point. I'm knackered.'

'Well, you know you said we needed another body for the Airport job?'

'Yeah.'

'Well, I've got someone. He's downstairs.'

'Good. I better come down then.'

I lead Harry over to where Beardsley and Trevor are sitting. They seem to be getting along. Beardsley's taken his hat off and let Trevor touch the fuzzy little pelt of his barnet. Trev's all wide eyed and giggling but he straightens up and looks serious as soon as he clocks Harry and me.

'There he is,' I mutter to Harry.

Harry frowns and talks though the side of his mouth to me.

'But he's just a kid, Jack.'

Bareheaded Beardsley does look younger than ever. Innocent even. I try to reassure Harry.

'He's all right. Honest. Got a right nasty streak in him. Can handle himself too.'

'You sure, Jack?'

'Yeah. Of course.'

'Well, I'm holding you responsible if anything goes wrong.'

Then we go over to the table. Introductions. Harry, Beardsley. Beardsley, Harry. Harry has this stern demeanour. This kind of quiet fierceness he puts on when he meets people. His I-mean-business look. Beardsley's impressed, tries to mirror it a bit himself.

'The crop looks great, doesn't it Harry?' Trevor pipes up.

'Yeah,' mutters Harry. 'Look Trevor, we've got some business to discuss so make yourself scarce.'

Trev wanders off in a bit of a huff and we get down to it. Plan to meet up next day and pay a visit to a certain car-park supervisor.

Next day. We take the Daimler over to an address in Brentford. I'm in the front, driving. Harry likes to be chauffeured on jobs like this. I don't mind. Lovely motor, handles beautifully. Harry's in the back with Beardsley explaining the scam, of how the car-park staff have been on the fiddle, manipulating the time clock mechanism of the ticket machines. Also, detailing how we're going to persuade them to hand over a percentage.

'Remember,' he says finally. 'I do the talking.'

We arrive in the middle of suburbia. Nice little semi-detached houses with well-trimmed hedges around them. Follow Harry up the garden path of one of them. Neatly mown front lawn. A gang of gnomes hanging around a stupid little fish pond.

Harry presses the bell. Ding dong. Avon calling. Sound of footsteps. Door opens a crack and Harry gives it an almighty shove just in case the bloke has second thoughts, and we pile into the hallway.

'Hello Charlie,' Harry announces with a big frightening grin.

Charlie's on his hands and knees. I close the front door behind us. Harry points at the door to the front room.

'Come on, Charlie,' he says. 'Show us through.'

He gives Charlie a kick up the arse and he crawls through into the lounge.

'What do you want?' Charlie sobs up at us.

'Now, that ain't very friendly, is it? Not very hospitable. You should say, "Make yourselves at home."'

'What?'

'I said,' Harry goes on very deliberate like, 'you should say, "Make yourselves at home."'

'Make yourselves at home,' Charlie whimpers.

'Well thanks, Charlie. We will and all.'

Harry gives us a nod and we grab the settee. Beardsley plonks his steel-toe-capped boots on the smoked-glass-topped coffee table. Harry goes over to the bay window and peeps out through the net curtains.

'Nice neighbourhood, Charlie,' he says. 'What's a nasty little thief like you doing in a place like this?'

He starts to draw the chintzy curtains.

'Don't want to upset the neighbours, do we?'

The room darkens. A few shafts of daylight spread out across the wall-to-wall carpet. Harry turns around and looks down at Charlie crouched on the floor.

'Time to talk business, Charlie. A new business arrangement.'

'What do you mean?'

'You know what I mean. Our cut of all the money you've been filching from National Car Parks Limited.'

'That's all finished with.'

'What, because a certain firm's been banged up?'

'Yeah, that's right.'

Harry sighs and shakes his head.

'It ain't finished, Charlie. Why don't you show us around the house?'

We go upstairs. Charlie's a gibbering wreck. Harry sniffs about, looking in the bedroom, the bathroom.

'What's in there?' He nods at another door.

'Spare room.'

Harry grabs the door handle, rattles it about. The door stays put.

'It's locked, Charlie.'

Charlie stutters something. Harry nods over at Beardsley who gives it a good kicking. The frame splits and it swings open.

'Well, what do we have here?'

The room was a sort of office with a little desk and a chair. On the desk were piles of papers. Harry sorts through them, tossing about account statements and flipping through bank books.

'Look at all this.'

He opens a drawer and takes out a handful of bank notes. He waves them in front of Charlie's face and then lets them sail to the floor. He spots a tea chest in the corner and goes over. He looks in and starts to laugh. He puts a hand in and scoops up a handful of silver coins. He lets them slip out through his fingers and clatter into the chest in a pantomime of richness. He tries to lift the tea chest but it doesn't budge. He grunts.

'Give us a hand with this, Jack,' he says.

I go over and we grab it each side. It still won't give so we tip it over. All the silver comes sushing out all over the floor.

'I think we hit the jackpot,' Harry declares.

Charlie starts to yack.

'I, I wanted to stop, I really wanted to, but we couldn't, you see.'

'Shut it,' Harry orders. 'Come over here and sit down.'

Harry grabs the chair and turns it round. Standing behind it he draws it back a little, like a waiter in a posh restaurant.

'Take a seat, Charles.'

Charlie reluctantly comes over and sits down. Harry walks around him and fishes out a few lengths of rope from his pocket, handing them to me and Beardsley.

'Make him comfortable,' he tells us.

I go around the back and start to tie his wrists together. Charlie starts to protest.

'Don't say a fucking word!' Harry orders sharply.

'You'll have time to have your say,' he continues in a softer tone. 'I just need to say a few things. Beardsley, tie his ankles together. You haven't been looking after your accounts very well, have you? You need somebody to help you in putting your finances in order, don't you? Take his shoes and socks off.'

Beardsley does as he says. Charlie starts to giggle as his bare feet are handled.

'Shut him up, Jack,' says Harry.

I grab the socks from off the floor and shove them in Charlie's mouth.

'Hold his feet up.'

Beardsley lifts up the pair of yellowy plates of meat. There's a corn plaster on the right little toe. Harry crouches down in front of Charlie, looking at him with that mad stare of his.

'Naughty of you, lying to us like that. Don't want that to happen again, do we? We want to establish an amicable business arrangement. Don't we?'

Charlie nods frantically, straining to speak through the woollen gag. Harry tuts and shakes his head.

'Don't talk with your mouth full, Charlie. It ain't polite.'

He brings out a cigarette lighter from his pocket. Gold-plated Ronson, very flash.

'Hold him steady,' he says.

He flicks open the top and sparks it up. Charlie strains against us as he sees the flame. Harry lets it lick against the sole of each foot. Muffled shrieks from the car-park supervisor.

After a few seconds Harry clicks it shut. Charlie goes limp on us, heaving heavily through his nostrils.

'See, it's quite simple really. We can do business together. Everything sorted out nice and proper. You just need to know who the guvnor is.'

Harry flicks the lighter on and warms up the feet again. Charlie tenses up. Chewing at the smelly socks in his gob. A choked scream tearing at the back of his throat. Sounds distant.

'This is just a taste. Just a little taste of what will happen if you fuck around with us. If you lie to us. Grass us up. If you do *anything* out of line.'

He stops again. Looks straight into Charlie's eyes.

'All you've got to do is hand over our cut. That's all.'

Charlie's nodding, tears streaming down his face.

'Good.' Harry pats him on the head. 'Good boy. Now, just one more go for good measure, eh?'

Harry burns him again. I catch a whiff of toasted foot. Horrible cheesy stench. Then we're finished. We let go of Charlie and Harry pulls the socks out of his mouth. He's quivering away, wheezing and sobbing. He starts to gibber. Harry nods.

'Yeah, yeah,' he says. 'Tell us all about it.'

'We wanted to stop it,' Charlie blubbers. 'Really we did. Thing is, we couldn't. If we stopped fiddling the machines there'd be such a leap in the takings that head office would have got suspicious.'

'So you just carried on.'

'Yeah, we'd got into a routine. Everyone was getting their whack. It kept everyone happy.'

'Except with certain people away, the main whack wasn't going anywhere, was it?'

Charlie nodded.

'You just didn't know what to do with all this money, did you Charles?'

Charlie shook his head.

'Well, your troubles are over. We'll take care of that now. Let's get down to business. Beardsley, why don't you make us all a nice cup of tea?'

'Uh?' replied Beardsley.

'Put the kettle on son. Jack, untie Mr Charles. I'll bet he's gasping for a cuppa.'

'Right,' says Beardsley, a bit bewildered, and wanders off downstairs.

'And don't forget to warm the pot,' Harry calls after him.

We drive back east. Drop Beardsley off at Shepherd's Bush. Harry slips him a wad by way of a sub. He can afford to be generous. He's set to take a grand a week off the car-park fiddle. Easy money. Get onto the Westway Flyover and bomb down into the City. The Westway. Think about the rumour about Jimmy.

'All right, Jack?' asks Harry.

'Yeah.'

Feel like asking: It true that Jimmy Murphy's helping to hold this thing up? Think better of it.

'Fancy a drink?' Harry offers.

'Yeah, why not?'

Get off the Flyover at Paddington. Go to one of the seedy little drinking clubs in Praed Street that Harry's protecting. A handful of second-rate Lisson Grove faces trying not to gawk. Everyone nervous and polite. Drinks on the house. Respect, that's what it's all about.

'Well, your boy seemed all right,' says Harry as we grab a second bacardi.

'Beardsley? Yeah, he'll be fine.'

'Thing is, it's not going to be so easy when we go up against the baggage handlers. Some of them are proper villains. There's more at stake and they might not be so eager to hand over the swag.'

'Yeah, well, we'll see, eh?'

Beam a big nutty grin over at Harry.

'Silly cunts think they can fence all that stuff themselves,' he says. 'Jewellery, industrial diamonds. You need proper organisation to offload gear like that.'

'Yeah, well, we'll just have to point out the error of their ways, won't we?'

Laughter. We have another drink. Then Harry goes all quiet. Thoughtful.

'There was another thing I wanted to chat about, Jack.'

'Oh yeah?'

'It's a matter of some delicacy,' he says softly, looking around the room.

I frown. What the fuck's he on about?

'The other night at the club. What Mooney was going on about.'

'Dirty Squad business? You thinking of heavying into the Maltese?'

'No, no. Well, not at the moment, anyway. No, the other matter.'

I suddenly get it.

'Oh, the Suitcase Murder,' I blurt out, a little too loud for Harry's comfort.

He winces and puts a finger up to his mouth.

'That kid who got sliced up?' I whisper. 'What about it?'

'Well, as I said,' he goes on, 'it's a matter of some delicacy. I need a hand.'

Hang on a minute, I think to myself. What's all this about? I don't want to get involved in any of this. Maybe he did have a hand in it and wants to cover his tracks. Never know what these queers are into. I don't want to know. And I know what Harry's capable of. This afternoon, that was just kid's play. He's done nasty things, worse things than that. Jimmy Murphy propping up the Westway

Flyover. We've all done horrible things. Madge. I crippled her. Poor cow, she didn't deserve that.

'Jack?'

'I don't know, Harry. I don't want to get involved in that.'

'What's the matter?'

'Well . . .'

'Come on. I just want to make a few inquiries of my own. And I need a hand.'

Shrug.

'I don't know, Harry.'

And I don't. I can't fathom this homo business. Nothing against them, mind, long as they keep it all to themselves.

'Come on, Jack.'

He gets up. I heave a sigh and go along with it. Agree to drive him down to Piccadilly. Feel a bit sluggish so I pop a couple of black bombers on the sly.

It's dark by the time we get to the Dilly. Bright lights swirling patterns on advertisement hoardings, extra sharp as the speed rush comes up. *Chicka, chicka, chicka.* Bright lights luring naughty boys away from Mum and Dad and into all kinds of nasty vices. Groups of long hairs sitting around the statue of Eros. Junkies strung out by the entrance of Boots 24-hour chemists, hoping to score a bent script. We cruise by the Meat Rack and one of the Dilly boys comes out to the motor. Harry gives him a nod and he gets in the back of the limo and I pull away.

'What do you want?' asks the renter, all cocky like.

'I want to talk,' replies Harry.

'Oh yeah? Dirty talk?'

'No, nothing like that. I want to talk about the kid who got killed.'

I check the rear view mirror. The kid is looking scared.

'Bernie,' Harry goes on. 'You knew him?'

The kid nods, frightened.

'So did I,' says Harry.

'I don't know anything,' the kid says, terrified, all cockiness gone now. He pleads in a whisper, 'I won't say anything.'

'Look, son . . .'

Harry goes to grab his arm but the kid makes for the door. Trying to get out as we're cruising down the Haymarket. Madge, I think, flinching. I hit the brakes. Tyre squeal, hooter blaring from the motor behind us. Harry and the boy are thrown forward.

'Jack!' Harry shouts.

The boy gets up, hysterical. Harry slaps him.

'Jack!' he shouts again. 'For fuck's sake move us on.'

And I pull away. The boy's sobbing quietly in the back now and Harry's talking softly, trying to reassure him.

'Look, I won't hurt you. Just tell me what you know,' he says, handing him a handkerchief.

The kid calms down a bit. Blows his nose. Then starts the spiel.

'Yeah, I knew Bernie. Not very well. Just that he was on the game like me. Nice kid. Quiet, a bit dreamy. Haven't seen him round the Dilly recently. Last time I saw him he said he wasn't doing trade no more. Said he was going to be a pop star. Found some rich homo record producer he was going to cut a record with. Just like Bernie. Always dreaming. Only thing he'd ever starred in was some tacky porn smudges he'd done with some bloke in Old Compton Street. Even then he was going around saying that he was going to be a famous model one day. But I don't know anything about what happened. Honest.'

'Right,' says Harry. 'Take us back around, Jack. Look, son, what's your name?'

'Phil.'

'Look, Phil. If anyone asks any questions, keep shtum. But ask around on the quiet if anyone knows anything. If you find out anything then let me know.'

Harry hands him a business card and a few notes as we come around Piccadilly Circus again. As we pull up to the Meat Rack, Harry pats Phil on the shoulder.

'Don't forget, anything you hear, let me know.'

Phil shoves the money and the card into his pocket and gets out of the Daimler. Harry squeezes his arm as he goes.

'Take care of yourself,' he says.

'Where to now?' I ask, hoping that we can go for a drink somewhere.

'Take us up Shaftesbury Avenue. I think we should have a shufti around Old Compton Street.'

Yeah, well the kid was involved in porn so maybe that's a lead. Another reason why Moody's been dragged into the investigation. Detective work. I can see why it's so appealing. But I don't want to get caught up in all this. What's Harry up to? Maybe he's – nah, I don't want to think about it.

We get into Soho. Go up Wardour Street, past The Flamingo. Hang a right into Old Compton Street.

'Pull up here,' says Harry.

I park by a seedy-looking shopfront. ADULT BOOKSHOP, it says in big white letters. We go in. Soft porn in the front part of the shop. Musclemen posing against Greek columns, that sort of thing. Bead-curtained doorway into the back where the heavier stuff is, no doubt. Weedy-looking queen hunched over a book by the till. Looks up and sees Harry.

'Harry!' he whines in a sing-song simper.

Harry nods, grunts.

'Jeff.'

'And what can I do you for?'

'I want a word,' he replies all serious.

The queen blinks and pushes his specs back into the ridge of his nose.

'Better come through here then,' he says.

The curtain makes a little clattering noise as we go through into the back room. Stacks of hard-core books and magazines shrink-wrapped. A pile of rollers in the corner, Super 8 films with titles like *Dark Desires* and *Forbidden Love*.

'What's all this about?' asks Jeff.

'Has a certain OPS officer been around asking questions about this Suitcase Murder?'

'George Mooney? Yeah, he's been in.'

'And what did you tell him?'

'Not a lot. He was more interested in upping his normal licence fee to keep me out of the investigation.'

'And anyone else been around asking questions?'

'No.'

'Good. Right. Well, tell us what you know.'

'Well, Mooney was in and out of here quick as a ten bob wank. In such a hurry to get his money he didn't give me a chance to show him this.'

He rummages about in a pile of glossies and comes up with a handful.

'I don't do much of my own stuff any more. A lot of the stuff is from the States or Scans, you know, Scandinavian. But I meet this kid and he's into it, so I do a session with him. Pretty kid, not really butch enough to tell you the truth, still he looks a lot younger than he is so I figure it would work for the juve market.'

He holds up one of the smudges. Skinny kid looking shyly at the camera. Mop of blond hair, one hand on hip, the other holding on to a hard cock. I look away. Harry grabs the photo and examines it closely.

'It's Bernie,' he says.

'That's right. Poor old Bernie. Or, rather, poor young Bernie.'

Harry looking at the smudge. Frowns all funny like. Looks up at Jeff.

'You weren't involved in anything heavier than this with him, were you?'

'Look, I do a bit of bondage, a bit of fladge, that's it. All harmless fun. I only did the session with Bernie because I ain't going to use real juves. Sure, I get some right weirdos in here. Get offered some pretty heavy stuff as well. But that's all import.'

'So you don't know anything else?'

'On my life.'

'Yeah,' Harry gives him this nutty grin. 'Well, let's hope it doesn't come to that.'

We walk through into the front of the shop.

'Any trouble off the Maltese, Jeff?' Harry asks.

'No, they only deal with the straight stuff. Tight-arsed catholicism, I reckon. Can't say the same thing for the Dirty Squad, though. They're very broadminded. So long as they get their licence fee.'

'I'm thinking of expanding my operations, Jeff,' Harry announces.

'Well, I'm a bit specialised here,' Jeff lisps. 'Not a big market, really.'

'No, I mean the straight stuff.'

Jeff wrinkles his nose.

'I see.'

'I want to start arranging leases on a chain of bookshops sometime soon. Might need a hand in setting up front men.'

'Of course, darling.'

We go to the door and Jeff sees us out. All eyes and teeth. Gives me a big wink as I go out.

'I'll keep hold of this picture, if you don't mind,' Harry says, holding up the glossy. 'And if anyone comes asking about this suitcase thing, let me know.'

We drive back to Harry's flat in Chelsea. Harry's in the front, brooding. I try to snap him out of it.

'So, you are moving into the porn racket,' I say.

'Yeah,' he mutters all faraway. 'I guess.'

'Means having to deal with that cunt Mooney, though.'

'Let's sort out the Airport first. And this.'

He taps the picture of Bernie propped up on the glove compartment. Shy little teenage face peeking out under a blond fringe, staring out at oblivion.

We get to Harry's place. He peels off a few notes. My share plus a little extra.

'Thanks for all your help, Jack. I'll get in touch regarding the baggage handlers. You can get hold of Beardsley when we need him?'

I nod.

'Right then.' Weary sigh. 'I'll see you, then.'

A hard day's work and home to Trevor. What time is it? Just gone eleven. The night is still young and I've still got a bit of a buzz. *Chicka, chicka, chicka.* Time for an after-hours' nightcap. Need a drink, all this queer business leaves a bad taste in my mouth. Nothing against Harry, mind, but you know what I mean. Pick up the Zodiac and head north.

Stoke Newington. The Regency. Big sign says, 'North London's Smartest Rendezvous'. My arse. Three floors of tacky nightclub, more like. Favoured meeting place for many well-respected faces, though. Gets a bit lively on Saturday night when it fills up with young hooligans trying to act tough to impress the birds. But it's Tuesday night so it's bound to be quiet. Yeah. Take it easy, Jack. Just a couple of drinks then fuck off home.

It's half empty in the downstairs after-hours' drinker. A few of the Kray firm are about, lording it over. Nods, grins, all right Jack and all that pony but I can tell they're a bit wary. Yeah, I'm all right. Don't trust any of this lot. No sign of the Other Two, thank Christ. Shouldn't have come here. Harry's right, I should steer clear of all their firm. But fuck it, I ain't afraid of them. The Lambrianou brothers come over. Tony and Chris. Obviously well in with the Twins now. Chris is friendly enough, gentle sort of a bloke really. Tony's a bit more sly. Suddenly feel all alone, eyes darting at me, people whispering: *Jack the Hat, he's a troublemaker, he's got it coming to him.* I'm on my own and I ain't even tooled up. Finish the drink and get out of there.

Get home to my flat. The place is in a right state. A shithole. Can't sleep. Feel uneasy. Maybe it's the pills. Maybe it's something else. Get up and reach up into the chimney breast. Pull out my shooter all wrapped in cloth. Give it a clean. Long-nosed Colt 45. Spin the cylinder slowly. *Click, click, click.* Feel a lot better for giving it a good oiling. Then put it back in its hidey hole. Feel safe it being there. That and the sawn-off under the floor boards. Eventually I drift off. Half sleep. Mad dreams. Luggage going around the Airport carousel. Two suitcases come around, like the ones that kid was cut up and put into. But when I go to pick them up I see that it's my name on the tags.

Get up late the next day. Try and sort out the flat a bit. Take a bag of smelly old clothes down to the laundrette, drop a couple of suits off at the cleaners. Have something to eat in a nearby caff then spend most of the afternoon picking losers out in the bookies. Do a bit of shopping on the way home. Crack open a new bottle of vodka and watch a bit of telly. Stare at the fuzzy old screen until it's all over. National anthem, then that sharp tone to wake up the dozy fuckers who've fallen asleep in front of the box. An empty signal buzzing in my head. Closedown. Drink to stave off nightmares. Go to bed alone.

Lunchtime, Harry calls up to arrange the meet at the Airport. Get a full tank in the Zodiac and drive out west. Get hold of Beardsley and he says to pick him up at a pub just south of Dalston junction. He's outside when I pull up. Looking right flash. New crombie, Ben Sherman shirt, tightly tailored with buttoned-down collar, Sta-Press trousers with razor-sharp creases, a bit short in the leg to show off the lethal-looking ox-blood polished boots. Well, he's been spending some of his newly earned gelt on this get up. No hat this time but he wears his brand-new number-one crop with a well-studied glare. Obviously been practising the look. Learning off the grown-up gangsters. Other little touches too. A silk handkerchief in the top pocket of the crombie held there with a tie pin. And a steel comb poking out from there as well. No doubt its rat-tail end sharpened up just in case there's no time to get his Stanley blade out. Every detail of style spelt violence.

And there's this gang of kids hanging around him. All trying to look like him, act like him. They ain't as flash, of course. Donkey jackets, monkey boots, that sort of thing. But they've all got the regulation crop. It must be a new craze, I suppose. But I ain't seen nothing about it in the papers or on the telly. They're all fannying on about long hair and swinging London. Kind of reassuring to bald Jack that you don't have to have much of a barnet to be fashionable.

150

So, anyway, Beardsley hops in and I ask him about it.

'So, what? Ain't you a mod no more?'

'Nah, I told you, it's all over now. All that lot down The Flamingo have gone all hairy. Beads and flowers. Peace and Love. Fuck that.'

'So what are you lot called?'

'We ain't got a name yet. We're into aggro.'

'Aggro?'

'Yeah, you know, aggression, aggravation. Aggro.'

'Oh yeah,' I give a little chuckle. 'Aggro.'

We go across town, get onto the Great West Road at Hammersmith.

'So what about the shooter, Jack?' asks Beardsley, a bit too cocky for his own good.

'I told you son,' I reply. 'You got to do your apprenticeship first.'

He goes into a bit of a huff about this.

'Look Beardsley, don't worry. You'll have plenty of opportunity to prove yourself. You're into the, er, ag, what do you call it?'

'Aggro.'

'Yeah, aggro. Well, there'll be plenty of that this afternoon.'

I give him a wide grin and he smiles back. I feel a bit queasy though, to tell you the truth.

Harry's got Mr Charles, the car-park supervisor, to set up a meeting with the main baggage handler. It's a set up of course. We're in the basement level of the multi-storey car park waiting for this mug who fancies himself as boss of all the thieving. Charlie's closed this level to the public so we've got it all for ourselves. We're waiting in the shadows, half hidden by concrete pillars, back lit by sickly yellow sodium lights. Harry likes to stage manage the fear.

Beardsley's a bit twitchy, raring to go. I crack each set of knuckles and give him a wink. Harry's calm as ever, leaning against the Daimler all nonchalant.

Echoed footsteps coming down the ramp. We're on.

'Charlie!' this voice booms around the concrete.

'Over here!' Harry hisses, stage whisper.

This geezer walks into a pool of yellow light. Overalls, loading hook slung over one shoulder. Harry reaches into his motor and turns on the headlights full beam. The baggage handler shields his eyes.

'Charlie? What the fuck's going on?'

'Mr Charles couldn't make it,' Harry announces softly.

Me and Beardsley fan out each side of the baggage handler.

'Who the fuck are you?' the man demands looking each way as we circle around him.

'I'm your new guvnor, Derek,' says Harry.

Derek grabs his hook and blindly makes a swing with it in a wide arc. Harry steps back from it. I come around the back and kick Derek's legs from under him. He's down on his knees and Beardsley follows in. Putting the boot in. I step on the hand still holding the hook and it lets go. Kick the thing across the floor of the car park. Harry nods at Beardsley to stop kicking. He walks up and stands over Derek who's now curled up in a ball snivelling. Looks down his nose at him.

'We've got to discuss our new business arrangement,' he says, gently prodding Derek with his toe cap.

We tie his hands behind his back and tape up his gob. Harry gets a big sack from the Daimler and chucks it over at me.

'Put him in this.'

Me and Beardsley bundle him into the sack and secure it with some twine. Derek's making muffled noises. Harry kicks the bag and tells him to shut up.

'Right,' says Harry. 'Put him in the boot of the Daimler.'

Then we're off. Beardsley goes with Harry in the Daimler and I follow on in my Zodiac. End up at a disused warehouse in Bermondsey. Unload Derek like he's dry goods. Upstairs, a long dusty space with cast-iron pillars. Empty, except for a table with a few things on it and some chairs. One of the chairs is right in the middle of the room. All on its own. It's been nailed down there.

We get Derek out of the bag and tie him to this chair. Still gagged.

Then Harry brings out the black box. It's got a little handle on the top of it and wires coming out with little crocodile clips on the end. The Black Box. I've heard about it. Never sure it was true. The Crank Up, I'd heard it called. Rumours. Not from anyone who ever had it done to him, mind. I mean, that was the whole point, wasn't it? Funny really, you get the idea, like in all them war films and that, that torture's used to make people talk. But Harry uses it for the opposite reason. The whole point's they don't talk, ain't it? Don't grass.

'Take his overalls and his pants down,' Harry says to Beardsley.

Derek tries to protest through the tape gag but he doesn't struggle.

'You want to do the honours, Jack?' Harry asks.

He holds up the wires by the clips, moving their hinged ends so that they snap like two little pairs of jaws. I try not to flinch. Big grin to hide any lack of bottle.

'Why don't we let the young apprentice have a go?' I suggest.

Harry nods.

'Beardsley,' he says, holding up the clips for him to see. 'Attach these to our friend here.'

Beardsley frowns as he takes the wires off Harry.

'Uh – Where do I put them?'

Harry smiles.

'Where do you think?'

And so they get on with it. Harry delivers this long lecture about business, stopping every so often to nod at Beardsley to give Derek a crank up. Derek goes into this sort of short fit every time he's given the electric. The rest of the time he's nodding or shaking his head frantically at what Harry is saying. Desperately trying to agree with him, except he can't because his mouth's taped up. At one point there's some talk of dousing Derek with water or something to increase the conductivity but he's already pissed himself so it wouldn't make much difference. I watch and try not to think about it too much. It will all be over soon. There's a bottle of Johnny Walker on the table and I pour myself one. Take a few sips as Harry delivers his spiel. All this psychology makes me feel a bit sick.

When they finish, Beardsley rips off the tape from Derek's mouth and he's gasping and blubbering away. We untie his hands and chuck him a cloth to wipe up the piss off his legs. We get him to clean up the chair and the floor around it as well. Then we let him get back into his overalls and give him a drink. Let him have about two fifths of the Johnny Walker. He's like a zombie now. He nods, wide eyed, as Harry explains how things are to be organised.

Later, me and Harry have a drink at The Stardust. A sort of celebration, like. H proposes a toast, holding up a tall glass of bacardi and Coke.

'To Thiefrow,' he says.

'Thiefrow,' I repeat.

Clink.

'And to the theft of valuables in transit,' says Harry.

Yeah, looks like that racket's all sewn up for a while. Harry reckons Beardsley's all right for the pick up. I say I'll keep an eye on him. The Stardust's dead as ever. This place must be losing Harry money. It's quiet as fuck and Harry's just sitting there. Thinking about something. Brooding. I hope he's not having one of his black moods. Heard horror stories about him 'going into one'. I get up.

'Just going to put something on the jukebox,' I say.

'Uh?' says Harry, only half out of his trance.

'Just going to put a record on.'

'Yeah.' Harry nodding, all thoughtful. 'Wait a minute.'

He grabs my arm.

'What's up Harry?'

'Remember what that kid said down in the Dilly the other night.'

He's off on *that* business again.

'What?'

'He said Bernie had talked about a "rich homo record producer".'

'So?'

'Well, that could be a lead.'

'So, who do you fancy for this "rich homo record producer"?' I ask.

Must be plenty to choose from, I think.

'Meek,' replies Harry. 'Joe Meek. You know him don't you Jack?'

'Yeah. Sold him pills a while back.'

Big amphetamine customer. Practically bought in bulk.

'Well, it could be him, couldn't it?'

'What?'

Harry sighs, impatient.

'The "rich homo record producer", of course.'

I shrug. So what?

'We should go and see him.'

'We?'

'Come on, Jack. I need a hand with this.'

So I get talked into all this palaver once again. I don't like it. Something wrong about the whole thing. Anyway, before you know it, we're off up the Holloway Road to Joe's flat cum studio. Pokey little place above a leather goods shop. Intercom on the door. Harry buzzes.

'What do you want?'

Joe's yokel voice crackles on the little speaker.

'It's Harry. Harry Starks.'

'Go away.'

'Come on, Joe. Open the door.'

'Leave me alone.'

Harry slips the lock and shoulders it open. Up the stairs. Strange electronic music echoing about the flat. Broken crockery, smashed records and odd bits of recording equipment strewn everywhere. Promotional pictures of Heinz, blond pop star in silver suit, scattered about the floor. Face crossed out with angry black lines. Music's weird, like a soundtrack for a science-fiction film.

'Joe?' Harry calls out.

Suddenly he's there at a doorway. Dressed all in black. Shiny black shirt open at the neck. Face as white as a ghost. Eyes popping out of his head. He's holding a single-barrelled shotgun at waist level.

I look over at Harry. Nod. I'm ready to rush Joe. Harry holds up a hand. Easy. Madness, he understands it.

'It's all right, Joe,' he says softly. 'We just want to talk.'

'It ain't safe to talk,' Joe says in his west country drawl. 'They're listening in.'

'Who are, Joe?' asks Harry, humouring him.

'The police,' replies Joe. 'And EMI.'

Harry slowly moves towards Joe.

'It's all right,' he says, soothingly. 'It's all right.'

He comes right up to him with his hands out.

'Give us the gun, Joe.'

Joe shrugs and zombie-like hands it over.

'You can have it,' he says. 'It isn't mine anyway. It belongs to Heinz.'

Joe starts to sob quietly. Harry hands the shotgun back to me and pats Joe on the back.

'There, there,' he whispers.

'Ungrateful bastard. After all I did for him,' says Joe.

'Come on Joe, he ain't worth it.'

Harry leads Joe to the settee. Chucks some of the junk piled on it off onto the floor and gets him to sit down. I stash the shotgun behind it. Harry sits next to him.

'We need to talk,' says Harry.

'I told you, it ain't safe to talk. They've got this place bugged.'

'Well, we'll whisper then. They ain't going to hear us above this racket.'

The air is still full of this electronic din.

'It ain't a racket. It's my space symphony. It's called "I Hear A New World". I did it back in 1960. Nobody liked it. The rotten pigs.'

'Well I think it's very, er, interesting. And if we talk quietly they won't be able to hear us above it.'

'I hear voices all the time,' says Joe, getting agitated again. 'They're trying to steal my sound. Steal it out of my head.'

'Shh,' shushes Harry. 'It's all right. We're friends, aren't we?'

He pats Joe on the leg and Joe smiles.

'So what do you want to talk about, Harry?'

'Bernie. Bernie Oliver.'

Joe stiffens up, lurches forward. Harry holds on to him.

'Poor little Bernie,' says Joe. 'Chopped up and put in a couple of suitcases.'

'That's right, Joe. And we want to find whoever did that to him.'

'They've got stuff on me. I'm a known sexual offender, Harry.'

'Who's got stuff on you?'

'The police. Highgate nick are in on the investigation, Bernie was from round here, you see?'

'What have they got on you, Joe?'

'They nicked me. Back in '64.'

'What for?'

'"Persistently importuning for an immoral purpose".'

Harry laughs.

'What, at that cottage on Holloway Road?'

'Yeah. But I wasn't being persistent, I can tell you. He was nothing to write home about.'

And they're both giggling like girls on the settee.

'Thing is,' Joe goes on, 'I met Bernie there one night. So I'm a suspect. They want me to go in and make a statement.'

'Who, Highgate nick?'

'Yeah. But then this other copper turns up. Plain clothes.'

'Not out of Highgate nick?'

'Didn't say.'

'Murder Squad?'

'Yeah, maybe. I don't know. Told me I was eliminated from their inquiries.'

'Did he ask any questions?'

'No. He just told me to keep quiet about the whole thing. If I knew what was good for me.'

Harry frowned. Joe went on.

'Maybe he was one of *them*.'

'What?'

'You know, maybe he was trying to steal my sound.'

'Yeah, yeah. So did you make a statement at Highgate?'

'No, no. I'm frightened of leaving the flat, Harry. I'm scared.'

'Well Joe,' says Harry, patting him on the back again all reassuring like. 'Why don't you give me your statement?'

Joe shrugs. OK.

'I meet Bernie at the cottage. You know, the one up the road. He comes home with me. When he finds out who I am he wants me to record him singing. He's a lovely kid, lovely long blond hair. But he can't sing. I play back the tapes for him and we have a good laugh. He says if I play around with the recording enough, put plenty of echo and compression on and that, it'll sound OK. I humour him. I like the kid and he shows a bit of appreciation. Not like some of these selfish bastards who've made a career out of me. So I tell him to come back next week and we'll try again. That was the last I saw of him.'

'Any idea of where he went after that?'

'He said he was going to this party in a big house out in the country. Rich people.'

'Where?'

'I don't know . . . strange name . . . nightmare . . . just a . . . just a . . . heart . . . well . . . just a mare . . . just a . . . nightmare.'

Joe's gabbling. Speed talk. Madness. Harry waits for him to finish.

'And that's the last you saw of him?' he asks.

'Yeah, honest. Next thing I know he's in the papers. Just a, just a nightmare. Do you think they got him, Harry?'

'Who?'

'You know, *them*.'

Harry gets up and looks down at Joe.

'I don't know, Joe. We're going to try and find them, though.'

Harry gives me a look. Time to go.

'I know who might know,' says Joe.

Harry's ears prick up.

'Who?'

'Buddy Holly,' Joe gets up off the settee and starts to move around the room. 'I need to get in touch with Buddy,' he says, suddenly urgent again. 'He'll know.'

Harry nods over at me. We make our way out of there, leaving Joe to mutter away to himself as all this space music is floating around the place.

'Just a, just a—' stutters Joe as we leave. 'Nightmare.'

We go downstairs and get into the motor.

'He's sick, Jack,' Harry says in the motor as if he needs to explain it to me. 'We need to talk to him again when he's not in such a state. He needs help. I know a shrink. Maybe . . .'

Harry's voice drifts off into brooding.

Maybe he could do with some of those loony pills of yours, I think. The ones I saw in your bathroom cabinet. Don't say anything, though. Harry's a bit touchy. But maybe Joe could do with some pills like that. Something to bring him down a bit. All that speed isn't good for you. Sends you loopy.

A week later and I'm driving Beardsley out to the Airport in the Zodiac. Making sure the pick up runs sweet. Beardsley's sporting a holiday look as cover. The bovver boy look might raise a few too many eyebrows. Probably scare the shit out of the British Airports Authority Police but we don't want to upset anyone, do we? So he's wearing a straw pork-pie hat and wraparound shades. Sta-Press but with loafers instead of boots. Bottle-green Fred Perry shirt and a windcheater jacket. Little holdall bag looking like hand luggage for the loot.

Beardsley makes the pick up in a gift shop in the Arrivals area. Derek goes in and leaves a package hidden between the rows of little dolls dressed in national costume all lined up in see-through plastic cylinders. Beardsley follows in and stuffs the package in his holdall on the sly. Picks up a doll to avoid suspicion and pays for it at the counter. Easy. We make our way out to the car park as the Arrivals board clatters away behind us. Beardsley's swinging this little doll by its string tassle.

'You going to chuck that?' I ask him.

Beardsley holds it up and looks at it. It's all dressed up like a Dutch girl. He grins.

'Nah. I'll give it to me kid sister.'

Then the car park. At the barrier we hand in our ticket and the bloke in the booth slips us a big fat envelope. Then we're away. Nothing simpler.

We drop off the stuff with Harry and take out cut. Everything's running sweet but Harry's brooding away. Preoccupied with this other business, no doubt. I worry about him 'going into one'. Don't want things to fuck up now when everything should be just ticking over fine and earning us easy money. Still, there's nothing to be done so we leave him to it. I agree to give Beardsley a lift.

Driving back across town Beardsley talks about our own little racket. Drugs. Pills and that. Might as well keep that scam going in case this one falls apart. Had a little trouble on the supply side, though. Certain people wanting their share of everything. The Other Two. Greedy bastards. Kind of fucks things up. Still, me and Beardsley are on a roll, feel a bit cocky. So we decide to pay a visit to Marty the dealer.

'Need to pick something up from my gaff first,' I tell Beardsley.

Get to my drum and have to wade through all the junk I haven't got around to clearing up yet.

'Christ, Jack,' Beardsley gasps. 'Your place is in a bit of a state, ain't it?'

'Never mind that,' I tell him. 'I've got something to show you.'

I lead him through into the bedroom and reach up into the chimney flue. Pull out the shooter. Unwrap it and hold it up to his face. He gives this little noise of excitement in the back of his throat.

'There you are son. Colt 45.'

Give the cylinder a little spin. *Click, click, click.*

'That's a real fucking shooter. You could blow someone's face off with that.'

Beardsley's all wide eyed like a little kid. I load it up with shells and hand it to him.

'Go on,' I tell him. 'Have a pop. I can tell you're dying to.'

Beardsley feels the weight of the thing in his hands.

'Go on. Fire it into the chimney breast.'

Beardsley's gripping the revolver, squinting and gritting his teeth.

'Keep your arm straight. Squeeze the trigger, don't pull it too sharp.'

Bang. A big flat bang fills the room. Little clouds of blue smoke and plaster dust. The recoil's knocked Beardsley back a couple of footsteps. He's giving a mad little giggle.

'Quite a kick hasn't it, son?'

I take it off him and slip the safety on. Shove it in my waistband and do up my jacket.

'Right,' I say. 'Let's go and pay a little visit to Marty.'

I can tell Marty ain't pleased to see me when he opens up but he puts on this stupid smile to try and fool me otherwise.

'Jack,' he tries to say all friendly but it sticks in his throat. 'How you been?'

'Busy. That's why I ain't been around much, Marty. But me and the kid here want to resume our little arrangement.'

'Want a drink?'

'Let's get down to business.'

'Thing is, Jack,' Marty starts up, trying to be diplomatic. 'Thing is, things are difficult.'

'Oh yeah? Like what?'

'The Twins. I had to pay them off last time I dealt with you.'

'So? That's your business.'

'Well I thought it was sorted out with you.'

'What?'

'That's why I dealt with you. You said it was sorted with them. You were sticking their name up. I dealt to you because I thought it was sorted with them.'

'I don't understand.'

'Well, I've had to pay them off, haven't I? They said you weren't on their firm no more and I have to deal through them in future.'

'So what are you saying, Marty?'

'I'm saying that I can't afford to fuck around, Jack. I don't want to mess with the Twins.'

'You saying you ain't going to deal to me?'

'Jack, this puts me in a difficult position.'

'Well let me make it easy for you, Marty.'

I pull out the shooter and press its long barrel against his nut. Beardsley gives a mean little laugh.

'Let's stop fannying around and do business, shall we?'

'All right, all right,' stutters Marty, shitting himself. 'Point that thing somewhere else, can't you.'

Marty goes off to get some stuff, shaking his head and sighing. 'This could bring a lot of trouble, Jack,' he says as he comes back.

'Don't you worry about the Krays,' I tell him, tucking the shooter back in my waistband. 'They're on their way out. They don't bother me.'

Bravado. Still, I'm not afraid of them am I? Am I?

'Well,' Marty goes on, sighing like he's resigned to his fate. 'Since I ain't got much choice you might as well have something a bit special.'

Marty's beady little eyes light up as he takes out a sheaf of brightly coloured paper. I take one off him. It's blotting paper, marked off in little squares.

'What the fuck's this?' I ask him.

'LSD, Jack. It's the new thing. A couple of chemistry students are knocking up this stuff in a makeshift lab in Canning Town. All the Beautiful People are mad for it.'

'Beautiful People,' Beardsley snorts.

'I'm telling you Jack, it's the height of fashion. Cut them up into little squares and sell them to longhairs for ten bob or a quid a piece.'

'What is it, speed?'

'Nah. It makes you see things brighter. Colours and that. Gets you into all of this peace and love shit. Lasts for hours and all. You only need a tiny bit. Just a drop of it on the blotting paper, that's all.'

What the hell. Have to keep up with the times. We buy a load of it even though Beardsley doesn't look too keen. Get some black bombers and all. Largely for personal use. Though I'm going to cut down. Don't want to end up like Joe Meek.

'Great,' says Beardsley in a huff as we drive off. 'This means we've got to deal with the fucking hairies.'

'Don't worry about it, son,' I tell him. 'Business is business.'

A couple of days later Harry calls me up.

'I've got a meet fixed with Mooney,' he says. 'Want to sit in?'

So Harry's serious about moving into the porn racket. Wants me in on that as well. I'm flattered but also wary. Not sure if I want to be on his firm permanent. Prefer being freelance, me. Still, it's worth sussing out so I say: 'Yeah, sure.'

And I bomb over to The Stardust in the Zodiac. Harry's on the top table all laid out dead flash. Champagne in an ice bucket.

'Kid worked out on the drop all right?' he asks.

'Yeah, no bother.'

Beardsley's working out fine. Don't mention our little drug enterprise though. Never sure if Harry might be greedy and want his cut like the Other Two.

'Seen the papers?' he asks me all agitated.

Shrug.

'Just looked at the racing page.'

'Well take a load of this,' he says handing over tonight's *Evening Standard*.

TOP OF THE POPS COMPOSER AND A WIFE SHOT DEAD, reads the

headline. *Joe Meek in double tragedy at recording studio*, in a line above it. I read on: *Joe Meek, 36-year-old composer of the Top Ten hit Telstar and promoter of three pop groups, was found dead today at the Holloway, London, recording studios he always called The Bathroom.*

Beside him on the landing of his flat was a 12-bore shotgun. Down the stairs nearby, dying from shotgun wounds in the back, was Mrs Violet Shenton aged about 52 . . .

I put the paper down.

'Well, Harry,' I say. 'He finally flipped.'

'Yeah, poor old Joe. Thing is, I'm sure he knew something. He was trying to tell us something. Just something. That's what he kept saying. "Just a just a . . ." I don't know what it all means.'

'You think he had anything to do with it?'

'Joe? Nah, I don't think so.'

'It'd explain him topping himself like that.'

Harry shakes his head. Mooney arrives. Strolls in with this superior copper look on his face like he's above it all. He ain't fooling nobody. I hate dealing with filth like him. I know Harry ain't keen himself but he can fake it better than me.

Harry's all gracious charm, pouring out the expensive bubbly for this bent DI. A few pleasantries exchanged then we're down to business.

'Well, if I can speak freely,' announces Mooney, looking around him then looking at me.

'Of course,' says Harry. 'You know Jack, don't you? He's in on this.'

Mooney nods in my direction, grudgingly. Gives a little sniff as if I'm dogshit on his well-polished PC plod shoes. I feel like giving him a slap but hold back. Easy, I think. Have to deal with scum like him. Take a sip of this posh fizzy stuff. Don't know what all the fuss is about. Tastes like Tizer.

'So,' Mooney says. 'The good news is that the Suitcase Inquiry is being wound up. We can all breathe easily now.'

'They didn't find anything?'

'No. The Suitcase is closed.'

A little smile plays across Mooney's lips. Harry frowns. He don't get the joke.

'What about Joe Meek?'

'Yes, I heard about that. An unfortunate business. But he was eliminated as a suspect, I believe.'

'So they didn't turn anything up?'

Harry looks incredulous.

'Well,' says Mooney, all reasonable and shit. 'As I've said, the Murder Squad are winding down their investigation. They haven't managed to find any more tangible leads. There's a considerable concentration of manpower required in maintaining a murder inquiry.'

'And a seventeen-year-old rent boy isn't really worth bothering about,' mutters Harry.

'I'm sure the Murder Squad have their priorities,' Mooney replies softly. 'The thing is, with this messy business out of the way the spotlight is off Soho for a while. We can get on with the main business in hand.'

'Porn,' says Harry bluntly.

Mooney coughs.

'Quite. This permissive society that everyone's talking about means that business is booming. The squad's scale of operations has increased considerably.'

'So have the kickbacks I bet,' I chip in.

Mooney gives me a dull stare.

'I prefer to see it as a work incentive for keeping the lid on things. We can't afford to let things get out of hand. There are dirty bookshops springing up all over Soho and nobody's controlling it properly from your side. The Maltese are so busy with clip joints and prostitution they don't seem to realise what a growing market there is for pornography.'

'So you want someone to take over the porn rackets?'

'It would be a lot easier all round if we just had to deal with one firm.'

'And what if some of these bookshops needed leaning on?'

'That's your business. I'm sure you could persuade them to come into line.'

Mooney's green light on putting the frighteners on.

'And what if the Maltese get riled that someone is taking over their pitch?' asks Harry.

'As I've said, that's your business. You do your job and I'll do mine. Your methods don't concern me. The OPS wants to deal with an organisation that can control all of this. I'm sure, as a businessman, you understand the need for a balance of free trade and protection. Particularly protection.'

Harry grins and fills another glass of champers for Mooney. The bottle's empty and he waves at a waiter for another bottle.

'Well, I'm sure we can work something out,' says Harry, giving me a nod. I grin back. Mooney catches the look and sighs.

'I want all of this done quietly. I can't afford to have some sort of gang warfare on my pitch. As I said, my job is to keep the lid on things.'

'Don't worry, George,' says Harry with a grin. 'We'll be real subtle.'

'Hm. Well make sure that you are. Then we can negotiate our percentage. Remember, if you work with us you'll not only be immune from official prosecution, you'll be immune from narks as well. Any grassing that comes our way can come straight back to you. It's a bloody good deal and we'll expect a reasonable share from it.'

Mooney slurps down his bubbly and gets up.

'I really must be getting off,' he announces. 'We'll talk figures once you've got your side of this arrangement sorted.'

'Yeah,' Harry agrees.

Then we all stand up together, handshakes all round and Mooney's off. Harry slumps back down in his chair. A bit mad about the eyes. Picks up the champagne bottle.

'Fancy another Jack?' he asks.

'Nah. Let's have a proper drink,' I reply.

*   *   *

Next few weeks me and Beardsley are putting the frighteners on a few porno bookshops. Offering them new terms and conditions, reminding them of their fire regulations, that sort of thing. Sticking up the Starks trademark helps but some of these filth pedlars aren't playing. Fannying on about already having protection. So we firebomb a couple of them. Harry's not pleased. We didn't consult with him first. Doesn't want things to get too lairy. I don't know what he's complaining about.

In the meantime me and Beardsley are dealing the funny drugs to the Beautiful People. Those chemistry students in Canning Town are knocking up this stuff on overtime since these hairies can't get enough of it. Acid trips. Looking all lairy in their beads and kaftans and crochet knit dresses. It's all Wow and Flower Power and Peace, Man. Which is fine by me. We don't get anything unnecessary off these fuckers. No aggro, as Beardsley would put it. The weather's getting warmer and everyone's talking about the Summer of Love. Beardsley can barely disguise his contempt but business is business, I remind him.

'I hate the Beautiful People,' he says.

But we're having our own Summer of Love. What with the drugs money and the Airport rackets earning us an easy life and the porn trade about to take off. It's dodgy but it's swinging. Can't seem to do anything with all this bad money though. It all goes on the horses or on the dogs at Hackney or White City. And if I'm still ahead I usually find myself pissing it away in a casino. Get into a spot of bother at the 211 in Balham one night and pull a knife on a croupier. Silly really. Brown Bread Fred gets right narked. He's in with the Twins so it's bound to get back to the Other Two. I need to calm down.

Still, everything's swinging in the West End so I don't have to worry about the East End for a while. Harry should be happy too but he's still brooding about this dead kid. One time I go around to his place I see Trevor's sporting a black eye. Harry's black moods. Been taking it out on Trev no doubt. No fucking good. Just makes him moodier and full of guilt. Trevor's looking sullen.

A sad, fuck-the-rest-of-the-world look on his bruised face. Same as the look on Madge's face when I knocked her about.

Then Beardsley hears something from the Airport. The word from Derek the baggage handler is that a huge consignment of industrial diamonds is due in in a couple of days. A massive haul. Something we could all retire on.

Harry arranges a meet. Derek's nervous, no doubt keen memories of the Crank Up. He goes through all the arrangements in great detail and we start to make plans. This is the big one. No discreet pilfering this time. We're going to take the lot.

Me and Beardsley are in cargo loader overalls as Derek leads us out onto the runway. He's straightened a couple of security passes with the British Airports Authority Police. We get into this little truck with a trailer on it and drive out to this big fat jet plane. It's like a huge bus with stubby little wings on it. Don't know how they get these things off the ground.

The truck's got an electric motor, like a milk float, and it hums away and I hum along to it. A few nerves but nothing to worry about. It's all been planned. We've been through it several times. Harry's worked it out down to the last detail. Not that he's had much experience at this sort of villainy. As I said, more used to just taking a percentage out of thieving. That and fraud and protection rackets is more his style. Still, this one's too big to let pass, so Harry's been playing the big criminal genius. Meetings at his place going over the MO. Maps, little Dinky toys, the lot.

Not that H is with us on the big day, of course. It's just me, Beardsley, Derek and a couple of baggage handlers Derek can trust. They're waiting for us in the cargo hold of the plane. I'm humming along to this electric motor. Look over at Beardsley. He's got a manic grin on his face. Jaw clenched with nerves and maybe the black bombers we've downed this morning. Well, you need a bit of speed for a caper like this. Keeps you sharp.

It's all worked out. We get into the hold and then this conveyer-belt truck pulls up and starts loading the loot. We get it passed through sharpish and drop it out onto the trailer on the back of our truck. Then we tie up Derek and the other cargo loaders. Give them a bit of cosh to make it look like we've overpowered them. Then we're away with a truckload of industrial diamonds over to the maintenance vehicle yard where there's a driver waiting for us in a transit van. We should be halfway down the Great West Road before the alarm's sounded. Need to put the cosh about a bit lively to make it look convincing. Still, the cargo boys won't mind a few lumps for the percentage they'll be getting. We're talking about hundreds of thousands for the haul if it's fenced right. Maybe a million. But best not to think about that. The Train Robbers started to lose it a bit when they realised that they'd got a lot more than they'd been counting on. It went to their heads and they got a bit sloppy. Best not to think about it at all. Just get the job done and then wait. Then wait some more until the fuss has died down.

So we get into the hold with the loading crew. The conveyor-belt thing comes up and is connected into place. It starts moving and the first of the packages come up on it. It's pass-the-parcel time all the way to the back of the plane and dropped out through a hatch onto the trailer. They're a bit lighter than I expected and I suddenly feel something's wrong. Like there's nothing in them or something. I try not to worry about it. How should I know how much these things weigh? Everyone's concentrating on getting it all loaded and unloaded as quickly as possible. Eyes down at the matter in hand. I happen to look up at the loading hatch for a second. I see a head appear at the top of the conveyor belt. Then a body. Somebody crouching on the moving belt. Somebody loading themselves into the cargo hold. I try to call out but the body beats me to it.

'Police!' he shouts.

He tumbles out into the plane, landing on the first baggage handler. He's got a truncheon out and he's trying to get a swing on the overalled body beneath him but he's all tangled up. Then another copper follows him in and there's a pile up. Shouting and bodies rolling around in the hold. One of the coppers is on his feet whilst the other is holding down a cargo loader. They're plainclothes. They ain't British Airports Authority, that's for sure. Flying Squad or something. The whole thing's a fucking set up. The one standing is whacking the next cargo loader with his truncheon as a couple more of this serious filth are pouring in from the conveyor belt. Beardsley's nearest the exit hatch so I give him a shove towards it.

'Out! Out! Out!' I scream at him.

He squeezes himself through the little doorway and drops down onto the trailer below. Derek's coming down along the plane trying to get to the escape hatch followed by all the filth in single file with their truncheons out.

'Got you, you bastard!' the leading one shouts as he grabs Derek by the scruff of his overalls and gives him a knock about the side of the head. Derek balls up and the copper nearly topples over him. I get my cosh out and clock the hunched-over copper right in the gob. He groans as he goes down, spitting teeth and blood as the filth behind him pile up, Keystone style, over him and Derek. I make it to the hatch and swing down onto the trailer. Beardsley's at the wheel of the truck in front.

'Come on son!' I shout. 'Get us out of here.'

He drives off as one of the Old Bill on the tarmac gives chase on foot. He manages to get to the back of the trailer and tries to jump on. I give him a whack with the cosh and he falls rolling onto the runway. (Madge falling onto the Great North Road, for fuck sake, Jack, don't think about that now.) I climb back to the front. Get onto the truck. Sit in the little seat next to Beardsley. I'm facing backwards and I can see a little group of filth about fifty yards back.

'Can't you get this milk float to go any faster?' I ask.

'Jack,' replies Beardsley nervously.

We're starting to slow down. Plod are beginning to gain on us.

'Come on son! For fuck's sake, put your foot down!'

'Jack,' Beardsley repeats. 'Look!'

'What the fuck's the matter with you?' I shout as I turn around.

Then I see what the matter is. A huge VC10 is taxiing out on the runway in front of us. We're heading straight for its front undercarriage. Behind us a load of filth are running after us.

'Fuck!' I say and grab the wheel off Beardsley. I stamp my foot on his and onto the accelerator. He screams, more from fear than pain as we go straight towards the big wheels of the landing gear ahead.

I slam the wheel over hard so we just miss the front undercarriage and then I zig zag around the two even heavier sets of landing gear behind. I'm laughing hysterical now, like a kid on the dodgems and we come out around the back of the jet. Its tail engines are screaming as it brings itself to a halt. We've lost the coppers for a while as all sorts of palaver breaks out behind us. We make for one of the loading bays, dump the truck and leg it back into the Airport buildings.

We slow down a bit and walk down one of the corridors. Try to act nonchalant. Give the old leer to a couple of stewardesses that pass. Somehow manage to find our way out to Arrivals. Go into the gents and get out of our overalls. Normal clothes underneath as planned which is just as well. The place is swarming with filth, though. Uniforms at all the exits, plainclothes snooping around. Just as well the place is really crowded. Don't know how we're going to get out, though.

Just then we hear all this screaming. Sounds like some sort of a riot. High-pitched voices wailing by one of the Arrival gates. Decide to go with the commotion. Might give us some cover. Find a whole mob of teenage girls screaming at a pop group just arrived home from a European tour. Flashbulbs popping, placards saying WELCOME HOME THE STONES, MICK WE LOVE YOU. Me and Beardsley try and blend in.

'Fucking hairies!' Beardsley mutters.

But the police are lost in the crush and we manage to get out to the main exit amidst this gaggle of teenage tarts, screaming and calling out the names of their idols. I join in for the hell of it.

'Aren't you a bit old for this sort of thing?' asks this girl in a mini skirt.

'Nah, I've always been a fan of the boys.'

The uniformed coppers at the foyer are mostly crowd control

now, so we manage to slip out unnoticed and grab a cab back to London.

'We were fucking set up, Harry!'

I'm shouting. I'm bloody livid to tell the truth.

'Somebody grassed! Or set the whole fucking thing up with the Old Bill!'

Harry's trying to calm me down. Pours me and Beardsley another brandy. Waits for us to calm down a bit. He shrugs.

'You reckon Derek stitched us?'

'I don't know. I don't think so.'

'So what you reckon happened?'

'Well, I heard something,' he says.

'What?'

'Bit of inside information from a friend on the force. Change of security arrangements at Heathrow. Airports Authority Police are out. It's CID Number Two Area's patch now. I think people were beginning to notice how much stuff was going missing.'

'Well, it couldn't last for ever I suppose. And would your bent copper happen to know who it was that stitched us, Harry?'

'Leave it, Jack. A caper gone wrong. It's no big story. Let's just wipe our mouth and get on with it. Best thing is to lie low for a while as far as the Airport's concerned. Chances are they'll be pulling in the car-park mob and all. We just need to make sure no one can finger us for anything.'

'Yeah, I guess so. Well that's the end of Thiefrow then.'

'Yeah. It was good while it lasted.'

'And now we've got other rackets to attend to.'

'Yeah,' says Harry. 'And I want you to take it easy. No more petrol bombing bookshops without my go ahead.'

Porn. And me and Beardsley's little drugs operation. With the Airport gone at least there'll be money coming in from them. Maybe we should cut Harry into the acid racket. Could do with some whole-sale protection if we come up against any opposition. Not that we have any bother with the hairy Peace and Love types we deal to.

Beardsley gets off and we arrange to meet up later. I stay for another drink. I can tell Harry wants to talk. He pours me another brandy and then goes out and comes back with a map. More big-time criminal plans, I think. I hope not, if the Airport fiasco is anything to go by.

'I want to show you something, Jack,' says Harry.

'Oh yeah? What?'

Harry smooths out the unfolded map on the coffee table. Chubby finger points at a bit of green.

'Here's where they found Bernie. That kid in the suitcase.'

'Oh yeah?'

That again.

'Tattingstone,' he says, pointing to a little dot of a village. 'And just along from it, here,' he goes on, tracing a fat finger to a slightly larger dot next to a whole lot of blue, 'is Hartwell-juxta-Mare.'

'Hartwell.'

Juxta-Mare. It's Latin for, by the sea. Remember Joe Meek kept saying "just a, just a" after he told us that Bernie was going to a party in a big house out in the country. Maybe he was trying to tell us something.'

'It's a bit of a long shot, Harry.'

Harry Starks as Sherlock Holmes. I think not.

'No it ain't, Jack. I know of a big country house there where they have just the kind of party Bernie might have gone to. And whose house it is. We're going to pay him a little visit.'

Trevor drives us over in the Daimler but we could of walked. It's only a couple of streets away. Eaton Square. Dead flash. Park the motor and Harry leads us up to the front door of one of these big houses. Trevor comes with us. Harry leans on the bell and after a while someone comes to the door. I'm half expecting a butler or a footman or something but instead there's this flabby-faced fellow in a bow tie, grey hair swept back. He gives a little start when he sees us but you'd hardly notice as he quickly goes into genial mode.

'Harry!' he announces in a posh jolly voice. Sounds a bit ginned up. 'This is a pleasure. Do come in.'

He leads us into a small hallway and I realise that it's just a flat, not the whole house, that he lives in. Harry does the introductions. 'Lord Thursby,' he says. 'Call me Teddy,' insists the jolly little man, beaming a greedy grin at young Trevor.

'Can I take your hat, Jack?' he asks as he shows us through into his drawing room.

'Er, no. I'll keep it on if you don't mind.'

I feel clumsy and awkward. Should really take my hat off. The done thing in posh society, I suppose. I half expect a ticking off. Instead Teddy gives me another of his grins.

'Of course,' he says.

This civil manner, all cultivated to put people at ease, makes me feel uneasy. I ain't used to all this politeness. It's intimidating. Teddy seems so relaxed and unflappable. I do notice his hand shakes a little as he pushes the door open for us, though.

We go through and Harry and Trevor settle down on a settee next to a big marble fireplace. I grab an armchair. Sort of perch on it uneasily. Its rich upholstery making me feel uncomfortable and out of place. Teddy gets us all a drink. Gin and tonics all round. He settles in the chair across from mine with a self-satisfied sigh.

'Cheers,' says Teddy all jovial, lifting his cut-glass tumbler.

We all repeat it like zombies. Like he's got the upper hand.

'So,' he says in this rich voice of his. 'To what do I owe the pleasure of your company, Harry? And of your charming friends of course.'

'Well, it ain't a social call, Teddy.'

'No,' Teddy says with a hint of regret in his voice. 'I somehow thought it wouldn't be.'

Harry takes a sip of gin and plonks his glass on the coffee table.

'Let's stop fucking about and come to the point, Teddy,' he says impatiently.

'Oh dear.' Teddy flinches a little but keeps up his polite front.

'I do hope this isn't going to be unpleasant. I do detest any unpleasantness.'

'That's precisely what it's about. It's very unpleasant.'

Teddy's nervousness is beginning to show. He looks into his gin.

'Then you better tell me what this is about,' he says quietly.

'Bernard Oliver,' says Harry looking for a reaction.

Teddy shrugs.

'Seventeen-year-old rent boy. Found cut up and in two suitcases in a field not more than five miles away from your country seat.'

Teddy traces a finger around the lip of his glass. Looks up slowly.

'Oh,' he says.

'Yes. Oh. He was at one of your parties, wasn't he Teddy?'

Teddy doesn't look so jolly now.

'Well he might have been.'

'What do you mean "might have been"?'

'Well, you can't expect me to remember all these boys' names. But Scotland Yard seem to think he might have been.'

'Scotland Yard? You mean to say they've been to see you?'

'Oh yes. A very high-level investigation, needless to say. The Murder Squad was kept out of it. There were some very high-ranking people at that party. The important thing was to avoid any sort of scandal. Everyone was very keen to avoid that.'

'The murderer could have been one of the guests.'

'It's a possibility. Look, nothing happened at Hartwell Lodge. Nothing like that, anyway. But when the connection was made between this, well, regrettable incident and a party attended by ministers of Church and State, it was decided that the investigation would be wound down.'

'So there was a cover up?'

'Harry, you make it sound like there's some sort of conspiracy. Of course there isn't. There never is. Nobody knows what happened to this unfortunate boy. And everyone wants to keep it that way.'

'And protect some sick bastard who might be well connected.'

'Harry, I'd hardly expect you to get squeamish over another unsolved murder.'

Harry tenses up, eyebrows furrowing with fury, hands clenched. He's about to say something but then he just seethes through gritted teeth. A hand unclenches to pick up his glass. Takes a big slug of gin.

'It's a terrible thing to have happened,' Teddy goes on calmly. 'But there's nothing we can do about it now. And there are other things at stake. There's a Bill for homosexual law reform going through the Lower House at the moment. A scandal like this involving important public figures could do untold damage to it.'

'You're involved in that?'

'I'm championing it in the Lords,' says Teddy a bit smug.

'Doesn't that rather blow your cover, Teddy?'

'Well,' Teddy gives a little chuckle, 'I always insist on my disinterest in these matters. My amateur status as it were. I always declare myself as a non-playing captain.'

'Very fucking funny, Teddy.'

'Now Harry, don't be tiresome. You know that discretion is the better part of valour. And it's an important change in the law.'

'What, consenting adults over twenty-one? Doesn't make me and Trevor legal. Or little Bernie for that matter.'

'But it's a start, isn't it? If we remain discreet and behave ourselves, the law will leave us alone.'

Harry grunts dismissively then gives Thursby his coldest stare.

'Look at me, Teddy,' he says. 'You say no one knows who murdered Bernie. You sure about that?'

Teddy looks him in the eyes and nods.

'Yes.'

Harry gets up and grabs Teddy by the throat. Eyes bulge and flabby face goes all red.

'You better not be lying, Teddy.'

'Please, Harry.' Thursby's deep rich voice gone all high pitched. 'I'm telling the truth.'

Harry lets go of him and sits back down. Teddy sighs and brushes himself down. Trying to regain his composure. His bow tie's come undone. He takes out a matching handkerchief from his top pocket and mops at his sweaty brow.

'Any ideas?' Harry continues.

Thursby shrugs.

'Well, it was odd that the body was so carefully cut up and packed into these cases and then left in the middle of a ploughed field,' he says a bit wheezy. 'As if whoever left it there wanted it to be found. Could be blackmail of some kind. Double blackmail even. But really, Harry, I don't know anything. It's best left well alone.'

Harry stands up to go. Me and Trevor follow suit.

'One more thing,' says Harry. 'Who supplied the boys to the party?'

Teddy's stood up now too. He roars with laughter.

'Don't you remember? It was you, Harry.'

Harry looks shocked. Sways a little like a stunned bull. Trevor's gone pale.

'I don't remember,' mutters Harry frowning.

Trevor looks like he's going to be sick. Instead he suddenly says: 'He's right. I organised it. We'd just met. I was still on the game then. You gave me two hundred quid to gather together some boys for this party. I was going to go down myself. You gave me another fifty to stay with you instead.'

'You see?' Teddy declares a little triumphantly. 'You're implicated in this as well, Harry.'

Harry starts asking Trevor questions as soon as we get back to his flat.

'Why didn't you tell me before?'

'Tell you what? I'd forgotten all about it. I never thought it had anything to do with Bernie's murder.'

'You should have thought.'

This is becoming like an interrogation. Trevor looks pale.

'I was thinking of going down,' he says quietly, full of fear for what might have been. 'Could have been me what got cut up.'

177

Harry ignores the comment. Carries on the questioning. Time for me to go. Got to meet Beardsley in Tottenham.

'Tell me all the names of the other boys that went down,' Harry demands, hardly noticing me make my excuses.

'I don't remember, Harry.'

'Then start remembering.'

We're in this pub with a little dancehall attached to it just off Tottenham High Road. Full of Beardsley types. Cropped hair, boots and braces, Crombies and Sta-Press trousers. A few sporting little pork-pie hats like junior versions of old Jack. Baldheads, I decide to call them. Mad *chicka-chicka-chicka* music on the jukebox. Baldheads stomping along to it in formation boot dance.

Me and Beardsley recounting the Airport fuck up with post-job bravado. We can laugh about it now. Beardsley's got no idea who might have grassed. We both make filthy oaths of nasty revenge even though it's unlikely we'll ever get our hands on the nark.

Then on to the main item of business. Beardsley's made contact with a couple of big acid customers. A hippy party in Hampstead in the next couple of nights and a fellah over in Ladbroke Grove. I just got to get the gear off Marty and we'll meet up the day after tomorrow in the Mildmay Tavern.

Go for a piss. Fresh graffiti above the urinal. PAKIS OUT. Hear a ruckus in the car park as I come out of the bogs. A small gang of greasers is shaping up. Baldheads pouring out of the boozer. The greebos are game enough, swinging motorbike chains and putting it about a bit lively. But they're outnumbered. Beardsley leads the charge and they go down for a right good kicking.

Get into the Zodiac and head east. Stop off at the Regency for a late one. Take it easy. Don't want to ruffle any feathers there. One of the Kray firm lets it drop that there's a job going. The Twins want somebody doing. A hint that it could be a ticket to being back on their firm. I say I'll think about it.

*   *   *

Next day and Harry wants me to drive out with him to Suffolk to where this kid's body was found. I ain't keen.

'Come on, Harry,' I say. 'You know what that toff friend of yours said. It's best left alone.'

'I promise, Jack,' he says. 'This is the last time. I just want to see for myself.'

See what? Maybe he just needs to put it all to rest somehow.

So off we go for a drive in the country. Up through Essex. Past Colchester and into East Anglia. The land flattens out and the sky gets bigger. Big bright clouds hang above the long horizon, gloomy fields of sugar beet stretch out below. We reach Hartwell-juxta-Mare. Pretty little seaside village. Cliffside road takes us up to Hartwell Lodge. Big mansion with a good view of the North Sea.

'Right,' says Harry, taking the next turn. 'This is the road to Tattingstone. The killing could have happened somewhere along here. So keep your eyes peeled.'

'What are we looking for?'

'I don't know,' Harry mutters. 'I don't know.'

We drive along to the actual field where the kid was found. Harry's got map references and everything. But we don't spot nothing. We get out of the motor and Harry snoops about the hedgerow gloomily.

Well, that's it then, I think. We can go home and forget about it. Get on with some serious business. But Harry wants to drive back along the route just to make sure.

About three miles up the road from Tattingstone, Harry notices a little track leading off into a patch of woodland. Didn't notice it on the way over. Harry stops the car, reverses back and turns up into it.

'Let's have a little shufti up here,' he says.

The bumpy old track winds up into a little clearing among a few weatherbeaten trees. There's a battered old caravan sitting there. Harry looks at me, eyes bulging a bit with tension as we pull up. Harry reaches down to in front of the driver's seat and pulls out

179

a shooter he's got tucked away by the pedals. Tucks it into his waistband and winks over at me.

'Let's see if anyone's at home.'

We get out and walk slowly up to the caravan. Filthy curtains drawn on all its windows. Harry raps on the door.

'Hello?' he calls, one hand fingering at the gun butt poking out of his trousers.

I nearly laugh. All this suspense and it's probably just some gyppo's doss hole. Harry knocks again.

'Anybody there?'

No reply. Nothing.

Harry tries the door, rattling the little handle. Locked. Starts to make to force it with his shoulder then thinks again. Fishes in his pocket and pulls out the car keys. Hands them to me.

'There's a crowbar in the boot,' he says.

I fetch it and jemmy open the little metal door. We go in. Nasty butcher's-shop pong. Harry clicks on a gloomy little lightbulb. A chamber of horrors. Pages of homo porn mags torn out and sellotaped all over blood-smeared walls and windows. Hacksaw and set of butcher's knives on a little table in the middle of the room. A coil of rope and a pair of handcuffs on the floor. A couple of blood-caked scalpels rusting in a tiny wash basin. Kilner jars with things floating in them. Human organs. Suitcase Murder newspaper clippings scattered everywhere. Anatomy textbook lying open on a chair.

I nearly puke. Harry's got this mad gleam in his eye.

'We've got the bastard,' he hisses.

'How did the Murder Squad miss all of this?' I ask.

'Well, they weren't looking, were they? They were put off the scent once the Hartwell Lodge party was covered up. It'll be no use going to them now.'

Harry goes over and touches the kettle on the stove.

'So what are we going to do?' I ask.

'Feel that.'

I put my hand to the kettle. There's an ever so faint warmth to it.

'Someone's been here recently. That means they might be coming back.'

'So we're going to wait for them?'

'Yeah. But first I've got to hide the motor. We give the game away if they see that.'

He walks to the door.

'Wait a minute,' I say. 'You leaving me here?'

'What's the matter? You scared?'

Harry's grinning. Goading me.

'Course not.'

Harry laughs and pulls out the gun.

'Here, take this,' he says, handing it to me. 'You might need it if anyone turns up. Don't kill them. I want them alive.'

And he goes. I pick up the anatomy book and sit down in the chair. Try to make myself comfortable. The gun's a .38 revolver. The weight of it in my hand is reassuring. I pull the broken door to and settle back down again. Watching the door. Listening out. It's starting to get dark. Strange hooting country noises in the air. Otherwise it's quiet. Dead quiet. I start to feel tired. Search my pocket for black bombers but just come up with lint and old betting slips. I'm knackered. Haven't had a proper night's sleep in a donkey's age. Stretch and yawn. Put the revolver down on the table near to where I can get it and lean back a bit. Fingers lace behind my neck, cradling it. Pull some hat-brim down and give my eyes a bit of a rest from the bare lightbulb. Harry's taking his time. Drift off a bit.

Feel someone prod my arm and give a bit of a start like you do sometimes when you're just nodding off.

'Harry?' I mutter, pushing back the hat from my brow.

I blink and see the barrel of the gun pointing at my face.

'Don't fuck about, Harry,' I say, a bit tetchy.

I blink again and see that it ain't Harry holding the gun. It's a little weasel-faced bloke grinning down at me.

'What the fuck?' I gasp.

'Expecting someone else, were we? And who would that be?'

He clicks the hammer back for emphasis.

'No . . . n . . . no one,' I stammer. 'My dog. Harry's the name of my dog. I was just taking it for a walk. It ran off and I was looking for it when I got tired, and I just thought I'd have a little rest until it came back.'

'And what was this for?' he asks, waving the pistol at me. 'Pigeon shooting?'

'Yeah,' I reply with a nervous laugh. 'That's right.'

Weasel Face presses the barrel of the shooter against my forehead.

'Shut it,' he says.

He picks up the handcuffs and clicks one manacle around my left wrist. Still keeping the gun against my head, he takes the bracelets around the back of the chair.

'Put your other hand in here,' he orders and both hands are now secured behind me and against the backrest.

He backs off, aiming the gun at my head. He picks up a bloodstained rag from the floor and pushes it into my gob.

'There,' he says. 'Let's wait for your little doggie now, shall we?'

Footsteps outside. Weasel Face goes to the side of the door to be behind it when Harry comes in. I try to make a noise but gag against the filthy cloth. Taste stale blood in the back of my throat and feel like retching.

Door opens. Harry frowns at me. I nod like a loony at him. He swings around to see Weasel Face and the gun.

'Put your hands up!' he snaps.

Harry slowly lifts his big paws.

'So who are you?' Weasel asks. 'Old Bill? You don't look like Old Bill. Did they send you?'

Harry frowns, then plays along.

'That's right. They sent us.'

Weasel laughs in his face.

'And who would they be?'

Harry shrugs. Weasel laughs again.

'You don't know anything about this, do you? Do you?'

Weasel sniggers.

'Why don't you tell us about it?' Harry asks softly, managing to stay calm.

'Oh yeah. Tell you about it. Tell you all about it.'

More sniggering.

'I didn't kill the kid, you know. They did it. Left me with this boy's body to get rid of. I know how, you see. Know how to butcher. Let the butcher take care of it, they says. He likes that. Give me some money and the body and think I'll be happy with that. Butcher boy. Delivery boy. Chop, chop. Get the job done. But I'm not happy, see. Don't want to get rid of it all. Want to keep some for myself. Want to show people what a good job I've done. So I pack him up in a suitcase. All cut up perfect into choice cuts. Everyone can see what a good job I made of it. Then they're not happy. Say butcher should have got rid of it properly. Say butcher's greedy, keeping choice cuts for himself. And butcher *is* a greedy boy. Wants more money otherwise he'll tell. They say it doesn't matter. They got powerful friends and don't need to worry about Old Bill.'

'Who are they?' asks Harry.

'Shh. Show you something. Kept the best bits for myself.'

Weasel creeps over and picks up one of the Kilner jars. He holds it up against the lightbulb. The gun's pointing away from us now and I look over at Harry. He holds his breath. Wait.

'See.' Weasel sniggers, distracted by his trophy. 'It's his heart.'

The purple and grey lump bobs in the murky fluid. A tiny stream of bubbles glows silver in the light. Harry nods at me and I throw myself at Weasel. The jar smashes on the floor releasing a sharp tang of embalming fluid. Weasel staggers back waving the revolver about madly. Harry's made a grab for one of the knives on the table. Comes up with it slashing Weasel across the throat. He clutches at his neck, wide eyed with shock, tries to work a finger into the trigger guard. Harry knocks the shooter out of his hand. Weasel falls to the floor, blood spurting out, splattering onto glossy pictures of naked men. Harry crouches down next to him, trying to avoid the blood spurts as he holds Weasel's throat.

'Who are they?' he demands, shouting. 'Who are they?'

But Weasel just gurgles and chokes, the blood bubbling out of his mouth and out of the gaping wound. His vocal cords slashed. He'll never tell now.

He takes a long time to die. Nearly half an hour before all his blood pumps out of him. His breath slows into a rasping wheeze. Then one last sigh and it's over.

Then we set to work silently. Harry finds the keys to the cuffs and I rub at my wrists where the ratchets have cut into them. I try to spit out the clotted blood from my mouth but I feel that the taste of it will be with me for a long time. Even when I've taken a mouthful of petrol and spat it out when I'm siphoning some out of the tank in Harry's motor, it's still there. We spread it all over the caravan and pour the remaining down Weasel's throat, hoping he'll burn really well and there won't be any forensic.

Then we torch the trailer. A gypsy funeral. We watch it go up in a fireball. I feel the heat of it against my face and hope that it burns away all of the evidence. Pray that it burns away the horror that we've witnessed. Then we get in the motor and drive as fast as we can back to the Smoke. Harry's brooding face looking ghostly in the dashboard lights. Cheated. He'll never know now.

We get back to Harry's place at about two in the morning. Trevor's waiting up, looking sullen. Harry undresses in the hallway and goes through to take a shower.

'Get rid of them,' he tells Trevor, nodding at the pile of bloodstained clothes.

Wish I could get rid of the bloodstained taste in my mouth.

Harry comes through into the drawing room in a dressing gown and Trevor gets us drinks. Nobody says much. We just concentrate on drinking enough to blot it all out.

'I've remembered some more names of the boys who went to that party, Harry,' says Trevor.

Harry shrugs.

'That's finished with now,' he says.

'It could have been me,' Trev continues. 'I nearly went to that party. It could have been me what got cut up.'

'Don't talk about it,' Harry orders gruffly. 'It's done with now.'

It takes us a long while to get drunk enough to think about turning in.

'You can kip here if you like, Jack,' says Harry. 'You know where the spare room is.'

Can't sleep. Weasel-faced horrors keep jolting me awake just as I'm about to nod off.

Morning. Breakfast with Harry and Trev. Newspaper headline: DETROIT BURNING *Dead Toll Mounts As Race Riots Sweep US*. Harry gets a phone call. Anxious looks as he speaks down the blower.

'Come on, Jack,' he says as he slams down the receiver. 'We got to get over to Soho. We've had some trouble.'

The homo porn bookshop Harry's been nipping off has been burned down. Gutted. Blackened photos of musclemen, their glossiness charred away, scattered everywhere. Petrol bomb, no doubt about it. Maltese revenge.

'This was personal. It would have made more sense to attack the new shops I've got leaseholds on. But they know that I'm queer so they're trying to wind me up.'

'What we going to do about it, Harry?'

'Nothing. Not yet anyway.'

'But we can't let the Maltesers get away with this. We got to do something.'

'Look, Jack. I told you not to get lairy with this racket. You start chucking petrol bombs and this is what happens. Mooney ain't going to like this.'

'Mooney.' Repeat that filth's name with contempt.

'Yeah, Mooney. That's who we've got to deal with on this.'

Hide a sneer. Harry cosying up to Old Bill.

'So what do you want me to do?'

'I don't want you to do anything. Leave all of this alone, Jack.'

Tempted to question Harry's bottle but I keep my thoughts to myself. This porn racket's taking longer than I thought to build up, and with the Airport gone, I'm running short of cash. Just as well I've got the drugs business going with Beardsley. Can't really afford to cut Harry into that yet, though. And then there is that Kray job someone mentioned the other night in the Regency.

Go home and try to get some proper kip. Wake up around five. Sluggish. Have a bath and get something to eat. Still feel lousy. Take a couple of bombers. There we go. *Chicka, chicka, chicka.*

Get the gear and meet Beardsley in the Mildmay Tavern. This party want a hundred quid's worth. The fellah over in Ladbroke Grove is down for two hundred and fifty. Paying Marty a ton for the gear that's two hundred and fifty quid profit. Half a monkey split two ways. Not bad for a night's work.

We drive to this place in Hampstead. Huge house up by the Heath. Weird music blaring out. Beardsley gives the name of his contact at the door and we're led in. Some bird with her face painted and her tits hanging out hands me a flower. Put it in my buttonhole. Beardsley drops his on the floor and stubs it out with his boot.

We pass through a crowd of hairies. Kaftans and crochet-knit mini dresses, headscarves and flowers. Bleeding flowers everywhere. Spacey music echoing through these big, high-ceilinged rooms. Inkblot light show projected on the walls. Diabolical.

We find a quiet room and Beardsley's contact turns up. He peels off a wad and gives it to Beardsley. I hand over the goods.

'Wow,' he says. 'Thanks, man.'

Beardsley sneers and makes to leave.

'Stay for a bit, if you like,' this geezer offers.

Yeah, why not? I think.

'Nah,' says Beardsley. 'We've got to get off.'

'We could stay for a drink though,' I say.

'Nah. I don't fancy it.'

'Come on, Beardsley. Just a drink.'

I could do with some recreation. Especially after last night's horrors. And this place is mob-handed with half-naked birds.

'We've got business to attend to, Jack. Remember?'

'Yeah, yeah. Relax. We ain't meeting this geezer until midnight. We've got time to enjoy ourselves a bit.'

'I ain't hanging around here.'

'Well, I'm staying for a drink.'

'I'll meet you there later then. You know where it is?'

Plan to meet this bloke in an all-night caff on Ladbroke Grove.

'Yeah, I'll find it.'

Beardsley shrugs and I hand him over the rest of the gear.

'I'll see you later then, Jack,' he says, rolling his eyes in disapproval. 'Behave yourself.'

Then Beardsley's off, shoving his way through the hairy crowd.

'I can see that this isn't your friend's scene,' says this bloke we've just sold the drugs to. 'He seems a bit uptight. But you're welcome here, man. We're all free here. You can turn on with us.'

I'm not quite sure what this geezer is fannying on about but I think I get his drift. He shows me through and gets me a drink. Someone passes me a joint and I take a couple of puffs of it.

Some bird with flowers in her hair starts chatting to me.

'Love the outfit, man,' she says pointing at the suit and hat. 'You look like some sort of gangster.'

'Yeah, well, you could say that.'

'Wow.'

Everyone fannying on with *wow* and *yeah* and *out of sight*. All on the happy drugs that we've been peddling, no doubt.

'Are you tripping?' asks this bird.

'What?'

'Are you turned on?'

'I'm not with you.'

'You know,' she says. 'Acid. It's psychedelic.'

'Nah. I ain't into that.'

'Why don't you try?'

Before I know it she's got a tab of LSD on her finger pointing up at my face.

'Go on,' she says. 'Turn on with me.'

I look down at her smiling face. At her young tits, braless and

187

peeking out of her chiffon blouse. Why not? Everybody seems so happy. I have some of that myself. I put my tongue out and she dabs this little blotter on it like a communion wafer.

'Yeah,' she says.

I chew it up and swallow it. Nothing happens for about half an hour and then, *whoosh!* Suddenly all these lairy colours come to life. Swirling patterns all around me. Dots before my eyes exploding like flowers blooming. Weird music throbbing around in my skull.

Suddenly I'm dancing with this bird. Joining in with this funny old moving around everyone's doing. Waving hands and fingers about like music-hall conjurers. Like we've all got some sort of magic power. And it feels like we have. Of course, it makes sense now. Wow, I'm thinking. It's all right. Everything is all right.

I start taking my clothes off. Don't need them any more. I'm free. Free of the badness. Naked and free. The bird grins at me as I get my kit off.

'Yeah,' she says. 'Let it all hang out.'

I kiss her on the lips. Feel so happy.

'What's your name?' I ask her.

'Samantha.'

'I love you, Samantha,' I say and kiss her again.

'Yeah,' she says. 'Love, love, love.'

And I really do love her. It's not just randiness. Not dirty old Jack the Lad. I want to be with her. To love her always. Love. It's all suddenly clear to me now.

'Let's go upstairs,' I suggest.

Samantha giggles. I take her hand.

'Come on,' I say.

We find an empty bedroom. Samantha looks wide eyed at me as I help her take off her clothes. Then we just stand there looking at each other. Starkers. Like Adam and Eve. Would you Adam and Eve it? Slowly tracing hands around the shapes of our bodies. Fingers meeting and parting. I put a hand on her breast. Squeeze it gently. She stares at me. Chews at her lower lip. Then grins.

'You still got your hat on,' she says with a giggle.

I take it off. Throw the hat across the room. No more Jack the Hat. No more. Jack's head is bare. He's bareheaded, baldheaded, boneheaded. His head is free of The Hat. My mind is fannying on and I can't stop it. The Hat lies on the floor. No more Jack the Hat. *You've got it coming to you.* Suddenly feel scared. No hat, no head. No face. *You're not a face, you're a fucking head case.* No head, no face. No body, no case. A nobody. Cut up and packed in a suitcase. Nobody. I'm a nobody.

'Hey,' says Samantha. 'You OK?'

I look up at her. Her face is all blurred. I try to focus on it. Then it turns into something else. It becomes Madge's face. Oh God no. It's Madge looking at me. Yakking on at me.

You destroyed me, Jack the Hat. You destroyed my mind and then you destroyed my body. All those times I stuck by you when you got into trouble. You thought it was bad for you. Going inside. Well, what about me, left behind to face it all? The Law always coming around. Looking everywhere. Questions. Dates, times, everything. It made me a nervous wreck. You just walked away from it. I tried to explain but you said I was just nagging you. Yakking on at you. You couldn't see that it was destroying my mind. So you pushed me out of the car and destroyed my body as well. You've got it coming to you, Jack the Hat.

'I didn't mean it,' I say. 'It was an accident.'

'It's all right,' says the face, suddenly turning back into Samantha again.

I back into a corner. I'm frightened. Worried that this bird will turn back into Madge again. Scared that something horrible might happen.

'I'm sorry. I'm sorry,' I sob, curling up in the corner of the room.

'Shh,' says Samantha, leaning over me. 'It's OK. It's just a bad trip, that's all.'

Her naked body looks huge, towering over me. Tits dangling over my bald head. I figure that if I can press myself into this corner I'll be safe.

'You want to stay here for a while?'

Nod nod nod.

'I'll get you a blanket.'

She pulls one off the bed and brings it over. I wrap it around me. Rocking backwards and forwards. Trying to keep the horrors at bay.

'You want anything else?'

Nod nod. Point at The Hat. She passes it over and I put it back on.

Try to calm my head down. Horrors come and go. Torture. The Crank Up. Electric shocks of fear running riot through my shivering body. *We all done bad things, Jack.* Bottle gone. All the fear come back to haunt me. Kilner jars with internal organs bobbing about in them. My organs cut out and floating in fluid. My body cut up and got rid of. No body, no case. Nobody. *You've got it coming to you, Jack the Hat.* Hold on to The Hat and try and keep it all in.

Curled up and rocking backwards and forwards in the corner. Mind yakking on at me. Red demons out to get me. Diabolical liberty. Crippled Madge points the finger. *Chicka, chicka, chicka.* Nonsense horror driving me mad. Jack the Hat is in Hell.

Hours of jabbering terror. Seems like years. Then it eases off a bit. Still flashes of fear and horror. Mad bright colours. Bobbing and weaving. Lairy patterns coming at me at odd moments but I feel I'm coming out of it.

The bloke what we sold the drugs to comes up with my clothes and a cup of tea. I get dressed.

'Bad trip, eh man?' he says. 'Well, it happens.'

'What time is it?' I ask, taking a shaky glug of tea.

'I don't know, man. It's nearly dawn.'

Fuck. Beardsley.

I get the rest of my gear on and run down the stairs. Push my way through what's left of the party. Painted faces. Shadows dancing huge against the oily lightshow. A naked threesome writhe about on the floor.

Get into the Zodiac and drive down the Finchley Road towards West London. Mind still flaky but I hold it together. Streetlamps melting, dripping yellow pools of sorrow. Traffic signs leaping out at me like dreadful warnings. Ignore it all. Concentrate on driving.

Get to the caff and the owner is sweeping up debris. Broken crockery and splintered furniture. Blood on the lino floor.

'What the fuck happened here?' I ask him.

'Fucking greasers causing trouble again. Hell's Angels. Jumped a skinhead guy sat here on his own.'

Fuck. Beardsley.

'Was he badly hurt?'

Guilt. Fear. Panic. Got to hold it together.

'He got a right good beating. Ambulance job.'

Get the name of the hospital and get back to the motor. Gloomy purple dawn coming up over Portobello Road as market traders set up their stalls.

Beardsley's a right mess. Head bandaged, face stitched up. Broken nose, broken ribs, broken jaw, broken teeth. Sat up in a hospital bed, glaring at me. It was my fault. Should have run this racket properly. Should have known it was too easy to be true. Should have cut Harry in and made sure that we were properly protected. And I should have been there, for fucksakes.

'What happened to you?' I ask Beardsley.

'More to the point, Jack,' he mumbles through wrecked jaw and teeth. 'What happened to you?'

He's right. I should have been there.

'It was a fucking set up, Jack. They were saying that it was their racket. They took the money and the acid and beat the shit out of me.'

Fuck. Money gone. Acid gone. We end up owing Marty a hundred nicker with nothing to show for it.

'We've got to get those bastards, Jack.'

Beardsley mouthing vehement through the pain.

'Yeah,' I humour him. 'Sure.'

But I'm thinking: this racket's over. Cut our losses. Acid is bad news. Don't want to deal with that diabolical stuff no more.

'Get me a shooter, Jack. I'll fucking straighten them.'

'Take it easy, son. You just worry about getting yourself mended.'

Beardsley's eyes burning fierce through the bandages. His mind full of revenge.

'Just get me a shooter, Jack.'

On me own again. No more rackets. Airport gone, drugs gone. Harry stitching something up with the Dirty Squad about the porn. Probably doesn't need to cut me in. The Summer of Love is over, leaving poor old Jack skint. Weather's turning colder and I'm damn near boracic. The word keeps coming. A job for the Other Two. Someone needs doing. And I'm up for it. I could get back on their firm. I know I've bad mouthed them but this could straighten things out. Maybe get me back on a pension. Whatever, I need the money.

Arrange a meet. Get ready. New shirt bought for the occasion. Strap on a shoulder holster over it. Put on my best suit and hat. Get out the long-nosed Colt .45 from the chimney flue. Unwrap it and slip it in under the suit jacket. Practise a couple of draws in front of the mirror. Down a few bombers. *Chicka, chicka, chicka.* Pull a bit of hat-brim down. I'm ready.

The meet is at the Grave Maurice in Whitechapel. The Twins are there with some of the firm. Predictable show of strength. Never subtle when it comes to front. Try to stay calm but I'm pilled so I'm flapping about like crazy. Talking too much. Mr Payne, their business front, wants topping. The geezer who runs their long firms is looking dodgy. The Twins are worried that he's going to grass so they want him snuffed out. The Man with The Suitcase has got to go. I get handed a package. £250 up front and then there's another £250 when the job's done. There's something heavy in there. A shooter no doubt.

Billy Exley's doing the driving. We've got an address in Dulwich, so we set off over the water. Billy was a good middleweight in his day but he's past it now. Looks ill.

'It's my heart, Jack,' he says, as if explaining his state to me. 'I got a bad heart.'

I unwrap the package and pocket the money. Pull out the shooter. It's a poxy little automatic. A .32 or something.

'These things are no good,' I tell Billy. 'Automatics are always jamming. And they leave too much forensic. Cartridge cases all over the place.'

I slip the little automatic into my pocket

'This is more like it.'

I pull out the .45 and cock the hammer. Billy gives a start and nearly swerves off the road. He pulls over to the kerb and starts fishing about in his pockets.

'Oh my God,' he mutters, red faced. 'I don't think my heart can take it. For fucksakes Jack, put that thing away.'

He gets out a bottle of pills and downs a couple. I offer him a black bomber but he shakes his head.

'Come on, Jack, let's not fuck about. Let's get this done quickly and quietly.'

We head off again, through Camberwell. I hope old Billy doesn't have a heart attack on me. Some hit squad we turned out to be. Truth is, I've never shot anyone. Still, it should be straightforward enough. I go through it in my mind. Knock, knock. Who's there? Door opens. Bang, bang. And we're away. What could be simpler? Just need to keep my bottle. This will prove I've still got it.

We get to Dulwich and find the address. A nice big house for a nice big businessman. Billy parks up. I go through the routine with him. Get the motor started when you hear the shots. Stay calm, that's the main thing. I'll walk, not run, back to the car. Then we're away.

I get out and go up to the house. Heart pounding away like fuck. Wrought iron gate squeaks open. Gravel drive crunching away underfoot. Slip my hand into my jacket. Ready. Get to the door. Hit the doorbell. Bing bong. Avon calling.

Hear footsteps in the hallway. See distorted outline of person through mottled-glass panel. Ready to pull out the shooter. Wait.

Wait till I see them proper. Then I shoot them. Bang, bang, you're dead. *We all done bad things, Jack.* Never killed anyone before. But I got to do this. Got to. Get your bottle together, Jack.

Door swings open.

'Yes?'

It's a woman. It's a fucking woman standing in the doorway.

'Can I help you?' she asks.

'Er, is Mr Payne in?'

What am I going to do? She's seen my face. I'll have to kill them both.

'He's not here,' she says.

Fuck. Fuck. Fuck.

'Do you know when he'll be back?'

'He won't be back all evening, I'm afraid.'

'Oh, right. Well, sorry to trouble you.'

'Who shall I say called?' she asks but I'm already legging it down the gravel driveway.

'What happened?' asks Billy when I get back in the motor.

'He wasn't in.'

'What?'

'I said, "He wasn't in." Now let's get the fuck out of here.'

What a fuck up. Why does it always happen to me? Still, I've still got the £250 advance. I can keep that and go back and finish the job some other time.

'What are we going to tell The Twins?' asks Bad Heart Billy as we motor back up north.

'You mean, what are *you* going to tell them, Billy?'

'Jack, you can't do this to me.'

'Look, they said he'd be there tonight. I kept my part of the bargain. Tell them to set it up again properly. And tell them to get their information right. Then I'll finish the job.'

'They ain't going to like this, Jack.'

'Well that ain't my problem, is it Billy?'

Poor Billy's shaking his head and rubbing his chest.

'I don't think my heart can take much more of this.'

*   *   *

Beardsley's out of hospital. Meet him in the Mildmay Tavern. His stitches are out but he still looks a right state. Broken nose gives him a new look. He looks proper tough now. Sad really, to see his youthful looks all gone. Even his expression looks old. Bitter and full of hateful brooding. He's done his apprenticeship. He's earned what I'm going to give him.

A few faces in the boozer. Kray hangers-on. Giving me moody little smiles. Not sure whether I'm in on the firm or not. Fuck them.

Me and Beardsley have a bit of a chat about setting something up together. He's got a fix on getting his own back on those greasers. I go along with it but think: some quiet little racket, that's what we want to be looking for.

'I got you something,' I tell him.

'What?'

'Something you've always wanted.' I tap myself under the armpit. Poxy little automatic's almost too small for the shoulder holster.

Beardsley smiles for the first time this evening. His nasty little face beaming. Evil eyes lighting up with joy.

'Let's have a look, Jack,' he says.

I look around the taproom, at all the second-rate faces, all the little Kray spies.

'Not here son. Later. Outside.'

'Fancy another one?' I ask Beardsley.

'They just called Time.'

'Don't worry about that, son.'

I go to the bar.

'Same again.'

'Sorry Jack, we're closed.'

'Come on, don't fuck about. I want a drink.'

'I said, "We're closed."'

'You've done afters before.'

'Yeah, well not tonight. If you want a late one you can go up the Regency.'

'I don't want to go up the fucking Regency. I want a fucking drink.'

'There's no need for that, Jack,' someone says.

Muttering in the bar. *Troublemaker*, a voice says. Cunts. You want trouble? I pull out the shooter. Point it at the barman.

'Just get me a fucking drink.'

He starts pouring out the bacardi sharpish. Everyone's gawking. Turn the shooter on them.

'And you lot,' I say, grinning like a maniac. 'Drop 'em. Go on, you stupid cunts. Drop your trousers.'

And they fucking do and all. Pass a glass over to Beardsley and pick up mine.

'Cheers,' I say, raising my drink and waving the shooter about.

Beardsley's laughing away like a drain. We drink up.

'Come on Jack,' he says. 'Let's get out of here.'

I hold up the pistol. Haven't cleaned it or checked it since it was handed over to me in the Grave Maurice. Common knowledge: Kray firearms notoriously unreliable.

'Poxy little thing probably doesn't even work. Probably jammed or something.'

I aim it at the optics and pull the trigger. BANG. A whole row of bottles explode. Everyone ducks except me and Beardsley.

'Fuck,' I say. 'I didn't expect that to happen.'

'You fucking nutter, Jack,' says Beardsley. 'Come on, let's go.'

Beardsley examines his new toy as I'm driving down the Ball's Pond Road. Pulls out the clip, shoves it back in again. Clicks on and off the safety. He's happy.

'Thanks, Jack.'

'Well, you be careful with that.'

Winston Churchill on the gramophone when I go around to see Harry. Bad sign. Empty bottles of Stematol and Napoleon brandy lying around. Anti-depressants with cognac chasers, a desperate attempt to stave off his gloomy madness. I figure all that grief has come to the surface with this Suitcase thing. And he never really found out what happened in the end.

Trevor's gone. Harry feels he's driven him away. The horror of it all frightened him off.

'He kept saying, "It could have been me that got cut up like poor little Bernie,"' says Harry. 'And after a while I felt he was accusing me. Like he was saying, "It could have been you that did something as terrible as that."'

Trevor's gone and Harry's going into one. Not the best of times to bring up the subject of work. I want Harry to cut me into his porn racket. Figure it would be an easy little number. Keep me out of trouble.

'Thing is, Jack. Word gets around. You've been acting lairy a few too many times. I can't afford for things to get out of hand just as I'm getting started on this. I've got to keep a respectable front.'

'I'll behave myself, Harry. Promise.'

'Jack, you've been winding up the Twins. I told you I didn't want to get into any of that. I can do without another enemy in Soho. I've got enough on my hands with the Maltese.'

Here we go again. The Other Two. Fucking everything up for me again.

'And, well,' Harry goes on awkward like, 'well a certain somebody isn't too happy with you being involved in all of this.'

'Mooney.'

Harry shrugs.

'Yeah. Look. I need someone who the OPS fancy. Someone who can keep his head down. And someone who knows the trade. I'm using Wally Peters.'

Fat Wally. Rumour has it he was running a blue-film racket with George Cornell just before George had the top of his head taken off by a luger in Whitechapel.

'Harry—'

'Times are changing, Jack. It's the Dirty Squad what are calling the shots with this one. Being polite to the Old Bill isn't exactly your style, is it?'

'Yeah, well.'

What he means is: Jack the Hat is bad news. Trouble. A bringer of bad luck. A Jonah.

Shrug.

'So this is it, then, eh?'

Harry sighs.

'Jack, look, sort yourself out. Deal with it. Straighten things with the Twins. There'll be other jobs in the future.'

'Right then,' I say and make a move to get going.

No point in making a fuss. Wipe your face and move on. That's the thing.

'Business is business, Jack.'

What he means is: times change. You're a dinosaur. And he's right and all.

Double handshake at the door. Folded wad slipped into my palm. Rude, and downright stupid, to refuse.

'Be lucky, Jack,' he says.

And I'm off.

Page four headline in the *Evening Standard* a few days later:

MAN HELD IN ARCADE SHOOTING.

Two men were seriously wounded yesterday when an assailant walked into The Golden Goose amusement arcade in London's West End and fired a pistol at them as they were playing on a pinball table. Gunfire caused panic in the crowded arcade. Witnesses say that the victims were both members of a motorcycle gang. Both men are in a critical condition. Police have arrested Simon Beardsley in connection with the incident and he is being held for questioning . . .

Silly cunt. He's gone and done it now. All my fault. Should never have given him that shooter. Well, I'm well and truly on my own now. Doesn't matter. I can look after myself. Feel uneasy, though. Bad thoughts. It's dangerous to be alone.

Can't sleep at night. Can't stay awake during the day without the black bombers. Keep taking the pills. They fuck me up but I can't do without them.

Word gets around. Jack the Hat. Jack the Troublemaker. Had the Twins over one time too many. Making trouble in pubs and clubs they're giving protection to. Still owe them for the bungled hit. Not my fucking fault he wasn't there.

Staying in. Watching telly. Spending what cash I've got left on the horses and bottles of bacardi to help me sleep. Got to get out. Worried about getting into bother. Need some sort of job. Ready for anything. Need to be seen. Need to let it be known I'm still a face.

Fuck it, I'll go to the Regency. *They* might be there, so I need to watch my back. It's dangerous to be alone. Take a load of bombers to shore up my bottle. *Chicka, chicka, chicka.* I ain't afraid of nobody. Nobody. Pull up the floorboards and get the sawn off out. Shell in both barrels. Shove it in the shoulder holster. Doesn't fit quite right but it'll have to do.

JACK THE HAT'S GUNS DON'T ARGUE!

Chicka, chicka, chicka.

Drive up to Stoke Newington. The Regency. *North London's Smartest Rendezvous.* Walk up to the upstairs bar. If any of the firm are here they'll be in the private bar in the basement. Mind throbbing with pills and bacardi. Shotgun butt poking out of suit jacket. People looking at me with fear. Backing away. Giving me a wide berth. Get a drink and stand at the bar, looking around. *Chicka, chicka, chicka.* One of the Barrys comes over. Moody grin. All polite with nervousness.

'All right, Jack?'

'Yeah, yeah.'

'Anything the matter?'

'Should anything be?'

Look around. Shotgun hanging out between the lapels. People backing away. Drifting out of the bar.

'Any of the firm here?' I ask him.

Palms out, big smile. Black and White Minstrel gesture.

'I'll go see,' he says and walks off.

Faces peeping out from behind upholstered booths. Read their minds. *What's he going to do?* I lean back against the bar and sip at my bacardi and Coke. Room swirling around me. I'm on my own now. Pill madness buzzing in my head. People looking at me. Clocking the fact I still exist. I'm still here. I'm Jack the Hat.

Barry comes back.

'There's no one here, Jack,' he says.

'None of the firm?'

'Yeah, that's right. None of the firm.'

'Oh.'

'Why don't you get off home, Jack? You're in a bit of a state.'

'Yeah, right.'

Yeah, right. He's right. What the fuck am I doing? Push myself off the bar. Nearly tumble over onto the floor. Stumble out. People edging out the way like I got the plague or something. Get into the Zodiac and weave my way home.

Hungover. Broke. Find myself driving up West in the afternoon. Looking for a clue. No ideas. Piccadilly. Junkies and tourist gathered around the statue of Eros. Rent boys lined up along the meatrack. Boarded-up window on Golden Goose arcade. Head up into Soho. There's got to be something for me up here. Something to keep me away from the East End and the Other Two.

Old Compton Street. Pull up outside Fat Wally's bookshop. You never know. He might know something. Wally's all smiles and pleased to see me. A little nervous. Knows that I'm bad luck to have around.

Have a chat. Nothing doing.

'I'll let you know if I hear anything Jack, but . . .'

Plastic strip-curtain flutters. Someone coming in.

'Heads up,' Wally mutters softly.

It's DCI Mooney. Doing his milk round no doubt. I hate that fucker.

'Hello Wally,' he announces all casual.

Then he sees me.

'Jack.' He frowns. 'What are you doing here?'

'It's a free fucking country.'

Wally hands over an envelope.

'I don't know where you get that idea,' says Mooney.

He wanders out to the back of the shop. Where all the hard-core stuff is. I follow him through. He starts picking up shrink-wrapped mags. *Schoolgirl Lust*, *Animal Farm*.

'Did you tell Harry Starks you didn't want me on this racket?' I ask him.

'This is my patch, Jack. I think I can have my say about who I deal with.'

'And you told him you didn't want to deal with me?'

'I said that you were unsuitable, yes. That you have a problem with authority.'

He turns to face me. A bundle of smut in his arms.

'You cunt,' I hiss at him.

'You're a hooligan, Jack the Hat. You're just a second-rate thug.'

I lunge forward. Wally grabs hold of me.

'Easy, Jack,' he says. 'Not in here, eh?'

I shrug him off. No, not in here. I make for the door.

'I'm confiscating this material.' Mooney talking to Wally behind me. 'It's far too strong.'

Out on the street. Walking back to the Zodiac. Rage in my eyes. I'll get that cunt. Wait for him to come out. Brown paper bag under one arm. Dirty fucker. Taking his work home with him no doubt. Doesn't see me. Goes to his car parked across the road. Pulls off. I follow him.

It's starting to get dark. Mooney's heading west. Through Victoria. Chelsea. Maybe he's going to see Harry. Wait a minute. He's pulled into a little square. Parks up in front of this big house. I recognise it. Where from? Mooney's going to the front door. Grey-haired man with puffy face opens up. Bow tie askew. It's that posh fucker me and Harry and Trev went to see that night. Lord something or other. One of Harry's friends in high places. Thursby, that's it. What's going on?

Curious. I wait for them to go inside. See a light go on in the front room. Go up to the house myself. Ease the front gate so it doesn't squeak. Tip toe up to the front door. Slip the Yale lock and creep slowly inside. Easy does it.

I'm in the hallway. Dark. Little wedge of light fanning out from under the door to the front room. Voices. Sidle up to the crack and listen in.

'We haven't heard from our friend the butcher in a while.' Mooney's dull, flat voice.

'Yes, well, that *was* rather unfortunate.' Thursby's rich, fruity tone. 'I thought that the body was being disposed of properly.'

'I didn't know that he was going to get awkward. Anyway, he seems to have disappeared himself. And the inquiry's over. So all that remains is our little arrangement.'

'Yes. I've got the money here.'

'I don't just mean the money.' Mooney's voice whining, hateful. 'I've had to deal with you and your friend's disgusting little vices. I've had to clean up the mess. That boy was still breathing when you called me over. I had to strangle the little fairy myself.'

Thursby sobbing quietly.

'Please . . .'

'I have your filthy sin on my hands. I have to find my own redemption for that. All around me is filth and degradation. I've done your dirty work. So, you and your friends owe me. Not just in money but in influence. In patronage, if you like.'

Thursby blows his nose. Sniffs.

'What do you mean?'

'I don't mean anything just now. But a time might come when I'll be calling up favours. Remember that.'

'Of course.'

'So, it's over for now. You'll have to live with your conscience, Teddy. My sins are those of expedience. I'm surrounded by foul obscenity and the corruption it causes. My job is to contain it. I'll be going. You'll be hearing from me.'

Sounds of Mooney getting up to go. I back off. Make for the door through to the kitchen. Get behind it. They come through into the hall.

'Just one thing, George.' Thursby.

'Yes?'

'Harry Starks was around here. About a week or so ago. Asking questions. I thought we were keeping him out of this.'

'Ah, well, I got Harry to check on a few people. Make sure they were keeping quiet about the whole thing. He got a little over zealous. That's all.'

Thursby sees him to the door. Coldly polite goodbyes. Thursby wanders back through into the front room. Hear the soda siphon shh. Think. Mooney in on the Suitcase Murder. First thought: tell Harry. Gloomy bulb throws light on grubby kitchen. Dirty plates stacked in sink. Empty whisky bottles and box of Complan on the kitchen table. Tell Harry. He'll want to know. But Harry's gone into one. Black mood. No sense from him for a few weeks. Maybe never on this one. Yeah, Harry will want to know. But he won't thank me for telling him. He's in with Mooney for fucksakes. Think: I got something on this cunt Mooney. But that's dangerous for me. He wouldn't hesitate in having me done. Lined up with some powerful fuckers now. He's right, I'm just a second-rate thug. Think: I'll have to think about it.

Thursby's out in the hall. Wandering about. Pissed. Getting ready to hit the pit. Turning off lights. Hand reaches around kitchen door. Click. Darkness.

Think: let's have a shufti in his front room. Wait till Thursby's upstairs then tip toe through. Turn the light on. Pick up a few bits of silver. Use a tablecloth to gather it up in. The drunken lord's forgotten to double lock the front door so I ease the Yale open quietly and fuck off back to the Zodiac.

Too many pills. Dope myself with booze but feel like I'm sleeping with my eyes open. Like the speed's given me X-ray vision. See through my own eyelids. Nightmares coming anyway. Madge yakking at me just before I pushed her. Weasel Face choking blood all over the caravan floor. Little Jack, age six, holding up jam jar full of tadpoles turning into bits of body. Mooney strangling a blond-haired boy.

Sleep through the day. Wake up, it's the night again. Time all to cock. Like it's running backwards or something. Lose track. Sometimes not sure whether it's dusk or dawn. Dull greyness in the window. Is it getting lighter or darker?

Think about Mooney. Feel frightened by it all, somehow. Imagine myself getting done and chopped up. No body, no case. Stick to the East End. Want to avoid the Twins though.

Start going to boozers where I'm not known. Dodging anything connected to *them*. Still manage to bump into the odd face. My bottle's going. Fear of the Other Two. Don't want to show it so I mug them off in front of people they know. 'I'm not afraid of the Twins,' and even: 'I'll fucking kill them.' Bravado. Makes me feel better at the time. Feeds the fear later.

Going mad. Start to have nightmares about *them*. Can't stand it. Got to face them. Straighten it all out somehow. Go back to the Regency. Chinese restaurant on the middle floor. Some of the firm sitting at a long table like that picture of the Last Supper. Waiting for Jesus to arrive. Or Judas. Sit in the corner a bit away from them. A few nods in my direction. Moody grins. Wary.

Then suddenly it's heads up, someone's arrived. Everyone's sitting up straight. One of the Twins has just walked in. Difficult to say which one it is at first.

'All right, Reg?' says one of the firm.

He nods and, seeing me, comes over. Glad it's not Fat Ron. At least with Reg you've got some chance of talking things through. Hold on to the table so that he doesn't see me tremble. Smile. Try to act relaxed. Fuck, this is it.

'I want a word with you, Jack,' he says.

Chicken Chow Mein. Weird fucking nosh. Noodles, bean sprouts, bamboo shoots looking like fucking entrails. Strips of meat like bits of gut. Bring back horrible thoughts. Don't care because most of all right now I feel relief. Reggie's gone through it all. All the lairyness and me being out of order in places they've got a part of. All the mugging them off and not giving enough respect. All the drug deals and other scams I never cut them into. The Payne hit not mentioned directly but the gist is, we all keep well shtum about that. And I've sat there and nodded and said, 'Yeah, I've been out of order. I've not been well, my nerves are shot to pieces. But I'm going to change. I'm going to behave myself from now on.' I've said I'm sorry and I feel a lot better for it. Reggie's handed me fifty quid. Two weeks' pension. Back on the firm. I belong to them now.

Feel better already. I *am* going to change. Sort myself out. The Twins aren't bad lads after all. Reg even paid for this chinky meal. No more lairyness, Jack.

Finish the grub and get off home. It's all going to be all right now, I feel sure of it. Have a shit and this chow mein's floating in the pan. Entrails. Gone straight through me. Try not to think what my insides are like. But I'm going to get healthy again. I've been fucking myself up. Going to cut down on the booze and get off the pills. Suddenly feel tired. First time I've felt properly sleepy in weeks. Yawn. Sleep waiting for me like an old friend. No bad dreams this time. No. Everything's going to be all right.

Wake up mid morning well rested. Saturday. Tidy the flat up a bit and get myself some dinner. Money in my pocket so I have a bit of a flutter on the horses. Watch the racing on the telly. Manage to pick a couple of winners. Things are looking up. Collect my winnings and watch *Dr Who*.

Saturday night. I can go out and have a good time now. Put on my my best check suit. Brown trilby with brown hat band. Look sharp, feel sharp. Jack the Hat's back. Get into the Zodiac and zoom off up to the Regency.

The Regency's packed. Full of mouthy hooligans showing off, trying to impress the birds. Wankers. Still, I'm in a good mood. As long as none of them spills beer on my suit. *Behave yourself Jack.* Stay away from trouble. Look around to see who's around. See the Lambrianou brothers. Chris grins. Tony looks a bit shifty. Go over and say hello.

'What are you having, Jack?' Chris offers.

'Lager,' I say. Keep off the heavy booze early on, that's the idea.

He brings me a pint over and introduces me to a couple of chaps from Notting Hill. Tony's sloped off somewhere. Acting a bit suspicious. Something's up. I can feel it.

'I don't trust your brother, Chris,' a whisper to Chrissy.

He looks at me all shocked.

'Come on, Jack. He's as right as rain.'

Shake my head.

'I don't know, Chris. I don't trust him.'

Chrissy smiles.

'I've lived with him an awful long time, Jack. He's all right. Believe me.'

Yeah. Just the old bottle playing up again. Don't need to worry any more. It's all been straightened. I'm on the firm. The Lambrianous are on the firm. Nothing to worry about.

Tony's back. Been for a piss or something.

'There's a party at Blonde Carol's,' he says. 'Plenty of birds and the rest of it. Let's go there.'

'Party?' I say. 'What party? Come on, let's all go.'

So we push our way through the mob and out onto the street. Chrissy suggests we go in his motor but it's blocked in.

'Come on,' I say. 'We'll go in mine.'

So we all pile into the Zodiac. Me and Chris in the front and Tony and the Notting Hill lads in the back.

'You know where we're going, Jack?' asks Tony.

'Yeah. I know where Blonde Carol's is.' I laugh. 'Me and her go back.'

Blonde Carol. Had a thing with her a couple of years back. She knows how to throw a party. Suddenly feel frisky. Feel sure I'm in for a good time. Never know, might get lucky. Might be able to get it up. It's been a long time.

We're there already. It's only around the corner anyway. We pile out. Me taking the lead.

'Come on lads!' I call out.

Up the steps to the front door and in. Soul music coming up from the basement. Go downstairs. *Chicka, chicka chicka.*

'Where's the party?' I say. 'Jack's here. Where's all the booze. Where are all the birds?'

Go into the basement room. No birds. No booze. Just a couple of boys dancing together. Fat Ron sitting on a sofa watching them. Leering. Toad-like eyes blink over at me. Reg is behind me. Pulls a gun. Cold metal against my head. Fuck.

Then a click. The gun just goes click. Poxy Kray automatic gone and jammed again. Click. Like a joke gun. Half expect a little flag with BANG on it to come out of the barrel. It's just a joke. That's what it is. Just meant to scare me. Any minute now everyone's going to laugh. We had you there, Jack. I look to Ron. He ain't smiling. Heavy-lidded eyes glaring at me. The boys have stopped dancing. People standing around stock still, like time has stopped. Soul music blaring on. *Chicka, chicka, chicka.* Chrissy sitting on the stairs, starting to weep. No joke. Look at Fat Ron. Ugly lips flatten out like he's about to say something.

Fuck. What have I done? I'm sorry. Whatever it is, I'm sorry. I didn't mean it. *You've got it coming to you, Jack the Hat.* Sorry.

'Do him!' Ron hisses.

4

The Rank Charm School

Oh, we shall allow them even sin, they are weak and helpless, and they will love us like children, because we allow them to sin. We shall tell them that every sin will be expiated, if it is done with our permission . . .

Dostoevsky, *The Grand Inquisitor*

It was then that I realised I'd never be Britain's Blonde Bombshell.

Spring 1962, and I'm in the Kentucky Club on the Mile End Road. The Krays are hosting a party for the premiere of *Sparrers Can't Sing*. Joan Littlewood's sentimental Cockney comedy. Flashbulbs popping as the Twins line up with Barbara Windsor. And I think, well there it goes. Spend all this time waiting for Diana Dors to get past it and now someone's got there before me. Ronnie Kray's cooing around a gang of minor celebrities, trying to herd as many of them as he can into the frame.

'Fancy being in this one, Ruby?' someone calls over.

Shake my head. No thank you. Don't fancy it. Don't fancy being a false smile in the background. Don't need reminding that my career's going nowhere. Why did I bother coming? I hate going to these sort of parties on my own. My agent, bullying on the phone, 'contacts dear, contacts'.

Interesting mix of people, I suppose. The Joan Littlewood Theatre Workshop crowd slumming it prole style. East End villainy dressed up to the nines. The Krays crowing. Their big night. Even if Princess Margaret only came for the premiere and not to the party. Heavy-looking faces in dark suits congregating in little groups accorded by a protocol of respect. Gangsters on their best behaviour, struggling to make small talk with starlets and comedians.

And I'm swanning around, trying to keep the smile going. Trying not to look like my career's up the swannee. Poise, deportment, all that Charm School crap. I need a drink. Push my way through to the bar. Pass by someone I vaguely recognise from somewhere. Slicked-back hair and slightly battered features. Piercing eyes that click with mine as I go by him. Where do I know him from? Then it drops. Oh fuck, I think, *him*. Another bloody reminder. Glance back carefully. He's with a young man, not much more than a boy really. Well, that makes sense. He's watching. A shiver of fear, I try to suppress it. Concentrate on getting to the bar.

'Gin and tonic, please.'

'Let me get this.'

A hand waves a note over the counter. I look around. Him.

He's not with the boy any more but with one of the faces that I've spoken with earlier. Jimmy something.

'Ruby,' says Jimmy. 'Let me introduce . . .'

'Oh, it's all right,' I cut in. 'We've already met. Harry, isn't it? Harry Starks.'

Grinning at recognition brings out a thin scar line in his cheek. He's more thick set than he was back then. It makes him look all the more impressive.

'Yeah,' I say, with a sneer. 'We go back. Don't we Mr Starks?'

Go back. Three years earlier.

Peter must have sent him. I don't know whether he'd followed me or just been lying in wait somewhere. I'd come back to the flat and he walked up as I was unlocking the front door. I tried to get in and lock the door behind me but his hand was on the frame blocking me. He leant against the jam and muttered to me softly.

'We need to talk, Miss Ryder.'

It would have been stupid to offer any resistance. He was a lot bigger than me. He could have simply pushed me inside and followed me in without much fuss.

'You better come in then,' I said.

We went in through the hallway. I slumped into an armchair as he padded around the room.

'Why don't you make us both a drink?' I said, thinking: act friendly, charm him off.

As he poured two large scotches his eye caught a publicity photo on top of the cocktail cabinet. Me with blonde beehive and Diana Dors décolletage. The one I'd used for the quarter page in the young actresses section of *Spotlight 1958*. He picked it up and wagged it at me.

'You an actress then?'

He seemed impressed as he passed over the drink.

'Yeah, I suppose so,' I shrugged. 'Just walk-ons mostly.'

'Walk-ons?'

'Yeah, you know, background work. You walk on, say a few lines, walk off again. A bit like what you do I suppose.'

He frowned and then let a mirthless grin spread across his face.

'Yeah,' he nodded and sat down in the chair opposite. 'That's a good one.'

He held up the photo and studied it with a shrug.

'Well you got the looks for it,' he said. 'You want to take care of them.'

A cheap line. I sneered. He shrugged.

'I mean it. You could go places.'

'Yeah,' I said. 'That's a good one.'

Not the most illustrious of acting careers. At eighteen I'd been spotted by one of J. Arthur Rank's talent scouts at a Butlin's beauty contest. I got a year's contract with the Rank Organisation's Company of Youth. £20 a week. We were sent to this studio in Highbury to learn elocution and deportment. How to be stars. The Rank Charm School they called it. But after a year of walking about with books on our heads we found there wasn't much work to be had. I had a few walk-ons. Did a Lux soap commercial. I got a small speaking part in *Violent Playground* in 1957 but it wasn't the big break that I had imagined.

When the castings and the cash started to dry up I took a job in the Cabaret Club in Paddington. Dancing on stage. The low lighting hid the peeling decor and the tattiness of the sequined costumes. When you weren't dancing you could sit out in the audience and get an extra £5 hostess fee. You weren't supposed

to make any other arrangements with the customers but most of
the girls did. If you were discreet the management didn't seem to
mind. I was reluctant at first but the money was so easy. You didn't
always have to sleep with them anyway. One punter had me whip
him with a leather belt while he masturbated. I learnt a few tricks
that weren't taught at the Rank Charm School.

The man leant forward in his chair a little and gave me a stare
that was piercing and yet seemed to require little effort from him.
His nostrils dilated slightly and a frown furrowed a line where his
eyebrows met. He wasn't grinning any more.

'You know what all this is about, don't you?'

'Yeah,' I sighed. 'Peter.'

Rachman. I met him at a party in the Latin Quarter Club in
Soho. He set me up in the flat. Made me give up the club. 'It'll
wear you out,' he said. 'In a few years you'll have nothing to show
for it but a lined face, and then what'll you do?' He gave me enough
money so that I could start going to castings and auditions again.
He even got me a little MG sportscar. He didn't ask for much in
return. He would come around every so often and without much
ceremony lead me into the bedroom. He was short, fat and bald
and had an odd squeaky Polish accent. He always had me sitting
on top of him facing the other way so I didn't see his face when
we had sex. He'd been in a concentration camp during the war and
had never really got over the experience. He was stinking rich but
he still hoarded crusts of bread under his bed out of habit. His eyes
never lost their cold glittering hardness. I'd heard about his methods
as a landlord. Setting thugs with alsatians on tenants that wouldn't
pay. He shrugged as if he didn't realise what all the fuss was about.
'Business is business, Ruby,' he'd say. 'If someone agrees to pay ten
pounds a week then I am entitled to make sure payment is made.
I have my overheads, you know.'

For a while our arrangement worked well for me. I had the
time and money to try again with my acting career. Peter had
lots of contacts. Usually the wrong ones. And I had become his
possession. I lost any sense of pursuing things for myself. I no

longer felt that I had any control over my life. Being kept made me lazy.

He had other mistresses but he was insistent that I was not to see other men. He was suspicious of the most innocent circumstances. He could not imagine men taking any kind of interest in women unless it was sexual.

After a while it got too much for me. At first I made excuses to avoid seeing him, to put off his little visits to the flat. But when these ran out I just missed appointments that had been made, knowing that he would be infuriated turning up to an empty apartment. I'd been expecting a visit from one of his heavies for a while now.

'Mr Rachman wants to know where the hell you've been.'

The well-tailored thug spoke softly. He had more style than Peter's usual muscle.

'You don't look like one of Rachman's usual rent collectors,' I said.

The man shrugged and took a sip of whisky.

'I'm not,' he said. 'I'm freelance.'

'So Peter's hiring extras, is he? What's the matter? He in trouble?'

'Yeah, well, your boyfriend is having a spot of bother, actually. Not just from you. Some people are wanting a share in the profits. It doesn't pay to let a racket get too well known. People are liable to muscle in. I think he wants me on his firm.'

'For protection?'

'Something like that. But I ain't getting involved. It's bad business.'

'But you don't mind coming around here and scaring me for him?'

'Hell, he's paying me enough.'

'I still don't get it. Why's he gone to the bother of having you follow me? He could of sent one of his own men.'

'Well he wants this matter sorted with a bit of delicacy. And because . . .'

The man gave a little cough.

'He can trust me with you.'

'Really?' I said smiling. 'Immune to my charms, are you?'

'Yeah, something like that,' he replied rather tetchily.

I'd hit a nerve. For a second his gaze lost some of its toughness and became petulant. He pulled his head back a touch as if to regain his poise. His face tightened with menace as if to compensate for being caught off guard.

'He wants you to start behaving yourself.'

'Or else?'

The man suddenly slammed his glass on the coffee table and I gave a little jump.

'Look, darling. You've got a flat, a car, regular money from him. You know what Rachman's like. He expects you to keep your part of the bargain. It's not a good idea to fuck him around like this. He's liable to turn nasty.'

'Or to get someone to turn nasty for him.'

'Well I ain't here for my own good health.'

He picked up his glass, drained the rest of his scotch and put it back on the table.

'So, what's supposed to happen now?'

'You come with me and we go and see him.'

'And if I say no?'

'That wouldn't be a good idea,' he said flatly.

He looked around the room for a while and then stared back at me.

'So what's it going to be?' he demanded.

I suddenly found myself starting to sob. Real fear mostly but some of the tears were Charm School technique, like I was detached from it, acting it out. Just like he was. He sighed heavily and went over to the cabinet and poured another round of drinks. He handed me a glass and pulled the handkerchief out of the top pocket of his suit for me to blow my nose on.

'You've got yourself into a right fucking mess, Miss Ryder.'

'Ruby,' my voice quavered. 'Call me Ruby. What am I going to do?'

216

He sighed and shook his head. Then he sat down again and waited for me to catch his stare once more.

'We go and see him. Yeah? Come clean about finishing with him. Give him the car keys and the keys to the flat.'

I wiped my face and stared back.

'But he'll be angry. He'll want to hurt me.'

'Well, you should expect a couple of slaps for the way you've been carrying on. But that will probably be it.'

I nodded slowly as if trying to steady my head.

'OK,' I said. 'OK.'

He got up and patted my shoulder.

'Finish your drink and get ready. We'll go in my car.'

I looked up at him and chewed at my lower lip nervously. He grinned down at me.

'Don't worry about it. It'll soon be over.'

'Yeah, all right. Thanks, er . . .'

'Harry,' he said. 'Harry Starks.'

Harry drove us to an address in North Kensington. It was a crumbling Victorian terrace that smelt of damp. One of Peter's properties. Rachman pulled me by the arm and dragged me into the front room. He slapped me hard about the face while still holding me by the elbow and then pushed me onto a battered sofa.

'You stupid bloody bitch!' he shouted at me.

Harry had come into the room. Rachman turned away from me and walked over to him, peeling off notes from a bankroll he took from his back pocket.

'Thank you, Mr Starks,' he said, suddenly genial as he handed over a wad of money. 'A job well done. I only wish that I could employ you on a more permanent basis.'

'Rent collecting?'

'I was thinking more of using your, um, organisational skills.'

'This wouldn't have to do with a take-over bid from Bethnal Green, would it?'

'Tch, those twins. What am I going to do with them? They were always looking for twins in the camps, you know,' he remarked rather wistfully. 'Experiments.'

'If you want my advice, give them something to play with. Something to distract them.'

'Money?'

'No. They'll spend it quick and come back for more when it's used up. Give them something solid. A racket or something.'

'A property?'

'Yeah, something like that.'

Harry made a move to go. Rachman shook his hand.

'If you ever reconsider my offer, you know where I am.'

Harry looked over at me just before he turned to leave. He gave me a quick nod and then he was gone.

'So, have you come to your senses?' Rachman hissed at me.

'You could say that,' I replied and picked my handbag off the floor.

'Are you going to behave yourself?'

I took the keys to the car and the flat and handed them to him. He weighed them in his hand and narrowed his eyes at me.

'I see,' he said.

He pocketed the car keys and then, holding the flat keys by the fob, made to swing at me with them. Flinching, I curled up into the sofa, then uncoiled as I realised he was faking. He started laughing.

'You little bastard!' he hissed, tossing the keys in my lap.

'I can keep the flat?'

'Yes, you can keep it. But you start paying rent.'

Queenie Watts was belting out a song on the stage of the Kentucky. There was a glass in my hand. I took a gulp of gin without thinking. Reflex action.

'What do you want?' I asked.

What did he want? From what I'd gathered the obvious seemed out of the question. Uneasy thoughts. Blackmail. Was that it? Always edgy about my past. I worked so hard to cover it up. And here he was now like the ghost at the feast.

'I just wanted . . .'

A shrug and a grin. Putting on the friendly act.

'To buy you a drink.'

'And talk over old times? No thank you.'

'Look, I'm sorry. About what happened. It was just . . .'

Another shrug.

'Business.'

'And this is just sociable?'

'Yeah.'

I laughed.

'Go on then. Surprise me. Be sociable.'

'You were good in *Woman in the Shadows*.'

'You saw that?'

After Peter I got a film part. I'd played a tragic whore in a Gaumont feature in 1961. Cruel gossip was that I hadn't had to act very hard. Rumours dogged my attempts at a legitimate career. The film hadn't done much business anyway.

'Yeah, I saw it. You were good.'

'The tart with a heart. Well, as you know, I can play that one from memory.'

'I thought you didn't want to talk about old times.'

'Why not? We know each other's secrets. Where's your young friend, by the way?'

Harry lost his smile for a second. He coughed and looked across the room to where his boyfriend was talking animatedly to Victor Spinetti.

'He can look after himself,' he said gruffly.

'Yeah, you want to watch him.'

'So,' said Harry turning back to me. 'What are you working on at the moment?'

'Darling, I've had fuck all work for months. I think I'm getting past it.'

'Don't say that.'

'It's true. Anyway, never mind my so-called career. What about you? Who are you threatening these days?'

Harry laughed.

'I've come on a bit since then.'

'Not doing walk-on work any more then?'

'I've got my own interests now. I'm a businessman.'

'Of course.'

'No, really. I've got my own club now.'

'Really?'

'Yeah,' said Harry proudly. He did a quick scan of the Kentucky, flaring his nostrils slightly. 'In the West End.'

'Oh yeah.'

'Yeah. You should come down. I'm having a big do there next week. A charity night.'

'Well, I don't know about that.'

'Go on, Rube. It'll be a chance for me to make it up to you for, you know, that Rachman business. There's quite a lot of people in your line of business that come down. You could make some useful contacts.'

'I've heard that one before.'

The Stardust Club. It wasn't exactly part of the fashionable scene. But then it was a relief not to be surrounded by wafer-thin models and slumming public schoolboys. Charity night and Harry packed his club with 'personalities'. Politicians, showbiz types, all sorts of potential friends in high places that he could be photographed with. I realised then what Harry wanted. He had collected me. He wanted me as part of the group of minor celebrities that he liked to gather around him for a bit of social clout and cheap glamour.

There were others there too. People with improbable names up to all kinds of business. Thieves, touts, con men, dog dopers. Harry would introduce me to them, often with a whispered aside as to their status. 'A hoister,' he'd say, indicating a short, well-dressed woman, 'and a good one at that.' He was as proud of the form of the villains that frequented his premises as he was of the fame of his celebrities. And it seemed an active meeting place for criminals. All sorts of people would drop by to gather information. To 'get a clue', as they'd put it.

There was a sort of fairground or circus feel to the place. I have to admit that it was me that nicknamed it the Sawdust. I got to quite like the atmosphere there. I got treated with a lot more respect there than in the trendier places in London. There I was just a tarty actress with a shady past. In the Sawdust I felt legitimate.

And I got to know Harry. He was always charming in that slightly menacing way of his. I remained wary of him. He frightened me a bit – I heard all sorts of rumours about him. And I always had this nagging feeling that he had something on me.

I understood the value of the sort of power people like Harry wielded. I'd lived a precarious life and in the back of my mind I thought there might come a time when I'd need to call on it. I only worried about what it might cost me.

In November of that year Harry phoned me.

'Come for a drink, Ruby,' he insisted, bluntly.

'Harry?'

'Come over Rube,' he went on. 'We should celebrate.'

'Why?'

'You not seen the evening paper?'

'What's all this about, Harry?'

'Rachman. He's dead.'

'No.'

Harry laughed.

'Yeah, the old bastard's dead. Heart attack.'

'I didn't think he had one.'

So I got a cab over to the Sawdust and we held a bit of a wake for Peter. I felt relief that he was dead, that that part of my life was finally over. But I was shocked too. Someone so viciously dedicated to his own survival could suddenly drop dead without warning. I'd almost envied his ruthlessness. After a few gins I had this strange image of all the stale crusts of bread that he hoarded under his bed, blue with mould, being heaped like packing for him into his coffin.

'I can hardly believe that the old bugger's dead,' I said as Harry and I raised a glass together.

'Well,' said Harry. 'At least he brought us together, Rube.'

With Rachman dead, few people knew about me being a whore. Except Harry of course. Now me and Harry had a past. We went back. From then on we started to become close. From time to time we went out together. There were many social occasions where he liked to be seen with a woman. He liked to put on a straight front sometimes. And I was the ideal companion, I was in on the act and my Rank Charm School training came in handy after all. And Harry played his part too. He acted the real gentleman. It was nice to be taken out and fussed over, so it worked out for both of us. Neither of us felt that we were doing each other any favours.

We became friends. As well as wanting an escort now and then Harry liked to have someone to talk to. To confide in. To be able to talk about the boys that he'd fell for or fallen out with. It wasn't something he could discuss with his other friends. And I would confide in him as well. We seemed equally unlucky with men but we could rely on each other to some extent. Harry was prone to depression and at times, during one of his black moods, I'd have his heavy battered face sobbing gently into my shoulder.

In 1964 I was in a film called *A Bird in the Hand*. It was a trashy, very British sort of comedy. Full of innuendo and double entendre. I'd traded in my starlet persona for the blowsy dolly-bird act. I was the oversexed housewife opposite Gerald Wilman who played a travelling salesman selling sex hormones door to door. Gerald was famous for his part in the radio comedy *How's Your Father?* A complete queen but terribly repressed about it. It all got channelled into his performance. Hyperactively furtive, neurotically camp, it seemed to sum up the British fear of sex. And I was the dolly bird gone to seed, playing frustration as comedy.

When he wasn't having a tantrum Gerald could be great fun on set. He could make the most harmless comment or situation seem loaded. His manic behaviour implied a lustful potential that existed everywhere. Except in the act itself. I don't think Gerald ever had sex. Except with himself. He often mentioned masturbation. The 'J. Arthur', he called it, in a rhyming joke against my former employer, the methodist, ever so stainless, Mr Rank. I once said that Gerald should run the Wank Charm School, a that he found so funny that he later claimed it for himself

I introduced him to Harry who was keen to meet him and they got on like a house on fire. Harry tried to get Gerald to come to one of his 'parties' but Gerald would have none of it. He still lived with his mother. He was a bit of a sad case really.

Apart from *A Bird in the Hand*, I did a bit of telly work, but work was a bit thin on the ground. I thought about leaving the business for good but what would I do? Harry always looked after me, insisted that I took a bit of cash from him from time to time to tide me over.

In 1965 I met Eddie Doyle at The Stardust. Harry introduced us. Eddie would regularly call in at the club. It was a good place to meet other faces and exchange information about jobs. Maybe get a clue.

Eddie was a jewel thief. A climber. He'd made a fortune out of shinning up and down the plumbing of some of the best houses in London and the Home Counties. And it wasn't just drainpipes he was climbing. Eddie was from Deptford but he wore Savile Row suits and shirts by Washington Tremlett so that he could effect an entrance to the classier places in the city and mingle with his potential victims. He regularly read *Tatler* or *Harper's*, scanning features on social engagements, photographs of rich socialites and their splendid homes, sizing up future jobs.

His first interest in me was probably in the possibility of meeting the rich and famous. Even when we started dating, I always suspected that his attention would at any moment stray to a professional interest in any fur or costume jewellery on display in the restaurant or nightclub we were in.

I could tell that Harry became a little jealous when me and

Eddie started seeing each other. I still escorted Harry sometimes on social functions when he wanted to be seen with a woman but these occasions became rarer as I got more involved with Eddie. I realised that Harry had become quite possessive of me. But also I felt that Harry worried that he didn't have as much style as Eddie. Eddie was a thief, not a heavy, and consequently his style was sharp where Harry's was blunt. When they met they would talk in an almost competitive way about what to wear, what to drive, even what wine to order. Behind it all Harry always would have the upper hand, even if Eddie could point out that Cartier was not as sophisticated as Ulysses Jardin. Harry wielded real power and Eddie was always careful to defer to that. It was important for him to stay on good terms with people like Harry. Getting rid of stolen gear was often as risky as actual theft and Harry had more control over that end of the business. Gangsters would often prey on thieves if they got wind of a big haul. If Eddie made a lot of money from a particular job he'd often give some to Harry in exchange for protection.

Eddie never begrudged this. He had no interest whatsoever in getting involved in the heavy end of the business. He didn't want his looks spoiled. But he did get off on the risks that he took in burglary. I think he got an almost sexual thrill from a successful job. All that adrenalin. He always kept me slightly in the dark about his activities but I could usually tell if he'd pulled off a big one, a *coup* as he'd call it, because afterwards he'd be a bit lacklustre in bed.

Not that I had any complaints for the rest of the time. I had a very good time with Eddie. He made me feel special. I felt good about myself again. I lost weight, dressed well, felt attractive. I had a much more glamorous time then than I'd ever had with the other 'business'. I didn't worry any more about being a has-been actress.

I did have nagging doubts in the back of my mind that all of this was going to mean trouble in the long term but I paid them little heed.

We drove down to the South of France together in an Aston Martin. We headed for Nice first and stayed at the Hotel Westminster on the Promenade des Anglais. We both loved the open expanse of the boulevards, the palm trees swaying in an offshore breeze from the warm blue Mediterranean. We spent days lying in the sun, evenings happily struggling with the intricacies of *haute cuisine*. We mocked each other's phrasebook French but revelled in the life of acting so fucking sophisticated. Then we moved on to Cannes. Driving along the Croisette, past all the best hotels, the Majestic, the Carlton, the Martinez, Eddie turned to me.

'When I've pulled off the really big one,' he declared, 'me and you could retire down here.'

'It's a nice thought,' I replied lazily. Eddie would always talk of pulling off the really big one.

'I'm serious.'

'Of course,' I humoured him.

'No, I really mean it, Ruby. Me and you.'

'What do you mean?'

'I mean, I'm asking you to marry me.'

I said yes, in the end, after a bit of coaxing and joking that the ring he finally produced was probably a snide (a fake). I'd never imagined that Eddie was that serious about me. Perhaps that he thought it was all a bit of a laugh. I was good company and a useful companion at the social gatherings that he preyed on. I'd got used to being used. I always thought of myself as more of an accomplice than a girlfriend. And I did worry about getting married to a professional thief. He wasn't exactly going to make an honest woman of me, was he?

It was like a romantic dream. Maybe breathing in the clean air of the Côte d'Azur went to my head. But I felt relaxed and free for the first time in my life. It was almost like happiness. I convinced myself that me and Eddie could love each other.

So we went back to London and made the arrangements. Me and Eddie got married in the spring of 1966. It was Harry that gave me away in the church. My mother was in the front pew as we made our vows but Dad had died a few years back. I think that Mum was happy for me that day. She seemed glad that I'd finally found someone. And it was hard not to like Eddie.

'Make sure you look after her, young man,' she said to him at the reception at The Stardust Club.

And for a while, he did. We had a honeymoon in Tenerife. Then we moved into this lovely house in Greenwich that looked over the river. Eddie started an antiques business which was a good cover for his other activities and actually made us money too. And I got a bit of work here and there. A nice part in a television play.

Me and Harry didn't see so much of each other. And when I did see him then it would be with Eddie. Occasionally, after a few drinks, Harry would want to confide in me about something or someone. He was happy for me in my new life but I think he missed our old friendship.

In the summer Eddie and me went back to the South of France. We rented a villa in Haut de Cagnes. 'More sophisticated than St Paul de Vence,' Eddie assured me, 'more arty.' It was a beautiful place, built into the terraced hillside with a wonderful view of the Alpes Maritimes. Intoxicated with the scent of wild thyme and bougainvillea we went into a kind of dream. Eddie was the rich successful man with cosmopolitan tastes and I was his wonderful glamorous wife. But, of course, we'd need a *coup* to make it real. Eddie would have to pull off the really big one.

Back in London everything seemed so grey. It was good living near the river. The way that it curled around the Isle of Dogs out towards the sea gave us a sense of escape. We held on to our dream as the reality of living together became more strained. I never knew where Eddie was or what he was up to. And yet I was expected to provide some sort of security amidst his dangerous lifestyle, to keep house and cover for him. We never seemed to have a regular income. We'd either be flat broke or Eddie would be waving about a big wad of cash, proceeds of God knows what. Our relationship wasn't based on anything settled. The dream kept us going but it burned at us.

A year later we were finally and brutally woken up from that dream. And quite literally woken up. Six o'clock in the morning the Flying Squad raided our house and dragged Eddie out in handcuffs. They had a warrant to search the premises and they pulled everything apart from top to bottom. Eddie had been involved in an armed robbery. It wasn't his usual style but the dream had driven him to desperate measures. The job had all gone wrong and a cashier had been shot and wounded. It was all a horrible mess.

They found a wad of cash from the robbery in my handbag so they held me as an accessory after the fact. This was a way of getting at Eddie. He did a deal in return for all the charges to be dropped against me. He signed a statement admitting to the robbery and asked for eleven other offences to be taken into account, and I was released the same day. I should have been grateful in a way. I didn't fancy a stretch in Holloway, that's for sure. But I felt angry at him none the less. Angry at him for getting involved in something heavy. Someone had been hurt and that gave me a bad feeling. And most of all angry at him for being caught.

His case came to trial three months later. He pleaded guilty and his brief tried to make a strong case for mitigation. But he hadn't named anyone else in the robbery and not all of the loot had been recovered. His previous form went strongly against him as well. He was sentenced to seven years.

The press had a field day. Pictures of me leaving the courtroom in tears. Headlines: RUBY AND THE ROBBER. *Blonde Star Breaks Down As Husband Is Sentenced*. Since when was I a star? It was so humiliating. And just the sort of publicity that I did not need. There goes my so-called career, I thought for the umpteenth time.

I was on my own again. No work and no money. The antique business went into liquidation. The *Sunday People* offered to buy my story. Ruby tells all, that sort of thing. I was almost tempted but they were only offering £500, the cheapskates.

Eddie got sent to Wandsworth Prison. A horrible place. The cons nicknamed it the Hate Factory and for good reason. At least it was close for visits. Our dream of the South of France now seemed so stupid. It was all used up. Reality was like a bad hangover. I'd become a jailbird's wife. Eddie had become, what they called in the East End, an away. There were regular collections in pubs in that area, where villains congregated, for the aways. So every so often a couple of faces would turn up on my doorstep and hand over twenty-five quid or whatever to 'help out'. They always came in pairs in case a visit to an away's wife was misconstrued. They would never even cross the threshold. The implication was that with Eddie in nick I couldn't be seen with another man. I was supposed to lead a chaste life now, just waiting for the next visiting order. It wasn't as if I had any other prospects but I resented this sort of enforced abstinence. It was like fucking purdah or something. I took the money for a while though and tried to look grateful. I needed the cash.

So I got back in touch with Harry. I could be seen out and about with him. Him being queer meant that no one could point the finger. Also, he was well respected and well feared so I didn't have to worry about taking shit from anybody. I'd lost the house in Greenwich to the receiver so Harry found me a flat in Chelsea. He insisted on paying the rent. At least for as long as it took for me to get back on my feet. I didn't really know what I was going to do, though. There was no work coming in and I didn't even have an agent any more. I was off the books as soon as Eddie went down.

I worried about being in debt to Harry. Of owing favours. And I'd kind of promised myself after Eddie's trial that I'd try and keep away from villains. But I didn't really have any choice.

Harry was still pursuing his dream of being an impresario with The Stardust Club. I think that was one of the reasons he liked having me around. I was a link, however tenuous, with legitimate show business. But Harry's dreams of the big time on that score were about as ridiculous as mine had ever been.

His latest venture was booking Johnnie Ray for a two-week residency at the club. Poor old Johnnie Ray. His career was on the skids and his voice was going. He was off the booze but his liver was wrecked. Cirrhosis had nearly killed him. And he was still hooked on huge quantities of heavy-duty tranquillisers. He'd come to England to escape a pile of back taxes owed to the US Inland Revenue. And here, at least, he could get regular work. Even if it did mean doing the working men's club circuit up North. Harry thought he was lucky to book him. He somehow imagined that Johnnie was still a big-time performer. But he hadn't had a hit since the fifties. With his strange melodramatic gestures and wailing voice he was, at best, merely a novelty act.

On opening night Harry tried to scare up an impressive guest list. As it happened it was the usual mix of ex-boxers, minor celebrities and major-league villains. There was, however, a representative of a social group that had not been regular attenders at The Sawdust before. The police. I knew that Harry paid off policemen from time to time but I'd never expected to meet one in his club. This was how things were changing.

As I sat down at his table, Harry introduced me to a thick-set sullen-faced man in a cheap suit. He had eyes that seemed too small for his face.

'This is Detective Chief Inspector George Mooney,' Harry said.

Harry gave me a sly wink as Mooney took hold of my hand. His palm felt limp and clammy. I gave the Detective Chief Inspector my best Charm School smile. Eyes and teeth.

'Pleased to meet you, Miss Ryder,' he said.

His expression was impassive but there was something sly about how he looked around the room. He seemed to be watching everything but his little eyes gave nothing away. They were like peepholes.

'I've seen some of your films, Miss Ryder,' he said.

'Not exactly cinema classics.'

'No, but *you* had class. It's like you know they're trash and you're acting above it all.'

'Yes, well, that attitude always got me into trouble with directors. One reason my career never went anywhere. Being married to a convicted criminal didn't help either.'

'Yes,' said Mooney, coldly. 'That was unfortunate.'

His attention was distracted for a moment and I started to make a move to another seat, away from him, but I felt Harry's hand on my arm.

'Be nice to him,' he hissed in my ear.

So I sat back down in my seat. Mooney smiled at me and was about to say something but just then the band finished their overture to polite applause, and the compère came to the microphone.

'Thank you, ladies and gentlemen. Now, here he is, the man you've all been waiting for. The Cry Guy, The Prince of Wails, Mr Emotion himself. A warm welcome please, put your hands together and let's loudly laud the legendary Lachrymose Lochinvar, The Nabob of Sob, Mr Johnnie Ray!'

Johnnie skipped onto The Stardust stage, nearly tripping over the microphone lead, and launched into a song. His performances were always bound to be dramatic. With his degree of deafness he could never afford to be tentative or subtle about how he pitched his voice. He just had to throw it out there with all the conviction he could muster, hoping that he'd hit the right notes as his voice quavered around recklessly. His body flailed about as if it was following his vocal struggle. It was desperate. He became a parody of himself. In the middle of the second number the microphone picked up feedback from his hearing aid and the whole of the club was drowned out by a piercing shriek. He had to stop and start over again. Somehow he managed to get through his set and Harry led a loud and appreciative applause, which seemed more of an expression of relief that it was over than anything else. Except, perhaps, sympathy.

'Well, what did you think of tonight's show, Miss Ryder?' asked Mooney.

I shrugged.

'Johnnie had a bad night.'

'Are you a friend of Mr Ray's?'

I shook my head. I'd never actually met Johnnie. I knew him and Harry went back to a certain extent. Harry had set him up with boys when Johnnie had been in London in the past and Johnnie had been at some of Harry's infamous 'parties'.

'I much prefer Tony Bennett. These over-emotional performances aren't really to my taste.'

Mooney got up to go and talk to Harry. He gave me another limp, damp handshake.

'It's been a pleasure,' he said. 'I do hope we meet again.'

The Johnnie Ray residency was not a great success. Harry had managed to fill the club on the opening night but that was about it. After that nobody came. The Sawdust never did great trade anyway. It was in the wrong end of Soho and it had never managed to build enough of a reputation to draw a crowd. And Johnnie Ray wasn't a big enough attraction to reverse the trend despite Harry's desperate faith in him. When it came to show business he was just far too sentimental. He had some dewy-eyed notion of some magical world of entertainment. To be honest, I don't think Harry ever realised how ruthless you had to be to be a successful booker or an agent. Consequently he made silly and unprofitable decisions. Like booking Johnnie Ray. The thing was he actually *liked* performers, which goes against rule number one in show-business management. And he tended to book the acts that he liked, and that usually meant the ones that were woefully out of fashion.

So anyway, after a week of empty houses for Johnnie, Harry cancelled the residency and paid him off. It was all done very amicably and Johnnie actually appreciated having a bit of a break after all the gruelling trudge around the northern club circuit. Harry shut the Sawdust and put a sign on it: CLOSED FOR REFURBISHMENT. He had plans for it, he informed me.

The Stardust reopened after a few weeks as The Stardust Erotic Revue. Harry tried to appear enthusiastic about it but you could see his disappointment. His dream of legitimate show business had finally evaporated and there to replace it was a strip club.

He showed me around as they were getting ready for the reopening. It looked flash. All black and chrome with a completely rewired lighting system. It seemed cold and sterile now. It wasn't the Sawdust any more. A group of bored-looking girls were rehearsing their routines and out of curiosity I sat in. It was a bit of a shambles, really. Some of the girls could move quite well, obviously trained dancers down on their luck. But some of the others just didn't have any idea. It was all a bit slapdash and when I told Harry what I thought he grinned at me.

'Well Rube,' he said, 'why don't you take it in hand?'

And I thought, why not? I'd learnt enough back in my Cabaret Club days of what worked with the punters, even though we had kept more of our clothes on back then. So I started to knock it all into some sort of shape. Harry was impressed.

'You could be our choreographer,' he suggested.

It was a bit of a grand title for organising a tits-and-arse show. But I set about it with as much professionalism as I'd put into any other job. I used all sorts of things that I'd learnt from the business and parodied them. Routines and costumes that were like a joke version of sex and performance but would work for the punters. Artistic direction based on a simple premise: men are suckers. They'd think that it was all very tastefully done.

And the girls that didn't move so well I put through their paces. Basic things like posture and deportment that I'd been taught when I was under contract with the Rank Organisation all those years ago. Yeah, I even had some of these girls going up and down the catwalk with books on their heads. I couldn't help laughing when I thought about it: The Ruby Ryder Charm School.

I also sorted out the terms of employment of the girls with Harry. It only seemed right to treat them properly. Despite everything else that was going on in Soho those days, The Stardust was run on very orthodox business lines. The club paid the girls' National Insurance stamps and they had Equity contracts. Harry liked the idea that the strippers in his club would be able to go on and do legitimate theatre work.

So although they had to bare all to the dirty-raincoat brigade twice nightly, the girls were well treated, and for the most part didn't mind working for us. They knew they wouldn't get any hassle from Harry. The sight of naked female flesh did nothing for him after all. His detachment made the girls feel at ease and meant that he could be very business-like about the running of the club, unlike the old days when he'd been booking the has-beens of the cabaret circuit.

And I was on a wage. I could pay my own rent now. I felt a lot better about not being beholden to Harry even though I was a bit wary of becoming involved in his world. But it was a job. It wasn't exactly how I'd imagined my career to turn out but, hell, that's show business.

On the night we opened we had a full house. Things looked good. The Stardust could start making real money for Harry Starks at last. As the punters sneaked out, I noticed a cropped-haired man who remained seated at the back of the club. It was Detective Chief Inspector Mooney.

'Inspector Mooney,' I announced, all mock polite.

'George, please.'

'Is this business or pleasure?'

His little eyes twitched. He made a tutting sound and shook his head slightly.

'Now, Ruby,' he said chidingly. 'It's business of course.'

'Really?'

'Oh yes. All official and above board. I have to obtain author-isation from the Commissioner himself to attend theatrical perfor-mances that might be of an obscene nature.'

'And how was tonight's show?'

'You've got nothing to worry about. It was all very tastefully done. My report will recommend no further investigation.'

Harry had come over.

'George,' he said, deftly handing him a brown envelope.

'Harry. Congratulations on a successful new enterprise.'

Harry sat down on a chair next to George. I could see that they wanted to talk so I left them to it and went backstage to see the girls.

Harry called me up to the office later. He was sitting at his desk, brooding. For the first time The Stardust was making real money for Harry. Stacks of it. It was bringing the punters in, which it had never done before. But they were flocking in to see filth. It wasn't the club that he'd wanted it to be. There were no more opportunities for being photographed with celebrities or society types at charity evenings. Those pictures lined the walls of the office. He was staring at them wistfully as I went in.

'You wanted to see me,' I said.

He came out of his gloomy reverie and looked at me.

'Ruby,' he said and smiled.

He handed over a wad of notes.

'What's this?'

'It's a bonus, Rube.'

'Harry, you don't need.'

'Go on, take it.'

So I took it.

'How would you like to earn a lot more money, Ruby?'

I didn't like the sound of this.

'What do you mean?'

'I mean, becoming involved in some of my other business ventures.'

I'd never really pried into Harry's affairs. He'd told me that he'd 'gone into publishing'. I knew that this meant pornography.

'I don't think so, Harry.'

'Now wait a minute, Rube. Hear me out.'

Harry explained how he was paying off the Obscene Publications Squad in return for a free hand in running his porn racket. He needed a go-between.

'Why?'

'Well Rube,' Harry said with a sigh, 'I can't afford to be seen to be too close to Old Bill. Smacks of being a grass, see? Something goes down and people might point the finger. Word gets around that maybe I've been handing up bodies.'

'So why me?'

'Well . . .'

'What?'

'Well, old George Mooney's taken a bit of a shine to you.'

'Oh, great.'

Harry chuckled.

'Thing is Rube,' he said. 'Mooney's playing hard to get with me. And I've come up against more opposition than I'd bargained for. I thought that this was going to be an easy little racket. Something to retire on. It still can be, but I've just got to get tight with the Dirty Squad, that's all.'

'So you want me to get tight with Mooney?'

'Look, see it as a public relations exercise. Lay on a bit of charm. You're good at that.'

'And what if the Detective Chief Inspector wants a bit more than that?'

'You can look after yourself. See if you can find out what he's into. If we can get something on him then we can use it against him. I've tried setting him up with tarts but he doesn't want to know.'

'Is he queer?'

Harry laughed.

'No. I don't think so anyway. Rumour has it that he's, you know, into watching. He's a, what do you call it? A voyager.'

'A voyeur?'

'That's it. All this porn stuff. I suppose after all this time it's got to him.'

'Dirty old man.'

'Harmless though, I reckon.'

'So what does he see in an old dolly bird like me?'

Harry gave me this shocked look. He could be quite camp when he was laying on the charm.

'Rube,' he protested. 'You've got charisma, darling.'

'He knows about Eddie.'

'Of course. But I think that could be a winner and all. Being a villain's wife. He's bound to be drawn to that.'

'What makes you think that?'

'Just a hunch.'

'You should do a psychology degree.'

Harry smiled.

'So what do you say?' he asked.

'I don't know, Harry.'

'A favour, Rube,' he said softly.

I looked back at his face, caught that stare of his. I realised that 'favour' wasn't a request, it was a reminder. A reminder of all the favours he'd done me. I'd always known that this time might come. Time to pay back.

'I'll cut you in. As I've said, there's a lot of money in it. Plenty to go around. Honest Rube, we're looking at money to retire on.'

'I've heard that one before,' I said, bitterly.

Harry shrugged and nodded.

'Yeah, but we won't be taking any silly risks on this one.'

I realised then the difference between Harry and Eddie. Eddie's crime was driven by a doomed romanticism. Harry did business, coldly and ruthlessly.

'Just take him out and entertain him,' he said. 'Find out what his weaknesses are. And find out where I stand.'

I couldn't really refuse. I was in debt and scraping around for money. No career, no prospects except The Stardust. I relied on Harry. And his ruthlessness at least had a certainty to it. He was on to a sure thing. It didn't seem that I'd have to do very much. But I felt myself being drawn into something. A gravity that governed me. As if I'd always really belonged to seediness and the bad side of things.

Me and George Mooney dined at Kettner's. I chatted him up with showbiz gossip. Secrets of the stars I've worked with, all that crap. He lapped it up. George offered up some gossip of his own. The Krays. The Twins had been arrested back in May and committal proceedings had just been concluded. Nipper Read had stepped up police protection of witnesses. Some of their own firm were ready to go QE.

'No honour among thieves, Ruby,' he droned.

I thought about Eddie. But I didn't say anything. I was supposed to be being charming, after all. I hoped to God my husband didn't find out about me entertaining a bent copper.

'And what about your work, George?'

I tried to sound interested. I wanted to lead the conversation on to the business in hand.

'Well, it's not exactly as glamorous as the Flying Squad. But it does have its compensations.'

'Surely there can't be need for law enforcement in that area. Not now things have got more, well, permissive.'

'Permissive,' Mooney hissed the word back at me with relish. 'Yes, we live, as they say, in a permissive age. But, you see, as laws become more liberal they have to become more tightly regulated. The whole point of permissiveness is permission. We have to be careful what is permitted.'

'I see,' I said, nodding along with him.

'Filth, depravity, we can only allow so much. We can't stamp it out, we can only contain it. Control it. The courts are practically useless in defining what obscenity is. So it's up to the police to decide what's permitted.'

'So, this means you'll be granting permission to certain people.'

Mooney looked up and smiled. His little eyes gleamed at me across the table.

'Ruby,' he said, 'I know that you're here on behalf of Mr Starks. It pains me to think that the premise of our little tête à tête is this sordid business.'

'Now, George,' I purred at him. 'Don't be like that.'

'I'd like to think,' he went on, haltingly, 'that you could enjoy my company. Just a little bit.'

'Of course,' I replied, giving my best Charm School smile.

'Then we can be friends?'

His hand slithered across the tablecloth to rest limply on mine. I tried not to shudder. His palm was warm and clammy.

'Yes,' I agreed through a clenched grin.

'Then I will deal with you, Ruby, as a friend.'

I slipped my hand out from under his as casually as possible and folded my arms. I tilted my head engagingly to one side.

'So?' I asked softly.

Mooney's eyes darted to and fro as if he was checking the room.

'Permissiveness requires a necessary permit charge. It's big business we're dealing with here. "Licensing" we like to call it. Harry Starks knows all about it.'

'So, are you, well, granting him a licence?'

'Yes, to a certain extent. But we're not giving him free rein just yet.'

'Why not?'

'Certain reservations, shall we say.'

'Such as?'

'Well,' said Mooney, 'Mr Starks is a formidable operator, someone who can control the Soho rackets, someone we could definitely do business with on a large scale. This sort of thing needs a firm hand and Harry has a very good pedigree where that's concerned. But we don't want the boat rocked. We can't afford to be seen to be presiding over some sort of unseemly power struggle. This business with the Maltese. It needs to be sorted out.'

'And what do you suggest that he does?'

Mooney shrugged.

'Well, unless he can eliminate the opposition, swiftly and efficiently, I'd suggest some sort of accommodation. If both parties can be clear about who operates what, then we can be sure about who we're dealing with and settle our percentage accordingly. But, however, it needs to be done quickly and cleanly. We certainly can't sanction a messy gang war. That would definitely be bad for business. With the Twins banged up and awaiting trial, West End Central are under pressure to come down heavily on anything that looks like a power struggle. So I suggest that Mr Starks operate with some discretion.'

Mooney insisted on paying for the meal, even though Harry had given me plenty of cash to cover it. He showed me to my cab and I allowed him to peck me on the cheek.

'I look forward to our next date, Ruby,' he said as I got into the back.

I reported back to Harry and he set up a meet with the Maltese. I got back in touch with Mooney so that he could sit in on the negotiations. Harry cut me in as promised and he went through the sort of money he planned to make from this racket. There was a huge amount to be made and I would be on a percentage. It all started to make sense. All I would have to do was play at being nice to that creep Mooney. Hell, I'd done a lot worse for less cash. Now I could get together some capital of my own. I could set myself up with it and I wouldn't have to rely on anyone. I thought about Eddie again. I didn't love him any more. I didn't want to have to worry about him rotting away in the Hate Factory. I wanted to be free of all that.

The big meet took place at the Criterion Restaurant. Harry attended with two of his firm, Big Jock McCluskey and Manny Gould. Three of the Maltese firm were there and George Mooney turned up with a couple of junior officers from the Dirty Squad. And like some diplomatic summit, they carved it all up.

It was agreed that the Maltese would stick to their familiar territory, clip joints and prostitute flats. But they would only have a limited interest in pornographic bookshops. Harry would make few incursions into prostitution and clipping, mostly confined to running rent boys, which in any case the Maltese had no interest in. In return, he would take the biggest share in the pornography trade.

It was a shrewd deal on Harry's part. He knew that the porn trade was booming and was easy to run, and carried with it the minimum risk. Initially the Dirty Squad was to be paid, via Mooney, £5,000 – £3,000 from Harry and £2,000 from the Maltese, and then a continuing percentage from the shops and clubs.

To secure the deal and to make sure that there was less chance of rivalry in the future an arrangement was worked out giving both parties, the Maltese and Harry's firm, joint interest in some of each other's clubs. This meant that if any of the premises run by either group were attacked, the other operator would suffer by it as well. So the incentive for any further trouble was removed.

Everyone went away happy. The racketeers could continue to make a fortune out of vice with the minimum of harassment. The police would get their cut and be able to claim that they were keeping the lid on Soho. Anything that might too easily offend public morality, over-enthusiastic touting by a clip joint, shop-window displays that were too lairy, these could easily be curbed by having a quiet word. It made sense for the Dirty Squad to deal with organised crime, with crime that they themselves had helped to organise. It meant that their patch wouldn't get fucked up by irresponsible and unruly elements. The gangsters could do the majority of the policing for them, and the really dirty stuff at that.

At first I had worried about Eddie. Then I stopped worrying about him and just worried about not worrying. As the months went by with him inside, I felt a sort of emptiness towards him. My visits had already become much more important to him than they were for me. I felt guilty about that, which just made things worse, and I began to go and see him less and less. I started to think about getting a divorce.

By now I had money in the bank. A couple of years of this, I figured, and I could look after myself. The porn business was booming. I got to know how it all worked. How the shops were laid out. Soft core in the front, hard core out the back. And the real money was to be made in the shops. In retail. Especially the hard stuff. The wholesale racket was vulnerable, with risks at both ends, production and distribution. Harry could pressurise the people producing this filth into disposing of their stock at low prices whilst the punters were willing to buy it at any price. Buy cheap and sell dear, the classic profit formula. And there was much less risk involved as well. Harry didn't even own the shops that he ran, he leased them from what was known in the trade as 'the superior landlord'. Managers or wholesalers could be charged with 'possession for gain' but 'possession' or 'gain' could not be proved against Harry. And with the Dirty Squad paid off, Harry was laughing. It was hard not to admire his cunning in all of this. He was offering 'protection' and yet he was the most protected.

I got involved with it far more than I'd really wanted. I got to know the ludicrous nicknames – nobody used their real name if they could help it. And I got to know the slang for all the aspects of the business. Photographs were 'smudges', Super 8 films were 'rollers' and dirty books were 'yellow backs'. Most of the hard-core stuff at that time was imported from Scandinavia. 'Scans', they were called. Some stuff came from America but this was done by people going over to New York, buying up the heaviest porn they could find and smuggling back individual magazines which could be copied 'dot for dot' in some dingy printworks in London. Scans were shipped in in bulk, right under the noses of Customs and Excise. There were careful methods of importation. Smudges and yellow backs would come in in bales of wastepaper that were then being imported from Scandinavia. Rollers would often be hidden in refrigerator trucks carrying bacon. Flesh with 'Danish' written all over it.

Thankfully, I rarely had to handle this filth. Whenever I saw any of it, well, I felt a sort of sadness. It all seemed pathetic. It was hard not to pity the sad old raincoat brigade who lapped all of this stuff up. The really obscene thing was the huge piles of cash we were making. And most of all, I pitied the people these distorted bodies belonged to. I didn't imagine they were paid much or treated well.

I tried not to think about them or feel guilty in any way, and instead to concentrate on the thought that with enough capital I could set myself up somehow. I could divorce Eddie and, I don't know, maybe even start my own business. Something utterly legal and boring. I didn't have any idea of what, though. The money kept coming in, some of it in my name simply to protect Harry, but a fair percentage would be mine in the long term. Or so I hoped.

*   *   *

I wanted to talk to Harry about Eddie. But I couldn't get much sense out of him. He was in love again. He was stupid over this kid Tommy. I couldn't say I blamed him. Tommy was fucking gorgeous, that's for sure. Blond with pale blue eyes. A tight, muscled little figure. There was something very flirtatious in his manner. He had a slight squint, a lazy eye full of mischief.

Harry had met him a few years back in one of the boys' clubs that he'd donated a boxing trophy to. Harry had got him to give up boxing. 'It'll spoil your looks,' he'd told him. He'd been in trouble and done a bit of borstal. When he was out he came and found Harry.

He wanted to be an actor though I don't think he had any idea of how to go about it. He'd done some modelling and some extra work, that was all. He seemed very taken with me. I guess he thought, rather naively, that I could further his career. I told him straight out that I wasn't exactly a shining example of success when it came to show business but I promised that I'd do anything I could to help. I couldn't tell whether he had any real talent in that direction. He kind of performed with people, sort of craving their attention. He knew he was attractive all right, but he gave off a sort of nervousness, as if he was struggling with something.

Tommy had had a hard time. In and out of care most of his life. You'd often catch a hurt look about him that spoke of God knows what. And I suppose I worried about him. Harry's boyfriends could often have a rough deal.

I introduced Tommy to Gerald Wilman who agreed to help him out with his voice. Gerald had an incredible vocal range and was famous on the radio for his funny voices. He'd done legitimate theatre work as well so he knew all about proper technique. Gerald was very taken with Tommy's boyish good looks and Tommy played all of that up to the hilt. They made an arrangement to do a voice class every week. I warned Tommy of Gerald's notorious short temper.

I took Tommy out from time to time to the theatre or to see a movie. He was quite starstruck. He watched in the darkness with wonder, sometimes grabbing my hand as his eyes gazed upwards to the screen or the stage. It was nice to have the company of such a beautiful young man. It took my mind off worrying about Eddie and wondering how to act friendly with George Mooney. He had a great energy and enthusiasm about him, a curiosity about things. And he was very affectionate. It was as if he was making up for lost time.

At other times me, Harry and Tommy went out together as a threesome. One night we went around to Johnnie Ray's mews house in Chelsea for drinks. Johnnie and his boyfriend manager, Bill, had become quite settled there, even though Johnnie was about to do another god-forsaken tour of working men's clubs. Tommy was very impressed by Johnnie, even though he was hardly a big star any more. Even in small social gatherings Johnnie would go into a sort of scripted dialogue. With his deafness it was always hard to know how much he kept up with the conversation and I think he went into a repetitious patter as a kind of defence mechanism.

'You know,' he announced, for the umpteenth time, 'Sophie Tucker once said to me "Johnnie, you and I have paid our dues but these kids today, they all come up so fast."'

Tommy lapped it up. He nodded enthusiastically. It was as if in his own mad dreams of stardom he actually thought Johnnie was talking about him.

'How's the club?' asked Bill, unaware of the recent changes.

Harry explained rather sheepishly about the 'Stardust Erotic Revue'. Johnnie smiled.

'I used to go out with this high-class stripper back in the fifties,' he said. 'Tempest Storm. You may have heard of her.'

'That was when you were trying to bolster your straight image, wasn't it dear?' quipped Bill, and everyone laughed.

They all seemed happy enough. Harry loved Tommy. Johnnie loved Bill. And I felt like a double gooseberry all evening.

Mooney didn't bother checking the money that I handed over to him in the Celebrity Club off Bond Street. He let a sly smile play across his lips and his peephole eyes darted to and fro as he slipped the fat envelope in his inside jacket pocket.

'Please pass on my thanks to Mr Starks,' he said. 'But also, some of our concerns regarding some of his more, er, flamboyant window displays. There's a few we don't like the look of.'

He handed me a list of shops.

'Get them to tone it down a bit. We need to keep the lid on all of this. Then everybody's happy.'

He poured the champagne.

'And warn him that the *Sunday People* is doing an exposé of the porn trade in Soho. There's nothing that titillates the tabloid reader more than a moral crusade against filth. There's a bloke calling himself Fahmi, claims he's a rich Arab wanting to buy blue films in bulk. He's really a freelance journalist.'

'I'll tell him.'

Mooney smiled.

'It really is a pleasure doing business with you, Ruby.'

I forced a smile back.

'There is something else,' he said softly. 'Something I'd like to keep just between the two of us for the time being.'

He patted my hand.

'What?'

'Well, one of Mr Starks's former cohorts, a certain Tony Stavrakakis. He's in Brixton Prison and itching for an early release date. So he's started talking. Making statements about some of Harry's past activities. Looks like a case is being put together.'

'What sort of case?'

'Once this Kray business is dealt with, the word is that the Yard is going to be coming down heavily on any other organised crime. Don't want anyone filling the vacuum, if you see what I mean.'

He slurped at his champagne.

'We need to be careful, Ruby.'

'We?'

'Yes. You and me. If Harry Starks goes down we need to be

as far away from it all as possible. Don't want to get sucked under, do we?'

'Er, no,' I replied cautiously.

'Don't worry. I've started to make contingency plans. I've developed a fondness towards you, Ruby. I wouldn't want you to be implicated in anything nasty.'

1968 was nearly over. I had my last visit to Eddie of that year. Christmas was four days away so it didn't seem right telling him anything of what I thought of us splitting up. I think he knew that something was up, though. I found it hard to look him in the eye. I didn't mention what I was doing, other than to say that I'd got some work in stage management, which was near enough the truth.

Harry went back to Hoxton for Christmas and took Tommy with him. A sure sign that he was serious about the kid. He invited me as well but I stayed in Chelsea and had my mother over for a couple of days.

After Christmas we all went around to Johnnie's and Bill's for drinks. Johnnie had just finished a tour of the northern club circuit and didn't have any engagements until next year so they could relax and see in the new year together.

'How are you going to celebrate it?' Harry asked.

'Well,' replied Johnnie with a grin. 'Judy's in town.'

'Judy Garland?'

'Yeah. She's doing a residency at the Talk of the Town. We thought we'd go and give the old girl some support. She sure as hell needs it. It'll be like old times.'

'You know Judy?'

'Sure. Well, I know her daughter Liza better. But me and Judy go back. I met her when I was working on Sunset Strip. She said to me, "Johnnie, you and I have paid our dues, but these kids today, they all come up so fast."'

'You a fan, Harry?' asked Bill.

'Are you kidding?' Tommy interjected. 'Harry loves Judy. Don't you Harry?'

'Yeah, well,' replied Harry, slightly guarded. 'She's a great talent.'

'Well, we could introduce you,' suggested Johnnie with a smile.

'Could you?' Harry piped up, his voice suddenly full of child-like enthusiasm.

Harry couldn't help coming over all eager. Johnnie and Bill laughed at the expression on his face. He looked like a big kid.

'Well, lookee here,' Johnnie drawled in a Midwest twang, 'Harry's a real friend of Dorothy's, aren't you, Harry?'

Harry went all bashful. But you could tell he quite enjoyed being made fun of. In carefully controlled circumstances, of course. He could relax for a bit, laugh at himself.

Everyone was in a good mood. But I suddenly had this odd sense of foreboding about Judy. She seemed so doom laden. There were awful press stories about her. Breakdowns, disastrous marriages, pills and booze and suicide attempts. Her tax bill made what Johnnie owed in back taxes seem like milk money. The queens still loved her, but maybe all that drama and tragedy was part of the attraction. I was beginning to long for the quiet life myself. And I somehow felt that her coming was a bad omen.

New Year's Eve I went out with the strippers from the club. We went drinking in the West End. They were a good crew of girls to get drunk with. We staggered down Charing Cross Road arm in arm to join the crowds in Trafalgar Square just as Big Ben was pealing midnight.

'What's your New Year's resolution?' asked one.

'I'm going to get a proper West End show. A nice musical.'

'Fuck that! I'm going to marry a rich punter!'

Laughter.

Then one of the girls turned to me and asked me softly: 'What about you, Rube? You got a resolution?'

'Yeah,' I replied. 'I'm going to make me enough money out of this filthy game and then retire. Do something normal.'

I meant it too. But I couldn't help having these uneasy thoughts. I had a bad feeling about 1969.

*   *   *

On the night that Harry and Tommy had planned to go and see Judy at the Talk of the Town, Harry was called away on business. It must have been important to keep him from seeing Judy Garland. He called me up on the telephone.

'You take the kid,' he said. 'Tommy's been dying to see Judy. Wouldn't want to disappoint him.'

He sounded like he was under pressure.

'Is anything wrong?' I asked him.

'Nah,' he replied, distractedly. 'Nothing I can't handle. I'll get Tommy to pick you up.'

And so me and Tommy went to the Talk of the Town together. Harry didn't like Tommy going out on his own. He was jealous and possessive just as Rachman had been with me.

'I hope you don't mind going out with me,' I said to Tommy.

'Course not, Ruby.' He grinned at me with an off-centre stare. 'I can be your boyfriend for the evening.'

We had a good table, near the stage. There was a floorshow on first. Some silly revue with showgirls in feathery costumes. High-class bump and grind. Like The Stardust but they kept their clothes on.

Judy was due on at eleven. She was late. No surprise there. It gave me and Tommy a chance to chat. Tommy's career. It had started well enough. He'd got an agent. One of Harry's connections. And he'd had some nice new publicity photos done. But he'd had no luck with any castings. He'd come to my flat from an audition one afternoon virtually in tears. He obviously wanted reassurance. 'That director was a right bitch,' he'd said. I'd hugged him and said, 'Yeah, I know darling.' Deep down I suspected that he hadn't been any good. And Gerald Wilman had given up on the vocal training. He'd lost patience with Tommy's inability to form consonants, and ended up shouting at him. Tommy had fled, upset.

I tried to sound encouraging but deep down I wanted to warn him off. He didn't really have much going for himself apart from his looks. Someone needed to break it to him gently that he didn't really have any talent as an actor. I decided that I'd talk to Harry about it. I just felt that Tommy was setting himself up for a lot of humiliation and disappointment.

Judy finally made it onto the stage just past midnight and by now the crowd had become more than restless. The spotlight hit her spindly, quivering form as it tottered out in a red trouser suit. She didn't seem to be aware of where she was. The mob became ugly and started to bay. Someone threw an empty cigarette packet. A few bread rolls followed. Booing and catcalls.

Judy just stood there trembling.

'Oh dear,' she managed to squeak. 'Oh dear.'

It was obscene. Like some sort of awful ritual sacrifice. A man got up on stage and grabbed the microphone.

'If you can't turn up on time,' he bawled, 'why turn up at all?'

Judy rushed off the stage in tears. I was glad Harry wasn't there to see this. He'd have probably started a fight with the hecklers. Tommy was in a state of shock.

'Come on,' I said. 'Let's get out of here.'

We drove slowly back to Chelsea in silence. Tommy dropped me off and I invited him up for a nightcap. The poor kid could do with a drink after tonight's fiasco, I thought.

'Well, that was a bit of a disaster,' I said as Tommy poured us both a brandy.

'It was awful,' said Tommy, still wide eyed from it all. 'Those people were so horrible to Judy.'

'Well that's show business,' I said flatly. I felt a cruel satisfaction in his disillusionment.

'But Ruby . . .'

'But nothing. That's what it's like. You don't come up with the goods, and they'll tear you apart. You should remember that.'

Tommy looked hurt. He took a gulp of brandy and squinted at me.

'You don't think I'd be any good as an actor, do you?'

I sighed.

'I don't know, Tommy. Maybe you shouldn't set your heart on it too much. It's a tough business, believe me.'

'But I want to be somebody.'

I smiled at him.

'You are somebody, Tommy.'

He went to the window.

'No I'm not,' said Tommy. 'I'm a nobody. I don't even know who my parents were. I want to make something of my life. That's why I took up boxing. I thought that could be something.'

I turned around to look at him. Head down, eyes up looking at me in a dewy squint. I went over and touched his face.

'I'm glad Harry made you give up boxing. You are very handsome.'

Tommy pulled away.

'Harry,' he said resentfully. 'He'd make me give up everything. Give up myself. For him.'

'He cares about you,' I said.

'Does he?' Tommy's voice was suddenly cold. 'He doesn't even know me. I don't even know me. I've never—'

He stopped abruptly, turning away to look out of the window. A hollow reflection of his face in the darkened pane.

I put a hand on his shoulder. He turned back and looked at me. I was mesmerised by his squint. His pale-blue eyes. He was so pretty. I kissed him gently on the mouth. He kissed me back and before I knew it we were at it. Arms snaking around each other. Mouths greedy. We tore at each other's clothes and staggered into the bedroom.

This is crazy, I thought as we climbed onto the bed together. I think we both got carried away with the sheer recklessness of it. A passionate sense of danger. *Harry would kill us for this.* Tommy raked his fingers over me clumsily, sucking at my tits in a kind of blind hunger. I stroked his taut body, tracing the little ripples of muscle, and arched myself up against him as I guided him into me.

Afterwards we lay on the bed in silence for quite a while.

'Tommy?' I said finally. 'Are you all right?'

There was a strange low laugh in the darkness. I rolled over onto one side and tried to look at him.

'This is a very bad idea,' I said.

'It's all right,' Tommy whispered, stroking my hair.

'What's all this about, anyway?' I asked.

'What do you mean?'

'I mean, I thought you were, you know . . .'

'Queer?'

'Well, yeah.'

'I told you. I don't know what I am.'

I sighed heavily and rolled onto my back.

'Don't worry,' Tommy insisted. 'It'll all be all right. I promise it will, Ruby.'

I didn't know what on earth he meant by this. But I felt too exhausted to ask. All I knew was this could fuck everything up really badly. And all I could think was: Harry mustn't know.

Harry phoned me the next day sounding flustered and I had a sudden fear that he'd found out. He said that he needed to talk to me.

'What's the matter?' I asked.

'We've had a spot of bother.'

I felt a wave of relief. He was talking business.

'Meet me at the club,' said Harry, and I made my way over there.

I got to The Stardust and went up to the office. Harry was sitting at the desk glancing at the *Daily Mirror* and smoking a cigarette. KRAYS AT THE OLD BAILEY, read the headline. I could see the tension in his jaw.

'Shocking,' Harry said, tapping the paper. 'All these guys the prosecution's calling. All these faces going QE. It's a bad omen.'

He shook his head slowly and looked up at me.

'Glad you could come, Rube,' he said, agitatedly stubbing out the fag.

'What's happened, Harry?'

'We've been fucked over. That's what's happened.'

'What?'

'A whole shipment of Scans. Busted at Felixstowe. Customs and Excise. Somebody grassed. They had a tip off, that's for sure. Three lorries' worth, pinched. Worth fifty grand retail. I need to know what the fuck's going on.'

'What do you want me to do?'

'I want you to have a meet with Mooney, pronto. I want to know who grassed. I want to know where it's safe for me to bring this stuff in to.'

'Right.' I nodded.

'And I need to know what he's up to,' said Harry.

'What do you mean?'

'Something's up. I'm paying him off for the whole squad but I've heard a rumour that the Chief Super isn't getting his fair whack. Money we're giving him isn't going upstairs. If he's keeping it all for himself then I'm soon going to have his guvnor breathing down my neck. It's all a fucking mess.'

Harry was completely wound up. It wasn't like him.

'Is this what last night was all about?' I asked him.

Harry sighed.

'Nah,' he said, darkly. 'That's something else.'

He lit another cigarette.

'What is it, Harry?'

Harry sighed out a stream of smoke.

'Nothing you need to know about,' he muttered. 'Look, just get a meet with Mooney and find out what's going on.'

I didn't have any time to do anything about it that day, though. I had to go over to Wandsworth. I had a VO to see Eddie in the Hate Factory. Eddie looked well enough physically. A fine example of how jail keeps young men lean and fit, mean and ready for more crime once they're out again. Scores of plans for scams and really big ones trod out on the inner circle of the exercise yard.

The conversation began to flag once it went past the how are you, how's it going stage. Then we hit silence. After about a minute, I came right out and said it: 'I want a divorce, Eddie.'

He sighed. More silence.

'Ruby,'

'I'm sorry.'

He sighed again.

'Look,' he said, 'don't do it now. Not yet.'

'Eddie . . .'

'Think how it would look to the parole board. They might well think if they let me out, I'll be after you with a grudge. Give it a bit more time, eh?'

Eddie looked over at me desperately.

'Ruby, there's two ways you can do your time, you know? With love or with hate. Either one will keep you going. Don't make me hate you. At least let me pretend for a while.'

And we left it at that.

I met Mooney in a pub on Brewer Street. He gave a little show of surprise at me coming empty handed.

'What, no envelope?'

'No George. No envelope. As a matter of fact, Harry wants to know where all the money's been going. You've been keeping it all for yourself, haven't you?'

He smiled coyly.

'I've been a naughty boy, Ruby.'

'Cut it out, George. Some of that cash needs to go upstairs. That was the deal.'

Mooney shrugged, noncommittal.

'And a whole shipment from Scandinavia's been seized. What's going on?'

'I'm afraid Customs and Excise is a little out of my patch.'

'So who tipped them off?'

He shrugged again.

'Look,' I said. 'I thought the deal was that you'd be able to hand up grasses.'

'I can. If it's in my jurisdiction.'

'Can't you ask Customs for a name?'

Mooney laughed.

'I'm afraid that the Excise men don't really trust the Dirty Squad. They have this nasty notion that stuff we impound simply turns up on the market again with just an extra mark-up price.'

'Well, Harry needs to know where he can bring the stuff in safely.'

'He'll think of something.'

'And the money you owe your Chief Super?'

'Well, that's another matter. Mr Starks might just have to make another payment.'

'Harry won't like that.'

'No, I don't suppose he will. But then I would have thought that he has more pressing matters on his mind at the moment.'

'What do you mean?'

'Harry's headed for a fall. Tony Stavrakakis is now officially an RI.'

'RI?'

'Resident Informer. Doesn't fancy such a long stretch, so he's dictating his memoirs to the Serious Crime Squad.'

'Harry needs to know about this.'

'Oh, well, I've got the feeling he already does. Not much he can do, though. Not with Stavrakakis in a nice secure cell with a colour telly and all. Once this Kray trial is over and they're put away for good, Harry's next in the firing line. There's a lot of pressure from up top to make sure no one fills the vacuum. So maybe Mr Starks won't be with us for very much longer. We need to think how we might go about business without him.'

'You can't be serious.'

'Why not? We just need to find somebody who can take over. This racket won't last for ever. *The Sunday People* are snooping around, trying to stir up an anti-filth crusade. And some of the top rank of the Met are beginning to get suspicious about the Dirty Squad. It's good for a couple of years, I reckon. Plenty of time to make plenty of money, Ruby. Harry or no Harry.'

'And then what?'

'I'm thinking of taking early retirement. With all of this cash I should be able to find somewhere warm and quiet to live out my days. Southern Spain, I was thinking. Somewhere on the Costa del Sol.'

He gazed off, looking wistful. Then his eyes narrowed on me.

'It would be nice to have a companion, Ruby.'

'What?'

'I mean it, Ruby. Starks has run out of luck. I could offer you a safe haven. Protection. You never know, you might need it. I wouldn't ask much in return.'

'George . . .'

'Think about it, Ruby.'

I phoned Harry the next day.

'Harry, we need to talk.'

'Ruby!' he sounded excited. 'Come over. We're going for drinks with Johnnie. Guess where we're going?'

'Harry, this is important.'

He didn't seem to hear me.

'We're going around to see Judy.'

'Harry . . .'

'*Judy*, Ruby. Judy Garland. Can you believe that? Come and join us.'

Judy Garland was staying in a mews house just around the corner from Sloane Square with her new fiancé, Mickey Deans. Judy was wearing a psychedelic paisley trouser suit, her deathly pallid face framed by a shock of dyed-black hair. Mickey had carefully tousled shoulder-length hair and sideburns. He wore a polo-neck sweater under a mohair suit. He had a washed-out look about his face that made him look older than he was. He still looked a lot younger than Judy. But then everybody did.

Harry, of course, insisted on photographs. Finally completing his showbiz gallery with the long-sought-after prize of his collection. Harry with Judy Garland. The gangster looking stern but benevolent, Judy's death mask suddenly coming to life with instinctive eyes and teeth animation by the miraculous light of the flashbulb. Everybody took turns at lining up as if we were all old friends at a reunion.

Tommy was camera shy, which wasn't like him. It may have been because he was sporting a bit of a black eye but there was something else as well. He'd become kind of sullen in the past couple of days. He'd given up all his dreams of acting. Instead he'd started getting involved in Harry's businesses. He'd become serious. He seemed to be viewing the whole occasion with a newly found disdain. He sidled up to me and nodded towards Judy.

'Look at her,' he muttered conspiratorially. 'She's falling apart right in front of us.'

'Tommy,' I chided him softly.

'Well,' he said with a casual cruelty, 'who needs a healthy Judy Garland?'

Meanwhile Harry talked up his charity work to Judy.

'Boys' clubs, deprived kids, that sort of thing.'

'That sounds nn, very rewarding,' slurred Judy.

'In fact, I often organise special events. Charity evenings. If you could be a guest at one of them . . .'

'You mean nn, sing?'

'No, not sing. Well, you could if you wanted to. But I mean if you could make an appearance. The boys would really appreciate that.'

Judy smiled and nodded blankly.

'An appearance,' she repeated.

'At my club.'

'You run a club?' Judy asked. 'My fiancé runs a club in New York. Don't you, Mickey?'

Mickey nodded. Harry looked over and they sized each other up for a second, and then smiled. The talk was all Judy and Mickey getting married once the divorce had come through, Judy and Johnnie Ray working together. They'd done an impromptu duet one night at the Talk of the Town and brought the house down. No one mentioned what terrible shape she was obviously in or how she'd barely made it through her last residency. Everyone colluded in the Judy Garland Lazarus act.

I finally cornered Harry in the kitchen as he was preparing the next round of martinis. I told him about Mooney keeping the money.

'Bastard,' he hissed. 'Well there's not much we can do for now. I'll just have to pay his superiors direct. He thinks he can have me over. We'll find some way of dealing with Mooney. In the meantime, we need to get our hard-core stuff into the country. We need to know where we're safe bringing it in. Does he know anything?'

'He said it was out of his jurisdiction.'

'Well, we'll have to think of something otherwise no one's getting any gelt. Look, let's talk about this tomorrow.'

We went back into the drawing room. Johnnie and Judy were at the piano going through a rather shaky version of 'Am I Blue?' Harry talked with Mickey in a quiet, business-like intimacy. They talked up clubs and possible joint-business ventures.

I took a drink over to Tommy. I couldn't help staring at the yellow-edged bruise under his right eye.

'What happened to you?'

He frowned.

'Your face.'

'When he's in a bad mood he takes it out on me,' he replied flatly.

I felt a sudden stab of anger towards Harry. He could be a real bastard. I gently stroked Tommy's face, then quickly took my hand away, looking around guiltily.

Johnnie's and Judy's harmonies grated. Bill looked on, forcing encouragements. Harry and Mickey talked of a European tour. They're still big stars there.

'Can I walk you home after this?' asked Tommy. 'I want to talk to you.'

I nodded. Piano chords plodded like a funeral march. Harry mentioned Scandinavia. Judy squawked off key. Mickey winced.

'You'll have to do better than that!' he hollered. The music stopped.

'Now, Mickey that's not nn, very nice,' Judy muttered softly.

Then it all started to get ugly. Brandy, their alsatian dog, started to bark along to the row like he knew the routine. Johnnie and Bill looked on helpless. Me, Harry and Tommy made our excuses and left.

'What a bloody farce,' Tommy commented as he walked with me back to my flat.

'Tommy,' I said to him. 'We need to talk.'

'I know, Ruby,' he replied, almost indignantly. 'I know.'

'What happened the other night, well, it was a mistake. It's best if Harry doesn't know about it, though. It's best if we just forget it.'

'Ruby . . .'

'Please, Tommy. Let's be sensible about this.'

Tommy chuckled softly.

'You worry too much.'

'Yeah, and with good reason.'

'It'll all be all right, Ruby. I promise.'

We reached the door to my flat.

'I've got plans,' he said rather grandly. 'It'll all be fine.'

I didn't like the sound of this.

'Goodnight, Tommy,' I said and went to kiss him on the cheek.

He grabbed me and held me in an embrace, pressing his mouth into mine. I gave in to it. *Stupid cow*, I thought to myself. But I couldn't help it. My resolve just melted inside me. He drew his head back and looked at me. His eyes looked grey and determined.

'We'll be all right,' he said, and then he was gone.

I was going through a new routine with the girls at The Stardust. We spent most of the morning working on how to get tit tassels to rotate properly. Harry arrived about lunchtime. He looked terrible. His face was pallid, eyes all puffy from booze and anti-depressants.

'Very nice,' he commented wearily, looking up at the stage.

'OK girls,' I called out. 'Let's break for lunch.'

I followed him up to the office. He had a bundle of daily papers under one arm. He dropped them on the desk. All the headlines screamed out about the Krays. END OF A REIGN OF TERROR, THE FIRM THAT RULED THE EAST END BY FEAR, THE NEAREST WE CAME TO AL CAPONE.

'Thirty years for the Twins,' Harry muttered. 'They're really crowing over this one, Rube.'

'An end of an era.'

Harry gave a hollow laugh.

'Yeah. And no love lost there. But it means I'm vulnerable. I've got a feeling that I'm next in line.'

'Really?' I acted surprise.

'Yeah. Somebody's grassing. And I can't get to them. There's a case being built up against me. I need to start pulling a few strings myself. I want you to talk to Mooney about it.'

I nodded.

'See if he can't bring some influence to bear on the Serious Crime Squad,' he went on. 'Slow it all down a bit, at least. Buy me a bit of time.'

'I'll try.'

'In the meantime I need to sort out our wholesalers. We need to keep our supplies coming in, whatever else is happening. I might have to go abroad for a few days soon.'

He lit up a fag. I stood up.

'I'll talk to Mooney,' I said.

'Thanks. There is one other thing.'

'Yeah?'

'Tommy.'

I froze.

'I'm worried about the kid,' he said. 'Something's bothering him. I know he's disappointed about this acting business not working out.

He's got involved with the firm but he's acting all lairy. Throwing his weight about like he owns the racket. I don't know what's got into him.'

Harry took a drag and sighed the smoke out.

'I know I'm not easy to get on with. But it's like he's winding me up.'

'How?'

'I don't know, Rube. Little things. I don't know what he's talking about half the time. Could you have a word? I know you're close. And he talks to you.'

'Yeah, Harry,' I said. 'Sure.'

'Thanks, Rube.' He stared at me. 'I love that boy.'

Mickey Deans became Judy Garland's fifth husband at Chelsea Register Office at noon on March 15. They both looked slightly bewildered as the registrar droned out their real names. Will you, Michael De Vinko, take you, Frances Ethel Gumm? Judy slurred her words so that when she tried to repeat the line: 'I know of no lawful impediment why I cannot marry this man,' it came out as 'I know of no, nn *awful* impediment . . .'. One of the journalists sniggered and quickly scrawled something in shorthand.

Judy wore a chiffon mini dress festooned with ostrich feathers. Thick eye liner darkened sockets in a ghostly white face. She looked like some strange bird. Exotic and near extinction. She clung on desperately to Mickey with claw-like hands. He sported a plum-coloured suit with a regency-style collar and a cravat. Johnnie Ray was best man.

The reception was at Quaglino's. There was an impressive guest list, including many American stars who were currently working in Britain. Bette Davies, Veronica Lake, Ginger Rogers, Eva Gabor, as well as John Gielgud, James Mason, Peter Finch and Lawrence Harvey were all invited. None of them turned up. There was Glyn Jones and Bumbles Dawson, Johnnie Ray, Bill, me, Harry and Tommy. The small crowd of journalists and photographers present were unable to make the occasion look well attended. The only other guest was a crippled fan who believed that listening to Judy sing could make her walk. She was treated to a croaky rendition of 'You'll Never Walk Alone' but she remained in her chair throughout the reception.

The cake arrived, courtesy of the Talk of the Town, but it hadn't been defrosted. It was frozen solid and could not be cut. Judy got horribly drunk. Harry talked intently with Mickey Deans.

Judy and Mickey then left to fly off to Paris for a honeymoon. Four concert dates in Scandinavia with Johnnie Ray had been booked by Mickey, and they were all going to meet up in Stockholm for the beginning of the short tour.

After the party Harry broke it to us that he was going to go over to Sweden for a few days too. He'd been involved in the bookings in some way and he had some business lined up as well. No doubt sorting out a way of getting Scans into the country safely.

We saw him off at the airport a few days later. He and Tommy said their goodbyes awkwardly. Harry patting Tommy on the shoulder, wary of showing affection in public. Tommy nodding solemnly as Harry said a few words. Then Harry quickly leaned over and kissed me on the cheek.

'Keep an eye on the kid,' he whispered and turned to walk through to his Departure gate.

But I kept away from Tommy. Harry being away was a great temptation. I tried not to think about it. It was all too dangerous.

Instead I concentrated on business matters. I met Mooney in a hotel bar in South Kensington. Kray talk was still in the air.

'Nipper Read held this big party in a hotel in King's Cross. I wasn't invited. Once the celebrating's over, Harry will be definitely in the firing line.'

'Harry wants to know if there isn't anything you can do about that.'

'I doubt it. The squad is notoriously incorruptible. They're not even based at the Yard. They're running everything across the river at Tintagel House. Can't be got at. No, I think our mutual friend's days are numbered. He's out of the country, I believe.'

I nodded.

'Well, it's probably good for him to be out of the way for a while. And it's a good time to think about how we can work things out without him.'

'Come on, George.'

'I'm serious, Ruby. I've already talked to someone on his own firm who's ready to take over once he goes down.'

'And what if I tell Harry that you're planning to stitch him up?'

'Oh, you wouldn't do that, Ruby.'

'Wouldn't I, now?'

'No, I don't think so. You see, it might force me to let slip a certain bit of information.'

'Like what?'

'Like about you and this young lad, Tommy.'

Mooney gave an evil little smile. I sat staring with my mouth open. *How did he know?*

'He wouldn't like that, now. Would he?'

'How . . .'

'How do I know? Oh, you'd be surprised what I know about people. I can't say that I approve, Ruby. But I'm willing to keep quiet about it. For now. But maybe you'll consider my offer more seriously.'

'What do you mean?'

Mooney fished about in an inside pocket and pulled out a photograph. He handed it over to me. It was a picture of a whitewashed villa.

'Llanos de Nagueles,' he announced. 'It's near Marbella. My little place in the sun. A couple more years of making money out of filth and then I'll have somewhere to retire to. The day might come when you'll need somewhere to escape to.'

'I don't think so, George.'

'Oh, I can understand your reluctance. But you'll come around.

I can fix things, Ruby. I can fix things so that you come out of all
of this all right. Or, I could fix things so that—'

He shrugged. His little eyes blinked.

'Let's put it this way, you wouldn't want me as your enemy.'

I spent the next few days just trying to carry on and trying to figure
out what the hell to do. Everything was out of control. A husband
in prison I didn't love any more. Harry out of the country using
the Judy Garland/Johnnie Ray Scandinavian tour as a cover for
hard-core porn smuggling. The Serious Crime Squad all ready to
nick him for a list of past misdemeanours as long as your arm.
Detective Chief Inspector Mooney virtually trying to blackmail me
into becoming his 'companion'. I tried to think it all through. And
I kept coming back to Tommy.

How did Mooney know? Who else knew? Whatever happens, I
thought, we need to get our story straight. At first, when there was
no word from him, I felt relieved, as if I could put the whole thing
out of my mind. Then I started to worry. Then I had a thought as
disturbing as any of the others. I missed him.

Finally he phoned.

'Why are you avoiding me, Ruby?' he asked.

'Why do you think?'

'Harry's not back for a couple of days.'

'Yeah, I know.'

'Come over, Ruby. We need to talk.'

He was right about that, so I agreed. I went over to Harry's flat
with all the best intentions. I promised myself that I'd be sensible.
When I got there, Tommy got us some drinks and we made small
talk for a while. I found myself talking nervously about trivial things.
I hadn't realised how tense I was. I had a few more drinks to relax.
We sat on the sofa together. Tommy looked more handsome than
ever. He seemed strangely cool and collected. He talked softly as
if trying to calm me down. I wanted all the mad thoughts in my
head to go away and leave me alone. I let him put his arm around
me. We started kissing.

I remember thinking, as we went through into the bedroom, that this would be the last time. That this would be a way to finish it. And I felt a kind of sadness about that.

'Tommy,' I said afterwards. 'We've got to stop.'

'You don't mean that.'

'Yes I do. When Harry gets back . . .'

'Don't worry about Harry. He's finished. Old Bill are on to him. He'll be going away for a long time. Then it'll just be you and me.'

'Tommy,' I said sternly. 'Think about this for a second, will you? Harry could find out about us. Somebody already knows.'

'Yeah?'

'Yes. Mooney knows. We're in trouble.'

'Yeah, well, don't worry about Mooney.'

'What do you mean, "Don't worry about Mooney"?'

'I know he knows.'

'How do you know?'

'Because I told him.'

'You did what?' I nearly shouted at him.

'Calm down, Ruby. It's all under control. I told you I'd make things all right, didn't I? I talked to Mooney. I knew he was looking for somebody to take over the porn racket once Harry's put away. So I kind of put myself forward. He wants you in on it as well. So I told him about you and me.'

'You stupid fucker.'

'Don't get angry, Ruby. I did all this for us. Once Harry is inside, it can just be you and me running things.'

'And George Mooney.'

'Yeah.'

'And any number of faces lining up to move in. Tommy, this isn't a game you know. There are a lot of heavy people out there.'

'I can look after myself,' he said, petulantly.

'And what if Harry finds out about all of this while he's still at large?'

Tommy paused as if he was thinking something through.

'Then I'll kill him,' he said suddenly.

'What?'

'I mean it, Ruby. Look.' He reached under the bed and came up with a small automatic pistol. 'See?'

'Tommy, please—'

'He thinks he owns me. Thinks he can order me about. Knock me about. I'll show him.'

'Tommy, put that thing away.'

Then I heard a sharp click from the hallway.

'What was that?'

'What?' asked Tommy.

'That sound.'

Another click. A key was being turned in the door.

'Harry!' Tommy whispered. 'But he's not due back until the day after tomorrow.'

There was the sound of the door being opened and heavy bags dropped in the hallway.

'Tommy!' Harry called out. 'Come and give us a hand with these bags!'

I tried to gather the bedclothes around us. There was no time to do anything. We looked at each other, horrified. Harry was walking through the flat.

'Tommy! Where the fuck are you? Judy cancelled Göteborg, so I came back early.'

He was at the bedroom door.

'The flat's in a fucking mess. What you been doing while I've been away, eh?'

He came in and looked down at us naked in bed together.

'What?' he asked, bewildered. 'What?'

He just stood there staring. His face all creased up with disbelief. I got out of the bed and went up to him.

'Harry . . .' I started to speak.

Dull eyes registered me. His nostrils flared slightly. He slapped me hard across the cheek and I spun off away from him.

'Come here you,' he said softly to Tommy.

Tommy pulled the gun from out of the bedclothes. He pointed it at Harry. Harry snorted.

'Now, I've seen everything. Go on, shoot me you little fucker.'

He started to advance on Tommy. Tommy used both hands to keep the gun steady.

'Don't come any closer,' he said. 'I'll shoot.'

'You haven't got the fucking bottle. Come on,' he said, holding out his hand. 'Give me that fucking shooter.'

The gun went off, clipping Harry on the shoulder and sending him spinning. The recoil threw Tommy back as well and he fell back against the head of the bed. Harry was on the floor clutching at his uper arm, grunting in pain and anger. Tommy knelt up on the bed and took aim again, pointing the gun down towards Harry. Harry frowned at the blood on his hand and then looked fiercely up at Tommy.

'You bastard!' he hissed. 'Go on then, kill me!'

Tommy gritted his teeth and pulled his face back, away from the gun. His finger tightened on the trigger.

'No!' I shouted and dived onto the bed towards Tommy, grabbing for the gun.

It went off in his face. I don't remember hearing the shot, I must have sort of blacked out. But when I opened my eyes I was on top of Tommy's naked body on the bed. There was blood everywhere, splattered against the headboard and the walls. Half his face was blown off. His hand was still curled around the pistol. There were flecks of red all over the top half of my body.

'Tommy? Tommy?' I started to whimper, pressing my fingers against his body.

I don't remember much else. Harry had to pull me off and sit me down in a chair. I just sat there shaking and trembling in shock. Harry had taken off his jacket and put it over Tommy. There was a huge red stain all down one side of his white shirt. He took that off too and started to feel around the wound.

'You, you . . .' I stammered.

'I'm all right. It's gone through. Just a flesh wound.'

He tore off the clean arm of the shirt with his teeth and bound it around his wounded shoulder. He went out into the drawing room and came back with a bottle of brandy and a glass. He handed me the glass and filled it. My hand was shaking wildly and some of the booze sloshed onto the floor. He took a big swig from the bottle. He closed his eyes and tried to slow down his breathing.

'Fuck,' he said softly.

I drained the brandy in the glass in one gulp. Harry refilled it. I drank that down too.

'Right,' he said. 'Go and have a shower.'

I wandered numbly into the bathroom. I turned on the water and stood under it, shivering and gulping for breath. I lost track of time. When I came out into the drawing room Harry was on the telephone, talking calmly. My clothes were on the sofa, neatly folded.

'Yeah,' said Harry into the phone. 'Bring one of them up to the flat. Leave it in the hallway. Yes, right away.'

He replaced the receiver and looked over at me.

'You better get dressed.'

'What are we going to do?'

'It's all being dealt with. Put your clothes on.'

As I dried myself down and dressed, Harry got a first aid box. He unwound the sleeve from his shoulder and started to dress his own wound. He mopped at a small dark red hole with a cotton pad soaked in iodine, hissing with pain through clenched teeth. He taped a bit of gauze over it and then bandaged it. Blood seeped through at first so he wound it tighter. When he'd finished, we had another drink and sat for a long time in silence.

'He was going to kill me,' Harry said, finally.

'Harry, about—'

'I don't want to talk about it,' he cut in. 'This never happened. You understand?'

There was a knock on the door. Harry went out into the hallway. There were voices, instructions. Something heavy was lifted in and placed on the floor. The men who brought it left. Harry came through again.

'Right,' he said. 'You're going to have to help me.'

'What are we going to do?'

Harry sighed.

'We've got to get rid of the body.'

'But . . .'

'But nothing. We don't have any choice. Come on.'

He grabbed me firmly by the hand and led me into the hall.

'You've got to help me with this,' he said. 'No one else can know. I can't trust anybody else.'

There was a large steamer trunk by the front door. Harry opened it up. Inside were stacks of shrink-wrapped magazines. Hard-core porn. Scandinavian. Smuggled in as part of Judy Garland's luggage. Harry started to fish out the glossies with his good arm, handing them to me.

'Take them through into the drawing room,' he ordered.

It took us about a quarter of an hour to empty the trunk and stack all the magazines in a row of piles behind the sofa.

'Right. You need to help me again,' he said, and led me towards the bedroom.

I froze.

'I can't go in there, Harry.'

'Come on, I can't lift it by myself. I've only got one arm.'

'I can't.'

'Come on. We don't have any choice.'

We went into the bedroom. Harry had already rolled Tommy up in the bedclothes and cleaned some of the blood off the walls. We slid the body around on the mattress. I took the head end, lifting under the shoulders, Harry put his good arm under the knees and we shuffled it out to the trunk.

He closed the lid and locked it.

'Right. Someone's going to come and take this away. Only you and me know about this. We keep it like that, OK? This never happened. Tommy never had any family so no one's going to report him missing. If anyone asks, you don't know where he is.'

'Harry . . .'

267

'We don't talk about this. Not even to each other. I've got to finish clearing up. You go home now.'

Home. I had a dinner date that evening with Gerald Wilman. I had to go, I told myself. Mustn't let anyone know that anything's wrong. Pretend that everything's all right.

I went to the bedroom and sat down at the dressing table. A ghost face stared at me from out of the mirror. I pulled my hair back and slapped on a mask of foundation. Stuck on false eyelashes, drew eye liner across the top lids. Blue eye shadow, some eyebrow pencil. I concentrated on the process, tried not to think. I spat into a dried-up cake of mascara and was nearly sick. I swallowed hard and worked the mascara brush into the pigment and spittle, and painted it thickly on. A bit of rouge. Some powder. Deep-red Chanel lipstick.

The hair was a straggly mess. The roots needed doing. With plenty of backcombing and lacquer, I worked it all into some sort of shape.

Got out my favourite dress. A Belville Sassoon evening number in pink beaded organdie. I could still get into it. I looked OK. A little dab of Shalimar and I was ready. I went out.

The next few days passed in a blur. Alcohol numbness interspersed with anxiety and horror. I started having nightmares. I still have them from time to time. I got some yellow pills from the doctor to help me sleep.

And waited. I kept away from Soho. I didn't go into The Stardust. I kept away from Harry and from Detective Chief Inspector George Mooney. But nothing happened. I didn't know what was going on. I didn't want to know, but not knowing drove me even more crazy.

All sorts of horrible visions came to me. I kept seeing Tommy covered in blood, his face blown off. I imagined awful things that Harry might do to me.

So finally I went around to see him. He came to the door, his eyes all bloodshot and bleary.

'Ruby?' he croaked, as if he hardly recognised me.

He showed me through to the drawing room. 'Get Happy' was on the gramophone.

'You heard about Judy?'

I hadn't but I immediately knew what he meant. The only shocking thing about Judy Garland's death was that there was no shock. You just wondered how she'd lasted so long.

'She had an overdose. Mickey found her dead on the toilet.'

'Harry, about what happened . . .'

'I told you, Rube. I don't want to talk about it.'

'But . . .'

'But nothing. It's all over, Rube. The Dirty Squad have started raiding my bookshops. Mooney's incommunicado. Most of the firm's scarpered. I'm finished.'

'Isn't there something that can be done?'

'Nah.'

'But you could implicate the police. Accuse them of corruption.'

'Nah, the Dirty Squad have got nothing to do with the case they're building on me. It's all the long firms I did way back. Besides, it's no good screaming on about bent coppers. Doing that only means that you're not going to be able to deal with them in the future. You're a wrong 'un and they'll never do business with you again. One look at your file and then it's over, that's for fucking sure. No, you don't want to go at the Old Bill. You want them to fancy you for the next time. Sometimes you have to go down. You have to wipe your mouth, do your time, and the next time – and there will be a next time, Rube – you can start off again.'

'So what do you think will happen?'

'I don't know,' Harry sniffed. 'A seven stretch, maybe even ten if the beak's feeling brutal. I need to get my affairs in order.'

He smiled thinly at me. Garland croaked jauntily on the gramophone. *Forget your troubles c'mon get happy*. We never mentioned Tommy. Harry tapped his fingers in time to the record on the arm of his chair. *We're headed for the judgement day*.

'Poor Judy,' he said, as if it summed everything up. 'Poor, poor Judy.'

*　　*　　*

Harry was arrested the next day. One count of GBH, another of making an unwarranted menace. These were holding charges. Once he was away they could get more witnesses to come forward. By the time of the committal proceedings there were fourteen counts of Grievous Bodily Harm against him and several charges of fraud and uttering menaces.

It went to the Old Bailey, and the press had a field day. Reporting with relish all the testimony of the beatings, the pliers that pulled teeth, the black box that was used to give electric shocks. *The Daily Mirror* dubbed Harry THE TORTURE GANG BOSS.

As the trial continued it looked like Harry's own sentence prediction was a little on the optimistic side. But there was no mention of Harry's pornography racket. Mooney would have seen to that. And nothing was ever heard of Tommy again. There was no investigation. I don't think he was even reported as a missing person. Harry was right. He had no family, no permanent contacts. No one who missed him. Except Harry. And me.

So I sort of picked myself up and tried to start all over again. I managed to keep out of the way of George Mooney. And I got a casting. A part in a comedy filming out of Pinewood. Same old stuff but I really needed the work. I think Gerald Wilman put in a good word for me.

The last time I saw Harry was on the day of the verdict. I managed to get a seat in the packed public gallery of Old Bailey's Number One Court. The jury found him guilty. The judge passed sentence.

'Harold Starks,' he said. 'Over a period of years you led a disciplined and well-organised gang for the purpose of your own material interests and criminal desires. You terrorised those who crossed your path in a vicious and sadistic way. That you set yourself up as judge, jury and executioner in heinous attacks on innocent citizens is particularly odious and a disgrace to civilisation. Your punishment must be severe because it is the only way in which our society can show its repudiation of your crimes. I won't waste any more words with you. In my view society has earned a rest from your criminal activities. You will go to prison for twenty years.'

If the sentence was a shock to Harry he didn't show it. He casually scanned the court, nodding to the jury and gazing up at the gallery. As if two decades were just a shit and a shave.

'Thank you very much,' he said, like it was the end of a performance.

'Take him down,' boomed the judge.

5

Open University

After two hours the felt stub is removed, for the man no longer has the strength to scream. Here in this electrically heated bowl we put warm rice porridge, of which the man can, if he feels inclined, take as much as his tongue can reach. Not one of them misses the opportunity. I am aware of none, and my experience is considerable.

Franz Kafka, *In the Penal Colony*

THE TIMES FRIDAY NOVEMBER 30 1979

Harry Starks writes to The Times
Why I have escaped from prison

This extraordinary letter arrived at The Times yesterday from Harry Starks, the gang leader who broke out of Brixton Prison earlier this week. We publish it as it stands, as a unique contribution to the debate on the rehabilitation of offenders.

Sir, I am writing to provide an explanation as to why I escaped from HMP Brixton and to put into context the charges for which I was sentenced to 20 years' imprisonment. I hope to counter the image society has of me from the gutter press with their prurient and overstated reports of my alleged activities in an attempt, desperate as it may seem, to counter-balance the biased opinion of my case and bring attention to the unfair treatment which I have received in my application for a conditional release on parole.

Firstly, I would like to address the nature of the offences of assault for which I was convicted. It is important to bear in mind the environment in which I was socialised. A subculture in which conflicts were resolved without recourse to authoritative norms or judicial agencies. A harsh world maybe, but one whose logic can only fully be understood within the terms of differential association. I must stress that the individuals upon whom such assaults took place were themselves part of a system of closure, not unknowing members of normal society. I do not wish to excuse my behaviour but to point out that I was operating in accordance with, and necessarily guided by, the perspective of a value system that I, myself, was part of and ruled by. I was found guilty of assault, not murder, on men who themselves were far from blameless and yet I have served more time than many criminals who have murdered or raped innocent people. Given the nature of my transgressions, I feel that the price I have already paid (ten years) is far more than my debt to society.

These years of incarceration have certainly taken their toll, mentally as well as physically. In particular, the effects of sensory deprivation, the lack of stimulus, the sheer weight of mental confinement can be too much for many men to bear. Scandinavian studies on institutional environments have concluded that after seven years in such conditions a subject will suffer severe psychological deterioration.

I have managed to stave off mental atrophy through study. In the course of my sentence I have taken up education, culminating in an Open University degree. Through this process, I believe, I have rehabilitated myself, though at times it seemed the only way in which I could keep mind and spirit alive. The prospect of another ten years inside have driven me to despair and ultimately to take the desperate course of escape.

I do assert, however, that my attempts at rehabilitation have been genuine. In studying psychology, sociology and political philosophy I have learnt new perspectives and concepts that have challenged my hitherto negative and parochial mores. I am a changed man. I now accept that no man can be a law unto himself no matter what social category of deviance he is subject to. I was convicted for offences that arose through disputes within my entrepreneurial enterprises. As I have had time to reflect and adopt more positive attitudes and values I know now that my methods in resolving such disputes were entirely wrong and the process of self awareness that I have been subjected to means that the possibility of being involved in such situations again is negligible.

I realise that any freedom granted to me in the future will have necessary limitations. Given the attention paid by the popular press to me in the past, my own supposed notoriety in itself would secure a good deal of scrutiny and surveillance. I accept that my pariah status has formed part of my punishment, albeit somewhat excessive in its severity. I wish to put all of that behind me now. My only desire is to fulfil a useful role in society that could be afforded by a conditional release on licence.

In the final analysis, it's my assessment that this worthwhile opportunity to humanely rehabilitate effectively enough, now is nigh. Enough over-zealous legal deterrence. Continuation of my punishment thus only negates society's tentative reforms, exceeding equitable treatment.

Yours faithfully

Harry Starks

* * *

Of course I'd heard about Harry's escape. It was all over the papers. TORTURE GANG BOSS IN DRAMATIC BREAK-OUT. STARKS ESCAPE: BRIXTON SECURITY PROBE ORDERED. Police-file photographs in dot matrix reproduction. Blurred front and profile shots, hardly much use for identification as they were a decade old, but sending a little shiver of recognition up my spine none the less. The tabloids ran other pictures. Sixties highlife and lowlife grinning for the cameras. Nightclub line-ups, Harry phalanxed by 'personalities'. Stories ran all week. Grave-robbed scandal and nostalgic gossip made good copy for page six or seven. *Ruby Ryder Speaks Out On Escaped Gangster: Exclusive interview with busty blonde star of ITV's Beggar My Neighbour*. A graffiti campaign started up all over the East End: STARKS – 10 YEARS LONG ENOUGH.

All this coverage helped to quell my unease at the thought of Harry being out there somewhere. All the details of his criminal career, his public-enemy status, reassured me that I was a very small part in the story. Then came the letter to *The Times*. Suddenly I was involved again. I couldn't avoid it. It was a message.

I hadn't thought about Harry for a long time. We'd lost touch after his last parole knock-back. To be honest, I thought he'd had a serious breakdown. Something that he'd always dreaded. The fear of it had at least been partly the reason for taking up education. He had a desperate will to keep that phenomenal brain of his together through the long years of incarceration. And it was this that had brought us together in the first place. Though, to say 'brought us together', well, we were never exactly together at any time over those years. Letters, prison visits, even the sociology classes I did at Long Marsh where we'd first met, in every instance we'd occupied a very different reality.

And my interest had always tended to the academic. 'Your little experiment,' was how Karen described it. But then I'm a criminologist. It would hardly seem natural for someone like me not to be fascinated by someone like Harry. It was something that Karen and I argued about. 'Ethnographic work based on participant observation,' is how I justified my methodology. She called it 'zookeeping'.

I'd actually believed that the relationship that Harry and I formed had a sort of dialectic energy to it, that something essential could be learned from a discourse between a criminal and a criminologist. I was wrong of course.

I remember someone using a quote by Chekhov to explain our duty as radical sociologists: 'We must take the part of the guilty men.' That's what I'd tried to do with Harry. But it was I who had the problem with guilt. The Catholic upbringing, I suppose. I think it was this that attracted me to criminology in the first place. It offered me a way out from guilt.

Harry, as the letter confirmed, always seemed less troubled by his conscience. Consequently the general response to it was cynical. Harry was using sophisticated terminology to excuse his crimes. He wasn't showing adequate remorse for his wrongdoings. The press was mocking. One columnist joked about Harry's new vocabulary, contrasting it with the vernacular more commonly used to describe his activities. 'Sociology is a cruel and unnecessary punishment in Britain's prisons,' he concluded. 'It should be abolished forthwith.'

But they didn't see the real joke. The letter had its purposes, as a stunt to bring attention to his case, as a way that Harry could prove he was educated and 'reformed' and not just some mindless thug. But it was a wind up as well. He was taking the piss. The terms he used mocked my own lost faith in a theoretical system. A faith that he himself had shattered.

And there was a real meaning to what he wrote. In the final analysis. A message hidden in the text. Something that addressed itself to me. A semiology of sorts. Signs, signifiers, the lot. In the final analysis, that was the key phrase that unlocked it. *In the final analysis.*

Long Marsh Prison's maximum-security-section wing was known as the Submarine. After going through three sets of gates to get into the main prison, I was led down to a metal door. A small shutter in the door slid open to reveal a peephole. It scrutinised me and the two officers who formed my escort. The double-locked door was opened from the inside and we entered an antechamber. I waited as more routine signals were exchanged by officers on both sides of another double-locking door beyond. There was a row of closed-circuit television screens in the antechamber. A couple of bored-looking screws sat watching them. The blue light from the tubes flickered as the screens gave the occasional horizontal-hold blink. Then the next door was opened and we went down into the maximum-security section itself.

E Wing. The Submarine. A tunnel-like building about fifty yards long and twenty yards wide. An underground bunker that entombed twelve Category Double-A prisoners. Hiding some of the State's most dangerous criminals from the light of day. There was no natural light let in to any part of the wing. Instead, harsh artificial fluorescence flooded the grey mausoleum. The lighting had to be kept at a high level of brightness in order for the closed-circuit surveillance to work. All these famous villains were well lit for the cameras.

There was no natural air either. No windows that opened to the outside. A ventilation system throbbed incessantly throughout the concrete and steel vault. An unfathomable stench pervaded the whole wing. A sickly sweet smell.

I was led to the end of the wing. The workshop. In the corner were bags of kapok, of fake fur and shredded foam rubber. Making soft toys was one of the few activities the inmates of the wing were offered.

There had been a riot earlier that year. An inquiry had recommended some changes in security and also a 'liberalisation programme'. As well as stuffing furry animals, sociology classes were suggested as part of that programme and I had been employed by my University's Extra-Mural Department for this purpose. On my appointment, the Governor was nervously insistent that I should follow the rules and guidelines laid down for prison teachers. Prisoners were not allowed to keep notebooks, for instance. I wasn't to discuss anything connected to their personal lives.

I'd nodded solemnly in his office and tried to conceal my

enthusiasm as a criminologist to have privileged access to such an elite group of criminals. It had come just at the right time. It was an exciting period for criminology. Radical ideas were everywhere. The National Deviancy Conference in 1968 had really shaken things up. We didn't talk any more of criminology per se but of the sociology of deviance. We had made a clean break from positivism and with siding with the agents of state control. We spoke of attempting to create a society where the facts of human diversity would not be subject to the power to criminalise. *We must take the part of the guilty men.* Going into a maximum-security prison to teach sociology seemed to epitomise this approach. I thought, in a quietly determined way, that I could be at the sharp end of a whole movement.

I turned from the bags of fur and stuffing in the corner of the workshop and met the combined gaze of seven heavy-looking and strangely familiar guys, all with expressions of bored malevolence. The Guilty Men. I swallowed and gave a little cough. I nodded to the prison officer who had come in with me and who was about to sit down in a chair by the door.

'Thank you,' I croaked.

He frowned up at me from a half-crouching position over the seat. I smiled and shrugged at him. He stood up straight again.

'I should really sit in, sir,' he said.

'I really don't think that's necessary.'

'Hm.'

'Please,' I implored.

'Very well,' he replied wearily.

He picked up the chair and scanned the room. Stares of hardened boredom came back at him. He slowly made his way out of the workshop.

'I'll be outside the door,' he insisted.

As he left I raised my eyebrows mischievously. A few smirks appeared briefly on the faces in front of me. I'd hoped I'd broken the ice a little but the cold expressions returned as they turned their gaze from the departing screw back onto me. *Who the fuck's this hippy?* I could almost hear them thinking.

I coughed again and sat down in front of this class. I tried to make my body language as relaxed as possible. I thought I recognised some of the assembled. Faces that matched blurred newspaper photographs. Tabloid headlines involuntarily flashed up in my mind. I tried to ignore these strange images and got on with the matter in hand.

I introduced myself and, in a tentative and casual way, outlined what we would be looking at in the course. I tried to get them to ask questions but very few were forthcoming. Well, I reasoned, incarceration in maximum security was hardly a conducive atmosphere for open discussion. They eyed me suspiciously and made guarded comments, cautious of giving anything away, wary of ridicule from fellow inmates.

The most vocal member of the group was a thick-set man with streaks of grey in his slicked-back hair. Heavy-lidded eyes that stared intently beneath thick eyebrows joined in the middle. He seemed to be the dominant member of the group. Others deferred to him, glancing carefully at his reactions if they spoke. But there was an engaging quality to him as well. He smiled a lot even though his grinning often seemed a reminder that teeth had other uses.

I finished the lesson by saying that although I had my own ideas about what we would study, I'd welcome any suggestions from the group as to areas of interest.

'Well, Lenny,' this man announced with his trademark smile. 'If you can prove that it's society what's to blame for me being in here, then it would be worth my while, wouldn't it?'

There was laughter at this. I joined in, trying not to force it too much. I didn't mind a joke at my expense. Indeed, I naively thought then that this comment wasn't too far removed from what I intended myself. I felt relieved that the first session was over and it had gone, yeah, it had gone OK. Now we could get started.

'Thank you, gentlemen,' I announced, standing up. 'See you all next week I hope.'

*   *   *

On my way home my mind was racing. All sorts of ideas and theories swarmed around me. About symbolic interactionism and the labelling perspective. About the nature of imprisonment and the potential for real-live exponents of social deviancy to define themselves. But all these buzzing thoughts were swatted by something else. I couldn't help but dwell on the uniqueness of the men I had encountered. Rather than putting them in the context of social norms, I found it impossible not to be fascinated by their very criminality and its individual characteristics. Many of them were famous, after all. Their faces had become matrix dot icons, their identities bound up in thick block headlines. *The Train Robber, The Panther, The Shepherd's Bush Cop Killer*, and the man who smiled so much, *The Torture Gang Boss*. I tried to avoid thinking like this. It ran so contrary to my theoretical standpoint. Rather than being objective about labelling theory, I was doing the labelling myself. I was regressing into crime as pathology. As mythology even. I tried to ignore these thoughts and concentrated on my methodology. Then the faces of the Guilty Men came back to me. Their terrible and audacious crimes. Did they *feel* guilty? I knew that this was the wrong way to think about them but it was all part of the experience, after all. There was something exciting about it.

I stopped off at a pub near the University. I needed a drink. I needed to wind down. Cool out a bit. The pub was full of students. I stood at the bar with a pint, staring out into the middle distance. I found my face hardening into a gaze of the type that the men in the Submarine wore. A sort of numbed alertness. The bleak expression that spoke of the empty years of confinement. The *what-the-fuck-do-you-want?* look.

'Lenny?'

A girl's voice behind me. I turned around.

'What?' I said, somewhat sharply.

'Are you all right?'

It was one of the first-year sociology students. Janine. She had long blonde hair, wide green eyes and a big pouty mouth. I smiled.

'Yeah,' I replied. 'Sorry.'

'You look like you've seen a ghost, Lenny.'

I laughed flatly.

'Yeah, well, I've just been in a room full of them.'

I told her about my evening in E Wing.

'Wow,' she remarked.

She was impressed. I was the youngest lecturer in the faculty. The students liked me, trusted me. I could relate to them and they appreciated my radical credentials.

'Do you want to come over and join us?' she asked.

I was tempted but I declined.

'I'd love to,' I said. 'But I've really got to get back.'

'We're having a party at my house. Saturday week. You will come, won't you?'

There was a flirtatious lilt in her voice. I grinned and nodded.

'Sure.'

'See you then, Lenny.'

'Yeah, see you.'

I finished my pint. I really did have to get back home. Back to Karen.

Karen and I had met at the London School of Economics in 1966. We were both Sociology undergraduates. Heady days. Full of fervour and activity. Even the Chess Society defined itself as Marxist Leninist back then. We occupied the LSE in 1967. We went to Paris in May '68. We actually participated. SOYEZ RAISSONABLE, DEMANDEZ L´IMPOSSIBLE! And when we got back to London, Hornsey College was occupied, a 'state of anarchy' declared. We joined the International Socialists. There was something in the air. Revolution. And we were going to make it happen. Herbert Marcuse had said that the workers had become stupefied by the products of their own labour and so revolution must come from those outside the system. It was up to us: students, hippies, freaks.

The second demo at Grosvenor Square, in October, was to be the climax of the year. Officially an anti-Vietnam War protest outside the American Embassy, it was intended as a catalyst. We would take revolution to the streets of London. As it happened, after a brief battle, the police kept control. And at the end of the day we trudged home to lick our wounds.

Then the National Deviancy Conference happened. That was when we saw the potential for putting radical ideas into academic work. When the next LSE occupation, in January 1969, ended in failure, we resolved to concentrate on our studies.

I got a first and applied for a post-graduate post in Criminology at Leeds. Karen got a 2:1 and started a Diploma in Social Work. And so we headed North. That in itself seemed a political decision. We moved into a big communal house in Chapeltown with some members of the Agit Prop Theatre Group who had come up from London at about the same time.

The sixties came to an end. It was a bit of an anti-climax. A time of reaction. The Tories got into power again. It was necessary to regroup. Karen concentrated on radical social work and began to define herself as a feminist. I focused on the sociology of deviance and theories of resistance to oppressive social norms. But it didn't seem so exciting any more. Until the Long Marsh project came up. Now this was something that I could really get my teeth into.

Karen was in the kitchen when I came in.

'You're late,' she commented.

'I stopped off at the pub on my way home. It was quite a heavy evening. I needed a drink.'

'Uh huh. Well there's some food left. It's in the oven.'

I got myself a plate and retrieved what was left of the evening meal. I started to tell Karen about the high-security wing, about the famous villains I'd met. She nodded blankly for a while and then rubbed at her face.

'Look, Lenny,' she said wearily. 'I'm tired. I've had a hard day myself, you know.'

I shrugged.

'I'm sorry. I thought that you'd be, like, interested.'

'Yeah. Well, you don't take much interest in my work.'

'I do.'

'No you don't. You just nod for a bit then try to change the subject. You always think that your work is more important than mine.'

'No I don't.'

'Well, more glamorous then. It's like these criminals are exotic specimens or something. I have to deal with ordinary people struggling to survive day in and day out. Maybe that just seems boring to you.'

'I don't think that,' I protested. 'Of course your work's important. But mine is too. I just wanted to share it with you. It's very exciting.'

Karen sighed. She put both her elbows on the kitchen table and slumped over them.

'Yeah, well, maybe I don't get a great deal of excitement in what I do.'

I reached over and put a hand on her shoulder.

'I want to get involved in something,' she said.

'Of course,' I said, stroking her back. 'Once I've got this project rolling we can both get involved. Together.'

She straightened up and brushed my arm away.

'Yeah, well, I want to get involved in something that doesn't involve you.'

I didn't follow.

'What do you mean, "something that doesn't involve me"? You mean an affair?'

'Oh, Christ, Lenny.'

'Babe, it's all right,' I said soothingly. 'I won't be jealous. We're supposed to be an open relationship, after all.'

'Is that all you ever think about? Do you think that's all women are for?'

'It's just that you said "something that doesn't involve me". I thought . . .'

'Yeah, you thought. I meant political involvement. You think politics is all about men. Well it's not.'

'I didn't say that.'

'Yeah, but you thought it. Well, anyway, I'm not putting up with all that any more. I'm starting a women's group. And that won't involve you.'

I smiled and said I thought that it sounded like a good idea. She chided me for being 'patronising', But I did think that it was a good idea. I was glad for her to get involved in something. I did feel a bit disconcerted, though. I mean, what was she getting so angry at me for?

At the next class at Long Marsh E Wing I went through some of the fundamental ideas of sociology. I talked about Max Weber, the Protestant Work Ethic and the rise of capitalism. I wasn't sure at what level to pitch the classes but I was determined not to have any kind of patronising approach to these men. I treated the sessions as if they were like any other class at a further education institute. Some of the group had dropped out but those who remained proved to be very sharp. They were all experts in one area of criminology, after all.

The Torture Gang Boss, Harry Starks, seemed particularly intelligent and lively in discussion, if a bit domineering, as I'd noticed before. He told me that he was determined to keep his mind alert amidst the stupefying effects of high-security imprisonment. He was worried that his long sentence might turn him into a zombie.

'A lot of old lags, they get into exercise, body building, you know,' he said. 'They get obsessed by it. Some of them, I reckon, would prefer an extra inch on their biceps rather than a year off their sentence. Thing is, they neglect that very important muscle that lies gasping for exercise in their skull.'

The rest of the group agreed. One of the biggest fears of long-term imprisonment was mental deterioration. Education could be of some use, simply as a resistance to the mind-numbing effects of incarceration in the Submarine. I wanted it to be more than that.

I introduced Durkheim and the development of the concept of anomie that came with the growth of industrialisation. I mentioned the Chicago School and their studies of urban environments and social disorganisation. It was all leading somewhere. I wanted to guide the group into an understanding of deviancy theory. Then I could really take the part of the guilty men, or rather let them take their own part, in a discourse that would put their crimes in the context of a political struggle. That all forms of deviant behaviour were in some way a challenge to the normalised repression of the state.

But when I brought up the word deviant, there was a reaction in the group I hadn't foreseen.

'You mean we're not criminals but deviants?' someone asked.

'That could be a way of looking at it,' I replied.

'What do you mean, deviants?' Harry Starks demanded fiercely. 'Like fucking nonces or something?'

The group bristled with barely suppressed fury. I felt that it could get ugly.

'Are you saying we're weirdos or perverts or something?' someone called out. 'Is that it?'

'No,' I tried to placate them. 'That's not what I mean.'

I waited for the room to calm down. It gave me time to think.

'What I mean is,' I went on, 'all social groups make rules and find ways to enforce them. They decide what is normal for the group and what is deviant. Howard Becker talks about this in *Outsiders*. And when someone breaks a rule it's not only the action that is seen as being outside the law, the person is as well. That's what I mean by deviant. That someone is labelled as an outsider.'

The group chewed this over for a moment. Some looked towards Harry to see what he would say. He smiled.

'Our problem isn't that we're outsiders, Lenny,' he said, looking around the walls of the windowless workshop. 'It's that we're insiders.'

And the room broke into much-needed laughter.

'Right,' I said when it had all died down. 'Any other questions before we finish?'

'Yeah,' someone piped up from the back. 'Why are you such a scruff, Lenny?'

'What?'

'Yeah,' someone else chipped in. 'You must be on a fair whack but you come in here looking like a tramp.'

I realised that appearance was everything to these men. A raw atmosphere demanded that one looked sharp. Even in drab prison-regulation gear they made an effort. To appear in control. My hippy aesthetic didn't impress them at all. It didn't look confrontational, it merely looked sloppy.

So I resolved to take their advice and smarten up. I felt that it might empower the group to show that I respected their value systems. And I might gain a bit more of their respect myself. I got rid of my old army-surplus jacket and bought a fingertip-length black leather coat. I dug out an old pair of chelsea boots and wore them instead of the tattered desert boots I habitually wore. I trimmed my beard into a sharp Van Dyke style and gathered my long hair into a ponytail so that it resembled the swept-back look that Harry Starks sported.

But Karen was not impressed.

'You look like a pimp,' was her dismissive judgement.

I managed to meet with her disapproval at almost every turn these days. It was like she was laying all of this resentment onto me

'The problem with all of this deviancy theory,' she ranted on, 'is that it's all so male dominated. And it's always male environments that you study. Skinheads, football hooligans, bank robbers. I think you get off on all this machismo.'

'I think you can take this feminist critique a little bit too far,' I countered.

'Really? Well what about rapists?' she demanded. 'I suppose there's rapists in that place you go to.'

I hadn't thought about that. Were there rapists amongst the men that I taught? Again, ugly images of the Guilty Men and the bad things they had done flashed up in my mind.

'So where do they fit into your theory of deviancy?' Karen went on. 'Eh?'

'Well,' I tried to reason. 'Of course some things are, well, unacceptable. But maybe they're better treated by something other than simple long-term imprisonment.'

'Oh, I agree,' she said with a gleam in her eye. 'We think that they should be castrated.'

I didn't ask Karen if she wanted to come to the party at Janine's house. I didn't think that she'd enjoy it and I figured, the way thing's were, we needed a bit of space.

'You look great, Lenny,' Janine enthused as I came into the party clutching a bottle of wine.

At least she approved. She was wearing a tight flowery T-shirt and blue velvet hipster jeans.

'So do you,' I told her.

And I felt good about my new image. It gave me an edge. Some of the arrogance of the E Wing inmates had rubbed off.

A rather loud second-year cornered me in the kitchen.

'The things is, about your theoretical base,' he droned, 'is it's all American. The Chicago School, Goffman, Becker. All Yanks. It's like cultural imperialism.'

'So,' I shrugged casually. 'It's like Rock and Roll. We're taking American ideas and doing it better. That's all.'

That shut him up. Someone passed over a joint and I took a long toke, smiling at my own cleverness. I couldn't help feeling pleased with myself. Sociology was by far the most fashionable, the hippest subject in academia of the time. And here I was, young, cool and at the heart of it.

Janine was trying to open a big Party Seven can of bitter.

'Let me do that,' I said. 'You have some of this.'

I offered her the joint. She took it with a smile that showed a row of perfect white teeth. Someone put on 'Street Fighting Man' by the Stones.

'Come on,' I said to Janine. 'Let's have a dance.'

We strutted our stuff together in the tiny living room. Janine's eyes half closed, her mouth half open, as she wiggled about in front of me. Her breasts bobbed up and down in time to Keith Richards's power chords.

Later, we met on the stairs as I came out of the bathroom. She smiled up at me. I sat down on the top step so that our faces were level. I couldn't think quite what to say.

'Great party,' I declared.

'Yeah. Glad you came.'

'So am I.'

I moved my face closer to hers. She blinked and pouted slightly. I kissed her on the mouth and ran a hand gently against a velvet-encased thigh. She pulled back and blinked again.

'Not here,' she whispered.

She continued up the stairs past me and, taking my hand, helped me to my feet.

'Come on,' she said, and led me through the door next to the bathroom. She clicked on a light. There was a poster of Che Guevara over the bed.

'This is my room,' she announced.

It all happened very quickly. Janine giggled as we took all our clothes off together. She giggled as she lay on the bed and let me put myself slowly inside her. Then she pushed at my chest.

'Let me see,' she demanded. 'Let me see it going in and out.'

And when I had granted her request she giggled some more.

Afterwards we lay on the bed for a while and shared a cigarette. I tried to relax but I kept thinking that I had to get back. After a while I got up.

'I've got to go,' I said.

'Don't you want to do it again?'

I smiled thinly.

'I've really got to go.'

Janine frowned.

'Have you got a girlfriend, then?'

I nearly laughed. *Girlfriend*. Karen would love that.

'No,' I replied. 'Well I mean, not a girlfriend. I'm in a relationship. An open relationship.'

'So, they wouldn't mind?'

'No,' I lied. 'They'll be cool about it. But I really should be getting back.'

I travelled home in a taxi in a state of elated drowsiness. But as we pulled up in front of the house I found myself anxiously checking the windows to see if any lights were on. I felt something strange in the pit of my stomach as I paid the driver. The garden gate squeaked, delivering a verdict. Guilty.

There was much laughter at my next entrance to the workshop in the Submarine. Catcalls and wolf whistles greeted my sartorial transformation. But I felt a rough sort of camaraderie in it all.

'You look like a Maltese ponce,' commented Harry. 'Still, it's an improvement.'

I felt that I was beginning to gain their trust and that I was starting to get results from my work with them. Most of the class had already used some sort of reading or study or even writing in order to deal with the mental punishment of confinement. Now sociology gave them a structure within which they could understand their situation and a vocabulary with which they could resist it.

Power was at the heart of it, of course. Despite a constant assertion of authority over them, the men on E Wing always tried to display a superior attitude to the screws. They considered themselves both intellectually and culturally distinct. Being mostly from London, they endowed themselves with a metropolitan, or even cosmopolitan, smartness with which they looked down upon the dull, provincial mentality of their captors. They sometimes revelled in being pariahs since it gave them an elite status and even celebrity. Harry Starks once commented that: 'These poor screws, spending all their waking hours on the wing, watching me, then when they get home and jump into bed with the missus, all she wants to know is: "Darling, did you speak to Harry today?"'

And as they studied their own predicament they could use a

theoretical language in any verbal confrontation with prison staff or governors. A new-found articulacy could be a weapon for their embattled position in a power struggle that formed the very centre of gravity of prison life. Not as direct or as cathartic as the physical force they had used in the riot all those months ago, but a resistance of sorts none the less.

Sometimes its form would merely be humour.

'So, this screw, you know, the stupid Geordie, he asks me at the end of last week's class: "So Jeff, what did you learn tonight?" And I tell him, all straight-faced like, that we'd been discussing a report that gave conclusive evidence that prison officers are predominately authoritarian psychopaths. And the silly cunt just smiles at me and says: "Very good."'

We'd spend a good deal of time in the classes discussing words. Sometimes to be clear about defining terms but sometimes just for the pleasure that some of the men had for understanding their meaning. For their own sake. They would enjoy having new definitions which they could apply to their own condition. They would use these words to spar with each other. Harry was particularly obsessed with expanding his vocabulary and applying new terms to his own experience or the environment around him. *Recidivist* became a particular favourite of his, I suspect partly because he found it so hard to pronounce at first. Once he had mastered it, it became something that he threw around with great regularity, often using it as a mild put-down to other cons. 'That's just what a recidivist would say,' he'd retort to someone's comment or: 'Typical recidivist thinking.'

During one session he launched into an anecdote that he felt epitomised the definition of his new pet word.

'When I was in Durham I came across this bloke, right, who must have held the British record for recidivism. He's on the security wing and word gets around that he's in under the Sexual Offences Act. He ain't on Rule 43 with all the nonces, but if someone's Category A, and it's sexual, it's bound to be something heavy. So, some of the chaps take a bit of an interest in this bloke, Frank was his name.

He keeps himself to himself, but soon enough a couple of fellahs corner him on the landing. Looks nasty, like they're going to do him with a razor or something but first they want to know what heinous crime he's in for. They've got him up against the railings, he's pleading and shit, then suddenly, they let him go and come down into association, pissing themselves laughing.

'Turns out Frank wasn't into little boys or little girls. He was into pigs.'

There was some laughter at this. Harry looked about the room with a mischievous gleam in his eye.

'Yeah, old Frank had been making bacon in a big way,' he went on. 'Thing is, he couldn't stop himself. His first offence dated years back to when he was a young impressionable lad, working on a farm. The head pig man catches him at it, shops him, and he does a couple of months. But what do you think is going through his mind at night in his cell as he's doing the old five-knuckle shuffle? Yeah, his little curly-tailed friends. So as soon as he gets out he finds himself another job on another pig farm, and he's at it again. He keeps getting caught, keeps going back to it. Over the years he notches up over fifteen separate convictions for bestiality and a fair few for breaking and entering pig farms. The sentences pile up and he ends up Category A.

'He got a bit of stick on the wing, but it was mostly verbal. Mind you, I did give him a slap myself once. One day, just out of curiosity, I turned to him and asked, "Frank, tell me, all those pigs you fucked, were they male or female?" And he looks at me, all affronted, and says, "They were sows, Harry. What do you think I am, queer or something?"'

There was more laughter which quickly petered out as Harry glared at the group.

'So I decked the bastard. He said *that* to the wrong person, that's for sure.

'Anyway, the point I'm making is how fucked up this system is. I mean, it creates that sort of recidivism. Think about how much it costs society to keep Frank banged up every time he gets the urge.

Then there's the court costs, legal aid, police time. It's a fucking fortune over the years. And it's not as if Frank's a menace to society. A menace to those little piggies maybe, though he always said they never complained. So wouldn't it make more sense, in the long run, for the Home Office to buy Frank a couple of porkers and a little sty somewhere and let him get on with it?'

Harry had not only defined recidivism but had also outlined a fine example of deviancy theory. But the absurdity of the story seemed to undermine the very thesis that it proved. The sociology of deviance was already under attack from critics as a 'misfit paradigm' which deflected from any real attack on the power of the State. Anthony Platt accused us of 'trivia and politically irresponsible hipsterism'. Whilst Alexander Liazos condemned an apparent preoccupation with 'nuts, sluts, and perverts', as he put it. In this context, Harry's impromptu case study was vaguely disconcerting. And I couldn't help thinking that he'd made up the whole thing to wind me up.

But it was the first time Harry made any reference to his sexuality. I felt there was an opportunity for some sort of symbolic inter-actionism there. I was to be disappointed. I brought up Gay Liberation at the next class and after a bit of sniggering someone asked: 'What do you think of that then, Harry?'

Harry's nostrils widened slightly, his mouth flattened into an impassive sneer.

'I'm not *gay*,' he said sternly. 'I'm homosexual but I'm not *gay*.'

Oo, get madam, someone muttered behind him and his head swivelled sharply around. I pondered on his use of a pathological term in preference to a subcultural one, but I let it pass.

'Yeah, well,' he went on. 'At least I'm open about it. I know what goes on inside. I tell you, Lenny, I ain't queer in prison. It's normal in here. Just because I'm like this naturally some people think it gives them the edge over me. They actually imagine that in any kind of normal setting I'd fancy them. As if I could get any real hard on for the old lags in here.'

'So what do you think about Gay Liberation?' I asked.

'Nah,' he replied dismissively. 'They're all too poofy and scruffy. I'm not into long hair neither. I like a boy to be well turned out.'

'Yeah, but what about their ideas?' someone asked.

Harry chuckled darkly.

'Well,' he said with a gleam in his eye. 'Someone once called Ronnie Kray a fat poof. Ronnie took the top of his head off with a Luger. That's my sort of Gay Liberation. Though, to be honest, I think it was the fat part what got to him. Ron's, well, touchy about his weight.'

But I couldn't help but be fascinated by the concept of a homosexual gangster. I talked about it to Janine when we were in bed together one afternoon.

'Doesn't it surprise you?'

'No, not really. I mean, we're all a bit gay aren't we?'

'Not me,' I replied hastily.

'Well, I am.'

'Really?'

I smiled. The thought of it rather excited me.

'But surely, this guy's sexuality isn't that important. He's a man, and a very violent one at that. It just proves that all men are predisposed to violence. Gay or not.'

'So where have you been picking up these ideas?'

'Don't patronise me, Lenny. I've been learning a lot recently. Things that I never really thought about before but sort of knew all along. "Consciousness raising" we call it in the women's group.'

'In the what?'

I sat upright in the bed.

'Oh,' Janine sighed. 'Didn't I tell you? I've been going to Karen's women's group.'

I stared at her, open mouthed.

'You haven't,' I stuttered. 'You haven't told her, have you? About us?'

'No. I thought you might have. You did say it was an open relationship.'

'You're not going to tell her, are you?'

'Of course I'm going to tell her,' Janine replied, indignantly. 'It would be very unsisterly not to. Karen's a wonderful woman. I've learnt so much from her. The group's really changed my life.'

I felt suddenly sick. I got out of bed and started pulling on my jeans.

'What's the matter, Lenny?'

'What?' I choked. 'Oh Jesus!'

'You really do look silly, Lenny. Karen's right, you know. She always says men are like children.'

There was a power cut on the night of Karen's next women's group. I went about the house putting nightlights on saucers in strategic places for illumination. The smell of wax smoke conjured unwelcome altar-boy memories. I felt horribly guilty. I knew that I should have told Karen before Janine had had a chance to. But I didn't dare. The front door slammed. A group of little flames flickered on the kitchen table. Like votive candles lit for atonement. Karen walked in, her shadow dancing across the ceiling.

'What's going on?' she asked.

'It's the power workers. The unions are really starting to get militant. A few more months of this . . .'

'Yeah,' she cut in flatly.

'Karen, look . . .'

'You bastard,' she hissed at me in the half darkness.

'I'm sorry.'

'Oh, you're sorry, are you? Well, that's great. Men. You're all the fucking same.'

'Now look, don't make a political point out of this. It was just an affair.'

'The personal is political, Lenny.'

'It's not a serious thing . . .'

'I wonder what you do take seriously, Lenny.'

'Well, this never used to be an issue.'

'Oh right. Back in the swinging sixties. Some great sexual

revolution that turned out to be. We lost out, you know, Lenny. Women lost out. It was only men who gained any freedom. We were supposed to just lie back and pretend we were enjoying it. Men get to do all the fucking. Women just get to do the faking.'

'Karen, look . . .'

'You're pathetic, you know that? You think you're some kind of stud in your leather jacket and ponytail. You're just using, or rather abusing, your power on impressionable young women.'

'Now, wait a minute . . .'

'You are, Lenny. Like all men. You use your power to try to dominate women. You're an oppressor, don't you forget that, because I won't.'

And with that she stormed out and slammed the door.

Directly as I came in from the main gate of Long Marsh, I was escorted for a short distance along by the perimeter wall, past the main wings of the prison, on the way to the maximum-security section. As we passed each block there came a now familiar humming sound. Hundreds of indistinguishable voices hovered up from every cell, landing and wing. Like the buzzing of insects in a hive, strangely soothing. Then we went down into the Submarine.

I had begun to get worried about group dynamics in the classes. Jeff, a mild-mannered triple murderer, dropped out. He told me in the corridor at the end of a session that he didn't feel he was getting any proper attention. He felt Harry always took over the class.

'He always dominates everything,' he said, looking around to make sure no one was listening. 'It's like in the TV room. We'll have a vote, like, about which programme we're going to watch and then he'll come in and say, "What, we having the film on then?" and change it over. And nobody says anything because they know he could have a right row about it. I thought it'd be different, doing this class, like, but it's the same, him taking over as usual. It's like he's running the sessions, not you.'

'You think I let him dominate the group?'

'You know you fucking do, Lenny.'

'Well, I'll try not to let it happen so much.'

Jeff laughed flatly at this.

'You think you control him any better than we could? You're as intimidated by him as we are.'

'Well, I could try. I wouldn't want you to stop coming to the classes just because of this.'

'Nah,' Jeff replied with a shrug. 'I ain't that bothered, to tell you the truth. At least now there'll be one night a week that we can watch whatever channel we want.'

'Well, I'm sorry you feel that way.'

'Don't worry about it, Lenny. I mean, Harry, he's like your star pupil, isn't he?'

I was a bit disturbed by this observation. It was hard to deny that I could be intimidated by Harry Starks. The Torture Gang Boss had a fearsome reputation. I soon found out that in the nomenclature of villainy he was known as Mad Harry. His violence could be explosive and unexpected. I also found out that this referred to an actual history of mental illness. Again it was hard for me not to be intrigued by the potential application of deviancy theory to this. I brought up R.D. Laing's work in one of the sessions. We discussed conformity and how creative potential is often seen as madness. The social construct of mental health and the labelling perspective of mental illness. Harry was his usual critical self.

'Yeah, that's all very well,' he commented. 'But without my pills I go off the fucking rails.'

In fact, Harry had his own version of anti-psychiatry: if you go mad they can lock you up for good. He had a deep fear of ending up in Broadmoor with no fixed release date. And this fear was at the heart of his obsession with exercising his mental capacities. Education was a way of keeping on top of things.

And he had a very sharp mind. I suppose that Jeff was right, I didn't manage to do anything that effectively pulled him back from dominating the group. But he was so relentless in his questioning, so consistently full of ideas. This was as intimidating as his physical presence. He never let me off the hook nor let me assume any kind of expertise in what was, after all, as much his field as it was my subject. 'You've really crow-barred that idea, Lenny,' he'd complain if I ever appeared clumsy in my analysis. He kept me on my toes. As with other areas of his life, he demanded rigour.

And whilst many of the other inmates readily took to deviancy theory, sometimes as a way to explain their crimes, Harry was reluctant to go along with this. It was as if it represented an excuse for failure. For some of the group, a bank robber for instance, their actions could easily be seen, somewhat romantically perhaps, in the context of an attack on advanced capitalism and conformity. In Harry's case his career rather held up a mirror to it.

'I wasn't a gangster,' he insisted, with no conscious irony. 'I was a businessman.'

Despite this, I laboured through theory with the group. Harry went along with it, elusive and obscure as ever. And though he displayed a natural resistance to my central thesis, he remained fascinated by self-analysis. 'I've always been interested in psychology,' he said. And I felt that I'd planted a seed. He wanted to learn and I felt that his self-examination would bear fruit. I was sure that he actually embodied the argument I was advocating. There was something tantalising about the ambiguity of Harry's criminality. It seemed to go to the heart of the whole academic enterprise that I was engaged in. With all his contradictions, he was a living discourse on the sociology of deviance.

About this time I published a paper: *Gangsterism: The Deviancy of Capitalism*. I started by examining the roots of deviancy theory itself. It seemed no coincidence that its formation took place in the Chicago School of the '20s and '30s. A time and place of widespread racketeering and mob activity. Amidst a post-war boom, furious demographic changes and the chaos of commercial deregulation, moral uncertainties emerged. Al Capone could be seen in this light as the Godfather of the sociology of deviance. His criminal corporatism had so thoroughly confused images of normality with spectres of abnormality that there was an inevitable change in attitudes to social norms.

And so, the gangster provides a realignment of these norms. Placed at the edge of modern values, he reassures it, gently mocking it in his mimicry of the trappings of big business, the well-tailored suit, the fast car, etc. The gangster's very extremism co-operates with the everyday world of the free market. 'Their alienation from our reality frees them to be subtly induced into realising our moral fantasies' (Goffman, 1972:267). Furthermore, they can project a dynamic of character in order to reify the adventure of capitalism.

At this point enter, stage right, the Hollywood gangster. In his seminal essay of 1948, *The Gangster as Tragic Hero*, Robert Warshow asserts the startling idea of the gangster as fundamentally an aesthetic as much as a physical threat. 'The gangster, though there are real gangsters, is also, and primarily, a creature of the imagination' (ibid.).

I then used my inside knowledge of Harry to examine gangsters of our own time and culture and how they epitomised the contradictions of our own age. In a sense, Harry Starks, the Kray Twins, *et al.*, were already following in a tradition. In the context of a post-austerity boom, they represented a dark undercurrent beneath the so-called 'swinging sixties'. A brooding presence that undermined the notion of this era being one of liberation and permissiveness. Liminal behaviour kept the lid on a potential social revolution with superficial charm. The glamour, the style, the friends in high places and showbiz personalities were all shot through with a deep sense of menace. 'Extreme seductiveness is at the boundary of horror' (Bataille, 1932:17).

Presuming the authority of working-class culture, the gangster actually upholds the binary systems of late-stage capitalism. Charity work goes hand in hand with protection rackets. In seemingly opposing operations of extortion and philanthropy, he becomes both malevolent folk devil and benevolent folk hero. Furthermore, he resolves the dichotomy of the individual and the collective.

Despite semantically implying adherence to a gang, the gangster instead becomes a distillation of mass culture into an individual pathology. Like Robert Musil's criminal Moosbrugger in *The Man without Qualities*, the gang boss inhabits a psychological as well as a social underworld. 'If mankind could dream collectively, it would dream Moosbrugger.'

Thus he provides catharsis. In acting out the deep fears and potentially dangerous ambitions of the individual in the market economy, the very deviancy of the gangster allows capitalism to exorcise itself and reassert its moral normalcy.

The course came to the end of its allotted span and there was no indication from the Prison Education Department that it would be renewed as an activities option for the inmates of the Submarine. All I heard were rumours that the Governor and the Assistant Governor had decided that the project had a dangerous whiff of subversiveness to it. Officers had been complaining that the prisoners taking the course had become even more gobby than usual. They'd gained a further articulacy in asserting their rights. Stuffing soft toys was clearly a better way of encouraging rehabilitation.

Many of the men I got to know on E Wing said that they wanted to continue some sort of study. I was always encouraging, even though I thought at times I was merely being humoured. Harry was particularly enthusiastic about the idea. As usual, he had his reasons.

'You know those Scandinavian studies you talked about?' he said to me on the last day. 'You know, the psychological effects of long-term incarceration. Sensory deprivation and all that. Well, they reckon, what? Five years, seven years at best before you start to crack up. Seven years, that's all I've got. Seven years bad luck. But bad luck is better than no luck. You know what I mean?'

'I'm not sure that I do, Harry.'

'Listen,' he hissed, drawing my face closer to his with a casual beckoning gesture. His eyes narrowed on mine. 'I mean, I looked at you and thought the only thought that makes any kind of sense in here. I thought: are you my way out of here? Seven years, then I'm up for my first parole board. Eat your porridge every day, do your time the easy way. So what's this? I'm thinking: is this the easy way? You know, this education racket. O levels, A levels, Open University, open sesame. Know what I mean? If I educate myself, it's like I'm reforming, ain't it? It's bound to go down well with the board, isn't it?'

He smiled at me. There was an enacted confidence in his manner. He sounded desperate. I dreaded being the one responsible for getting his hopes up.

'Yeah,' I said cautiously. 'I guess.'

Harry sniffed doubt. His eyebrows knitted as he frowned piercingly at me.

'Yeah,' he insisted. 'But what do you think?'

'I think,' I replied quickly, wary of any tension that a pause might produce. 'I think that you want to do it anyway. You want to learn. You want to study, don't you?'

Harry grinned, for once sheepish rather than lupine.

'Yeah, I do,' he grudgingly admitted.

I promised to put in a good word with the Education Officer, for what it was worth. Harry suggested that we stay in touch. I said that it sounded like a good idea. After all, it seemed a logical thing, for a criminologist to get to know a criminal. And I felt sure that I could maintain a certain professionalism in our acquaintance.

So Harry started his O levels. I only managed one visit after the course had finished before he was moved to Leicester. This was part of the dispersal system whereby Category A prisoners were moved around to different maximum-security wings. It was a policy implemented to try to avoid the problems of the long-term concentration of groups of dangerous cons, and little warning was given before a prisoner was moved. It became known as The Ghost Train. Or, as Harry more grandly put it, The National Tour.

We started to write to each other. Over the next few years I was able to visit Harry only occasionally, but we kept up a fairly constant correspondence. The letters would often have a purely practical focus, he might want to discuss an essay he was writing on differential association for his sociology A level, for example. Otherwise he might simply want to let off steam, complain about conditions or conflicts with screws or other cons. All letters were subject to censorship, Category A correspondence being particularly closely vetted, so he had to be careful not to be too explicit in his criticisms or descriptions of prison life or references to criminal activity, anything, in fact, that the censor could deem 'objectionable' under Standing Orders.

So Harry developed a code. If he used the phrase 'in the final analysis', it meant that a message was contained in the initial letters of the words that followed. Usually it wasn't terribly subversive stuff but it provided Harry with another way of undermining the system that dominated him. A little game, a little system of his own.

The thing about writing to someone in prison is you don't really remember very well what you've said to them because your life is changing all the time. But theirs isn't. Harry would refer meticulously to some point or other of a previous letter which I would have completely forgotten. And so he became a marker, a sort of fixed point which I could remind myself by.

Things were changing. On the outside at least. As the seventies wore on I felt a growing confusion about ideas that had seemed so certain. My academic career was going well. I had papers published, articles in *New Society*, even a little broadcasting work. I was getting a few ideas together for a book. Everything seemed to be going so well and yet I felt insecure. All the excitement that had come out of the National Deviancy Conference had seemed to peter out. There were scarcely any meetings any more. All these great radical ideas had gone a bit stale. Notions that had once seemed controversial now began to look threadbare and otiose. A smell of revisionism hung in the air and academics now turned on each other. That sense of a collective enterprise had all but vanished.

And in the meantime Karen was more confident. More assertive. She'd been writing for *Case Con*, the radical social work journal. She talked of the need for consciousness raising and the important imput of new ideas from the Women's Movement for social change. She wrote of the implications that a feminist understanding of aspects of the family and child rearing could have for political understanding of social work. Feminist ideas were now in the ascendant and could no longer be ignored as a critical framework.

I couldn't help but feel somewhat undermined. I can't say that I took too kindly to my newly supposed status as oppressor. It bothered me, this 'all men are bastards' analysis. It was too familiar. A doctrine of original sin, where all men are profoundly bad.

So our relationship became frosty, to say the least. We had separate rooms in the house now. We still had sex but it would always have to be Karen who instigated it. A 're-alignment of the economy of sexual relations', she called it. The personal is political, she kept reminding me.

Though it struck me that rather, our politics had become personal. She always insisted she was involved in something positive, something that would 'make a difference', as she put it, whilst I was merely obsessed with the more exotic aspects of the male psyche. And it was at this time that she first started using the 'zookeeping' jibe against deviancy theory. She was particularly dismissive of my continued contact with Mr Starks. 'So, how's your pet experiment?' she asked me once when I'd finished intently reading a letter from him. And another time she declared: 'You wouldn't want him to be released, would you? That would spoil everything. He's like your little rat in a maze.'

And the awful thing was, she was right. I was fascinated by his predicament. It was hard to resist seeing him as a long-term project. As a subject. But what bothered me wasn't any desire for him to be incarcerated but rather an odd little fear at the back of my mind at the thought of him being given his freedom. The notion of Harry Starks at large scared me a little.

Then one evening Janine came to the house. I hadn't seen much of her since the affair. She was a second-year now so she wasn't at any of my lectures. To be honest I'd been avoiding her.

She'd cut her hair short which accentuated her wide eyes and full mouth and made her look quite gamine. She blinked mischievously as she stood on the doorstep.

'Janine,' I announced as cheerily as possible, hoping that she detected no nervousness in my tone. 'Good to see you.'

'Hi, Lenny,' she drawled as she walked past me into the hallway.

'Come in,' I said, stupidly, and closed the door.

She looked up at the walls and ceiling and gave a little sigh.

'What a lovely house,' she said.

'I wasn't expecting you,' I said, a little more frantically than I'd wanted. 'Can I get you a drink? Go through into the living room.'

She turned to me suddenly. Her eyes and mouth formed Os on her face.

'Oh,' she said. 'I haven't come to see *you*, Lenny.'

I frowned, and at that moment Karen came thundering down the stairs.

'Janine!' she called out.

Janine looked up and smiled. Karen virtually landed on her, planting a big wet kiss on her mouth.

'I'm so glad you've come,' said Karen breathily, not even acknowledging my presence. 'Come on. Let's go upstairs.'

Later that night as I lay in bed I could hear strange noises coming from Karen's room above mine. Tremulous moans, urgent cooing and deep-throated laughter. Distant night sounds murmuring through floorboards and plaster. I tried to ignore it all and get some sleep but I couldn't help myself straining to listen.

Harry had started a BSc in Sociology with the Open University in 1973. He wrote and told me he thought that the course 'would be a piece of piss. The work you did with us back at Long Marsh has really come in handy.' He seemed to have settled at Leicester, for the time being, so I could arrange visits with some sort of reliability.

'You look a bit fraught, Lenny,' he told me. 'Still having trouble with your bird?'

I'd written to him about my problems with Karen. He was easy to confide in. He was so blunt and oblivious to the intricacies of sexual politics.

'I think she might be becoming a lesbian.'

Harry gave me an open-mouthed stare, then burst into laughter.

'Sorry, Len,' he said, trying to straighten his face.

'I don't know what to do, Harry.'

He shrugged.

'Search me. I never had much truck with dykes, to tell you the truth. The Twins used to run a lesbian bar. In the basement of Esmeralda's. Right old dive, it was.'

'Well, anyway, how are you?'

'I dunno,' he said with a sigh. 'Doing my time, I suppose. Thing is, it's not my time I'm doing. I've had my time taken away from me. I'm doing their time. It's turning me into a zombie.'

'I don't know, Harry. You seem pretty sharp.'

'Oh yeah. Abstract thinking. I can do that, no bother. But if I start to think about anything real in my life, I feel I could crack up. I've seen it happen enough times. Remember Jeff? Little Jeff from the Submarine?'

I nodded. The mild-mannered murderer.

'He's flipped. He's only gone and found God, hasn't he? I suppose he thinks he's found some sort of reality. He said to me, "I have decided to live inside my head." I told him, "Well, I'm sure there's enough room inside there, Jeff old son."'

Harry laughed flatly.

'Thing is,' he went on, 'Jeff reckons he can escape from it all by going inside. Well I couldn't do that.'

'Yeah, but in a way, you're using the inside of your head as a refuge. By studying.'

'Nah, Lenny. You're missing the point. What's inside is neither here nor there. It's not what's inside of me that'll make a damn bit of difference. It's what I'm inside. That's the reality.'

Then, a few months later, when I turned up at Leicester with a

Visiting Order to see Harry, I was told that the visit was cancelled. Harry had had all privileges suspended for twenty-eight days. For offences against 'Good Order and Discipline', was all I was told. I had no idea what had happened. I wrote to him but got no reply. At first I worried about losing contact with him. But as the weeks went by I found myself forgetting him.

Yet unexpectedly, like a particularly vivid dream, strange images of Harry would begin to haunt me. If I concentrated on him, I figured that maybe he had, as he'd always feared, gone mad. It was a disturbing thought but there was nothing I could do about it, I reasoned.

Then, about three months later, I received a letter from Durham. Harry had been moved back there on the Ghost Train. I got a Visiting Order and went to see him. I dreaded what state he might be in. But as he was led out to meet me, he seemed in good enough spirits. His hair had got longer and he didn't seem to be making so much fuss about his appearance. But he looked almost relaxed with an indifferent air about him that I recognised from all my time at universities. He looked like an academic.

The suspension of privileges and a spell in solitary had come about, it turned out, from a fight with a fellow prisoner.

'What the hell happened?' I demanded, almost chidingly.

Harry shrugged.

'This bloke on the wing at Leicester. Poisoner. He's doing a post-grad Open University course and he reckons he knows it all. He was always winding me up. Kept going on that sociology was a soft option. How what I was studying wasn't rigorous enough. That I was just doing a mickey-mouse degree. Got right on my wick. So I did him. Gave him rigorous. Right in the goolies.'

'Harry . . .'

'I know, I know,' he protested. 'It was stupid. But he was driving me crazy. Going on about how social sciences didn't have the right to be called sciences. Acting all superior.'

'So, what's he studying?'

'Chemistry.'

I laughed.

'I know. A fucking poisoner studying chemistry. Show's you how stupid the Prison Service is. That cunt ought to be in Broadmoor. Still, it was a stupid thing to do. I've really got to stay out of trouble.'

'That wouldn't be a bad idea, Harry.'

'I don't mind punishment. I can take that. It's losing remission that bothers me. I don't want to add another second to my time in here. Thing is, Lenny, back in the fifties I'd probably have got the birch or the cat and that would have been that.'

I winced and Harry chuckled softly at my response. Of course, as a criminologist, I knew that corporal punishment hadn't been abolished in British prisons until the early sixties, but the thought of it still shocked me.

'Nah, it would have been better,' Harry went on. 'Because with corporal punishment you didn't lose any remission or have to do any other punishment. It hurt like fuck at the time, and of course it was humiliating.'

'It was barbaric.'

'Yeah, yeah, but then it was over with. To be honest Lenny, a lot of these reforms, they don't necessarily make it any easier for those condemned. It's more for the benefit of liberal fuckers like you, so you can sleep easily thinking that you're living in a civilised society. I mean, a few strokes over someone's bare arse, that's barbaric, but locking up some poor fucker for years, pretending that you're rehabilitating him, that's OK. It's all nicely hidden away and forgotten about. I mean, look at what I did. If someone owed me money and couldn't pay up in time, I'd smack them around a bit. Oh yeah, that's terrible. But look at what happens in normal society when someone's in debt. Their house gets repossessed or the bailiffs call around to take everything that's not bolted down. Which would you rather have?'

I shrugged, preferring to leave it as a rhetorical question.

'Yeah, anyway. I've lost a bit of remission which is a bit of a piss off. But I'm going to be a good boy from now on. Concentrate on my studies.'

He gave me a shark-like grin. I smiled back.

'Well, it's bound to go down well with the parole board, isn't it? And when you come to think of it, it does kind of let me off the hook and all. I mean, this sociology of deviance. I could tell them that my actions were consistent with the value system of the subculture within which I was socialised. Couldn't I?'

He looked at me intently. I didn't know what to say. He suddenly burst out laughing.

'Don't worry, Lenny. I ain't that stupid. Your face. No, I know that won't wash with any kind of board. Harry Starks, they'll think, still a criminal but now he knows why he does it. No, don't you worry, I'll be all remorseful and shit.'

'You've got to play along with the system.'

'Yeah, I know Lenny, I know. Thing is, I always have, in a way. But yeah, keep my head down. No more kicking the shit out of chemistry graduates. But to tell you the truth Lenny, it did get to me. What he said.'

'What do you mean?'

'I mean, maybe he's right, in a way. Maybe sociology isn't rigorous enough.'

'Do you think that?'

'Well, I don't know. Some things. Like deviancy theory. I wasn't doing all that to rebel, you know. I wanted to be legitimate. I was just a bit, you know, heavy handed.'

He looked down at his heavy hands.

'I just think,' he went on, 'you know, there's something missing in a lot of these theories.'

'Well, that's a good thing, surely,' I replied. 'It means you're developing a critical approach.'

Harry certainly developed a keen intellectual insight into sociological theory as time went on. I found myself wanting to run things by him now, as a way of checking my ideas. His comments were always direct and often quite ruthless but he came to represent a test to sloppy thinking, particularly on criminology. And I felt I needed that now more than ever.

For my part, I could still guide him to key texts and references that might be relevant to the rough ideas he started to formulate. He exhibited a strong tendency towards structuralism. It seemed almost instinctive and maybe, after all, he scarcely had any choice in this way of thinking. He'd spent years of experiencing movement through rigid structures in both time and space. This, for him, was where meaning resided. So I pointed him towards Levi-Strauss and some other French thinkers I thought might be useful to him.

We developed a strange kind of discourse through letters and occasional visits. I never envied his predicament but I was sometimes jealous of his ability to concentrate, with few distractions, on study. This was, of course, all bound up with the act of will he was exerting in order to get through his sentence without going mad.

He was constantly surprising me. I was astonished that he was able to articulate political as well as intellectual criticisms on deviancy theory.

'You're a Marxist, ain't you, Lenny?' he asked on one of my visits.

'Yeah,' I replied, somewhat hesitantly. 'Not an orthodox Marxist, but, yeah.'

'Well, it strikes me that old Karl wouldn't have much truck with the sociology of deviance. I mean, criminals, misfits, deviants. Now, my old man would have called them *lumpenproletariat*.'

'Your father was a communist?'

'Yeah. And an orthodox one at that. Party member. It was big in the East End back then.'

'So he was at Cable Street?'

Harry laughed.

'Christ yes. He was always bloody reliving it. "We turned them back." Yeah, it was like Stalingrad to him. Thing is, a lot of people credit Jack Spot and his gang for beating the blackshirts, but my old man always maintains it was the Communist Youth League.'

310

'Who was Jack Spot?'

'Jewish gangster. He ran the spielers and protection in the East End before the war.'

'So you were never tempted to join the Party?'

'Nah. The old man wanted me to, of course. I could never see the point myself. I mean, communism, it's a cheap racket. They've got nothing and they want to share it with you. Sorry to disappoint you, Len.'

'So you joined Jack Spot's gang instead.'

'Nah, I never liked Spotty. The Twins worked for him for a while. That was before they got this idea that they were going to take over the world. Nah, I worked for Billy Hill at first. Before I got set up on my own. Billy and Jack didn't exactly see eye to eye. Anyway, going back to my original point. How can you square Marxism with deviancy theory?'

'That's a good point.'

Harry cackled, knowing that he'd got me on this one.

'Strikes me,' he went on, 'that it lets too many people off the hook. Now I know you've got some sort of romantic notion about crime. Yeah, you have Lenny, don't try and deny it. I bet you wish that I was a bank robber, something glamorous like that. At the heavy like some sort of modern-day Robin Hood. But it wasn't like that. You see, crime, well what I did, it was just business with the gloves off.'

'Yes, but it's still labelled deviant if it breaks social norms . . .'

'Yeah, yeah,' Harry went on, impatiently. 'But what's important is what you can get away with.'

At the end of 1975 I started work on my book, *Doing Time: Social Control and Subcultural Resistance*. I used some of the observations I'd made of the men on Long Marsh's E Wing and made comparisons with ethnographic studies of other deviant groups. *The Subculture of the Submarine*, I titled this section (rather snappily, I thought). But I began to feel that it was the system itself that needed analysing, not just those groups of people who found themselves in opposition to it. I found myself using Harry's impromptu critique of Becker; *our problem isn't that we're outsiders, Lenny, it's that we're insiders*. I found that so many of Harry's opinions were informing my approach to my subject. The rat in the maze had yielded results. But his thoughts always seemed to challenge rather than confirm my theories.

Karen left and went to live in a women-only household. She now defined herself as a lesbian separatist. I felt quite empty about the whole thing. Inadequate. I tried therapy. Some Reichian nonsense which didn't get me very far. I even went along to a men's group meeting. Sat in a circle with a lot of other sad blokes. Talking about getting in touch with our feelings. It was embarrassing.

In 1976 Harry graduated from the Open University with a 2:1. No gown or graduation ceremony of course but Harry looked pleased with himself when I got a VO and went to congratulate him.

'Letters after my name,' Harry mused. 'That ought to impress them.'

I guessed that he meant the parole board. I smiled weakly, trying to hide my discomfort. There was that spasm of anxiety again. The thought of Harry getting released.

'So what will you do with your qualifications? Once you're on the, er . . .' I coughed, 'outside.'

'Dunno.' Harry shrugged then grinned. 'Maybe move in on your racket. You know, academia.'

'Really?'

Harry burst out laughing.

'Only joking, Len. Christ your face. Nah, don't you worry, old son. I was thinking of something more practical, you know.'

'What like?'

'Well, I was thinking, with the combination of my experience and my studies I could work in an advisory capacity. Management consultancy, something like that. I don't know what you think's so funny, Lenny. A lot of people would give their right arm to know what I know about business.'

*   *   *

Doing Time got published in 1977 and I sent Harry a copy. It had had mixed reviews but it was Harry's opinion that I was most interested in.

'So?' I asked him. 'What do you think?'

'Well,' Harry shrugged. 'It was interesting. Yeah, it was all right.'

He sounded noncommittal. Polite. So unlike Harry.

'Come on,' I urged him. 'Tell me what you really think. Be brutal.'

Harry sighed. His eyebrows knitted.

'To be perfectly frank, Lenny,' he said. 'It's a bit old hat.'

'Yeah?'

'And a lot of your arguments are confused. They don't seem to go nowhere.'

'Yeah, well . . .'

'Look, you wanted my opinion. Face it, Lenny. The bubble's burst. Deviancy theory is dead in the water. It's all over, bar the shouting. Maybe that's all it was anyway. It wants to be radicalism but it's just liberalism with a loud mouth. Sorry, Len.'

'Well I said "be brutal".'

'Yeah,' he grinned. 'Well I have got a bit of a reputation. I liked some of it. That bit about the institutionalisation of power and that. I tell you what, though—' He leaned forward, eyes darting to and fro – 'I've been reading something else. Something very tasty.'

His sudden enthusiasm for another writer compounded his excoriation of my own work. I felt a bit sick.

'Who?' I asked, swallowing.

He uttered something I couldn't recognise. *Foe cult*, it sounded like. I had strange images of oppositional subcultures.

'Oh, come on Lenny,' he protested as I squinted at him. 'You know I can never pronounce these names. French geezer. *Discipline and Punish.*'

'Foucault, you mean.'

'Yeah.'

He muttered *foo co*, *foo co*, under his breath a few times, making sure that he'd got it, then looked up at me.

'You seen it?' he demanded.

I had. I'd even tried to read it but had not got very far. It seemed deliberately obscure, the long description in the first section of an eighteenth-century judicial torture rebarbative and brutal. Designed to shock perhaps but all a bit *grand guignol*.

'It's a bit heavy going,' I said.

'Yeah, well,' Harry chuckled. 'It ain't for the squeamish.'

The irony of the Torture Gang Boss reading all of this suddenly hit me and I laughed. His knowledge of brutality gave him insight, perhaps. And, as I remembered, straight after the torture account in the book came a description of prison routine of some seventy years later. Something that he also had first-hand experience of. Foucault was setting out two very distinct penal styles, one shocking and one familiarly modern, and inviting the reader to reflect on how, in less than a century, such huge changes had taken place. This much I understood and that any notion of 'humanisation' was to be avoided in the subsequent analysis, but that's about as far as I'd got. Harry was very keen to explain it all to me.

'It's all about the economy of power, Lenny. The modern penal system can present itself as being more just, more rational, but in effect it can exercise far greater power over people. Everything is controlled much more efficiently as with all other forms of industrial institutions. Remember what I said about the cat and the birch. Losing remission is a far worse punishment but it's seen as being less brutal. In fact punishment isn't seen any more but instead becomes the most hidden part of the process. So you abolish corporal punishment, you know, punishment on the body. Instead you punish the soul.'

'The soul?'

'Yeah, you know, the psyche, the consciousness, whatever. When you're banged up you're allowed exercise, you can study and pretend you're not turning into a zombie. But all along your personality, that delicate sense of freedom and integrity, is constantly being exercised and disciplined in time and space. That's the soul. The effect and instrument of a political anatomy. They imprison it, it imprisons you. The soul is the prison of the body.'

I tried to take all of this in as Harry went on. He was determined to use the rest of the visiting time to conduct a brief lecture outlining the whole thing. He talked of Bentham and the Panoptican, his design for an ideal prison where each inmate could be clearly seen by a central observer.

'You saw what it was like in the Submarine. We were hidden away, our punishment was hidden away from civilised society, literally submerged, if you like. Yet at the same time we're under constant surveillance. Constantly aware of our visibility to the system. Constantly isolated, with the only real intimacy being our relationship with the power exercised over us. Now, of course, this system produces delinquents, recidivists, deviants. This is prison's vengeance on justice. So what do you do, in a scientific age? Come up with another science to keep a check on this new species. Criminology. Sociology. Study the deviants then you can extend the surveillance. That's where you fit in to all this, Lenny. All this radical posturing. You just help to maintain the system. Make it appear more liberal, more civilised, but ultimately make it work better.'

'That's pretty damning, Harry.'

'Yeah, I'm afraid it is. But it's all there. You really should read it. You see, the problem with deviancy theory is that it never really analyses the structures we're supposed to be deviating from. Oh, you love the subjects. So strange and exotic. Like going to the zoo. You love all of these wild creatures because they're behind bars and can't hurt you. You want to like us but deep down you're shit scared of us.'

'Yeah, maybe.'

'Sorry, Lenny. I'm being a bit hard on you. Fact is, I'm in a good mood.'

'Yeah?'

'Yeah. Well, I've got my first parole board coming up in a couple of months' time.'

'So, you're optimistic?'

'Well, Lenny, you know, you've got to be careful how you think about these things. You can't afford to be hopeful about your situation. That makes you vulnerable, and the fuckers can grind you down easily. But you can't afford to be hopeless, neither. Because then they've really got you beat. It's like Antonio Gramsci said: "Pessimism of the intellect, optimism of the will".'

I smiled.

'You've been reading Gramsci?'

'Yeah. Now don't get a hard on just 'cos I'm quoting a commie, Lenny. I didn't buy all of that hegemony stuff. But anyone who's done that much time and held it all together deserves some respect.'

My mind was reeling as I came away from that visit. It was as if our roles had been reversed. I had become a student to Harry's teacher. He had acquired such clarity in his analysis of things whereas I had become more and more confused. My whole theoretical base was challenged. I had to start again.

I struggled with Foucault. I was jealous of Harry's clear grasp of it. And I felt guilty because deep down I didn't really want him to get parole. In a strange way I wanted him kept where he was so that I could have occasional access to his understanding. I didn't want him on the outside, roaming free. The thought of that always left me with a twinge of fear.

I didn't have to worry. Harry got the knockback. Later that year, six weeks after his board had met, he received a letter. 'The Secretary of State has fully and sympathetically considered your case for release under licence, but has regretfully concluded not to authorise it on this occasion.'

I managed to get a visit with him near the end of 1977. He looked terribly depressed. Puffy eyes stared at me gloomily.

It was an awkward visit. There wasn't much I could say about his being turned down.

'Well, you can carry on with your studying,' I suggested, hoping that we could talk academically. There were things I wanted to discuss with him. But Harry wasn't in the mood.

'It's all been a waste of fucking time.'

He gave a hollow laugh.

'Not that there's anything to do in here but waste time. But you've loved it, haven't you? I bet it's really been interesting for you.'

'Harry,' I murmured.

'Do your own time, Lenny. I've fucking had enough of it all.'

There was silence for about a minute. I cleared my throat.

'They're bound to lessen your category, at least,' I ventured. 'You'll probably get moved to an open prison.'

Harry's nostrils widened and he glowered at me.

'Open fucking prison. Open fucking university. Yeah, every-thing's fucking open, isn't it? You know what the worst thing is? Cunts like you looking in on me thinking everything's going to be all right because of their fucking bleeding hearts.'

Harry was becoming quite agitated. A screw came over.

'Now, now, Starks. Turn it in. Otherwise visiting time's over.'

'Fuck you,' he said to the guard. 'Fuck the lot of you. I don't need visiting time, anyway. It's a waste of fucking time.'

A couple more screws came over and they started to manhandle Harry.

'Get your fucking hands off me!' he shouted as they dragged him away.

I lost touch with Harry after that. He had got into trouble again over Good Order and Discipline. The last I heard of him was that he had been moved to Brixton. I reasoned that he might have finally cracked up as he had feared he would. Thoughts of him troubled me from time to time. But after a while it all receded in my mind. And that peculiar fear I had of him in the back of my mind nearly disappeared altogether.

I was left with the legacy of what I had learnt from him. The seed that I'd planted bore bitter fruit. I lost faith with my ideas, my once treasured theories. He had proved them wrong. I tried to keep up with new bodies of thought, new paradigms. Harry was certainly right about Foucault. His influence was tremendous. And all these other French guys. Post-structuralism, post-modernism, everything became fractured. The very consensus that deviancy theory envisaged (and indeed relied upon) was falling apart, so deviancy theory itself petered out very quickly. I carried on lecturing, without much enthusiasm. I was going through the motions.

Punk arrived and suddenly I became old fashioned. Students started criticising me for being an 'old hippy' or even a 'boring old fart'.

Funnily enough, punk regurgitated all that situationalist stuff from the late sixties. All that King Mob anarchism. The self-proclaimed deviants seemed ready to be digested as the new folk-devil pariah elite. I started to write an article for *New Society* but it just turned out turgid and flat. Stan Cohen had already done all that years ago with the Mods anyhow. I was bored, but not like these kids with their blank generation aesthetic. I was bored because I had become boring.

The Tories got in again in 1979. That seemed to epitomise the lost opportunities of that decade. Some people on the Left said it was a good thing. That it would give the people something tangible to rebel against. I wasn't so sure. Consensus was dead and our radicalism seemed burned out. In fact it looked like the very idea of radicalism belonged to the Right now.

Then, that same year, Harry hit the headlines. TORTURE GANG BOSS IN DRAMATIC ESCAPE, read one headline. STARKS ESCAPE: BRIXTON SECURITY PROBE ORDERED. I felt a familiar shiver of fear up my spine. It gave me quite a thrill.

It had been a meticulously planned escape. At Brixton, Harry had noticed that the external wall at the end of his wing connected to a flat roof. By bribing a couple of key warders, Harry had engineered a change in allocation that got him the cell at the end of the block. He wanted a better view, he assured them. Then, with the patience of an archaeologist he set to work. He started to cut into the mortar around a whole patch of brickwork. He used drill bits, fragments of hacksaw blades, anything that could be smuggled in or bartered for with other prisoners. He worked slowly and carefully and at night. He stole sugar from the canteen and sprinkled it on the floor of the corridor in front of his door so that he could hear the crunch of the rubber-soled boots of an approaching screw. That way he could time the lengths of the landing patrols and know when it was safe to work.

At dawn he would carefully sweep up the brick dust and mortar rubble from the night's labours and dump it in his chamber pot. In the morning he would slop it all out undetected. He hid the growing hole by pushing a wooden locker up against the wall.

It took him nearly three months to chisel out around fifteen bricks that were to provide him his exit. But he knew that any haste might lead to mistakes or clumsiness. He had time on his side, after all.

On the night of his escape he gently pushed out the loosened brickwork and crawled through the hole onto the flat roof. He had attached a short rope to the back of the locker so that he could pull it up against the wall and cover his exit. On his bed was a dummy, prison clothes stuffed with newspapers to fool the night-duty warders inspecting the cells. His disappearance would not be detected till much later that morning.

He made his way across the roof, over the security fence. He then simply hailed a cab on Brixton Hill and he was away.

I followed all the news stories about Harry that week. When the letter to *The Times* was published it took me a while to suss it out. Then it glared right out at me. Our letter code. It had been such a long time since it had been used. *In the final analysis*, that was the trigger phrase. *In the final analysis, it's my assessment that this worthwhile opportunity to humanely rehabilitate effectively enough now, is nigh. Enough over-ʒealous legal deterrence. Continuation of my punishment thus only negates society's tentative reforms, exceeding equitable treatment.* I decoded it. Spelt it out.

IMATTWOTHREENINEOLDCOMPTONSTREET. *I'm at Two-Three-Nine Old Compton Street.* Soho. Harry was hiding out in the West End of London. And he wanted me to meet him there.

An invitation. A summons more like. For a moment I felt indignation at Harry's presumption that I was going to drop everything and go and meet him. Then I felt fear knowing that I couldn't resist the adventure of it. A sense of excitement I hadn't felt for years.

I made some oblique excuses to the faculty. Family crisis, affairs to be sorted, arrangements to be made. I could be gone for a few days, I warned them. I threw a few things into my car and drove down to London.

PRIVATE SHOP was the sign above the storefront that was 239 Old Compton Street. I parted the coloured strips of plastic forming a curtain at its doorway and went in. There were racks of shrink-wrapped magazines. *Danish Blue, Swedish Hardcore.* A man in an anorak was surreptitiously examining the covers. There was a glass case in front of the counter which displayed strange pink objects like holy relics. Behind the counter a very fat man with lank greasy hair and froggy eyes was reading *Exchange & Mart.* On the shelves above him were displayed Super 8 films. *Fanny Get Your Gun, Ranch of the Nymphomaniac Cowgirls.*

The anorak man wandered out. I sidled up to the counter. The fat man was absently picking his nose. I coughed. Froggy eyes looked up from the auto-spares section and he wiped a finger on his sleeve.

'There's more hard-core stuff out the back,' he said, thumbing at the doorway behind him.

I drew in close to the fat man.

'I'm Lenny,' I whispered, conspiratorially.

'Nice to meet you, Lenny,' he whispered back with a knowing smile. 'What is it, S&M? Animals? Whatever you want, Lenny. I'm sure I can find it for you.'

'No,' I sighed. 'I've come to see Harry.'

His heavy-lidded eyes flashed for half a second and then looked down, pretending to find something interesting amongst the small ads.

'Don't know what you're talking about,' the fat man said flatly.

'Tell Harry Lenny's here.'

He looked me up and down and chewed at his lower lip.

'Right,' he said finally, coming out from behind the counter. 'Mind the shop for me will yer?'

Harry paced up and down in a tight pattern in the flat above the shop. Still measuring cell dimensions. He looked lean and mean, his greying hair slicked back tight against his skull. He had evidently gone through a rigorous exercise regime in the run up to his escape. He grinned at me. His eyes had a wild and hunted gleam in them. His stare was as piercing as ever.

'Glad you could come, Lenny,' he said. 'I knew you would. I knew I could trust you.'

I didn't know quite what he meant by this. I had no idea what he wanted from me.

'Good to see you, Harry,' was all that I could think of to say.

'Yeah. Likewise. Look, I was hoping that you could help me with this campaign of mine. Get it noticed. You know, like that George Davis thing.'

'"Harry Starks is Innocent, OK"?'

Harry laughed darkly.

'Nah, I don't think that would stick. A few friends have been doing this graffiti: "Free Harry Starks", "Ten Years is Long Enough". That sort of thing. It just needs a bit of a boost.'

'Well I don't know what I could do.'

'I dunno, get a petition together, hold a public meeting, I don't fucking know. You know more about these things than I do.'

'I don't know . . .'

'Come on Lenny. I ain't asking much. It's a human rights issue. I need all the help I can get. And it'd be good for you and all. You might learn something.'

'Well . . .'

'Go on,' he urged, his eyes narrowing into mine.

'I'll see what I can do,' I replied, timidly.

'Thanks, Lenny,' he said, patting me on the shoulder. 'I appreciate it.'

That evening, making sure the coast was clear, we went to The Stardust. Wally, the fat man in the sex shop, provided cover as we moved quickly through the dark streets. The Stardust had been Harry's club in the sixties, and Wally was running it for him.

'There've been some changes,' Wally explained as we walked around to the club. He seemed a bit nervous.

'We ain't just doing the Erotic Revue any more. We've sort of, er, branched out.'

'You mean like proper cabaret?' Harry asked, his eyes lighting up.

'Yeah,' replied Wally, hesitantly. 'Sort of.'

The Comedy Club, the sign on the door announced as we arrived. We went in and stood at the back near the bar. Drinks were brought over. On stage was a tubby, crop-haired man in a tight-fitting suit and a pork-pie hat, jerking about in front of the microphone stand.

'Thing is,' Wally went on, almost apologetically, 'your tasteful striptease revue just ain't making money any more. Peepshows, that's the business these days. Smaller premises, fewer staff, faster turnover. And no choreography or nothing. Just some tart rubbing away at herself.'

Of course, you lot don't go down the pub, do yer? The man on stage had a thick scouse accent. *Oh no. It's down the wine bar, like. That's the new thing. Got them all over Hampstead.* Harry frowned.

'So this bloke, right,' Wally went on, 'he's seen this thing in the States. Comedy clubs. Really get the punters in.'

You know why they call them wine bars, don't yer? It refers to the conversation, like.

'What the fuck is this?' Harry demanded.

Whine, whine, whine. Laughter.

Wally looked uncomfortable.

'I think they're calling it "alternative comedy",' I suggested.

'Yeah,' Wally agreed, eagerly. 'That's it.'

'What, you mean alternative to funny?'

We didn't stay at The Stardust for very long. Harry had some business to attend to and suggested that I come along too. We walked through Soho and across Oxford Street into Charlotte Street. Harry turned into a doorway with a brass nameplate which announced: *G. J. Hurst, Chiropodists*. He buzzed the door and muttered something incomprehensible into the intercom. The door opened to let us in.

'A spieler,' Harry told me, as we mounted the staircase. 'Be good research for you to see what one of them looks like. Just don't start fannying on about "subcultures". Keep your head down and your gob shut.'

The spieler was on the third floor. The room stank of cigar smoke. In the corner there was a table with a card game in full swing. There were six men playing and maybe about ten others looking on. It was a hard game to follow. Cards were taken and discarded at high speed. There was a pile of ten- and twenty-pound notes in the centre of the table.

'Kalooki,' Harry explained. 'Jewish game. The old man ran a spieler when I was a kid. He used to say to me, "Look at that son, that's the death agony of capitalism."'

Hundreds of pounds changed hands in flurries. The well-dressed men at the table handled their playing cards with intense concentration and their money with absolute nonchalance.

Eyes darted about. People talked out of the side of their mouths in a language I didn't understand. This was the world I'd spent all these years studying. I felt out of place. Conspicuous. I'd only seen criminals in captivity before.

Everyone in the club was clearly aware of Harry's presence but the little greetings that were made were carefully understated. A firm but brief touch on the shoulder as someone passed. A whispered:

'Well done, Harry, good to see you.' One of the card players, a small man with round spectacles who sipped thoughtfully at a glass of milk by his side, looked up and winked. There was a hiatus in the game and he drained the milk in one. Throwing in his hand and picking up a pile of notes, he stood up and came over.

'Hersh,' he announced with a shrug.

'Manny,' replied Harry.

The two men hugged each other, Harry stooping to slap the little man on the back.

'Manny,' Harry said, 'this is Lenny. A friend. It's all right, he's kosher. He's running the "Free Harry Starks" campaign.'

Manny's magnified eyes blinked at me for a second. He nodded.

'Come,' he said, cocking his head towards a door behind the card table. 'Let's go out the back.'

'Yeah, right,' said Harry. 'Come on, Lenny.'

In the back room were a few leather-covered armchairs. Copies of *Sporting Life* and *The Financial Times* lay folded on a coffee table. Manny produced a bottle of Remy Martin and some glasses and poured us all a drink.

'Mazeltov,' he murmured, jerking up his glass.

'So?' Harry asked.

Manny took a sip of spirit and sharply exhaled. He gave a little shrug.

'So,' he replied. 'Your business affairs are in good order, Hersh. Fat Wally has been skimming the profits of the porn shops and the peepshows and sending it all down to Spain. Jock McCluskey's down there dealing with it all.'

'Wally's been behaving himself?'

'Yes, yes,' Manny nodded. 'If anything, it's the Scotsman I'm worried about.'

'What, Big Jock?'

'I know, I know, he's usually so reliable. Some of the figures don't seem to completely add up. He's said that he's had to pay some people off but even so. You know, sometimes I get, what you say, a gut feeling.'

'I know, Manny. That's what makes you indispensable. But it's all safe down there, isn't it?'

'Yes, yes. The extradition treaty between Britain and Spain fell apart last year and it doesn't look like it's going to be patched up for quite a while. It's a safe bolt hole. A lot of faces are already relocating to Andalusia.'

Harry sighed.

'It'll be heaving with East and South London recidivists in no time,' he lamented.

'Well, they're already calling it the "Costa Del Crime".'

'Hm.'

'Don't worry, Marbella has, I gather, largely escaped the worst excesses of the tourist industry. It's well situated for business as well. Big Jock's procured a lovely big villa. Swimming pool and everything.'

'You must come and visit, Manny.'

'I'm sorting out all the paperwork for your travel arrangements. I'll need a passport photo.'

'Of course,' Harry stood up. 'Look, we better be getting back.'

As we walked through the main part of the spieler, a short stocky man came up to Harry.

'We've had a whip,' he said, handing over a considerable wedge of notes.

'Thanks,' said Harry, taking the cash and patting him on the shoulder.

'Be lucky,' said the man.

We walked back to Soho.

'So, you're planning to skip the country?' I asked.

'Yeah, well it's not a bad idea, don't you think?'

'What about the "Free Harry Starks" campaign?'

Harry chuckled.

'Well, it's not a bad smokescreen. I mean, if I can persuade people that my escape is some sort of publicity stunt to bring attention to my case, that I might be ready to turn myself in after a few days, then the Old Bill aren't going to be wasting too much manpower in looking for me are they?'

'I guess not.'

'Besides, I'm making a point. I don't expect much from the British justice system but I'm making my fucking point, ain't I?'

As we came into Old Compton Street, Harry slowed down. He led me into a shop doorway.

'What's the matter?' I asked.

Harry peered out of the alcove and cocked his head towards Wally's shop.

'Something's up,' he said. 'There's a couple of moody-looking cars parked up there.'

I peeped out myself. Two saloon cars were pulled up on the curb outside the shop. A man was standing by one of the cars looking down the street in our direction. Suddenly there was a commotion at the doorway of the shop. It was easy to make out the considerable figure of Fat Wally, surrounded by smaller figures who were awkwardly bundling him into the back of one of the cars. It drove off quickly. A siren started up and it wailed off into the night. The other car pulled off the curb and parked itself opposite the shop.

'Fuck,' Harry muttered. 'Where's your motor?'

I'd parked it at the other end of Old Compton Street.

'It's up the other end, Harry.'

'Well, go and get it and bring it back here.'

I walked up the street and passed the car parked across the road from Fat Wally's shop. I felt my legs almost buckling with nerves. I could barely stop myself from looking in at the men waiting in the car. I felt them watch me pass.

I drove back and picked Harry up. Harry laughed as he got into the passenger seat of my Citroën 2CV.

'Classy motor, Lenny,' he said.

'Yeah. Sorry about that.'

'No, this is perfect. No one's going to suspect Britain's most wanted gang boss being driven around in this jalopy.'

He told me to drive north, to Tottenham.

'I thought you said that the police weren't going to do a big manhunt for you,' I said.

'Hm, that weren't no fucking manhunt. They aren't that fucking clever. Somebody grassed, that's for sure.'

We reached Tottenham High Road and Harry checked in my *London A – Z* and gave directions.

'Thing is,' he spoke softly, as if to himself, 'only Wally, Manny, and Jock knew where I was.'

He looked up from the map book and stared at the road ahead.

'And you of course,' he said, bluntly.

We reached our destination. It was a row of large Victorian terraced houses. I parked up in front of them.

'Right,' said Harry briskly. 'Come on.'

'Wait a minute, Harry. Look, I think I've got more involved in all this than I planned to, Harry. Maybe it's best if I leave you here and I get off. All right?'

Harry frowned and slowly turned his head towards me.

'What the fuck are you talking about?' he demanded.

'I just thought, you know . . .'

'You just thought. You just thought. What? Drop me off here and go and make a little phone call. Is that it?'

'No, Harry. Of course not.'

'I trusted you, Lenny. If I ever found out that you betrayed that trust,' he whispered gravely, his face now close to mine.

'Honestly, Harry, I never . . .' I found myself pleading.

Harry suddenly grinned and tapped me on the side of my face.

'Good,' he said and drew back. 'Now come on.'

We went up the stone steps of one of the houses. Harry rapped on the door. It was opened by a cropped-haired man in a Lacoste cardigan.

'Yeah?' he said vaguely, then peered more closely. 'Harry? Fuck me, Harry Starks.'

'Hello Beardsley,' Harry said with a smile. 'How's it going?'

'Fucking hell, Harry. Come in, for fuck's sake.'

He ushered us into the hallway, and checked out the street as he closed the door. We went through to his living room. Beardsley produced a bottle of scotch and he and Harry caught up on old times for a while.

'Anything I can do, H?' Beardsley said.

'Well, we were wondering if you could put us up. Just for a couple of days.'

Beardsley drew in a breath and looked fraught for a second. Then he nodded.

'Yeah, fucking hell, of course you can. It's just the missus, you see. I've gone straight, as far as she's concerned. As long as she doesn't know nothing.'

'And have you? I mean, gone straight?' Harry asked.

'Yeah, well, mostly. I'm in the music business now. I'm managing this band called Earthquake. They're doing all this ska stuff. You know, all that skinhead music I used to be into. It's all the rage again. I'll tell her you're a couple of session musicians. You can share the spare bedroom. But keep your heads down. I don't want her kicking off at me again.'

The next morning I went out and bought all of the papers. Some of the dailies ran a small piece on Wally's arrest. The headline on page 5 of *The Sun:* STARKS SLIPS NET IN SOHO SEX SHOP SWOOP. *Police acting on a tip-off raided the premises of a pornographic bookshop in London's West End last night, believing it to be the hide-out of escaped gangster Harry Starks. But the notorious Torture Gang Boss evaded capture. The proprietor, Walter Peters, is helping police with their inquiries.*

'Right, let's get a press release together today, Lenny. Let them think I'm going to turn myself in.'

Beardsley brought up a meal for each of us on a tray.

'The wife's getting suspicious,' he said. 'There's all this stuff in the papers and she knows I used to run around with you.'

'Just a couple of days, Beardsley. Then I'm fucking off out of this poxy country.'

'Spain is it?'

'How do you know?'

'I don't. I just figured. You know, this extradition thing.'

'Yeah, well, you might as well know. Got a villa in Marbella all lined up.'

'Lovely. Weather's fucking lovely down there. My cousin runs an English Bar down that way. Fuengirola. It's great. Full English Breakfast, Sunday Roast, English beer and a proper cup of tea when you get homesick.'

'Right,' Harry said, giving me a sideways glance.

'"Pete's English Bar" it's called. You should check it out.'

'Yeah, sure. Look, thanks for putting us up B.'

Harry fished out a bundle of notes and offered them to Beardsley.

'Look, Harry,' said Beardsley, putting up his hands. 'There's no need. Old times and all that.'

'Go on, take it. Buy the missus something nice. Keep her sweet.'

We worked on Harry's press release through the day. Harry spent most of the time coaxing and cajoling ideas from me that he would then proceed to attack vociferously. There was heated debate over lines of argument, ordering of points and the choice of words. The habitual and mind-numbing questioning of every assertion and every subsequent criticism. It was just like old times.

Finally we hammered something out and we went through it together. Harry shrugged and pursed his lips.

'Yeah,' he admitted. 'It'll do.'

'You sure you don't want to change that last bit? You said you thought it sounded a bit weak.'

'Nah, it's fine. The main thing is that they should think that I'm going to come quietly.'

'Who do we send it to?'

'*The Times*, I guess. They ran my letter, after all.'

'Yeah,' I agreed.

We sat in silence for a while enjoying, for a moment at least, the calm blankness of having finished something. Finished business, I thought wistfully. I could go now. I looked up at Harry. Our eyes met.

'Right,' I said. 'Well . . .'

'Come to Spain,' said Harry.

'What?'

'Look, I'll level with you. I need something bringing back.'

'You've got to be joking.'

'It's nothing. Just some, you know, paperwork.'

'Paperwork?'

'Stuff for Manny. Look, the less you know the better.'

'Harry, I don't want to know about this at all.'

'Come on,' he implored. 'Come to Spain. Just for a few days. It'll be a bit of a holiday.'

'I've got to get back. The University.'

'Listen to you. The University. Fuck me. I thought I was becoming institutionalised.'

'Harry . . .'

'You need a bit of extra-mural activity, Len. Think of the research value. You're a criminologist for fuck's sake. Here's a chance to really know your subject. Extend your methodology a bit. Fieldwork, if you like. What do you call it? Ethnographic study based on participant observation.'

'This is a wind up.'

'Well, granted, it's bullshit if it's just intellectual analysis. This is a chance to really experience something. Admit it, you're tempted.'

'I don't think so.'

'Come on. You're drawn to the excitement of it. That's what got you interested in the first place.'

'Maybe. But I can't just drop everything and go to Spain.'

'Why not? Christ Lenny, you've spent all these years studying deviant behaviour and yet you've always acted according to social norms. You're supposed to be a fucking radical. When did you ever do anything radical in your life?'

'Harry . . .'

'Nah, it's true, isn't it? You're scared of doing anything that might constitute an adventure, anything that might upset that safe little life of yours.'

I sighed. Harry grinned that grin of his.

'Well, anyway,' I retorted. 'I can't leave the country. I haven't got my passport with me.'

Harry laughed.

'Don't worry, old son. We can get you one.'

My stomach sank as we dropped in altitude. Not air sickness. Ground sickness. Coming down to earth. I suddenly thought: *what the fuck am I doing?* Gone was the heady sense of escapism I'd felt when I'd first agreed to go along with Harry. I'd somehow found myself in a dilemma. My freedom had seemed as much at stake as Harry's. I'd felt a fatalistic tranquillity in recklessness. I'd calmly phoned the faculty again, answering frantic inquiries with obscure reasons for my absence. I needed time to think. Things had got on top of me. Compassionate leave was extended. They probably imagined that I was having some sort of nervous breakdown. They wouldn't be far off the mark there.

But it was as we were making our final descent on Malaga Airport that I felt the gravity of it all. Coming in to land. *Please fasten your seatbelts and extinguish all cigarettes.* Landing is the most dangerous part of flying. *What the fuck am I doing?* In a foreign country with a fake passport, accompanying a fugitive of British justice. Harry sensed my rediscovered nerves.

'Keep calm, Lenny.' His voice hoarse and soft. 'For fuck's sake.'

We were only carrying hand luggage so we could go straight through to customs. We cleared it quickly and without incident. A driver was waiting for us.

The drive to Marbella took about an hour. We caught occasional glimpses of the dull-blue Mediterranean usually accompanied by huge white concrete developments.

'The Costa Del Sol is a bit trashy,' Harry commented. 'But we could go inland for a couple of days. Go to Granada, have a look at the Alhambra.'

I nodded and closed my eyes, seeing a red glow.

We finally arrived at the villa. Marble steps led up to a series of whitewashed blocks. There was a cylindrical turret inlaid with coloured glass. By the wrought-iron gates at the top of the stairs we were met by a short balding muscular man. The sun had par-boiled his battered face. An open Hawaiian shirt revealed a greying hairy chest and a pot belly that hung over elasticated shorts.

'Harry,' he growled.

'Jock,' replied Harry, hugging the burly man. 'How the fuck are you? This is Lenny. He's in charge of public relations.'

'Pleased to meet you Lenny. Come on in.'

He led us through the gates, we passed through a tiny courtyard with a font heavy with dark-green foliage, then through panelled and studded doors. Portuguese pink marble floors, textured-plaster wall with a dado of ornamental tiles and clusters of more coloured glass inlay. A stone fireplace with a driftwood sculpture above it. Huge urns at each corner of the room. Moroccan wall hangings. A smoked-glass and tubular-steel coffee table surrounded by a massive sofa and armchairs in white leather. There were sliding french windows at the far end. Beyond, a turquoise swimming pool shimmered in a blue-tiled patio.

'Very nice,' said Harry, scanning it all. 'Yeah. It's all been very tastefully done.'

Jock produced a bottle of Krug and some glasses. He popped the cork and filled a glass full of foam. His hands were shaking as he guided the neck of the bottle. He picked up a glass, his hand a bit more steady now.

'Well, here's to crime,' he proposed, and we all drank the toast.

A roll call passed between them. A litany of names, of faces, of those 'away'. When it seemed exhausted, Harry sighed.

'So, let's get down to business,' he said. 'I want to go through everything I've got down here.'

'Yeah, sure, Harry,' Jock replied. 'But you'll want to relax a bit first, eh? It's been a long journey.'

'Yeah, well, let's get it all sorted and then I can relax.'

Jock cleared his throat.

'Yeah,' he said, nodding, rubbing his fat hands on the front of his shorts. 'Of course.'

Just then there was a shout from the patio. *¡Señor Yock! ¡Señor Yock!* Jock grumbled and rubbed his face.

'The pool boy,' he explained. 'There's something wrong with the filter.'

He stood up.

'I just need to see to this. I won't be long.'

And he went out through the sliding french windows.

Harry stared straight ahead and sipped at his champagne.

'Something's up,' he muttered. 'Jock's in a fucking funny mood.'

Agitated voices out on the patio. Two sharp cracks like heavy branches breaking and then a loud splash.

Harry was on his feet and racing to the glass doors. I followed him. We came out onto the patio. Someone was vaulting over the high stone wall.

'Oi!' Harry shouted.

There was the sound of undergrowth breaking. A motorcycle starting up and screaming off into the hot afternoon. Jock was face down in the swimming pool. Dark clouds of blood diffused in the water.

'Fuck!' said Harry, looking down at the floating body.

There was an automatic pistol lying on the poolside. Harry picked it up and looked at it. He sniffed.

'Fuck!' he whispered harshly.

He pocketed the gun and started to move quickly, back to the house.

'Shouldn't we get him out of the water?' I asked.

He beckoned to me.

'Come on,' he insisted.

I gazed at the bobbing body. I frowned.

'Something wrong with the filter,' I muttered.

'Come on!' Harry repeated.

He went into the house and pulled at the white fur rug in front of the fireplace. He lifted up a small section of marble to reveal a floor safe, worked the combination and opened it. Reaching down, he scooped his hand around it. It was empty.

'Fuck! We've been cleaned out.'

He stood up and adjusted the gun in his pocket. The sound of police sirens came from not too far off.

'Come on,' he ordered and made for the front door. 'We've been set up.'

We ran down the steps and down the street. Behind us cars were screeching to a halt in front of the villa. Another police car came racing from the direction we were headed. Harry pulled me in by a hedge and we watched it pass. We found ourselves in a small square. There was a taxi at the corner. We jumped in.

'¡Vamos!' Harry demanded.

'¿Adonde?' the driver inquired.

Harry pointed ahead.

'That way,' he said.

The driver pulled away and started down the road ahead.

'You English?' he asked.

'Si, yes,' Harry replied. 'English, yes.'

'Where you want go, English?'

'Oh, I don't fucking know,' he complained, rubbing his face with his hand.

Suddenly his hand stopped in front of his mouth. His eyes lit up.

'Fuengirola,' he gasped with a look of inspiration.

'Sure,' replied the driver. 'Fuengirola is 800 pesetas.'

'Take us there. Take us to Pete's English Bar, Fuengirola.'

FULL ENGLISH BREAKFAST, promised Pete's English Bar. FISH 'N' CHIPS 200 PSTS. SUNDAY ROAST SERVED DAILY. FULL RANGE OF ENGLISH BEERS. The interior was half-timbered white plaster. Horse brasses, a Union Jack and a portrait of Her Majesty framed by an alcove. A formal photograph of two ranks of a football team, one standing, one squatting. A maroon scarf tacked above with the legend VIVA EL FULHAM. Framed pictures of Henry Cooper and Winston Churchill. 'Una Paloma Blanca' was blaring out of the jukebox. A ruddily tanned man with a bleached-blond perm was wiping the bar. He looked up and smiled wearily at us.

'What can I get you, gents?' he offered.

'Are you Pete?' Harry asked.

He stopped wiping and squinted at us.

'Who wants to know?'

'A friend of Beardsley's.'

He smiled.

'Right. How is the old cunt? Keeping out of trouble I hope. Wait a minute . . .'

Pete craned forward and studied Harry's face.

'You're . . .' Pete began.

'Yes,' said Harry, holding a finger up to the side of his nose. 'I'm.'

Pete looked about shiftily then cocked his head backwards.

'Come out the back,' he said.

We went through the kitchen. It reeked of bacon and chip fat.

'We need somewhere to lie low for a bit,' said Harry, handing him a wad of notes.

'Sure,' said Pete, pocketing the money. 'I've got a room upstairs.'

Harry took off his jacket as Pete showed us the room. The pistol fell clattering onto the floor. Pete jumped back.

'Fucking hell,' he gasped.

'Don't worry,' said Harry. 'We won't be staying long. I need to get across the water to Morocco. You know anyone who can take me? Someone who won't ask too many questions.'

Pete nodded.

'Yeah. I know someone.'

Someone arrived three hours later.

'Hi, I'm Giles,' he announced in a lazy public school drawl. 'Mind if I skin up?'

'Be my guest,' Harry said.

'I understand you want to hitch a lift across the Straits of Gibraltar.'

'Yeah, that's right. You got a boat?'

'Yah,' Giles affirmed licking a rizla. 'Absolutely. Moored down at Puerto Banus. Planning to set off dawn tomorrow, actually.'

'So you could take me?'

'Oh, yah. For a price of course.'

'And nobody else needs to know about this?'

'Absolutely. There's my crew of course, but Juanalito's terribly loyal. I can trust him.'

'And can I trust you?'

Giles flicked open a brass zippo and lit the joint. He took a sharp pull. A smile emerged from a wreath of hash smoke.

'Don't worry, man. I'm terribly discreet. I have to be.'

'And why's that?' Harry demanded, with a slight edge to his voice.

'Because I'm picking up half a ton of resin from the Rif mountains next week and bringing it back over here. If you're planning to relocate to Morocco, perhaps we could do business sometime.'

He handed the joint to Harry.

'Yeah,' Harry toked thoughtfully. 'Maybe. Look, Giles, you know who I am, don't you?'

'Not necessarily.'

'Yeah, but just supposing that you do. What's being said?'

'That you shot Jock McCluskey by his swimming pool.'

'Right. Well I didn't. OK?'

'I'm very glad to hear it.'

Harry passed me the joint. I took a drag and held the smoke in my lungs.

'You knew Jock?' Harry asked Giles.

'Knew of him. And that weird guy he was doing business with.'

'What guy?'

'Calls himself the Major. Supposed to be ex-army. Looks more like ex-Old Bill to me.' Giles gave a stoned little giggle. *'El Viejo Guillermo.'*

'What sort of business were they doing?'

I exhaled and felt the hashish rush into my bloodstream, a prickly warmth rising up from my legs.

'Well, this Major guy, he's supposed to be well connected, knows all the bent *policia* down here. He's been approaching all the villains who are moving down here and offering protection. You know, acting as liaison with the authorities.'

'And Jock was dealing with him?'

'That's what I heard.'

'And where might one find this Major chap?'

'He's got a place up in Llanos de Nagueles. I could find the address if you want.'

'Yeah, you do that.'

At nightfall we drove up to a moresque villa overlooking the sea. It seemed dark and empty. We got out of the car. Cicadas chirped in an expectant rhythm. There was a firework display down by the beach.

Harry went up to the front door and rapped on it. He peered up at the windows. Nobody stirred. He came back out.

'Nobody home,' he said. 'Let's have a look at the back.'

He told the driver to wait and we walked around the premises. A burst of green cinders blossomed against the skyline and a gentle patter of thunder rolled up from the seafront. There was a low pillared balcony at the back of the house.

'Right then,' he muttered. 'Let's have a little look, shall we?'

'You're going to break in?'

'We're going to break in.'

'Harry, look . . .'

'Shut up and listen. A bit of practical work for you. Now concentrate. I'm going to explain breaking in. Here's the *modus operandi*. A team of three. Right?' Harry held up three fingers.

337

'Driver, minder, goer.' He counted off. 'The driver's obviously Pepe over there, I'm going in, so that leaves you to mind. Keep watch and keep your wits about you. If anything turns up, give me a shout. And then make sure the motor's ready to go when I come out. OK? Remember, rule number one, no one gets left behind.'

'I'm really not sure about this.'

'Don't worry. You're nervous, that's natural. Use your nerves to keep you on your toes. Oh,' he added, 'and you get to hold on to this.'

He slipped something into my hand. I felt cold heavy metal. It was the gun.

'Oh, fuck,' I groaned.

'Don't worry. I put the safety catch on.'

He padded across to the balcony and started to scale it. A rocket whooped up into the night. A bright orange star shell dropped slowly behind a row of palm trees. I could hear Harry rattling the shutters, forcing an entry.

Cars passing. A group of revellers in the distance breaking into a terrace chant. Syncopated pyrotechnic clattering. An engine sighed to a halt in front of the house. The sound of a car door clumping.

I walked briskly around to the front, clutching the pistol in my pocket. Someone was at the front door. Keys jingled, slotted, ratcheted. I ran back to the balcony.

'Harry!' I whispered harshly.

No response. A light went on.

'Harry!' I repeated, a little louder.

Still nothing. I started to climb up the balcony myself. The light went on in the room beyond. I crawled to the french windows and crouched behind the shutter Harry had forced open.

Harry was stooped over an open suitcase on the bed. It was full of money. There was a stocky man with close-cropped grey hair and piercing little eyes standing by the door. He had a gun in his hand.

'Hello, Harry,' he said. 'Long time no see.'

Harry gave a little start. He looked up.

'Mooney,' he moaned. 'Fuck.'

'I see you've found your legacy.'

Harry picked up a sheaf of notes and let it drop back into the suitcase.

'You had Jock killed, didn't you?' he asked.

Mooney sighed.

'Jock,' he said, shaking his head. 'Yes, that was unfortunate. I tried to work things out with him but he could so easily have fucked things up. And after I'd done so much for him. When he first came down here he really stuck out like a sore prick. It was easy to track him down. I've been here for quite a while, you know, established some very useful friends in the *guardia civil*. I could have had him thrown out on his ear. Instead I suggested a more co-operative approach. I helped him get set up. So much gelt coming in from Soho. Some of it owing to me now, let's face it. Plenty to go around. Then you break out of Brixton and Jock gets all flustered. Like an old woman. I say it's simple, let me know where you are and I'll just make a little call to some old pals at West End Central. And he's whining on about not wanting to grass you up. Dreary petty-criminal morality. When he does finally squeal, it's too late, you've already moved on. Then Jock gets near enough hysterical. You're on your way, what are we going to do. Like it's always up to me to sort all the shit out. I could have had you arrested at Malaga. But then I think, why not get rid of you both? Jock's becoming far too unreliable. I get him to hand over the loot to me for safe keeping. Tell him not to worry, I'll deal with you.'

'And then you have him bumped off?'

'Yes.' Mooney smiled. 'It seemed such a perfect solution. To do it while you're at the house. You're the most obvious suspect, after all. And it has been pinned on you, you know. There's a very good set of fingerprints on a glass found in the villa. Scotland Yard have already confirmed that they belong to you.

'But once again you have evaded capture. You've become quite a desperado, Harry. Now I can bring you in myself. A bit of glory. Retired detective collars the Torture Gang Boss. It'll do my reputation no end of good. You know, there's still some nasty rumours about my past, my time in the force. This will shut all of that up for good. And it'll impress my friends in the *policia*. A minor gang war cleared up. Just the sort of thing that they're dreading with this extradition difficulty. I can persuade them to let me have a free rein. Keep in line all the old lags that'll be coming down here to lie about like lizards in the sun. It'll be quite like old times, really. Familiar faces, just a bit of suntan. And bigger and better deals. It'll be my duty to properly police the expatriate criminal community. And it'll make me very rich. Now, put your hands up where I can see them.'

'Isn't there something that can be done?' Harry asked.

'Ah! That ancient phrase. It quite takes me back, it really does. You're of the old school, Harry, I'll give you that. I'd really like to be able to say yes, just for old times' sake. But I'm afraid, I'm going to have to hand you over. A little offering, as it were. Don't try anything. I've got a licence for this thing and using it to shoot a dangerous intruder would suit me just as well.'

Keeping his pistol trained on Harry, Mooney picked up the receiver of the telephone on the bedside table. He clutched it, then used the forefinger of the same hand to start to dial a number. I pulled out the pistol Harry had given me and edged forward. Suddenly the window shutter that obscured me swung inwards noisily. Mooney looked across, his little eyes narrowing in on me. I raised my gun and pointed it at him.

'Go on,' Harry urged gruffly. 'Shoot the fucker.'

I pulled at the trigger but it wouldn't budge. I tried again. Mooney swung his pistol around in my direction and fired.

Glass exploded next to my face. I staggered back out onto the balcony.

'The safety catch, you stupid cunt!' Harry called out.

Mooney followed me out, bearing down on me, both hands holding his gun, steadying its aim on me. My arms dangled at my sides uselessly. I still felt the weight of my pistol at the end of one of them.

Mooney pointed his gun at my face. I stared at the little hole at the end of it. Mooney grinned at me. I gasped a breath. My brain screamed with fear.

Then, with a thud, he fell forward, collapsed into a sprawling heap in front of me. Harry had hurled the suitcase against his back. Its hinged shells now gaped open, spilling out bundles of money onto the tiled floor and all over the back of the ex-policeman. Mooney stirred, coughing. He looked up over his shoulder at me. I only needed to lift my weighted arm a few degrees to bring the barrel of the gun in line with his view. I clicked off the safety catch.

Mooney curled up foetal. His beady eyes gleamed in panic. He made little palsied spasms of terror.

'Please,' he squealed.

All my fear turn into disgust. I felt a surge of animal loathing for weakness. Aerial maroons exploded in the sky behind me. My shoulder spastic with recoil. Cordite stinging the back of my throat. The gun was hot in my hand. I don't know how many bullets I put into Mooney. Harry got hold of me.

'That's enough, Lenny,' he shouted in my ear, pulling the gun arm gently down. 'That's enough.'

He carefully prised the pistol from my tense grip. Unthreading the forefinger from out of the trigger guard, unclawing the rest from the butt. There were neat little wounds in Mooney's face. The back of his head was a red and pink pulp. Blood grouted the tilework floor of the balcony.

I started to hyperventilate. Harry pulled me away from the body and slapped me across the face a couple of times.

'Come on. Breathe out slowly. That's it,' he spoke softly, soothingly. 'Let it go.'

I grabbed the window frame to steady myself and retched a couple of times. Not much came up. I drooled a few drops of bile over Mooney's well-polished shoes. Warm, sickly sweet odours wafted up from the voided body beneath me. My head throbbed with knowledge. I had killed. I had killed without mercy.

'Right,' said Harry, crouching down to repack the suitcase. 'We're going out the front door. Nice and calm now.'

Puerto Banus Marina. It was nearly dawn. Giles was loading his yacht. He nodded at Harry's suitcase.

'Is that all you're taking?' he asked.

'It's all I'll need,' Harry replied.

I was still shaking a bit. I chain smoked bitter Spanish cigarettes and paced up and down the quayside. Harry came over. He was carrying a holdall that he had been using for hand luggage.

'The bullets in Mooney will match the ones in Jock. Same forensic. They've already pinned McCluskey on me, so I'll be in the frame for Mooney and all.'

I nodded blankly, then suddenly thought about what Harry was saying. He was going to take the blame. My blame. He handed me the holdall.

'There's stuff in there for Manny,' he said. 'And something for you.'

I unzipped the bag and peered inside. There was a sheaf of papers and a few bundles of cash.

'Your cut,' Harry explained. 'Be careful taking that back home.'

'Where will you go?' I asked him.

He shrugged.

'Tangiers, I guess. Still got a few contacts there. Some of Billy Hill's old mob.'

The sky was getting lighter in degrees of purple. The morning star burned low in the sky. My mind was calm. Horrible clarity. I was a murderer. I would go back to England and carry on with my unremarkable life. Happy enough as a boring academic. No one would suspect a thing. The dreadful knowledge of it would sometimes haunt me amidst empty theorising about social taboos and individual transgressions. A hidden pathological self. A guilty secret. I was one of the Guilty Men now. But Harry would take the blame. I would become the type of criminal that criminologists never study. The ones that get away with it.

Harry jumped down onto the deck of the boat. Giles started up the outboard.

'See you,' Harry called as they chugged slowly out of the mooring. 'Be lucky.'

I stood and watched them sail out into the bay. There was a faint phosphorescence in the wake of the yacht. Like a silvery snail trail. A trace. Soon the water washed over it leaving only a homeopathic mark: the trace of a trace. But unlike me, Harry would leave some sort of imprint on the world. Most of us will vanish, leaving no real signs that we ever really existed. A fugitive leaves behind some clues. They disappear from view but leave evidence of their flight. A desired trail. They are wanted men.

A red blob of sun strained against the horizon. I lost sight of the boat. That was the last I ever saw or heard of Harry directly. But in time a whole series of rumours and stories emerged. He was an unsolved mystery. A regular feature in 'true crime' books or articles about the 'underworld'. He was in Morocco, running a huge drugs cartel. He was seen in the Congo, organising a treasure hunt for millions of dollars of gold buried by mercenaries in the jungle south of Brazzaville. He was running mercenaries himself for UNITA in Angola. He was running guns from Libya to Southern Ireland. He was the real brains behind the Brinks Mat robbery. I somehow knew that he was the source for at least some of these stories, not just to confuse the scent but also because he loved their smell.